MOTTY'S VOW

A Novel

Diane Wahn Shotton

ISBN: 979-8-9999465-0-8
Independently published

First Edition

To the women of my family,
past and present—
Your strength, resilience, and love
continue to inspire me.
This story is for you.

"There's truths you have to grow into." —
H.G. Wells, Love and Mr. Lewisham

PART ONE

Chapter One

After supper, Papa thrust today's edition of the *Cincinnati Daily Press* at me, pointing to an article in the Highly Important News column. "Read, Motty."

"The rebels at Charleston opened fire upon Fort Sumter yesterday," I read. "They fired the first gun, declaring war against the government of the United States in the insane hope of coercing the government into recognizing their independence." I looked up. "War? What does the *Volksfreund* say?"

"The same." Papa waved his German paper in the air with one hand and pounded the table with the other. "An attack on federal troops is against the law. Lincoln must declare war."

I peeked at Mama, gauging her reaction to Papa's opinion. Eyes flashing, she opened her mouth. A tart reply gained momentum. I asked Papa, "What happens if Lincoln declares war?"

Mama's jaw cracked as her mouth snapped shut.

"The President will activate the military. But he'll need more men."

"All this over slavery." Mama shook her head.

"You must agree, Retta." Papa folded the paper. "The southern states refuse to abolish this hateful practice, and it must end."

"I agree, but war? Is it necessary?"

Papa chuckled and winked at me. "She doesn't read the papers like we do. It will be over in a matter of months."

For once, Mama held her tongue. Her sideways glance warned me to hold mine as well.

"I'm going to the Republic. I want to hear what everyone is saying." He grabbed his coat from the wall peg. "Don't wait up."

"Go on! Drink with your friends and leave me here." Mama's eyes narrowed.

When he opened the door, the wind blew in, as frosty as his stare. The calendar read April, but winter's chill held fast.

"Close the damn door!" Mama yelled. "It's as cold out there as your Dutch heart."

The door slammed behind Papa. The flimsy walls of our three-room home shuddered as he stomped down the steps to Linn Street.

Papa's abrupt exit suspended all activity. Mama fixed her gaze on the door, the tight line of her mouth saying everything her voice didn't. I stared at the newsprint before me, the words blurring together as tension filled the room like smoke.

Sensing danger, my siblings retreated into themselves. Eight-year-old Lizzie, normally bursting with questions, focused on her hair ribbon with unusual intensity, her fingers working to tie the perfect bow. Mary, twelve but with a child's mind, paged through her picture book as if it held all the answers. She spoke only in single words, spun in circles when upset, and needed constant watching. Today she sat unnaturally still.

My parents' quarrels always circled back to the same things - Papa's low-paying job at the shoe factory, Mama's dreams of a better life. We'd learned to stay quiet during these moments, to make ourselves small and unnoticed.

Henry, not yet old enough to understand, left his blocks scattered on the floor and tugged at Mama's dress. "Eat," he demanded.

His simple need cut through the heavy air. I released a long, slow breath, feeling my shoulders drop as the tension eased.

"You're always hungry," Mama said, laying him in her lap, where he rooted at her breast to feed.

As Henry suckled, Mama stared out the window, murmuring to herself, "If Lincoln calls for men, he'll sign up."

Talk of war stirred anxiety, but Papa enlisting terrified me. He complained about his job at the shoe factory, stamping out shoe soles, his dream of owning a shop out of reach. Would he join to escape Mama's nagging? These tiny rooms? Could he earn more in the Army? A hundred other questions flooded my mind. Asking Mama might satisfy my need for information, but it would only worry her. Or worse, make her angry.

I agreed with Mama's assessment. A passionate Lincoln supporter, Papa attended the President's address in February, where he called for unity and thanked the German community for their votes in the election.

Without warning, Mary popped from her chair and presented Mama with her book, shoving it close to her face. Mama drew back and pushed it away. "What?"

Ignoring Mama's reaction, Mary said, "Cat." Beaming from ear to ear, she waited for a word of praise.

"Martha, take care of her. I'm going to bed." Her chair scratched across the floor. She shuffled to her bedroom, the door closing with a click. No goodnight, no instructions for bedtime.

My sister's face fell, as did her arm with the book. Mama's callous dismissal cast a shadow of defeat over blue eyes created for smiling.

"Show me," Lizzie said.

She drew Mary onto the floor and paged through the book. Thrilled at the attention, Mary kissed the tip of her forefinger, laid it on Lizzie's cheek, and smacked her lips, her way of saying thank you. And I love you. And sorry. One gesture, many meanings.

We dressed in our nightclothes, said our prayers, and climbed into bed. Instead of disturbing Mama to put Henry in his basket, I brought him into our bed, lining up on our sides to make space for four bodies on the thin, square mattress.

I worried about Papa going to war and Mama caring for us without him. And Mary, sweet Mary, unintentionally stirring up trouble. I sensed a shift in my world, a subtle yet tangible change suggesting significant challenges lay ahead.

The next morning, Papa sat at the kitchen table, the smell of freshly brewed coffee greeting me.

I poured a cup of coffee for myself and asked, "Mama awake?"

"She's stirring."

"What did you hear from your friends?" I moved the coffee pot from the stovetop, replaced it with a pan of water, added oats, and stoked the fire.

"Most think Lincoln will declare war and call for volunteers." He sipped his coffee. "Turner Hall is full of men eager to show off their military and athletic abilities."

"Will you go?"

"Perhaps. There's talk of raising an all-German unit. August Willich is speaking at a rally at Workingmen's Hall this evening." An editor of the *Cincinnati Republikaner,* and a staunch supporter of workingmen's rights, Papa admired Willich's views.

"From what I've read, he's a convincing man."

"Don't worry. I'm not signing up tonight." He finished his coffee. "See you at supper."

He dropped a kiss on my forehead, buttoned his coat, and shoved his hat over his curly auburn hair. Quick as a cat, he slipped out the door.

Papa didn't come home for supper. Mama made us sit at the kitchen table, food in front of us, waiting for over an hour. She paced, hurling questions at me.

"Where is he?"

"I guess he went to the rally."

"Where's the rally?"

"At Workingmen's Hall. Willich is speaking."

Mama's face froze at the name. "Willich? The editor?"

I dismissed her concern. "He said he wanted to hear his speech. Don't worry. He told me he wasn't signing up."

"He worships that man."

Trying again to make light of Willich's influence over Papa, I shrugged. "It's just a speech."

"You don't know him." Mama leaned over the table, her forefinger stabbing the air between us. "Mark my words, Martha. One day, you will regret believing everything your father says."

Escaping her piercing gaze, I lowered my head over my dinner, my mind racing. Why would Papa lie about something this important?

Waving a hand over the table, she said, "Eat. I'm going to Workingmen's Hall."

Shoes scuffled and skirts swished as a blast of chilly air swept into the kitchen. The door banged shut, followed by Mama's feet tapping down the stairs.

Raising my head, I saw Lizzie and Mary's hands, fingers threaded into one fist on the table - forced solidarity in the face of Mama's rants. I reached across and covered their hands with mine.

"She's gone."

Lizzie blew out a long breath as if to say, Thank God.

Wondering how sleeping Henry fared with the door slamming, I peeked into Mama's room. A slit of light over his basket revealed closed eyes and relaxed limbs. Returning to the kitchen, I tore off a piece of bread and went into the front room, leaving the girls to finish their meal. I squared a chair against the windows overlooking the comings and goings of our West End neighborhood. The windows in the building across the street reflected the pink and gold of the setting sun, a stark contrast to the inner turmoil Mama's words stirred in me.

I reflected on the statement she threw down like a gauntlet, challenging Papa's honesty, my gullibility. Unlike Mama, I trusted Papa, calm and logical. Whereas Mama's mood swings had Lizzie and me betting on which mother would show up for breakfast. The cheerful life-is-good-let's-have-fun, Mama, or the sullen world-is-out-to-get-me-no-one-loves-me Mama.

If she found Papa, they would visit a saloon and have a few beers. If she didn't, she'd come home angry, maudlin, and full of self-pity. On my knees next to the bed, I prayed for beer.

I awoke to someone shaking my shoulder. "What? What is it?" I jerked upright, expecting Henry beside the bed, his diaper at his ankles. Instead, an insistent whisper seeped into my consciousness. Lizzie.

"Motty! Listen!"

Voices. Outside. On the street below. My parents.

"Did you have to embarrass me in front of my friends?" Papa berated Mama.

"Did you have to ignore me?"

"You should not have come looking for me like an errant schoolboy. I'm a grown man," he growled and slurred, like a drunken bear.

"You always do what you want. I'm stuck at home, turning scraps of food into a meal and taking care of your brats. While you're out with your friends, spending money we don't have."

Papa didn't respond.

"You told Martha you'd be home for supper," Mama said, her voice low, tinged with heartbreak. "We waited an hour."

"I met some friends before the rally. Stop nagging."

They fell silent until Mama said, "I'm tired, George. Of war talk, of you going out, of not having the life I dreamt of."

"What did you think it would be, Retta?" Papa's screech echoed into our rooms. "Dancing? Parties? Making love every night? You're a fool."

A crack echoed beneath our windows. I winced, touching my cheek. Did she slap him?

"I signed up." His voice lacked embellishment or explanation.

I gasped, recalling Mama's prediction.

"You signed up. How nice for you." Her voice rose sharply, disbelief seeping into her mock approval.

"Lincoln asked for volunteers today, so yes, I joined the Ninth Ohio Infantry, a German regiment." I imagined his chest puffing out like a rooster courting a hen.

"It's only three months, Retta."

"Three months," Mama managed a shaky laugh. "That's a long time, George."

Lizzie interrupted my eavesdropping and held up three fingers.

"When is three months?"

I counted the time in my head. "After Independence Day, when the days are long and hot."

Papa spoke again. "Not so long, Retta. I'll make more money in the Army. Thirteen dollars a month. And you'll not have me to feed." Papa laid out the practicalities.

"I'd rather feed you and not have as much income," Mama told him.

Their voices, below the windows, melted into unintelligible murmurs. I imagined them leaning on the wall, heads close, a private conversation on a public street. I flopped back on the mattress, wide awake, staring at the ceiling, ready to close my eyes should the door open, pretending to be asleep. Lizzie rested her head on my shoulder and before long, her breathing came slow and regular.

A million thoughts ran through my mind. What did it mean for Papa to enlist? How will Mama be? Would he have to leave us? Would he be safe? Questions with no answers, only guesses.

I heard the door click shut, then muffled laughter, grunts, and creaking bed springs sifted through the thin walls. Mama and Papa could rip each other's heart out, or, as they did now, fill it with love and affection.

Chapter Two

Reaching over, I pulled aside the curtain to confirm rain splashed the windows, the roof, and streets below. I longed to stay in bed, close my eyes, and appreciate the watery melody. But it was not to be.

Papa tapped me on the shoulder. "Morning, daughter."

I smiled at him. "Morning, Papa."

"I'm going to work. Mama's a little under the weather. Help her, won't you?"

"We have school," I said, yawning and stretching. "What's wrong with her?"

"I have to go. I'll see you tonight."

"Papa?"

"Goodbye." The door shut behind him.

Sighing, I got up, wrapped my shawl around my shoulders, and padded into the kitchen to start the stove to warm the kitchen and put the kettle on. Waiting for the water to heat, I recalled the conversation, I wasn't meant to hear.

"Coffee?" Mama said, startling me from my reverie.

"Morning, Mama." I rose, wet the tip of my forefinger, and tapped it on the kettle. "Almost."

She pulled out a chair and slumped into it. A loose, messy braid of mousy brown hair lay over one shoulder.

Placing two cups on the table, I studied her, looking for signs of illness. "How are you feeling?" I asked, treading lightly.

"Why?" her head snapped up like a puppet's strings pulled by the puppeteer.

"Nothing," I murmured.

I poured our coffees. Leaving her in the kitchen, I took mine into the front room. Mary and Lizzie needed to get up. They stirred as I sipped my coffee, washed my face, redid my braid, and wound it into a bun on the back of my neck.

"Lizzie Bell! Mary Anna! Open your pretty blue eyes!" I used their nicknames to nudge them from sleep.

Lizzie grunted and turned away from me.

Mary's eyes slitted open. "Wain?"

"Yes, it's raining," I said.

"Rain starts with R," Mama yelled from the kitchen, "not W. Do it right or don't do it at all."

"Wain," Mary whispered, so Mama couldn't hear her try it again.

I smiled. "You'll get it. Now poke Lizzie for me."

Mary rolled over and stuck her finger in her sister's ear.

"Ow!" Lizzie grumbled. "Stop!"

Mama stomped into the room, hands on hips. "Can't I have one moment's peace and quiet?"

"Yes, Mama," we said in unison.

Lizzie flung the covers back and leapt out of bed. Mary sat up, her feet dangling over the side.

"Get dressed and go to school," Mama ordered.

"Can I have something to eat?" Lizzie whined.

"There's food in the kitchen."

"Thank you, Mama," Lizzie's sickening sweet reply curdled my stomach.

"Martha, did you speak with your father this morning?"

The day began like any other. Papa's hasty departure, followed by Mama's relentless interrogation. The hairbrush I pulled through Mary's hair stilled as I thought how best to answer. "Yes, before he left for work."

"Did he say what he's gone and done?"

I caught Lizzie's eye, subtly shaking my head. If we let on we overheard, Mama would have a fit.

Without waiting for a reply, she barked, "He joined the Army," choking back a bitter laugh at the folly of it.

"Papa's going to war?" I asked, innocently.

"Seems so. Everyone in the city is excited, like war is a grand party and they're all invited. Let's dress up and sing and dance to celebrate."

"Sounds like fun," Lizzie blurted.

Mama stared at her youngest girl, a wry smile on her lips, a wary look in her eye. "War is not fun."

Curious, I asked, "How do you know, Mama?"

"Because I lived through it. The young men in our village were called to fight the French, and many never returned. We paid extra taxes, and our farms were pillaged for food and supplies. War is poverty, and it makes you a widow." Her words landed like punches in the gut.

"What's a widow?" I rolled my eyes at Lizzie's innocent but stirring question.

Intercepting, I said, "It's what a woman is called when her husband…"

"Dies," Mama finished, her voice barely above a whisper. The word fell between us, heavy as a stone.

"Oh," Lizzie gasped.

"Let's go, we're going to be late," I clapped my hands, disturbing the quiet fear Mama's words evoked. "Mary, put on your skirt and I'll help do the hooks. Lizzie, wash your face."

Mama disappeared into her room when Henry cried, while we focused on our tasks.

Lizzie said, her face dripping. "Mama won't be a widow, will she? Papa can't die."

"No, of course not." I kept my tone light, hiding my uncertainty. But I wondered the same. Papa could be hurt or killed. As Mama said, everyone thought war a grand gesture to teach the South a lesson and make them bend to what the North thought best.

Mama's words of war scared me. How foolish of me to share Papa's excitement.

Papa and Henry greeted us, waving from the open window over Linn Street.

"Hello, my darlings!" Papa shouted.

We rushed up the stairs, threw our schoolbooks aside, and pounced on Papa for hugs.

"You're home early," I said. "Mama?"

"At the market. We have a few minutes to talk. Kitchen?"

I followed and gave him my full attention.

"Mama tell you?"

"About enlisting? Yes. And she told us war isn't exciting. It's people dying and not having anything to eat."

His eyebrows shot upwards. "Huh, she told you that."

"Yes, and if you die, she'll be a widow. I don't want you to die, Papa." And I certainly did not want Mama to be a widow.

"I will not die."

"But you could."

"Let's put the dying part aside and I'll tell you what's happening."

I drew a ladleful of water from the bucket and sipped. "Drink?"

He raised his hand and shook his head. "I signed up for three months and effective today, I'm on the military payroll. I quit my job and went to Turner Hall to meet with our unit's officers, including Willich. There are many unknowns as the Army is figuring out how and when we'll be paid, where we'll train, and when we'll be issued uniforms and firearms. The plan for the moment is to meet every morning, starting tomorrow, in the empty field behind the Hall. I'll sleep here at home until a camp is built to house us."

"A camp?"

"A bunch of tents to sleep in and an area where we can train and drill. I need to tell your mother my nights at home are almost over."

If Papa didn't come home at night, when would we see him next? "Will it be long until this camp is built?"

"They are saying a week, two at most. I know this is a big change. You know your Mama. She needs to be handled," he paused, "um, carefully. I want to take her out tonight. Can you mind the children?"

"Again? Can't I go too?"

"And who would watch the others?" Papa raised his hands.

"Mrs. Eiflert would. I'll go ask her." Out of my chair and lifting my coat from the peg, I stopped in my tracks at Papa's laugh.

"No, not tonight. I need time with Mama alone. Tell her what's going to happen. At least as much as I know."

"Why Papa? Why are you going away? Don't you love us anymore?" I returned to my chair, and put my elbows on the table, and cupped my chin in my hands.

"Of course I love you," he said. "It's not that. I raised my hand and swore allegiance to the United States Army for two reasons. One, the pay is far better than working in a shoe factory and two, I owe a debt to this country. America took me in with nothing but the clothes on my back and a dream in my heart. While all my dreams haven't come true, one has. The promise of freedom. A man is free to think as he wants, to speak for or against the government without retribution, and to organize with other men for fair working conditions and wages. I can vote for a man of my choice, one who

14

represents my way of thinking."

Papa filled the ladle and drank, locking his eyes with mine.

"And there's one more reason. Slavery is wrong. The Black man is a man, just like me. He should have the same rights as I do, but he does not. I will use my rights to defend the Negro and, in doing so, uphold the beliefs of my country and fight for their freedom."

A few words stuck out. Dreams. Freedom. Rights.

"I see the gears turning behind those pretty blue eyes. I've given you much to think about."

Sighing, I nodded, distracted. Something he said bothered me more than the rest. "Does Mama owe the same debt?"

"Interesting question." He rubbed his chin. "She does, but her way of repaying will be different."

"Good to know she's not going to war, too!" I jested.

"Her job will be far more difficult. While I obey orders and leave decisions to the officers, Mama will have four children underfoot with no man in the house. I think I'm getting the better end of the deal."

"I see." I didn't.

"She's going to need your help."

Blowing out an exasperated breath, I said, "You know how she is."

"You'll need to care for your sisters and brother."

"And who takes care of me? Mama berates me, belittles me, scolds me for no reason, and stomps off into the bedroom, leaving us alone. Anything that needs to be done falls to me, meals, school, bedtime, discipline. The only thing I can't do is feed Henry and if she could give that task away, she'd do it!" As my tirade gained momentum, I rose from my chair.

"She's not well." Papa sighed.

I leaned across the table, palms pressed against its worn surface and thrust my face nose to nose with his. "There isn't a day ends in y, she's in a good mood!"

"That bad?" He chuckled, firing my anger like the bellows to the stove.

I pulled up a chair and sat on its edge, my knees positioned between Papa's splayed legs. "Papa, you're not here like I am. Mama hides her moods from you. You get the good Mama, the gay and happy one. Unless, of course, you displease her. Like, join the army. Trust me, our lives, er, my life, will be hell when you leave."

His eyes hardened at my use of a curse word, but despite it, he raised a hand to my cheek and his thumb rubbed my chin. "We have no choice."

"Who's we? What you mean is I have no choice."

"It's the right thing to do for my country."

"It's the wrong thing to ask of your daughter." I crossed my arms and sat back in the chair.

Papa ran his hand through his hair, slicking it back. "I guess we've reached an impasse."

Our heads snapped toward the door as it creaked open, Mama's voice halting our conversation. "I'm home."

I glanced at Papa. "Sounds like she's in a good mood. We'll see how long it lasts."

Chapter Three

The next evening, Papa slumped into a chair, eyes darting around the room. "Mama?" he asked, nostrils flaring as he realized no meal awaited his arrival.

I pointed to the bedroom.

Stomping into their room, his voice echoed down the hallway, "Retta! Get out of bed and tend to your children. And me! We're hungry!"

I heard my name in her response, assuming she blamed me for not making the meal.

"No. This has to stop!" A scuffle ensued. Mama crying, "No." Papa yelling, "Now!"

The children and I huddled in the corner, clinging to each other, trying to evade the tension between our parents.

In the hallway, my disheveled mother appeared in her nightgown, eyes squinting in the light from the windows. Behind her, with his hands on her shoulders, Papa steered her into the kitchen.

"Make supper," Papa commanded.

Huffing, he stood outside the kitchen door. His gaze found us in the corner. "What are you doing over there?"

"N-n-nothing," Lizzie stammered.

"Oh, dear God! What have I done?" he pinched the bridge of his nose between his forefinger and thumb.

A pot clanked onto the stove, a cabinet door slammed, and muttered curses reached our ears. Papa, instead of confronting her again, fell into a chair. He looked skyward, as if the answer to his problems were in the ceiling.

"Papa?" I asked, my voice low to keep Mama from hearing.

Without moving, he said, "Yes?"

"Do you think she's like this because you're leaving?"

He sat up, folding his hands between his knees. "Partly. But she's been like this since Henry came two years ago. I don't know what to do."

"Are you leaving because she's, um, unwell?" I asked.

His head jerked up, and his outstretched arms drew me onto his lap. "No. I've told you why."

"We'll be all right with her," I said, pausing. "Won't we?"

Papa exhaled a slow breath carrying the weight of his worries. "Retta!" his booming voice startled me for the nearness of his bellow in my ears.

Mama shuffled into the front room, hands covered in flour. With lifted brows over narrowed blue eyes, she asked what he wanted without a word.

"Sit!" He commanded and pulled a chair from under the table.

"Get out of bed, make food, sit. Anything else you'd like me to do, George? I'm not a trained monkey."

"All right. I know. Please." His hand gestured to the chair.

Mama sat holding her floury hands above her lap.

"Children, come here and sit next to Mama." Papa waved his hand. "It's all right." Fearful of Mama's long arms, we inched closer, the little ones at Mama's feet while Mary and I sat cross-legged.

"Retta, I'm aware my joining the Army is upsetting you. I know you are afraid not only for me, but for yourself and our children. Since I'll be leaving soon, I think it best we talk about what it means."

Mama nodded. "George, I don't want to be this way, but I'm worried. Your leaving scares me."

"Let's start there. What scares you the most?" Papa went to take her hand and laughed when Mama held it up and away from him. "Give me your hand, dearest. A little flour won't hurt."

18

Mama managed a reluctant smile and laid her floury hand in his. "My greatest worry is you, George. You could get hurt or killed."

Papa patted her hand and said, "I'll do my best to avoid those unfortunate circumstances. The officers of the Ninth are confident this conflict will be short. What else worries you?"

"Money."

Papa glanced at me. "Bring me the tin."

I darted into the bedroom, reached under the bed, grabbed the cold metal box, and ran back to Papa.

He opened it and counted the coins. "Three dollars and seventy-two cents."

"Not much," Mama said.

"We've got some mending money coming this week," I said, excited to add to the conversation. "Mrs. Simmons owes us fifty cents."

Papa replaced the coins. "I read in the paper a committee is being formed to help the families left behind. It's unorganized, but Retta, you'll need to register your name and address with the Ward commissioners."

Mama retracted her hand from Papa's, needing it to convey her thoughts and feelings. "I wonder how our friends at St. Mattheus can help. I'll have a word with Hannah Eiflert tomorrow after the service."

"Good idea!" Papa rose and paced the room. "What else can we do? Children?"

"We can find more customers!" I clapped my hands together. "Let's ask at church tomorrow."

Mama nodded her assent to my idea.

Lizzie's face transformed from a blank stare into scrunched

brows over thoughtful eyes. "I've got an idea."

"Tell us," Papa encouraged.

"Well, my way is to save money," she said. "We could use less coal."

"Good idea, Lizzie! Cutting a scoop a day is a bucket by the end of the week."

Lizzie beamed from ear to ear. "We'll wear an extra sweater if it gets too cold."

"We could put her in the lunatic asylum," Mama said, head tilted toward Mary. "One less mouth to feed."

What in the world was she saying? Send Mary away? How could she think of doing that? I reached for Mary's hand.

Papa stood stock still, glaring at Mama. "You're joking, aren't you?"

Mama's hands stopped gesturing, a floury cloud puffing as they landed in her lap. Her chin dropped to her chest, avoiding Papa's gaze.

"I only meant," she said, her voice one note above a whisper, "if things get really bad."

Papa exploded with a roar, his face flushing crimson as he lunged at Mama. She recoiled and toppled backwards off her chair onto the floor and lay like a bug on its back, trying to right itself before the shoe crushed it.

Papa loomed over Mama, the scene slowly unfolding as in a dream, my parent's actions and reactions puzzling and surreal.

Mama groveled. "I'm sorry, George. I didn't mean it. It was a joke."

Papa stood over her, his voice a growl laden with misery. "If you ever do that to Mary, or if those words ever cross your lips, you will never see me again."

Mary recognized her name along with emotions she didn't understand. She seized my chin and yanked it square with mine. "Me, Mary." Her eyes were wide with worry.

"Don't worry, Mary. We're here."

Papa turned from Mama and squatted in front of us. "Motty. You must promise me something."

Eager to please, I nodded, agreeing to whatever he wanted.

"No matter what happens," he said, "Mary must never, ever, go to the asylum."

What did I agree to? "A-sy-lum?" I tested the foreign word.

Papa glared at Mama as if she needed to understand. "An asylum is a place where children go when they are orphaned or mad."

"Mad?" Lizzie piped up.

"Not the angry kind. Like Mary, who's different from other children her age," Papa explained.

"She's not so different," Lizzie defended her sister. "She's just, well, she's Mary."

Mama got to her feet, righted the toppled chair, and sat with arms crossed over her chest, observing the scene as an innocent bystander instead of the cause.

Papa resisted a retort and closed his eyes for a moment. "I only know this. Mary is special in ways many don't understand. They think she's stupid, because she doesn't say words like we do. They say she's crazy because she twirls on her toes and offers everyone a finger kiss. They want to put her in the lunatic asylum," he emphasized the word with a drop in his tone, "because she…"

"Because she's always going to need care," Mama cut in. "The kind I've been giving her since she was born. Took her three years to walk, still can't talk, and hangs onto my skirts like a clingy old tomcat. The census taker confirmed my suspicions last year. She's insane."

"Retta!" Papa sprang up from his crouched position and pressed his nose against Mama's. "This is your flesh and blood! Your daughter!"

"Mary will always be with me," I shouted. Mama glared at me, blue ice hardening like a glacier. Undaunted, I lifted my chin and repeated, "Always." And for good measure, added, "and forever."

I hadn't promised exactly what Papa asked, that Mary would never go to an asylum. But as I didn't intend to go, the promise could be kept by assuring Mary stayed with me.

Papa laid a hand over his heart and tipped his head. "Thank you, Motty."

I beamed up at him. Pleasing Papa meant more to me than complying with Mama's irrational demands. Sneaking a peek at Mama's reaction, I recoiled. Her eyes, glacial blue moments ago, now blazed with intensity.

"Retta?" Papa clasped Mama by the shoulders and gave her his full attention. "As I am brave enough to go off and put myself in harm's way, so must you be brave in caring for our family." Papa's arm swept the room. "You must all be strong, or our family will be lost."

Mama let her arms fall to her sides, head dangling as she studied the floor. "I'm sorry." A tear slid down her cheek.

He pulled her into his arms, her head settling into the crook of his neck, her arms around his waist. "I love you, Retta. Everything will be all right." He rubbed her back, his stubby fingers circling round and round. He forgave her in an instant. As if she'd never

22

muttered those foul words.

"I love you, too." She sniffed and jerked her head back far enough to meet his eye. "You better come back!" Mama slapped him playfully on the chest.

Papa pushed her head back onto his chest, looked at his children, and winked. "I'll be back."

Chapter Four

Papa said that on Wednesday, three days hence, he would leave for Camp Harrison, a temporary training area for the regiments formed in Cincinnati.

"I'll sleep at the camp, which means I'll not be coming home at night. Let's make these last days our best!"

And we did.

Papa met us at school with Henry in tow and took us to Washington Park. We fed the ducks, played hopscotch on a court I scratched into the dirt, and Papa chased us in a game of tag. Mama put her worries aside and joined in the fun. Lines of joy accentuated her blue eyes, her cheeks rosy with laughter. She and Papa exchanged little signs of love. Father playfully touched Mama's chin before planting a quick kiss on her nose, while she cupped his bearded face and pressed her forehead tenderly against his.

Lizzie stuck her tongue out. "I'm never gonna do that mushy stuff. Yuck!"

"But that's what love looks like, Lizzie," I said and wished my parents would always be this affectionate. But, in the back of my mind, I knew this Mama wouldn't stay around for long.

The night before Papa was scheduled to leave, Mama's

moodiness returned. I couldn't blame her. My spirits drooped, and I fretted, not getting any time alone with Papa. The little time with Papa wound down into our final evening, every other phrase starting or ending with, "When you come home, Papa."

Mama's cheeks never dried for her constant crying. Lizzie climbed into Papa's lap whenever he sat. Mary, oblivious to what Papa's departure meant, but alert to the coming change, showered his cheeks with countless finger kisses. Papa talked to Henry like a boy, not a baby, telling him he was the man of the house. He taught Henry how to salute and click his heels together.

Though Papa lavished the little time left on all his children, the absence of a private moment left me cross and jealous.

After supper, he took me aside. "Let's take a walk."

Mama said, "Wear your shawl, Martha. The night is cool."

Taken aback by her attentiveness to my health, I laid the strip of gray wool across my shoulders. "Thank you, Mama." My appreciation had nothing to do with staying warm.

We strolled north on Linn Street, the closely packed buildings giving way to scattered houses and vacant lots, leaving the bustling heart of town behind.

"I changed my mind," I said, keeping my eyes locked on the ground to avoid a twisted ankle or a fall on the uneven cobblestones.

"About what?" Papa asked.

"Taking care of my sisters and brother."

"And Mary?"

"Will always be with me."

He nodded. "Your mother will need you."

Sighing, I said, "I'll do what I can. No promises we'll get along!"

"I'll not hold you to it."

"Please stay safe," I pleaded, my voice wavering. "We need you. I need you to come home."

"I'll do my very best, for I like my life. As grim as it is sometimes, I have my children, your mother, and unlike Bavaria, I'm free."

"I didn't know freedom was so important to you."

"I didn't realize it either until I stepped off the boat in New Orleans. It's where I first saw black men, women, and children, naked and chained together, walking down the street on their way to the slave market."

"Market? Like Wade market?" Most of our meat and vegetables came from the covered space two blocks south of our home.

"No. This was an auction. A human auction. I didn't understand the words the man yelled from the box he stood upon, pointing to a boy about your age. Men in the crowd raised their hands or yelled their bids for him. Sickened, I turned away when a man in a white suit and hat dragged the crying boy away as he screamed for his mother on her knees, empty arms reaching toward her son."

"Oh no. You never told me that, Papa."

"A horrible sight I prefer to forget. I tell you now, so you understand how important ending slavery is to me. Why I'm going."

We turned toward the canal, a waterway stretching from Lake Erie to the Ohio River, dividing Cincinnati into two halves. On the path atop the west side berm, we matched the pace of a pair of mules towing a coal barge.

"I'm proud of you, Motty," Papa said.

I beamed at him and took his hand. "Thank you, Papa."

"Do you have any questions?"

"Only one. Any thoughts on how to handle Mama?"

Laughing under his breath, he said, "Distract her. Take her mind off her worries or whatever's making her mad. She's a planner. Perhaps between the two of you, the mending business will grow."

I nodded, thinking of the sewing Mama took in before Henry came. Learning how to sew at her feet, we worked well together. She handled the demanding tasks while I did the easy stitches. Over time, my skills improved enough to teach Mary and Lizzie simple stitches for darning and basting.

"I can do that," I answered, my voice stronger than I felt. "And Mary? What can I do about her and Mama?"

Papa's brow furrowed as he considered my question. He shook his head, exhaling a weary sigh. "Mary is work. Keep teaching Mary how to do things. Lizzie can help. It will take time, but in the long run, I think Mary will be a woman who adds beauty to this world, not detract from it."

"I like that! Mary's differences aren't to be mocked. They should be celebrated."

"You and I know it, but many do not. Beware, Motty. Prepare to be cajoled, tempted, and at times, believe you're better off by putting her away."

"Never!" I said, shaking my head.

"I will count on it." Papa kept my hand in his, while thoughts of never holding his hand again blurred my vision.

Chapter Five

At eight o'clock on the 18th of May 1861, the Ninth gathered at Washington Park, the designated starting point of the six-mile march to Camp Harrison. Mama looped her arm through Papa's, walking shoulder to shoulder. Behind them, Lizzie linked hands with Mary, their faces a mix of excitement and confusion while I brought up the rear, Henry on my hip.

The park overflowed with family and friends bidding tearful farewells to these new soldiers. An air of festivity permeated the park despite the grim intention of the gathering. The fine spring day masked the solemnity of the occasion, a cheerful atmosphere summoning the congregation to games, food, and music, as if it were a church picnic.

"There!" Papa shouted and pointed. Over the heads of the crowd, I caught sight of a white cloth fastened to what appeared to be a broomstick, the letter H printed in German cursive. "There's my company. Follow me."

Papa grabbed Mama's hand, and in single file, we wove through the crowd like a needle pulling thread. At the flag, Papa greeted fellow soldiers with handshakes and slaps on the back, steering us toward a cluster of women and children under a shady maple. A band struck the opening chords of "Yankee Doodle."

"This is where we must part, meine Lieblinge." He opened his arms, and we stepped into his embrace. Kisses fell on us, his lips pecking our foreheads, cheeks and lips.

I moved back, placed my hand on his cheek, and said, "Be safe, Papa." Eyes glassy, he bobbed his head.

Mary touched his cheek with a finger, and Papa's thick hand held it there, the thumb of his other hand swiping across her jaw.

Prying Lizzie's arms from his right leg, he bent down and squeezed his youngest daughter. "Must you go, Papa?" she asked. His Adam's apple bobbed once, then again. He fought for words. "I do. But I can only do my best if I can count on you, Lizzie. Help your Mama and Motty. Do well in school. I expect an excellent report when I return."

"Oh, I will, Papa!" She lunged at him once more, emphasizing her squeeze with a grunt. She let go and stood next to me.

A miniature of my father, Henry clicked his heels and saluted, his auburn curls glinting in the sun. Papa mimicked his son, returning the salute. Dropping his salute first, Henry relaxed and jumped into Papa's arms.

My eyes watered, blinding me. I dropped Mary's hand to dig for the handkerchief in my pocket.

Papa held Mama in his arms, their embrace unusual for a public setting. But all around, men and women said farewell with tears, desperate clutches, and passionate kisses defying decorum and restraint that normally ruled their lives.

"Mary," I reached for her, expecting her at my hip. But my hand met air. Turning my head, I stared at the space where Mary stood only moments before. "Mary?" I scanned the immediate area. Almost every woman wore a dark dress and hat, and from behind, they all looked alike, the one exception being their height.

"Lizzie," I whispered, careful to keep my voice low for fear of my parents overhearing. "Keep hold of Henry and stay close to Mama."

My sister, ever sensitive to tension and trouble, whispered back. "What's wrong?"

"Mary. I have to find her."

"What?" the volume of her voice rising to normal. "You lost Mary?"

I put my finger to my lips, hushing her. "No. Stay here."

Not waiting for a response, I turned my back on my family and scanned the proximity. Where would she go? Mary had her favorite spots in the park, but with people covering every aspect, none were identifiable. Along Elm Street, near where Company H gathered, budding maple trees lined the outer edge of the park. I pushed my way through, commenting, "Pardon me. Excuse me." I stepped on someone's foot. "I'm sorry."

The roots of one tree provided a slight rise above the crowd, and on my tiptoes, I peered over their heads. I hesitated to call out her name, for a dozen heads would turn, her name a common one.

A bugle's sharp notes pierced the air, a crisp, commanding call signaling something important. The din in the park lessened as heads swiveled toward the sound.

A man and woman beside me embraced. "It's time to go."

Frustration boiled over as I stretched on my tiptoes, craning my neck to peer over a sea of heads, my adjusted height inadequate. "Where the hell are you, Mary?" I said under my breath. If didn't return to my family, I'd miss seeing Papa one last time. But where was she? I hurried to my marker tree and pushed through the crowd, abandoning apologies in my urgency.

"Where have you been?" Mama hissed and grabbed my ear. "You cost me goodbye time. Your father had to rescue Mary from the duck pond."

"The duck pond? Huh?" I stammered, and in my peripheral vision spotted them edging their way through the crowd.

The disappointment in Papa's features, from the downward curve of his lips to the worry clouding his eyes, confirmed my failure.

"I'm sorry, Papa. She was next to me one minute and gone the next. I searched everywhere."

"Sam Wagner saw her and alerted me." He placed Mary's hand

in mine, and I jerked it into my skirts, signaling my anger at her running off. She tried to pull away, but I held fast.

His voice dropped, heavy with meaning. "This is what we talked about. You must watch over her, always."

My throat constricted, head shaking side to side, denying I'd lost his trust. He pecked a kiss on my head, disappointment evident in its brevity.

Papa clutched Mama to him, kissed her, and along with nine hundred other men, lined up for the march to Camp Harrison. A bugle sounded, the drum beat a marching cadence, and, on command, Company H of the Ninth Ohio Volunteer Infantry lifted their feet and filed out of the park.

In silence, we viewed the haphazard parade until Company K, the last of the Ninth, marched out of sight, leaving behind the human litter of the departing army. Bawling women, sniffling children, boys saluting and refusing to drop their stance. Families of two or six and even eight children snuggled in tight groups until the drumbeat faded into the hills of Cincinnati.

The picnic-like atmosphere of a few minutes ago collapsed under the weight of two truths. That fathers and sons counted on for protection and livelihood deserted their families today, destined for greatness or demise. Their wives and mothers, ill-equipped to care for their families, reluctantly shouldered the mantle of responsibility thrust upon them.

Could Mama make sure we survived? Could I keep the promise I'd already blemished by letting go of Mary?

Looking at the back of Mama's head as we trudged home, silent and mournful, I realized we had only one choice. To buck up and do what needed to be done. No matter what.

Chapter Six

The Saturday after Papa's departure, Mama remained in bed, moaning about a headache keeping her from facing the world. With seventy-five cents and a regular income at stake, it fell to me to deliver the week's batch of mending to Mama's first customer, Mrs. Simmons.

When Papa lost his job two years ago, Mama, a seamstress who learned her skills from her Oma, thought she could add income by taking in mending. Families in our neighborhood did their own sewing, so Mama knocked on doors in an affluent area. After a week with no luck, she did something drastic. Taking me into her confidence as I would be involved in doing the actual work, she said, "Let's offer to do work for free. If they like the results, I'll have proven my skills, and the ladies can recommend me."

Mama and I walked south to West Fourth, where large mansions and boarding houses lined the street. Many women turned us down, and at some houses, we didn't get beyond the servant who answered the door. As the sun fell behind the multi-storied buildings, tired and bereft of getting any business, we approached a simple yet handsome brick house. Mama dropped the brass knocker on the polished hardwood door. "Last one."

A petite woman wearing an apron appeared. Locks of brown hair escaped her bun, tendrils falling around her face, her forehead dotted with beads of sweat.

"Yes, can I help you?" Wiping her hands on her apron, she eyed us warily.

Mama introduced herself, charging right in. "My name is

Margaretta Hesch. May I see the lady of the house?"

"I'm the lady. Mrs. Jonathan Simmons."

Mama explained her mission. "I'm a skilled seamstress looking to help busy women like yourself with little time for mending. Would you be interested in trying my services for free?"

"Free?" The woman scrunched her brow over scoffing eyes. "Nothing is ever free."

"A free trial," Mama said with urgency. "I propose to mend a few pieces, and assuming you are pleased with my work, we can discuss future arrangements to meet your needs."

Mrs. Simmons stared at her, contemplating. "Well, I have a pile of mending I have no time for. And several dresses need to be lengthened for my girls."

A bright smile lit up Mama's face.

Tilting her head, her eyes looking above our heads, Mrs. Simmons pondered Mama's offer. "Wait here." She closed the door, leaving us on the porch wondering if we'd finally won a customer.

A few minutes later, Mrs. Simmons invited us in. We entered the foyer, where she pulled items from a chair and showed Mama the needed repairs.

"This is truly free? You won't take this, and I'll never see you again?" Mrs. Simmons asked.

"No, Mrs. Simmons," Mama said, her voice exuding confidence. "I live near Linn and Liberty Streets above Locke's Boots and Shoes. You can come find me there if I don't bring these back to you in, let's say, two days."

My eyes grew round at the quick turnaround. All other housework would be suspended until we finished.

"Very well. I expect you on Monday by noon." Mrs. Simmons

smiled and escorted us out. The heavy knocker clacked as she closed the door.

The memory of Mrs. Simmons' grim face when we missed a delivery promise clear in my mind, I had no choice but to take Mary along, leaving Lizzie with Henry. After packing the canvas bag we used to carry the mending, I stepped into the bedroom. "Mama."

No response. "Mama!" I raised my voice and shook her shoulder.

"What?" she replied, her voice muffled in the bedclothes.

"Mary and I are going to see Mrs. Simmons. Lizzie is in the front room with Henry."

A snort dismissed me. Her frequent ailments and lethargy worried me, but I could not deal with her now.

On the stairs from our rooms, Mary placed her right foot on the step below, lowered her left beside the right, and repeated the process. Her way of feeling safe, I waited an eternity until her last foot touched the ground. Her stride, shorter and more deliberate than mine, added fifteen minutes to the errand, but dragging her along to match my pace often resulted in her stopping without notice and refusing to move.

Saturday traffic was chaotic. I gripped Mary's hand as we dodged carriages, mule-driven wagons, and unpredictable men on horseback, who could change course and trample us. We made several of these busy crossings on our route and only after we arrived at the Simmons' house did my heart stop racing and my palms dry.

"Me?" Mary pointed to the door and poked herself in the chest. Not waiting for an answer, she grabbed the knocker and banged it on the brass plate twice. She giggled at her accomplishment.

Mrs. Simmons greeted us. "Hello, Martha. And who is this

young lady?"

"This is my sister, Mary. She helps with your mending."

The older woman nodded. "Nice to meet you, Mary. Please come in."

We stepped into the foyer, where I laid the mending bag on a table and extracted a nightgown, three sets of stockings, and two blouses. Mrs. Simmons didn't scrutinize them as she trusted our work.

"I did but-tons!" Mary announced. Two or more syllables required concentration.

Mrs. Simmons smiled at her and fingered the buttons on a blouse. "These are perfect."

As I placed the new mending in the bag, ten-year-old Sylvia Simmons entered the hall.

Mary lunged at Sylvia like a bird snatching a crumb of bread. "Hello!" she screeched, her face inches from Sylvia's startled eyes.

Sylvia shrunk back, looking for help, cried, "Mama!"

Mary said, "Mama."

Sylvia's jaw dropped. When she recovered, she shouted, "She's my mama, not yours."

Mary pointed to Mrs. Simmons. "Mama."

"What are you talking about? She's my mama."

Mrs. Simmons took charge. "Sylvia, this is Mary. She's Martha's sister."

"She's strange. I don't like her." Sylvia sneered and crossed her arms over her chest.

Our business concluded, I grasped Mary's upper arm and drew her to the door. "Thank you, Mrs. Simmons. We'll be here next week."

As we let ourselves out, Mrs. Simmons said, "Yes, my dear, Mary is odd, and I'm sorry she scared you. Maybe we shouldn't let her come again."

We depended on Mrs. Simmons' business and Papa's warning about people who didn't understand Mary echoed in my mind. Must family loyalty yield to financial security?

Maneuvering through traffic toward home, I thought about the incident with Sylvia and knew to expect more of the same. I berated myself for not stepping in to help Mary or confront Sylvia and resolved to shield my sister from situations like today. Better yet, surround her with people who accepted her. I needed to do a better job of defending her. Mary deserved defending.

Chapter Seven

Mama's health improved enough to visit our Ward Councilman and apply for relief money offered to families of Ohio Volunteers. He filed her application for approval, but Mr. Kleiner expected no problems, as Papa was in one of the first regiments. He instructed her to check back in a week.

At church, Mama asked several ladies, Mrs. Eiflert, among them, to let her know if they knew of anyone who needed mending help. With school recessed for the summer, and Papa not expected to return till mid-July, we hoped to fill our spare time with as much work as we could turn out.

With eighth grade completed, my formal schooling ended in early June. Some boys in my class would attend high school in the fall, but without the means and being a girl, I'd reached the limits of my education.

At age six, when Mary started school, Papa spoke to the schoolmaster, telling him I would help her in class. Mary learned best with repetition, and with constant practice, she could print her name and recite her letters and numbers. With school finished for me, Mary's formal education ended too, leaving it up to me to use daily life as teaching moments.

With Papa's enlistment and departure, spring cleaning yet to be undertaken, Mama suggested Mary and I launder our household goods. In the yard beside our building, I built a fire under the washtub and stabbed a set of sheets into the scalding water with a wooden paddle.

"Martha!" A gruff male voice at our yard's entrance, I whirled around to find Mr. Locke, our landlord, approaching.

Stocky and well-built, he held up a white envelope. "You have a letter." As he handed it to me, his eyes lingered on my chest, where the heat had unbuttoned my dress. I felt exposed. A chill ran through me despite the steam rising from the washtub. I snatched the letter and turned away, my cheeks burning.

"Tell your mama to see me about the rent," he called as he walked away.

My knees weak, I used the paddle for support.

Mary put an arm around my waist. "Motty, sad?"

"No, not sad." My shaking hands and thundering heart betrayed my fright. "Let's get these on the line. We have a letter from Papa!"

Rushing into our rooms, I held the envelope aloft. "Mama, a letter came!"

"A letter?"

My hand shook like a leaf in the wind, the lechery in Locke's eyes seared on my mind. Keeping my voice steady, Mama didn't notice.

She took the envelope, glanced at the address, and said, "George." Mama bit her bottom lip as she perused her husband's handwriting. "Letters are never good news."

"Since Papa wrote it himself, it's likely he's fine," I assured her. "Would you like me to read it first?"

"No, read it aloud," Mama said and handed it to me with great care, something to be treasured.

Instead of tearing the envelope, I picked up a knife from the table and slid it under the red wax, loosening it. The flap popped up. I pinched the paper between my forefinger and thumb, drew it out, and handed the envelope back to Mama.

Four pairs of eyes focused on the paper, folded in half, waiting for Papa's news. Mama's right hand covered her mouth, the knuckles on her left white as she gripped her skirt. She nodded for me to begin.

Papa's fine German cursive filled the front page. Clearing my throat, I read his words, imagining his low, melodious voice.

28 May 1861

Hallo meine Lieben,

After marching from Camp Harrison ten days ago, we arrived at Camp Dennison near Miamiville. We are known by our nickname, *Die Neuners*, because every man, except Colonel McCook speaks German. Adjutant August Willich trains us on modern military methods, preparing us to fight and win battles.

I paused and looked at the anxious faces of my family.

"Is there more?" Mama asked.

I opened the sheet to reveal a column of writing on each half of the page.

> When we arrived in camp, Governor Dennison, on behalf of President Lincoln, asked the entire regiment to enlist for three years instead of three months. I hesitated, knowing how much I am needed at home, but every man except a few stayed. I will stay too. At the end of my service, I will receive one hundred dollars.

"One hundred dollars!" Mama's eyes grew wide with disbelief at the outrageous sum.

I turned the letter over to the final set of handwriting on the back. Only a few lines remained above Papa's signature.

> When I am paid, I will send a pay ticket you can cash at the Paymaster's office. Please write the news from home and send it to the address on the envelope. I am well but miss you.
>
> Mit Liebe,
>
> Papa

I folded the letter and handed it to Mama. She pressed it to her chest as tears streamed down her pale cheeks. She stared into space, her expression neutral yet profoundly tragic.

Pulling a handkerchief from my pocket, I swiped at my lashes. Three years. Three months was long enough, but three years. I'd be, what, seventeen by the time he got out.

"How long is three years?" Lizzie asked.

"Let's see, you'll be around ten," I said.

"How old will I be when Mama's not sad anymore?"

Mama overheard and turned on Lizzie, venom coating her voice. "I'll be sad, I'll be angry. And I will not tolerate impudent children!" In one quick step, she towered over her youngest daughter.

Lizzie scooted back on the bed, away from Mama's threat. Mary scuttled next to her, knowing her mother's temper better than anyone.

"No," Mary said, eyes locked on Mama's, a spark of defiance flitting across her face.

"Mama," I said with compassion, an attempt to distract her from Lizzie. "We're all sad Papa is not coming home."

Mama's mood shifted again, overwhelmed by Papa's news. She paced. "Why would he leave us? Three years? How will we manage?"

At fourteen, I had little experience to draw upon, but I did know two things. One, we had to work together, which meant Mama could not hibernate in her room. Two, I promised to take care of the family. For the second to be true, the first had to be handled.

Inhaling, I led Mama to a chair. As she sat, her eyes locked onto mine, like a child looking for guidance.

"What are our options? Are they different from yesterday when we thought Papa would be home in three months?" I sat next to her, held her hand, and spoke without judgment.

From the corner of my eye, I saw Lizzie gather Henry and Mary in a circle for a game of jacks. Thanking her silently for the favor of time alone with Mama, I focused all my attention on discussing our dilemma with her.

"What's different today than yesterday?" I asked.

"He'll be gone longer than he said."

"Yes. So, what does that mean?"

"What do you mean, what does that mean? It means my husband has a greater chance of dying."

"Oh!" My plan to focus on how we'd survive backfired. Of course, Mama would think of Papa and his safety.

Aghast at my apparent lack of concern for Papa, Mama rose and fled from the room.

Staring after her, Lizzie's voice, thick with sarcasm, penetrated the horror of my blunder. "Well done, Motty."

Why did I bother trying to understand Mama? It always ended up in tears.

Chapter Eight

Papa's news shattered Mama. She closeted herself in her room, leaving me to cope with the children.

Henry refused to eat, Lizzie backtalked, and Mary flung her oatmeal onto the floor. At my wit's end, I escaped outside, and after a dozen turns around the yard, I decided we needed help.

I scribbled a few words on a scrap of paper. "Lizzie, can you take this to Mrs. Eiflert?"

Eager to be outdoors and escape our tiny rooms, she grabbed the note and bolted for the door.

"Stick to the streets. No alleys!" I called after her.

An hour later, the door flew open, unleashing a gust of warm air as Lizzie bounded in, Mama's friend in tow.

Offering to take her hat and shawl, I said, "Thank you for

coming."

"Happy to help." Despite her portly figure and advanced age she bustled about the room, peppering me with questions. "Have the children eaten?" "What's in the larder?" "Is anyone ill?"

I fired back the answers. Yes. Very little. No.

Satisfied the basics were covered, she fixed her piercing gaze on me and demanded, "Where's your mother?"

I pointed to the door at the end of the hall.

"How long?"

"Three days."

"Dear me! That's too long."

"Yes." I struggled with loyalty to Mama and honesty with her friend and figured a half-truth wouldn't hurt my chances of getting into heaven. "She's tired."

Lizzie interrupted, "She's got another headache. Says it's our fault."

With a sharp glance, I signaled my sister to hush.

Mrs. Eiflert folded her hands in front of her, silent, waiting for me to tell her the reason I'd asked her to come.

"She has headaches most days. Or at least she says she does. I don't know for sure if she suffers from them or if they are, um," I faltered, "an excuse to avoid things."

"Things?"

"You must know most of the Ninth signed up for three years. Did your Frank sign up too?"

"Yes, yes he did," her voice clipped, an edge to it indicating she didn't wish to discuss her eighteen-year-old son's frivolous actions. "I can understand how your father's absence would be upsetting. Can you let her know I'm here?"

I stepped down the short hall and knocked on the bedroom door, nudging it open. A sliver of light widened in the dark, windowless room. "Mama?"

"What?" Expecting a muffled grunt from under the covers, she was sitting, a quilt over her legs, squinting against the glare from the doorway. "You're awake?"

"I heard voices. Who's here?"

Her hair hung loosely over her shoulders, brushed and free of tangles. "Mrs. Eiflert's come." I neglected my part in her presence.

"I'll dress."

"No need, Retta." Mrs. Eiflert, said from behind me. "Hello, Retta. Martha tells me you aren't feeling well. I thought you could use a visitor. May I come in for a few minutes?"

Mama nodded, and Mrs. Eiflert squeezed past me.

"Martha, could you make us some tea?"

"Yes, Ma'am." I left the door open, hoping to catch some of their conversation and readied the tea. As I re-entered Mama's room, she hastily wiped her eyes, her fingers fluttering over her lashes before grasping the teacup.

"Thank you, Martha," Mrs. Eiflert dismissed me with a glance at the door.

I left the door open an inch and eavesdropped, straining to hear.

"Think of it, Hannah. I could find a job, and so could Martha." Mama's voice carried a hint of excitement, as if a windfall were on the horizon.

Mrs. Eiflert's usually stoic and forceful voice faltered with a hint of alarm. "Isn't it too soon for drastic measures? How would you manage the younger children?"

"I've been lying here thinking about it. It would be best if I put them in the orphan asylum."

Mrs. Eiflert and I gasped at the same moment. Berating myself for possibly giving away my position at the door, I covered my mouth and held my breath.

"Just until George comes home," Mama relented. "Then we'll get them back."

"But what if George doesn't come..."

"I'll worry about that if it happens. Right now, we can't afford to live here with no money coming in."

"It is a solution," Mrs. Eiflert conceded the point, and attempted to steer her in a different direction. "But surely, they will be paid soon."

"Another option is to leave Martha with the children while I work. But I'm not sure I'll earn enough."

"What if Martha worked and you stayed with the children? She could work as a domestic servant and have a place to live."

A cup clinked on a saucer. "No, I want to get away from the children. Especially Mary."

Poor Mary! Mama had little desire to spend time with her second daughter.

"Retta, I think you're making a mistake. Splitting up your family for the sake of a few dollars would not make your husband happy."

"That's what's holding me back." Mama said with a sigh. "George. I believe he'd kill me."

Mrs. Eiflert chuckled under her breath. "Hardly."

The swish of skirts alerted me to movement in the bedroom and I prepared to dash to the kitchen. But no footsteps signaled the older woman's exit from the room. I hovered at the door.

Deepening her voice with authority, Mrs. Eiflert said, "Here's what I suggest. The Relief Aid will be funded in a week or two, so you'll have money. The Turners are organizing donations of clothing and household goods, and Father Knochelmann asked me to help collect food for families in our congregation. You have your mending business, too. Why don't you wait? See how things go and then, if you can't make it, revisit your options."

Skirts swished again, this time followed by footsteps. Knowing how much Mama hated eavesdroppers, I scrambled into the kitchen and banged a pan on the stove for good measure. Tears burned as I fought them back. How could Mama think of sending my sisters and brother to the asylum, especially after Papa's threat that she'd never see him again? And Mary couldn't go, or I'd be breaking the promise to keep her with me.

A few minutes later, Mrs. Eiflert entered the kitchen. "Martha, your mama's ready to rejoin the world."

"Thank you for coming," I said, taking the teacups from her outstretched hands and asked innocently, "What did you talk about?"

"How to get along until your father's pay comes through. I've given your mother a few ideas, and I'll leave it to her to explain. I must go."

Having kept her hat on, she slipped dove gray gloves over her surprisingly small hands contrasting with her ample frame. "I'll see you at church. And Martha, don't hesitate to call on me again."

I nodded, dislodging a single tear, and swiped it away with the back of my hand.

My back to the door after Mrs. Eiflert left, I leaned against it, wondering how I could pretend ignorance to Mama's plan for putting the children in the asylum. How long until we ran out of money and supplies? I closed my eyes, exhaustion threatening to overwhelm me, when a creak from Mama's door jolted me alert. Footsteps padded down the hall, growing louder as they approached. I wiped my hands on my apron and turned to face whatever came next.

"Martha?" Mama's voice, clearer than it had been in days, called out, "What's for dinner?"

Mama resumed her motherly duties following Mrs. Eiflert's visit. That night, with the children asleep, she invited me for a cup of tea in the kitchen.

"I suppose sending for Mrs. Eiflert was difficult for you." Mama blew the steam from her cup, eyeing me over the rim.

Unable to meet her gaze, I fiddled with the cup handle and nodded.

"Thank you," she said, her voice steady and sincere. "She's a good friend. Reminded me we're not the only ones in this predicament. Men are joining the Army left and right, leaving families larger than ours behind."

Lowering her cup to the saucer, Mama put an open palm on the table and slid it toward me. "I'm sorry."

Suspicious, I stared at her outstretched hand. This unnatural gesture, as peculiar as snow falling in summer, gave me pause. Was this a trick? Did she know I'd overheard her confession to Mrs. Eiflert?

Her fingers wiggled impatiently. Accepting her apologetic hand betrayed my loyalty to Papa and my ideals of motherhood. I could not reward her, nor could I pretend ignorance of her scheme.

"Mrs. Eiflert said you discussed how to survive without Papa." I needed to know if her answer matched what I'd overheard.

A heavy sigh accompanied the withdrawal of her hand. She grasped her teacup with both hands, hovering over the contents as if the leaves foretold her future. "Oh, things like getting donations at Turners and St. Mattheus, checking on our application at the Relief Fund."

"Anything else?" I picked at a snagged cuticle, risking exposure to my eavesdropping.

Her chin snapped up, eyes locking onto mine, she said, "No. Why?"

I abandoned my injured finger and took a sip of tea. Setting down the cup, I shrugged nonchalantly. "Wondering how I can help."

"That's my girl," Mama said, a playful grin on her lips. Her hand slid across the table again.

Unwillingly, my hand went into hers. "Will we be all right, Mama? Three years is a long time." I needed reassurance from the only person I could rely upon until Papa returned. And 'all right' didn't include sending my siblings to the asylum.

Her cool fingers and gentle squeeze did nothing to allay my fears. Before I could reciprocate, she withdrew her hand. "I'll do my best."

Chapter Nine

Mama visited Mr. Kleiner and learned her weekly Relief Fund allotment amounted to two dollars. A wife with one child got a dollar twenty-five and each additional child, another twenty-five cents. Mr. Kleiner warned her the first payment would be disbursed the last Saturday in June, two weeks hence, a lifetime when we were already surviving on scraps and community donations.

Taking command of the situation for once, Mama issued clear instructions. "Tomorrow, you make the Simmons' delivery in the morning and ask if she knows anyone else in need of mending. When you return, I'll go to the church to pick up food and ask the women there for referrals."

Delivering her finished mending on Saturday, I asked if she knew of others who needed mending help.

"There's a boarding house down the street run by a widow, Mrs. Mitchell. She mentioned losing her mending girl and I told her I had a reliable woman who did good work. I'll write her address for you."

I loaded Mrs. Simmons' new batch of goods into the canvas bag and calculated the fee. A dollar! With three young girls and Mrs. Simmons' frugality keeping dresses and petticoats on them until they outgrew them, the income would last a few years.

"Here you are," Mrs. Simmons reentered the hall and handed me a slip of paper.

I read the address aloud. "422 West Fourth Street. Thank you, ma'am! It means the world to us to have another customer during times like these."

"I'm happy to help. But," she said, "I must insist my work be your priority. Will that be a problem?"

"No, Ma'am." My head shook like a baby rattle.

"Very well. Let Mrs. Mitchell know I sent you." She glided to the door and held it as I stepped onto the porch. "Give your mother my regards."

Curious about the Mitchell house, I walked two blocks west, verifying that the brass numbers on the door matched Mrs. Simmons' handwriting. "How grand!" I admired the imposing three-story red brick building, with a deep porch spanning its width and a gabled roof, the first and second floors lined with rows of windows. The amount of mending from this house could carry us until Papa's pay arrived and beyond. Excited to tell Mama, I raced home to share the news.

Smoke from the fire under the wash tub assailed my nostrils as I entered our yard. Mama jabbed at the contents with a paddle, a petticoat bubble rising to the surface.

"Mama!" I burst into the yard waving the Mitchell's address. "Mrs. Simmons gave us the name of a woman who needs mending help."

"Good. Where is it?"

"Down the street, less than two blocks away."

"I mean the mending. Didn't you go there?"

"No. I came straight home. I didn't think you'd want me to go by myself." I lifted the mending bag from my shoulder and laid it on the ground.

"Wasted time and energy!" she huffed. "Help me finish these."

With the paddle handle, she hooked a white blouse, dropped it into the rinse bucket, and swished it around. I plucked one end from the murky water, and Mama grabbed the other. Twisting in opposite directions, we wrung out the excess water, and I pinned it to the line. Repeating this process for the rest of the tub, we covered one of two lines stretched across the yard from our building to the one next door. As we worked in silence, I longed to explain myself, to make Mama understand my hesitation. But her rigid posture warned me off.

The tub empty, she ordered me to douse the fire. "I'll leave as soon as I'm presentable."

48

I smothered the hot coals with the rinse water. Upstairs, I placed the Simmons mending on its designated shelf, laid the Mitchell's address on the table and waited for Mama.

"I'm leaving." She wore a gray skirt with a white blouse, her favorite black silk shawl covering her shoulders.

"I should be back in an hour. Depends on what I find at the church." Standing at the table, she glanced at the Mitchell address as she plunged her hands into her gloves.

"Can we talk about the Mitchell work?" I asked, anxious to clear the air between us.

"Fine, walk down with me." Mama swept out the door and down the stairs.

At the bottom, she said, "What about it?"

"Did I do something wrong?" I picked at a loose cuticle.

"Nothing wrong. You did nothing. Nothing at all." Mama plucked a bit of lint from her skirt.

"I couldn't talk to the Mitchells without you. It wouldn't be right for me to meet them before you did." Propriety meant a lot to Mama, and I didn't want to overstep.

"These are difficult times, Martha. I thought we agreed to share the burden. I'll handle the church ladies, and you handle the rest."

This wasn't how I remembered our agreement. "I thought today we were splitting up, with the children and all."

Mama's dark brown eyebrows arched, bringing out the wrinkles on her forehead. An instant later they settled above her icy blue eyes. "You watched me deliver my speech a dozen times and were there when Mrs. Simmons agreed to try us. Do the same. It's not hard."

"But Mama, that was two years ago," I said. The cuticle bled. "I'm not good at meeting new people. You go and I'll handle things here."

Mama wagged her head. "Do what I did. Introduce yourself, tell her who sent you, and why you're there. Simple!"

"What if I mess up and ruin our chances?" Panic filled my chest. How could I possibly do what Mama did so easily?

"I'll make you a deal," Mama said. "If I get a new customer at church today, you go and meet Mrs. Mitchell. If it's not too late when I return, you'll have time today. Saturdays are best for back door trade."

"But." My argument dissolved before it took shape, cornered by Mama's expectations and my inexperience.

Mama eyed me, tapping her foot.

"Fine." I stomped my foot, the words bursting out before I could stop them. "I hope you come home empty-handed!"

Again, her brows arched. "You don't want your brother and sisters to eat?"

"No, of course not. I didn't mean it like that, Mama."

"I certainly hope not." She turned to go. Over her shoulder, she shouted, "Take the wash off the line. It looks like rain."

Mama marched in an hour later, a basket of supplies on her arm and a new customer's mending in her hand, a self-satisfied smirk dancing around her lips. "Mrs. Stickler's husband is a hog butcher. I've been promised fresh pork instead of cash payment."

I rewound my chignon, splashed cool water on my face, and slung the canvas bag over my shoulder, eager to depart before Mama added insult to injury.

The hot June afternoon darkened my underarms before I'd walked a block and after two, my drenched handkerchief merely smeared the perspiration across my brow instead of drying it. I weaved through a herd of grunting pigs, leaped over a dozen foul gutters, and narrowly avoided a rickety carriage hurtling around a corner on two wheels, derailing my plan to rehearse my introduction.

The cool shade of the porch at 422 West Fourth Street beckoned me. In front of the massive oak door, between me and a prospective customer, I muttered a few sentences aloud for practice. Even my mutter stuttered, my nerves raw at tackling this foreign task.

I recalled a trick Mama showed me about how to walk like a lady. "Imagine a string from the top of your head to the sky, like a puppeteer working a marionette. Your back straightens, your neck is long and lean, and your chin lifts."

Stretching with the imaginary string, I dotted my forehead with my useless handkerchief and patted my chignon for escaping locks. Clutching the heavy brass knocker, I tapped it twice in quick succession. I took a deep breath, held it, coaxed my lips into a somber smile, and exhaled slowly.

The door opened. A trim girl, a few years older than me, stepped into the doorway. She wore an apron over a striped blouse and skirt, the uniform of a house servant.

I opened my mouth to speak, but my tongue and brain wouldn't connect. "I, er, I'm—" I faltered, thinking myself a fool, unable to complete my introduction.

The girl smiled down at me, her hands crossed low over her apron. "There you go, t'will be better if you say your name, lass."

Her brogue and breezy way relaxed me a bit. I tried again. "I'm Martha. Martha Hesch."

She nodded. "Happy to meet you."

"Same to you. I'm here for Mrs. Mitchell."

"And the reason for your visit?"

"Mrs. Simmons said she needs help with mending."

"Nah. You'll be wantin' to speak with Miss Mitchell, not the Mrs." She pulled the door open wide, welcoming me into the house.

"I'm Rose. Please wait here." She motioned to two chairs set at an angle to each other. "I'll fetch Miss Jane."

Jane. Miss Jane Mitchell. Having gotten this far, a surge of confidence took hold of me. I could do this.

Ignoring Rose's invitation to sit, I scanned the foyer, turning slowly to absorb the grand hallway. A vase of fresh flowers sat atop a massive round table dominating the center of black and white checkered flooring. A bronze chandelier, fit for eight candles, hung suspended by a matching chain over the table. To the left of the front door, a steep and broad wooden staircase, banister gleaming, rose to a landing, with more steps beyond. If the hallway was this lavish, imagine the rest of the house! Circling the table, I mouthed my introduction, adding emphasis with hand gestures.

"Hello!" A woman's voice, light and melodic, came from behind me, accompanied by the swoosh of the swinging door Rose disappeared through.

Twirling to face the speaker, I planted a smile on my lips. "Hello." I dipped a small curtsy to a young woman, who returned my smile. A thick bun secured at the back of her neck appeared to hold a great length of glossy brown hair. A blue velvet ribbon encircled her head, complimenting her hairstyle, its bow askew but aligned with one of her dark blue eyes. She tipped her head forward, acknowledging my greeting.

Inhaling deeply, I focused on Miss Mitchell's neutral expression and launched into my speech. "I'm pleased to make your acquaintance, Miss Mitchell. I'm Martha Hesch. My mother and I work for your neighbor, Mrs. Jonathan Simmons, a few blocks east. She mentioned you needed help with mending." I'd done it! A self-congratulatory grin curled the corners of my mouth.

"It's a pleasure to meet you," she responded and sat in one of the hall chairs. "Please." She gestured for me to take the chair across from her.

I perched on the edge, spine straight, shoulders back, chin up, like Mama taught me. "Thank you. Are you interested?" I queried. I longed to wipe my sweaty palms on my skirt but refrained.

"We do need help, but first, tell me about your work." Her hands lay folded in her lap, eyes squinted with curiosity.

"My mother, Mrs. George Hesch, has been mending for women with busy households for over two years. Our prices are fair, we have references, and we can mend almost anything or sew from scratch."

"Tell me about the kind of mending you do."

"We mend all types of clothing - from shirts and nightclothes to skirts, trousers, and suit pieces. We also work on household items like sheets and tablecloths. We handle tasks like darning, alterations, repairing tears, as well as buttons, snaps, and hooks."

"Impressive range of skills, I must say! Let me explain what I, well, what we need." She gestured toward the rest of the house. "Mrs. Mitchell, my mother, runs our home as a boarding house. She and I, along with my brother, live here. At present, we have five male boarders rooming here."

The number of people surprised me. Eight meant a good amount of mending, therefore, a good amount of income.

"You must be busy, Miss Mitchell," I acknowledged.

"Yes, my duties are to oversee laundry and mending as well as a few others ensuring the house runs smoothly. The wash is done here, but we lost our mending woman recently. From what you've described, your and your mother's skills would suit our needs."

"It would be our pleasure to work for you." I wanted her to commit, but didn't know how to ask without being too forward.

"What if you take a few pieces on a trial basis?" she asked.

She suggested exactly what I intended to propose - the same way Mama won Mrs. Simmons' business.

"Yes, Ma'am. I can take what you like today."

Miss Mitchell patted my knee. "I'll be back in a moment."

She returned a few minutes later with an armful of white clothing. She showed me the problems with two shirts, a woman's nightdress, and a set of men's underwear, all clean and smelling like the outdoors on a spring day.

"When can you return these?" She stepped to the door and opened it for my exit.

"Would next Saturday suit you? I'll be in the neighborhood for Mrs. Simmons' delivery."

Miss Mitchell's grin spread to her eyes, tiny lines at the corners emphasized her dark lashes. "Saturday is fine. When you see Mrs. Simmons, give her my regards. I expect our arrangement will be a compliment to her excellent judgment of character."

I stepped out the door and onto the porch. "Thank you, Miss Mitchell. I'll be here Saturday morning."

Prancing down the steps and onto the sidewalk, I couldn't believe I'd done it. Or rather, I hadn't failed. Next Saturday I would collect a dollar twenty. As I counted future earnings, I realized she hadn't asked about our rates. Perhaps she assumed a fair price, or their wealth removed cost as a factor.

I liked Miss Mitchell, her easygoing demeanor, not snobby like some in her class. And Rose seemed the sort I'd like to get to know. Relief flooded through me. The deal Mama proposed proved successful after all. I wondered if all along she knew I could do this, even as I doubted myself.

Chapter Ten

As promised, I delivered the mending to Miss Mitchell on Saturday. Her enthusiastic praise, immediate payment, and more work secured our future with the boarding house. Mrs. Stickler, Mama's new customer, provided work infrequently, but she compensated with a ham, a string of sausages, or a chunk of lard, adding to our food supplies.

Week after week, Mama went to the county courthouse to collect her allotment from the Relief Fund. However, for the hundreds of women who relied on this money, the payments were unpredictable at best. On some occasions, Mama was fortunate enough to receive her share. Once, she waited for two hours, only to be informed that the funds had been exhausted. As the weeks turned into months, a disheartening sign frequently appeared in the pay window: "No Relief Fund disbursements today."

Arriving home one Saturday in late August, with no money in her pocket, Mama slumped into a chair, relaying the scene, the smell of beer lingering on her breath. "Women sobbed, screamed, and threw fruits and vegetables at the poor man who relayed the bad news."

While I understood Mama's need for momentary escape, my penny-pinching nature resented the waste of our precious earnings on a luxury we could ill afford.

"Did the man say when there would be more money?"

"No."

"Commissioner Kleiner will surely have an idea." Frantic to fill the tin with as many coins as possible, I prodded. "We have rent due."

"Don't you think I know?" Her angry words did not match the flash of something altogether different in her eyes. Fear? Desperation?

"I'm sorry." I reached for her hand, and she let me hold it. Her fingers were ice cold, as if she'd been throwing snowballs without gloves.

I examined her more closely. Sweat beaded her forehead, and her red lips contrasted sharply with her ashen complexion. Dark smudges circled the hollows of her eyes.

"Mama, are you ill?"

"Are you asking if I've been drinking?"

"No," I answered honestly, because I knew she had. I rubbed her hands in mine to warm them. "Can I feel your forehead?"

She tilted her head forward. I laid my fingers across her brow and drew them away as if from a hot coal. "You're burning up!"

"I'll go lie down for a bit. A nap will help."

We didn't see Mama till the next morning when she dragged herself into the kitchen asking for a drink of water.

"Are you feeling better?" I laid my hand on her forehead as she drained her cup. Cooler but too warm for normal.

"Some. Can I go back to bed? I should be fine in a little while."

It was clear she was truly ill, not just seeking escape from her worries, so I readily agreed.

By supper, Mama emerged, a little color in her cheeks, a shawl over her shoulders. "Hello, everyone."

Lizzie and Henry scampered to her and clung to her legs. Mary hesitated, waiting for my approval before approaching Mama. She'd been stung too many times, reaching for her mother only to be rebuffed or pushed away. But today, Mama gestured for Mary to join her siblings.

"I'm better. What's to eat?" she asked, a sure sign of improvement. Relieved Mama was on the mend, I monitored her over the next few days, but her fever abated, and our routine resumed.

A letter arrived from Papa, but our hopes plummeted when the envelope contained only a single sheet detailing war news instead of the long overdue pay ticket. He wrote of a battle at Rich Mountain, Virginia in July.

> After months of training and marching, we met the enemy. Several of our companies engaged with their soldiers and fought well. Three men were wounded, but none seriously. Most of the gunfire flew over our heads as we hid in the low brush of the forest. General Rosecrans, who led us with great honor and skill, commanded another regiment to the rear of the enemy, and after a short time, we defeated our foe.

> Our pay is on the way. I will send it as soon as it arrives.

> Mit Liebe,

Papa

He'd survived his first battle. The congregation of St. Mattheus buzzed with their opinion of the battle, calling it Feuer-und Bluttaufe, a baptism of fire and blood. I bowed my head offering up a prayer of gratitude to God for healing Mama and begged him to continue protecting Papa.

My weekly exchanges with Jane took on a rhythm I found efficient and pleasant. Rose met me at the door and led me straight to a little office behind the kitchen. While she retrieved Jane, I placed the finished pieces on a side table with the invoice I'd prepared.

"I like how you keep track of what's been mended and the price. It's helpful for mother, who passes the charge on to boarders for their repairs. I thought I'd do the same and prepare a list of what I'm giving you. That way, we both agree on what goes out and what returns."

Jane's inventory list streamlined our process, saving both paper and time. Check off the items returned, add the price, and tally the total. Simple.

"This is helpful, Miss Mitchell."

Jane gently touched my arm, her voice softening as she said, "I think it's time you called me Jane. Miss Mitchell is much too formal for our arrangement."

A mere seven weeks since we'd met, my heart swelled with pride. "I'd like that. Jane."

Rose rushed into the office. "Miss Jane, Mrs. Mitchell needs you in the parlor."

Jane nodded. "Thank you, Rose. Martha, I'll see you next week.

58

Please tell your mother how much we like your work and handling of our account. I hope to meet her one day."

Blushing, I stammered, "Th-thank you."

Jane sped off, leaving Rose and me in her wake.

"Mrs. Mitchell is quite demanding, isn't she?" I'd yet to meet the head of the house.

"Why no! It's just EB is coming home," Rose said. "The Mrs. is planning a grand party for his arrival tomorrow."

"Jane's brother?" I'd learned EB enlisted in the Second Ohio Volunteers for ninety days. Papa would be home now, too, if he hadn't signed up for three years.

"That's him." Rose motioned for me to follow her through the kitchen to the foyer. I stepped onto the front porch and turned to say goodbye. But instead of closing the door on my exit, she followed me.

Surprised by her presence on the porch, I stared at her.

"Nothing's amiss," she said. "I wanted a moment with you."

"Oh?" What did this girl want with me?

"Stay your worries, Martha. I thought I'd talk with you. Girl to girl."

"About what?"

"You are the one to be direct, aren't you?" She laughed and laid a hand on my arm. "How are you and your family doing?"

Her unexpected question caught me off guard, and I braced myself for where this might be heading. I'd mentioned my family members in passing, who did what mending, and explained Papa was in the Army. No one knew about our financial situation.

"Why? Why do you want to know?" I replied, my guard up.

"Over the short time I've known you, I've noticed a change in you."

"A change. In me? What do you mean?"

"Well, for starters, you're as jumpy as a cat with a dog on its tail. And the other is, your dress hangs on you where you once had a shape to fill it."

Her pointed observations struck uncomfortably close to the truth. "Did Miss Mitchell ask you to speak with me?"

"Nah," Rose soothed my fears. "I thought you might need a friendly ear. I'm a good listener, or so my brother says when he gets in trouble. Helps him figure stuff out."

I shook my head. "But I'm not in trouble."

"Glad to hear it." A knowing smile crossed her lips.

"I must go." I stepped off the porch and onto the sidewalk, wheeling around to check if she watched me, but the porch was empty.

I tortured myself on the walk home. What did she mean by jumpy? The strain of juggling the children's care, getting the mending done, and worrying about the cough Mama couldn't shake brought me little rest. I lay awake, figuring the last count of coins in the tin against our expenses as the relief money hadn't been replenished for over a month. More sleep, I told myself. A few more hours of rest, and I'd be fine.

She'd hit the mark about my dress, though. To save a few pennies and stretch our food, Mama cut us to two meals a day. I secretly halved my portions, ensuring the children got more. I could disguise my thinness with a few stitches in the waist and bodice of my delivery dress and Rose's insights would vanish.

Worries galore, I muttered as I navigated my way toward home. Though I would not share my problems, I appreciated Rose's kindness. Confiding in a near-stranger risked my words reaching Jane or Mrs. Mitchell. What if they decided to terminate our arrangement?

Stop! Stop worrying about something that's not happened yet. One of Papa's favorite sayings echoed in my head, "Kümmere dich nicht um ungelegte Eier." Don't worry about unlaid eggs. Easier said than done.

Chapter Eleven

"Retta, the Ninth is in town!" Mrs. Eiflert burst into our front room, hopping from foot to foot. "Our boys are home!"

Lizzie, the first to react, screamed, "Papa's home! Papa's home!"

Mama's careworn face lit up, her eyes igniting like kindling catching fire. The deep crevices on each side of her mouth disappeared into a broad smile and a flash of my younger, carefree mother appeared.

"George." Mama breathed Papa's name as if calling to him in a dream.

"They waited at the wharf all morning for permission to come ashore. They're on their way to Turner Hall now," Mrs. Eiflert said. "Come if you can. Tschüss!"

My heart crashed into my ribcage, each beat repeating, Papa's home. Papa's home.

"I must go to the Hall," she said. Her gaze fell to her stained, ill-fitting dress, and her joy faded from her face. "I can't go like this."

An idea struck me. "Mama, there's a skirt of Mrs. Simmons in the mending bag that should fit you."

"Do you think? Could I?" she stammered, unsure of the

consequences of borrowing a customer's clothing.

I rustled through the mending bag and pulled out a gray wool skirt. Mama held it to her waist while I judged her appearance. "It's perfect."

"We'll get ready while you dress," I said as she turned to go into her room.

Mama stopped mid-stride. "What? No. You're staying here."

"Won't take but a few minutes," I said, ignoring her statement while appraising Lizzie's mussed hair in need of a braid.

"I said, you're not going with me." Her hard eyes and pursed mouth challenged me.

Confused, she must know how we longed to see Papa. "Why not?" I retorted.

"I'll meet him, then we'll come home. I want time with him by myself." With finality, she flounced into her room and slammed the door.

"Motty, why can't we go?" Lizzie's lips quivered, her eyes brimming with unshed tears.

Baffled, I said, "I don't know."

Once again, I had two choices. Confront Mama or obey. Argue with her or do as I was told. I hated her for keeping us away from father after seven long months.

Mama entered the front room, cheeks glowing, hair trussed up in a tidy bun, the skirt a perfect fit. Papa would be pleased with this Mama, not the Mama of fifteen minutes ago, disheveled, fatigued, with a hacking cough that watered her eyes.

"We'll stay and wait for Papa," I conceded, swallowing the bitter awareness that Mama's happiness outweighed ours.

Lizzie screeched, "Take me with you." She clutched Mama's

legs, hindering her exit.

"Stop it, silly!" Mama gripped an arm and yanked Lizzie away. "You'll slobber all over the skirt."

Worried about the skirt. Not her daughter, her children, who wanted their father.

"I hate you!" Lizzie howled. My own thoughts came out of an eight-year-old's mouth.

"I don't care," Mama snarled, pulling on her gloves, her eyes settling on her hat.

"Mama," I said, anxious to tell her how it felt to be left out.

She stared at me. I glared at her. A bang against the wall broke our stalemate. I glimpsed Lizzie's brown dress as she streaked out the door.

Mama sighed, exasperated with her youngest daughter. "There she goes again. Always running when she doesn't get her way."

"Mama, please take her. I'll handle the others." Mary and Henry wouldn't care. Lizzie was Papa's favorite, and Mama knew it.

"No. She has to learn," Mama proclaimed with cold finality. She perched her hat atop her head and trounced out the door.

Standing at the window, I watched Mama stride toward the Hall, her pace brisk and determined. Mary pressed her hands on the other window, head swiveling left and right. "Wizzie! Where Wizzie?" she cried, tears streaming down her cheeks.

Lizzie gone. Mary distraught. Mama's dual blows leaving me to pick up the pieces. Again.

"I think I know where she is."

I spotted her hiding behind the smelly garbage barrels in the back corner of the yard. After all the yelling, I softened my voice and said, "She's gone." Wrinkling my nose, I added, "If you don't come out soon, someone might mistake you for a rotten onion."

She threw herself into my arms, declaring, "I'm telling Papa what she did."

I felt the same way but reasoned with her. "You could, but you might spoil his visit. We don't know how long he'll be here, but for sure, it won't be long."

"You mean he's not home for good?" Her lower lashes glistened with unshed tears.

"Do you remember Papa said he would be gone three years?"

Lizzie nodded, sniffing loudly.

"When the three years are up, you'll be almost ten. How old are you now?" I asked.

"Eight," she said, her chest puffing out.

"You can do the arithmetic."

"Two years. Or until this stupid war is over. Some boys in school say we'll win it before long." Lizzie pulled away, no longer needing my comforting arms.

"Yes, it's the best outcome." I put no stock in schoolyard predictions or the newspapers who prophesied a quick war, yet there was no end in sight.

"Can we go find Papa?" She fiddled with a twig she found on the ground.

It would be difficult to find him among all the men in the regiment, and dragging my siblings into that mess would end badly. "I have a better idea. But I'll need your help."

"If I have to watch Henry, then no." Lizzie's blue eyes sought a reprieve from the chore.

I chuckled, squeezing her shoulders reassuringly. "No, you won't have to watch Henry. We'll make it a real homecoming for

Papa."

We tidied up, made soup from what remained in the larder, and dressed in our best clothes. Expecting them by dinner time, we listened for Papa's boots stomping up the stairs, but they didn't arrive until dusk, the gray November sky fading to black.

We planned to surprise Papa. Henry would tuck under the kitchen table with Lizzie under the bed. Mary and I would stand behind the curtains. When finally, we heard footsteps on the stairs, we scrambled into position, Lizzie tittering and Henry squealing in anticipation.

"Sh," I admonished.

The handle clicked, releasing the lock. Peeking from my hiding place, I saw Papa step into the room, fists perched on his hips. He looked right, then left. "Wo sind meine Kinder?" he growled.

I'd hoped Papa would venture further into the room so we could shout surprise, but Lizzie, unable to constrain herself, screamed and shuffled out from under the bed. "Here, Papa! We're here!"

Papa enveloped each of us in bear hugs, peppering our faces with bearded kisses. I examined my father as he shed his blue uniform coat and slouch hat. Since he left in April, his cheeks were rosy but sunken, his chest and shoulders thinner but muscular. Same yet different.

Papa marveled at our growth, likening us to weeds, and homed in on Mary. He laid his hand flat on his head, moved it atop hers, gauging the difference in their heights, spreading his thumb and forefinger to measure three inches.

"You are catching up with me!" Papa said.

"Big girl," Mary agreed, duplicating Papa's actions with her hand on her head, then his.

Turning to me, Papa folded me in his arms, firm hands stroking my spine as I cried into his shoulder. All other sounds in the room faded, Papa's heartbeat vibrated against my face, its tempo steady and true.

Mama interrupted our lively reunion. "Bedtime everyone!" She clapped her hands briskly. "Out to the privy, and into your nightclothes."

"Aw, Mama! Papa just got home. Can we stay up for a while and visit?" Lizzie groaned.

"You can visit tomorrow. Papa needs his rest."

Papa opened his mouth to protest, but Mama's crossed arms and squinty eyes stayed him.

His face shifted from excitement to quiet resignation. "I'm looking forward to sleeping in a proper bed," he said, choosing to appease Mama over us.

Papa's presence breathed life into our home, filling it with laughter, hugs, compliments, and stories. Mary beamed as Papa praised her improved speech, newly learned letters, and ability to count to twenty. Henry showed off his block-building feats and Lizzie demanded to know what it was like to sleep outside, what he ate, how he bathed, his longest march, and more. At first, Papa obliged her interest and shared details, but as the day wore on, his responses grew shorter.

"Is your curiosity ever quenched?"

Lizzie shrugged her shoulders. "No. But now I can picture your life away from us."

Mama inhaled sharply, fixing Lizzie with a stern glare. "Enough questions for today."

Papa's gaze darted between them, landed on Lizzie, and a small, confident smile tugged at the corners of his lips, eyes soft with admiration.

He apologized for not sending any money, but said the paymaster would be at the wharf before they boarded the boat. "I expect about a hundred dollars."

Mama and I gasped at the huge amount. We'd survived on a few dollars a week. A hundred dollars changed everything! Worries about rent, food, and altering dresses skittered out of my mind.

Papa inquired how we made ends meet with no income. Mama described the undependable Relief Fund, the graciousness of St. Mattheus' congregation, and her generous pork customer. I explained the arrangement with the Mitchells and took special pride in touting an income of two to three dollars a week.

Papa told us about an encounter with the enemy at Cumberland, Maryland. "My company rarely saw action against the enemy, but in late August, Company H volunteered to root out some Rebel saboteurs who'd been wreaking havoc on our supply lines. Together with another company, we boarded a decoy train loaded with blankets and bayonets.

As we approached the bridge spanning the Potomac, the engine halted. A pile of railroad ties lay across the tracks—the Rebs' attempt to send us off the rails. Before we could reach the obstruction, a hail of bullets erupted from the tree line, peppering both sides of our cars. We returned fire from the train, providing cover for the men who cleared the tracks.

Afterwards, we chased them, slogging through chest-deep water in the Potomac. Despite our efforts, we couldn't lay hands on a single one of those damned saboteurs. They'd melted away into the countryside like ghosts."

"You got shot at, Papa?" Intrigued with Papa's story, Lizzie had questions.

"Yes," Papa said, lifting Lizzie onto his lap. "But don't you worry! Not a single bullet came anywhere near your Papa. I'm way too clever for those Reb soldiers. You can count on it!"

On the third day of Papa's visit, he told us it was time to go. My stomach knotted with dread at his impending absence and the terrifying thought of him facing enemy fire.

 He emptied his knapsack on the kitchen table, took stock of its contents, and repacked it. He asked Mama to fix a ripped seam along the arm of his wool jacket, which she started on immediately.

"And here's a button that fell off." He held it out to her, but before Mama could take it, Mary snatched it away.

"But-ton!" She inspected the dull shine of the brass disk in the weak light from the window.

"Give it to me!" Mama commanded, holding out her hand. But a coughing fit compelled her to cover her mouth.

"But-ton!" Mary repeated.

In between coughs, Mama screeched at Mary while I tried to pry the button from her hands. The racket overwhelmed Mary, driving her to squeeze her eyes shut and cover her ears to block out the chaos.

"Quiet!" Papa yelled. Instantly, the room fell silent. Tugging Mary's hands from her ears, he said softly, "Mary, open your eyes."

Lashes fluttering, she peeked warily at Papa.

"Tell me why you want the button."

"Sew," she said.

Brow furrowed, Papa asked, "So what?"

"George, this is ridiculous," Mama scoffed, her voice raspy. "Get the button."

Lizzie, Henry, and I stood rooted to the spot, eyes flickering from one parent to the other.

Papa ignored Mama. "Mary," his tone reassured her she did no wrong. "Tell me again. Why do you want the button?"

Pointing to Mama's sewing kit, she said, "Sew-ing," putting emphasis on the first syllable.

Papa's face broke into a broad grin, his booming laughter filling the room. "You want to sew on the button?"

"Sew. But-ton!"

Papa cupped her face in his hands and planted a fat kiss on Mary's forehead. "When Mama's done, I would love for you to sew the button on my coat, and when I fasten it, I'll think of my talented daughter."

With orders to report to the wharf by sunset, Papa donned his uniform, polished his boots, and jammed his cap over his unruly auburn hair. Until now, I hadn't spent any time alone with him and dearly wished to speak to him privately before he departed.

After supper, he tapped me on the shoulder. "Motty, walk down to the tobacco shop with me. I want some cigars."

I leapt to my feet, snatched my coat, and scurried down the stairs to Linn Street. Papa offered his arm, directing us north, the late afternoon sun throwing long shadows across our path.

"Papa, I'm glad we have time together. I've much to tell you and need your advice," I prattled on, barely taking a breath.

"I sensed you needed to talk." His steps matched mine. "Mary is thriving. Though I think both of you are too thin. We've eaten well during my visit. What's it like when I'm not here?"

"We, uh, we, well." Should I tell him the whole truth or a version of it?

"I want it all, Motty. I can't help if you don't talk to me."

Sighing, I stopped on the sidewalk. "We eat well when the Relief Fund pays. When it doesn't, we tighten our belts and make do on two meals a day."

Papa's brow furrowed.

"But I suspect Mama stops at the saloon after collecting the money. And sometimes she goes out after supper." Revealing this betrayed Mama.

"I met some of her acquaintances at the Republic this afternoon."

"Oh, so you know."

"I thought as much, but you've confirmed it."

"I'm sorry, Papa. I don't know what to do about that or money. We work hard at the mending. And with Lizzie back in school, it's one less pair of hands."

"How often does she go out?" Papa stared straight ahead, his face neutral.

"Maybe once a week. No more than twice."

He nodded. "I saw Mary and Mama firsthand today. Is it like that often?"

"I intervene and distract one or the other and smooth things over like you told me. Mary sews well, and we could not do the mending without her. She's slow but accurate."

"You didn't answer my question," he threw over his shoulder.

Divulging the truth would be betrayal number two, but Papa wanted it all. "She slapped Mary a time or two. Not because Mary's

70

been bad. Mostly because Mama loses her patience."

At the tobacco store, Papa left me on the walkway and went inside. On his return, he fisted six cigars. Taking one out, he sniffed it from top to bottom.

"Will you smoke one now?" I asked, knowing how he liked to relax with one.

"No, I'll keep them for when I'm in the field. Light one up when there's a reason to celebrate."

We strolled back to our rooms in heavy silence, my threadbare coat too thin to shield me from the biting autumn air.

"I'll speak with Mama." Papa said after walking a block.

"Please don't betray me! I'll never hear the end of it!"

"Not to worry. I've seen enough with my own eyes to keep your confidence."

"Thank you, Papa," I breathed a sigh of relief.

"One other thing," he said, an edge creeping into to his tone. "Mama's cough. It might be nothing but if it's not better by Christmas, find a doctor."

"But that's money we don't have." I berated myself putting money over Mama's health.

"You're smart enough to squirrel away a coin or two without Mama noticing. If her cough comes to nothing, use it to treat yourself."

I could have kicked myself for not doing this all along. Mama didn't check the Mitchell invoices, so anything I put aside would not be missed.

We reached the steps to our rooms. "Thank you, Papa. It's helped to have someone to talk to."

He drew me into his arms. Over my head, he said, "You should find someone you can trust and confide in them. Or I'm afraid what you've got pent up inside will burst one day."

Rose's offer of a sympathetic ear came to mind. And Jane was sincerely interested in my well-being.

"Promise to come home," my command muffled by his coat.

A long moment passed. Perhaps he hadn't heard.

"I'll come home as soon as I can." He held me away from him and kissed my forehead. "Let's say goodbye now. I'm afraid it will be too wild when it's time to go."

"Goodbye, Papa, and Godspeed."

"Goodbye Motty. Ich liebe dich."

I love you too, I whispered under my breath as we ascended the stairs.

Mama returned from seeing Papa off at the waterfront, clearly under the influence. I couldn't blame her and held my tongue. Her gaze swept over me, unseeing, feeling Papa's absence keenly.

"Mama?" I asked, trying to break through her haze.

"He's on the boat." She placed her hat on the rack and tugged her gloves off.

"Did he get paid?" I couldn't help asking.

"Yes. Colonel McCook held them hostage. Papa boarded the boat, signed for his pay, and handed me the money across the stern to the landing where I stood."

"How odd."

"Some soldiers weren't on the boat at the appointed time, so the Colonel used their pay as an incentive."

"Clever man," I acknowledged.

"I'm going to bed," Mama said. "Papa said to tell you he loves you."

Grateful for considering my feelings, I realized Mama's distress ran deeper than a few drinks.

"How are you?"

"I'm missing him already. I almost wish he hadn't come home, because seeing him leave again is breaking my heart."

Sensing Mama's need for comfort, I stepped forward, wrapping my arms around her waist, nestling my head into her shoulder. Prepared for rejection, my heart leaped when her cool lips touched my brow, and her arms encircled me. This used to be my favorite place on earth. Mama nuzzling, murmuring sweet sounds, strong arms supporting me. I missed this. I missed her. And now I missed Papa.

Chapter Twelve

Our despair at Papa's departure diminished gradually as Christmas approached. Mama paid the back rent, leaving us a balance of twenty-four dollars for future rent. Living on what mending brought in, we would enjoy a good Christmas.

Free from money troubles for the first time in months, I slept like the dead. We returned to three meals a day, and after a few weeks, plump as a dumpling, I removed the stitches in my delivery dress.

Two days before Christmas, Mary and I set out for the Mitchell's. As Mrs. Simmons had no mending, the timing was ideal for Mary to tag along. We enjoyed the walk, the winter sun warm enough to unbutton our coats.

I unfastened the gate between the houses, and we entered the kitchen. Mrs. Mitchell gave Jane explicit orders for all vendors to conduct business from the back door.

"Hello, Rose. Hello Cook." Her name was Mrs. Billings, but everyone called her Cook.

"I'll bring Miss Jane," Rose said and disappeared through the swinging door.

"Mary, dear. Would you like to help me roll out the dough for pies?" Cook asked.

Mary studied me expectantly. I nodded. "You know where to find me."

The cramped office Jane used to run the house flanked the kitchen. I laid the canvas bag on an old trunk and sorted the incoming and outgoing mending. The room had a desk, a wall with shelves stocked with books, and ledgers stacked every which way on a table in the corner.

Miss Jane bounded into the room. Always gay, with endless energy, I always left the Mitchell house in high spirits.

Halting at the doorway, her skirts swaying, she asked, "Are you all right with Mary up to her elbows in flour?"

"Cook invited her to help."

She dismissed her concern with a shrug and focused on the mending.

In her desk chair, she extracted the pen from its stand and dipped it into the ink well. She checked off each item against the invoice as I laid it on the trunk.

The clink of coins thrilled me as she meticulously counted the invoice amount into my outstretched palm.

"As it's Christmas, take next week off and deliver after the new year." Jane smiled as if she'd given me a gift. My head jerked up from loading the canvas bag.

"I see your wheels turning," Jane said. "Not to worry. I'll have enough work after the holidays to make up for the missing week. Besides, you work hard, and an easier week will do you good."

Relieved there would be no reduction in income, I stepped into the kitchen, where Mary moved a rolling pin across a thin sheet of dough, the heavenly scent of apples and cinnamon drifting from the oven. "How's it going?"

"We're nearly done. This is the last." Cook said. "Mary, you did a fine job."

Mary wiped her hands on her apron and tapped a finger kiss on Cook's cheek.

"Merry Christmas, child." Cook replicated the gesture.

As I arranged the canvas bag over my shoulder, the door swung in from the foyer.

"Merry Christmas!" Jane and Rose said simultaneously.

I stared in surprise at Jane cradling a long flat box, adorned in silver paper and red ribbon. Rose toted a large burlap sack bulging in odd places.

"Oh my." For me? Us?

Jane handed me the box, her eyes alight with excitement.

"Thank you." I flushed red, stammering, "I didn't get you anything."

"No need!" Jane said. "There's something inside for everyone. And here," Rose raised the bag, "are rolls, a ham, and cranberries for your Christmas dinner."

"Presents!" Mary cried with glee, clapping her hands.

"For you and your family as a thank you for your service. We truly love your work and working with you."

A mature, stately voice drifted elegantly from behind us. "Have you given her the present?"

"Mother, I thought you were napping. Yes, we've just done it." Jane said.

Mrs. Mitchell glided into the room, her crisp petticoats echoing softly against the polished floor, announcing her arrival. Of average build, her gray-streaked hair was knotted in a taut, severe bun emphasizing her sharp features. "Merry Christmas, Martha."

I dipped a small curtsy. "Same to you, Ma'am."

"And who do we have here? A face I don't recognize, though she favors you. I'd guess a sister?" Her right eyebrow arched high over one brown eye. The other stayed put.

"This is Mary. She's my younger sister by two years," I said and put an arm around her shoulders.

"I'm pleased to meet you, Mary."

Mary should have curtsied, but she forgot our etiquette lessons, leaving her unprepared for meeting someone who deserved respect. "Mary, this is Mrs. Mitchell. She's Jane's Mama."

"Mama," she mimicked and pointed to Jane.

"Yes, my Mama," Jane said, a hint of merriment in her eyes.

I squeezed Mary's shoulder, a signal she'd handled herself well.

"I heard your father visited a few weeks ago. You must miss him, especially this time of year. We hope our tokens of appreciation will make your Christmas a little brighter."

"I can't thank you enough," I said. The box under my arm, Mary carried the sack of food, and Rose escorted us out.

Mary waved. "Mewwy Chwistmas!"

At home, Lizzie stared wide-eyed at the silver-wrapped box while Henry's fingers pried at the paper, too curious to wait.

"Presents," Mary announced. "Jane."

"From the Mitchells?" Mama asked.

"Aren't they kind, Mama?" I asked, hoping for a sign of approval for my relationship with the Mitchell family. But her face remained impassive as she withdrew the food items and displayed them on the table. With a slight tilt of her head, as if conceding a point, she said, "They think highly of you. You've done well, Martha."

"Open! Present!" Mary squirmed in anticipation.

Mary pulled the ribbon, unraveling the bow and draping it around her neck. It would be a lovely accessory for her hair. I guided Henry's eager fingers, as we unfastened the paper and passed it to Mama for safekeeping. Quality paper like this was a treasure we'd use a dozen different ways.

The plain white box lid swooshed as I lifted it, revealing the contents. My siblings emitted gasps of delight, hands clapping in anticipation.

The box revealed a tin of sugar cookies shaped like trees and candy canes, alongside a fruit cake with nuts and fruit peeking through its golden crust. I removed a packet of cream-colored linen paper with matching envelopes. In a long thin box, I discovered a dip pen made of polished walnut and a bottle of jet-black ink.

Underneath lay another box. Affixed to it, a small white card in Jane's handwriting read, "To Martha, From Jane."

Opening the box, I stared, dumbfounded at the most magnificent shade of blue I'd ever seen, reminiscent of a bluebird I once spotted in Washington Park, its feathers bordering on indigo. I grazed my fingers lightly over the material. Poplin, finely woven with a silky, lustrous surface.

"What is it?" Lizzie looked over my shoulder, gaping in awe.

Unfolding the cloth, I gasped. "A dress!"

I stood, holding the dress against me. Its skirt gathered elegantly to a fixed waistband, while the bodice boasted a band collar and drop sleeves. It was, without doubt, the most glorious garment I'd ever owned.

"Oh, Mama! Can you believe this?" I held the dress to my breast and spun around, imagining me in it, swirling around a dancefloor.

"Pretty," Mama commented. "Won't be much use, though. Not very practical."

My face fell as I grappled with the truth in her words, though I bristled at her cynicism. When would I wear such a fine dress? Where could I possibly go that warranted such fashionable attire? Dances seemed like a far-off dream.

"Try it on!" encouraged Lizzie.

I shook my head, my initial excitement subdued. "Maybe later." As I carefully rewrapped the dress, my tears splattered on the box top. The joy of receiving a gift I might never use grieved me more than if I'd received nothing at all.

With the new year came the resumption of our routines. Lizzie attended school, Mary sewed and practiced her letters and numbers, while Mama mended for Mrs. Stickler and collected relief money when available. I darted about on errands, sewed until my fingers bled to meet deadlines, and helped Mama with household chores.

Winter's monotony preyed on our moods, leaving us peevish. Too cold to venture outdoors, the gray skies sapped all the color from our world. Rare sunny days or fresh snowfalls provided the only bright spots. When neither bitter cold nor sloppy streets confined us, I took the children to the park, or we met Lizzie at school.

Mama's health worsened in the weeks after Papa left. She complained of chills and sat for hours by the stove with heavy quilts layered over her shoulders. Thankfully, we had money for fuel as she burned through a bucket or two of coal daily.

Her coughing fits grew more frequent, worse at night, her hacking spasms waking everyone. The deep, rattling cough drained her energy and stole her appetite. Her bosom, once robust and firm, sagged in her corset, her scrawny waistline required altering her skirts. She shrunk in spirit, too. Missing Papa claimed her gaiety, but this illness, this wretched breath thief, robbed her of her strength, both mental and physical.

Anxious for help with Mama, but unwilling to disclose my troubles to Jane, I confided in Rose. "I need a doctor."

"There's one who came last year - Dr. Wilson, I think. Fixed up Mrs. Mitchell's rash. But I'm not sure where you'd find him now."

"Rash fixing is not what I need, but thank you."

Following Papa's advice, I'd set aside a few dollars for a doctor. With Mama only helping sporadically with the mending and no pay ticket from Papa, lean times loomed again. Mama and money chanted in time with my footsteps as I slogged through the mud and muck of busy midday streets toward home.

A letter arrived from Papa dated Christmas Day. He described his journey down the river and their long march to Lebanon, Kentucky where they made camp. He reported many men were sick with fever or dysentery, but he'd been spared these ailments thus far. His postscript was brief but disappointing: the pay master remains absent.

With the pen and stationery from the Mitchells, I wrote about our ordinary lives, minutiae about the children, that Mama's cough was worse, and taking his advice, I searched for a doctor.

In late January, the newspapers reported the Ninth Ohio, known as the German Regiment, under the command of Colonel Robert McCook, was in a battle at Somerset, Kentucky. The regiment turned the tide with an impetuous bayonet charge, earning acclaim for their gallantry in fierce hand-to-hand combat. Many men were killed or wounded but the papers only reported the fate of its officers. Papa's rank as private did not merit a word of his safety or demise.

As I scanned the Daily Press for other news of the Ninth, a brisk knock interrupted my reading. Visitors were rare. Only Mrs. Eiflert called or a neighborhood child wanting Lizzie to play. Praying it wasn't Locke looking for the rent, I unbolted the door and inched it open. A man in a dark suit, gray tufts of hair jutting from under his black hat, stood on the landing.

"Can I help you?" I asked through the gap.

"I'm Doctor Jenkins," he removed his hat, dipping his head.

"I haven't sent for a doctor." I'd yet to speak to Mrs. Eifert for a recommendation.

"Mrs. Mitchell, Mrs. Thomas Mitchell, asked me to visit. She said a woman is sick and needs examining." He grasped a small black bag in both hands, tipping back and forth heel to toe.

Mrs. Mitchell sent a doctor. God bless Rose for telling her.

"It's my mother." Relief washed over me as I yanked the door wide, gesturing for him to enter. "I'll see if she's awake."

Mama's room reeked of sweat, urine, and something

unidentifiable. She lay on her back, eyes slitted open, crusted at the corners and sunken into blue-black hollows.

"Mama, a doctor is here. I want him to examine you." I hoped she didn't reject his help.

She surprised me when her dry, cracked lips parted, her voice hoarse and raspy, "Yes. Please."

I pivoted and hurried to the front room. "Please come this way."

The doctor followed me to her bedside, where she attempted to sit up. I plumped up a pillow behind her back.

"Hello, Mrs.?" he paused, wishing to address her by name.

"Margaretta Hesch. Mama, this is Doctor Jenkins."

Standing at the foot of the bed, I took shallow breaths to fend off the unpleasant scent that lingered in the room. Mama answered the doctor's questions and let him examine her. He held a round metal disk connected to tubes in his ears to her chest. "Take a deep breath, Mrs. Hesch." As she inhaled, a coughing fit overtook her and covered her mouth with her handkerchief. Waiting for her cough to ease, he asked to see the handkerchief.

After he poked and prodded a little more, he put his medical tools into his bag, patted Mama on her arm, and said, "I'll give your daughter instructions on how to ease your cough."

She thanked him, her words raspy, nearly unintelligible. I led the doctor to the front room and offered him a cup of tea. He shook his head. "Miss Hesch, I'm sorry, but your mother is consumptive. At this stage, she is not likely to survive more than a few months at most."

My mind reeled, shifting from thoughts of tea to his confusing words. I echoed them, trying to understand. "Stage? A few months? Survive? Consumptive? Is that some winter ailment?

"No, I'm afraid not." He paused and asked, "Has she been vomiting?"

"Yes, some." I'd placed a bucket next to the bed after she'd spoiled the sheets.

"Keep her diet to liquids as best you can. She'll lose more weight, but it's a better alternative to throwing up solid food."

No food. Liquids. Why?

"Try to get her out of these rooms. Fresh air is favorable for those in her condition," he said as an afterthought.

Her condition. The word used in polite company for a pregnant woman, described a delicate condition. Putting two and two together, I smiled. A few months. Stage. Vomiting. Entirely possible with Papa's visit three months ago. "Mama's going to have a baby?" I watched the doctor intently, awaiting confirmation.

A flicker of comprehension crossed Doctor Jenkins's face. He shook his head slowly. "I wish it were that simple. Your mother has consumption. Her lungs are filling with fluid, and there is no way to ease its hold. There is no cure." Rising on his toes, he wobbled onto his heels and back again, swaying like a boat on a gentle sea.

His words, "a few months at most," struck me in the chest, the weight of an anvil. "But that's not possible. She can't be..." I paused, confused. "I don't understand."

"Do your best to make her comfortable. Give her tea with honey to soothe her throat."

"Are you saying she'll die? She can't die." My brain denied his words. I gripped his coat sleeve, desperate for him to change his diagnosis. "What will we do?"

"I'm afraid I don't know, Miss. I'm sorry." Doctor Jenkins reached for the doorknob, prepared to let himself out. As I fumbled for coins in my pocket, the clink of metal on metal caught his attention. He shook his head. "Mrs. Mitchell has taken care of my fee."

I followed him out the door, his footsteps thudding down the stairs. Tears welled in my eyes, blurring his retreating figure. At the bottom, he wheeled around and looked up at me on the landing. "I wish your mother a quick journey to meet her maker and will pray for you and your family. Good day." He tipped his hat.

His words, empathetic but blunt, tumbled over and over in my mind. A quick journey. Meet her maker. Pray for us. Only one absolute thought emerged: Papa. He needed to come home. To save Mama. Save us.

PART TWO

Chapter Thirteen

"Why me? What did I do to deserve this?" Mama whined. She shoved her bowl aside. Its watery contents sloshed onto the table. "I'm tired of this tasteless broth. I want ham and a biscuit."

"The doctor said…"

"I don't care what he said. Do you mean to kill me?" Mama's voice bounced off the kitchen walls. "I hate you. I hate this house. I haven't been out in weeks. Please, Motty. These four walls are suffocating me."

"It's cold, Mama."

Two weeks of relentless rain followed Doctor Jenkins' diagnosis. Dreary mists and heavy downpours seeped between the cracks of the poorly insulated walls. They crept into closets and dresser drawers, dampening clothing and bedding, leaving us cold and miserable. Cheap, wet wood in the stove, produced thick smoke, forcing us to open windows, and let in cool, damp air. The spring rains prohibited me from following the doctor's advice for Mama to breath fresh air.

"Where is your father? I've written, you've written. Why doesn't he answer? I need him." At this, she buried her head in her arms on the table, her body trembling as her sobs intensified. "Why, why, why?" A coughing fit interrupted her, and she clawed at her pocket for a handkerchief already sodden with blood.

I wept with her, for myself and my siblings. What would become of us? The thought of losing her was unbearable, a reality I struggled to accept. Who could I turn to? I didn't know if Papa received my urgent pleas to come home.

I rubbed her back, trying to soothe her misery as I wallowed in mine, recalling Mrs. Eiflert's visit last year, when Mama said it would be best if she put us in the orphan asylum. My resistance resurfaced, but the threat to Mama's health overshadowed my promise to keep Mary with me.

At church, Mrs. Eiflert inquired about Mama. "She's not been to services for several weeks. Is there something you're not telling me?"

Believing Mama wouldn't want anyone to see her haggard, thin appearance, I resisted telling her friend. But after many rounds of Mama's denial, anger, grief, and her recent refusal to eat, I was exhausted. In a moment of weariness, I realized Mama needed more than I could give her. She needed her closest friend.

"She's…Mama's got," I choked out, and named her nasty, irreversible disease: "consumption."

Mrs. Eiflert's eyes widened in shock. Her hand snapped up to cover a gasp. "Oh, no." Her head moved side to side, as if denying my words. "You know what that means?"

"I do. The doctor said," I raised my eyes to the heavens, showing God my distress, but doubtful He would, or could, change the outcome. "She's dying."

"I'll come this afternoon."

Grateful beyond measure, I bobbed my head vigorously, the lump in my throat stealing my voice.

"You go on home and tell her. I'll bring supplies."

My vision blurred and tears slipped down my cheeks, my head nodding uncontrollably.

"It will be all right."

The dam burst and my composure shattered. "How? How will it be all right?" My voice crackled with indignation.

"I don't know, but we'll take it one day at a time. I'll be there in an hour."

Blowing into our rooms like the wind before a storm, with a basket over her arm, Mrs. Eiflert only settled once the kettle whistled and she'd laid the supplies on the table.

"I'll see your mother now." Her broad hips swayed as she moved down the hall carrying a stiff canvas bag and a small brown bottle. She shut the door, excluding us from her ministrations.

When she emerged a little while later, pink rags spilled from the bag, and her rosy cheeks suggested considerable effort tending to Mama. Ignoring my inquiring look, she asked, "Martha, how are you for money?"

"We have a little. A pay ticket came from Papa, but Mama isn't sure how to cash it."

"Good. I'll take her to the paymaster this week. Are you still taking in mending?" Shooing Lizzie from her chair, she plopped her ample bottom next to me.

"We take in a dollar or two a week, but Mama's health prevents her from helping and sometimes we fall behind." Jane allowed an occasional late delivery but Mrs. Simmons detested tardiness.

"How much have you left to do?"

"A few odds and ends."

"Well, give me a needle and thread and show me what to do. I gave your mama laudanum to make her comfortable. I'll stay a while."

"Thank you!" I leaped from my chair and handed her a shirt with a ripped seam. Her assistance assured on time deliveries which posed another problem.

"Lizzie stays with Mary and Henry while I do deliveries on Saturdays. But I hate leaving them with an eight-year-old."

"Eight and two-thirds," Lizzie chimed in from across the room.

"Eight and two-thirds," I acknowledged her advanced age. To Mrs. Eiflert, I said, "Anything could happen."

"Well, you can bring them to me, or I could send Therese for an hour." Her fingers flew like lightning using a lock stitch to fix the rip.

Therese, a relative stranger, two years older than me, sparked hope. Mrs. Eiflert would not suggest her daughter unless she felt confident in her ability to handle the children and Mama. "Therese watching them would suit us well!" Elated with this solution, I wanted to hug the woman, but didn't want to take liberties.

"There's another problem," Mrs. Eiflert said, "Your mother may be too sick to cash the next pay ticket." Her nimble fingers stabbed, pulled, stabbed again.

"Why is that?" Absorbed in my task, I plunged my needle into a petticoat, attempting to match her pace, stitch for stitch.

"What if your mother isn't, um, here?" Her needle flashed.

My needle halted in mid-air. "Of course, she'll be here." I denied her logic, my voice sharper than intended.

Mrs. Eiflert paused, her eyes softening with understanding. Then, gently but firmly, she pressed on. "Your Mama should ask your father to change the payee. Just in case." She continued sewing with a calm, almost indifferent air, as if she were simply suggesting it was time to change the sheets.

Her words sank in. In case this illness took her away. In case she left us. In case she died. For once, reality disagreed with my practical nature. The doctor said a quick journey, a few months. Only two months had passed since his prediction. We had time. Or did we?

"I'll speak with her, but I suggest she designate someone like my husband. Mr. Eiflert would be happy to assist."

"Mama trusts me. I'll do it."

Tying a knot and cutting the residual thread with her teeth, she laid a hand on my arm. "I'm afraid you're too young."

I balked at putting Papa's money in the hands of a man I hardly knew, but I trusted Mrs. Eiflert. If Mama couldn't get to the office or she was, God forbid, dead, Locke could throw us out. The threat of the Orphan Asylum reared its ugly head.

"I'll speak with Mama and write to Papa." One more hurdle to overcome. Money. Mama's health. Mending. Children. Food. A roof over our head. Mrs. Eiflert helped, but her visit exposed an additional complication, one with lasting ramifications. What would we do if Mama couldn't cash the ticket?

I pushed the worrying thoughts aside, forcing a smile as I ushered Mrs. Eiflert to the door, exclaiming my heartfelt gratitude. I penned a letter to Papa, begging him to come home. Before it was too late.

Chapter Fourteen

Exiting the Mitchell house in early April, I tucked the canvas bag under my elbow and stepped into the backyard. Unprepared for the sudden spring shower, I sought shelter on the front porch. Cursing at my forgotten umbrella, I calculated a twenty-minute window was all I needed to get home. I checked the sky for a break, but dark clouds hovered low over Fourth Street, spilling their contents onto the street, gutters running fast. I could wait for the rain to let up or make a dash to the corner, where an awning over a storefront would protect me.

Behind me, the front door slammed closed, and a young man stepped beside me. I chose to ignore him favoring a plan to flee.

The man slipped on a pair of dove gray gloves as he scanned the sky. "Why are you on my porch?"

"I'm deciding," I said.

"Deciding what?"

I didn't recognize this man and debated stepping into the street despite the downpour. "Wait for it to let up or make a break for it."

"Where are you going?"

I wanted to tell him none of his business, but if he reported my impudence to Jane, I could lose her business. "Home."

"Where's home?"

Deciding to make eye contact, I wheeled around to face him. He stood closer than I expected, and my shoulder brushed against his fine fawn-colored coat. Taller than Papa, thin and wiry, the young man tilted his head and appraised me top to toe. Flustered and eager to escape his scrutiny of my shabby outfit, I lifted my skirts, planning to make a dash to the corner.

"Wait!" His voice exploded behind me. A hand clasped my elbow, staying my descent to the street.

Startled into motionlessness, I gaped at him. Wait for what? I needed to get home, rain or not. More than that, I needed to escape those dancing green eyes that held me captive.

"It's raining cats and dogs. Let me find you a cab." Not waiting for a response, he pulled his coat over his head and splashed down the steps and into the street. His arm shot up, hailing a taxi with its lantern lit. He waved for me to come and yelled. "Run!"

I heeded his command, lifting my skirts and picking my way through puddles to the young man holding the door. He offered a hand to help me into the cab.

He sprung in behind me and sat on the opposite seat. "May I join you? Finding a hack in the rain is tricky."

Paralyzed with indecision, my fears alternated between having no money for the cab and being alone with a strange man.

"Where to?" the young man asked, removing his hat and brushing off raindrops.

"Um, Liberty and Linn." I said, despite feeling he'd overstepped, I wanted to protect myself.

He slid the cab panel aside and shouted the address to the driver. The carriage jolted forward.

I shook out my skirt, water droplets sprinkling the upholstery and the man's trousers. "I don't know who you are, but I can't afford a cab. Perhaps we can stop, and I'll take shelter under an awning until..."

"I beg your pardon. I'm EB Mitchell." He leaned forward and tipped his head.

He'd called it his porch, and I chastised myself for missing the clue about the brother Jane adored, and the son Mrs. Mitchell supposedly spoiled to no end. In my comings and goings at the house, I'd overheard him talking in the dining room, yet we had never met. He and Jane resembled each other, both had curly, brown hair, square jaws, and dark lashes.

"And you are?" he relaxed into the corner.

"I'm Martha Hesch."

"Pleased to meet you, Miss, I assume Miss, Hesch?"

"Yes, Miss," I said.

"Why were you on my porch? Seeking shelter from the rain?" His questioning reminded me of Lizzie, curious, without judgment or rancor.

"I work for Miss Mitchell."

What might have been a hint of respect reserved for a lady dwindled to the dull gaze of meeting a servant. "Oh."

His reaction stirred an ember in my belly. A need to set this man straight. I mustered up my courage and said, "I do the mending for the house. I may have even sewn your britches, Mr. Mitchell." The words tumbled from my mouth. Good heavens, what's come over me? My hand flew to cover my insolent lips.

His face flushed from hairline to collar, but the twinkle in his eye signaled he appreciated my sense of humor.

"If we've been that intimate before meeting, we are destined to be friends." He winked, a deliberate crinkling of an eye.

It was my turn to blush. Eager to keep our banter going, I threw caution to the wind and said what I thought, rather than what I should. "I think you and I as friends, would turn heads and have tongues wagging."

"Why is that?" Head tilted; he studied me.

"I'm the daughter of poor German immigrants, forced to work because my father went off to war. Our social circles don't exactly overlap."

"What unit is your father in?"

"The Ninth."

"The Bloody Dutch!" He pulled himself erect on the opposite bench. "I've heard they're one of the finest regiments in all of Ohio with their discipline and skills on the battlefield. Brave men going after the Rebs with bayonets at Mill Springs."

His knowledge of Papa's regiment impressed me, especially about their crucial role in defeating the enemy in Kentucky.

"You are well informed."

"I was in the 2nd Ohio last year for three months. Now I do business with the Army quartermaster here in Cincinnati."

"What kind of business?" I focused on his lips, tuning out street noise, eager to learn about this young man's business. He couldn't be more than twenty-five.

"I buy goods from farmers and hog butchers and resell them to the public or the Army. I make it so the farmer can farm, the butcher can butch while I handle warehousing and sales."

I listened intently, his work interesting, his voice, passionate and educated. But too soon, the cab halted, and the driver announced, "Linn and Liberty."

"We're here," I said, slinging the canvas bag over my shoulder, as I searched my pocket for coins.

EB cleared his throat. "I'll take care of the cab. This stop is on my way."

"I'll pay you back," I said.

He opened the door and dropped to the street heedless of the rain, now only a light drizzle. I leaned into his outstretched arms, felt his hands clutch my waist, pluck me from the cab, and set me on the sidewalk. I felt weightless and something else. A mix of giddiness and fright rolled into a tight ball wedged behind my sternum.

94

"Where's your house?"

"Just over there." Purposefully vague, I waved toward the other side of Liberty. This fine man had no business knowing where I lived. For the first time in my life, I regretted the condition of our rooms, small, crowded, smelling of coal smoke, and reeking of consumption.

A bewildered frown creased his forehead, his eyes darting around. "We could have had the driver take you to your door."

"I have another errand," I lied. "Thank you for the ride."

Leaning toward me, he said, "If you're serious about paying me back, I just so happen to have a pair of drawers in need of repair." A conspiring smile settled on his lips. "We'll be better friends than ever."

I chuckled. "I'm certain of it."

"Goodbye, Miss Hesch," EB said from the window as the cab rolled away. "I hope to see you soon."

As the cab disappeared into traffic, I marveled at EB's looks, humor, and kindness. I also marveled at the luxury of taking a cab to one's destination.

Chapter Fifteen

Exhilarated from the cab ride with EB, reality set in as I arrived home and checked on Mama. Her chest rose and fell, showing she was alive. In just two short months, her breathing had grown more labored; she slept sitting up to avoid inhaling her vomit and had stopped asking for anything better than the thin soup my sisters and I spoon-fed her.

Therese gathered her belongings.

"Thank you for coming," I said.

"Happy to help." At the door, she turned and addressed Mary. "Your Mama likes it when you sing to her. You have a beautiful voice."

"Mary sings to Mama?" My eyelids fluttered in disbelief. This was new and I wasn't sure what to make of it. Mama had no use for Mary, and Mary feared her mother.

"She sits on the bed with her and sings. You should think about Mary joining the church choir."

As I sorted the mending and contemplated the development between Mama and Mary, three loud thuds rattled the door.

"Who is it?" I asked while wiping my hands on my apron.

"Your landlord." Locke's gruff, impatient voice penetrated our tiny rooms.

"Scheisse!"

"That's a bad word!" Lizzie said, her voice sharp with warning.

"That's the least of my worries right now. Watch your brother and sister while I deal with Locke."

Smoothing my skirts, I squared my shoulders, as if preparing for battle. I opened the door and stepped onto the stoop, forcing him to move back and down a few steps.

He handed me an envelope, a waft of stale beer and leather, shrouding Locke's form.

The sight of Papa's handwriting made my fingers itch to open it.

"Got a pay ticket in there? You owe twelve dollars." His beady eyes fixed on mine.

Plucking the letter from the envelope, I held it up. Nothing fell from its single fold.

Hiding my dismay, while delighting in his irritation, I shrugged and grasped the door handle. "Nothing today."

"Let me talk to your mother. She'll handle this." He came up a step.

My body and arm instinctively blocked the door, barring entry. "Mama's ill."

"I don't care. You get her out here or I'm coming in."

"You will not," I said, fighting to mask the tremor in my voice. If he came in, he'd frighten the children. "Wait here."

Charging in and throwing the bolt for extra measure, I approached Mama's sleeping form. Shaking her shoulder, I said, "Mama, Locke is here."

Mama stirred, one eye opened, her forehead wrinkled in confusion. "Here?"

"On the stoop. He wants the rent money, but we only have a few dollars."

"Give it to him," she said through her delirium. "Or he'll want something worse."

"Something worse?" I asked.

"Just…give it to him." Her eyes closed and her head fell to one side.

I took five dollars in coins from the money tin, unlocked the door, and pulled it to, blocking it from opening further with my foot. "This is all we have."

He counted it and dropped it into his pants pocket. "That's seven you owe. I'll knock off two if you come down to the shop. Show me some of your sewing."

"My sewing?" Confusion and unease clenched my stomach. Why would he want to see my sewing?

"Not that you have much, um, sewing, to look at, but I'm willing to make do." His tongue ran over his lips, then slithered back into his mouth.

Realization propelled me into action. I slammed the door in his face, shot the bolt and leaned against the door.

"Martha!" Locke hollered from the street. "Next Saturday."

I shivered, recalling last year's confrontation in the yard. His leer suggested I was a piece of meat he intended to devour. Mama's words about something worse haunted me. Had she allowed him to take liberties? I squeezed my eyes shut, trying to blot out a vision of her and Locke in the back room of his shop.

Later, the children asleep, Mama stirred.

"Locke?" she murmured, as I adjusted her pillows and quilts.

"I gave him five dollars."

"Nothing else?" Her eyes met mine. An unspoken understanding passed between us.

"Nothing else." I held the spoon with her medicine. She gulped it down, desperate for relief.

"Good girl." She patted my arm and slept.

The next afternoon, Lizzie came home from playing with a friend. "Letter from Papa!"

I snatched it out of her hand. "Where'd you get that?"

"Locke."

"Lizzie, don't you ever, ever, take anything from that man. If he approaches you, you get inside as fast as you can." I gripped her upper arms, shaking her to emphasize my words and instill the fear of God.

"Let me go!" she whined. "All right, I will."

98

I ripped open the envelope. A pay ticket tumbled out; Margaretta Hesch printed clearly on the payee line. Damn!

Chapter Sixteen

Mama's frailty prevented her from cashing the ticket alone. Weak and unstable, I dismissed the idea of Mrs. Eiflert and I escorting her to the paymaster's office. Sharing my predicament with Jane, she offered EB's services who agreed to meet us at the courthouse on Friday afternoon. A young man of his strength would get the deed done with minimal fuss.

Lizzie and I had Mama ready to go with an hour to spare. I broached the topic I'd yet to pursue with Lizzie. "Tell me about Mary and Mama. Therese said Mary sings to her."

Lizzie shrugged, as if Mary always sang to Mama. "Yeah, So?"

"Why didn't I know about this? She doesn't do it when I'm around."

She shrugged again. "I don't know."

Evidently, this revelation held little significance to Lizzie, despite its importance to me.

"When did this start?" I probed.

Exasperated, she huffed. "All I know is she sings to Mama. And Mama likes it."

What a riddle! Mama and Mary enjoying each other's company. Would wonders never cease?

The bells tolled three times. Time to go. Solving this mystery would have to wait.

"Are you ready, Mama?" I shook her shoulder to wake her.

She opened her eyes. "Mary?" The laudanum did its work, dulling her senses. Recognizing me and not my sister, she shoved my arm away. "I want Mary."

Suspicious, Lizzie and I exchanged glances over Mama's head. What did Mama intend?

"Mary, will you sing me a song and help me to the door?" Mama offered her hand to her daughter.

An island in the small room, Mary's gaze flitted from me to Mama, awaiting my instructions. Curious as to Mary's behavior in my absence, I stood silent, waiting for her to take the lead.

Of her own accord, she inched closer until she touched Mama's outstretched fingers, finally clasping her hand to help her rise from the bed. Struck with awe at Mama's need and Mary's independent response, I stood rooted to the floor.

Mary's voice, lush and warm, emitted the beginning notes of Rock-a-Bye Baby. Swallowing to hold back tears of joy, I stepped in to support Mama with an arm around her waist while Mary held her hand and we crept to the door, one painful step at a time.

"Wuv you," Mary said, giving Mama a finger kiss. I waited for Mama to correct Mary's pronunciation, but she only smiled and said, "Let's get this over with Martha."

Dapper in a summer suit, EB escorted Mama from the cab to the paymaster's office where a dozen men and women waited patiently for their turn. Wooden benches lined one wall, and two men observing Mama's struggle to stand, surrendered their seats.

After twenty minutes, EB reached the counter and explained Mama's situation. "This woman," he pointed to Mama, "is Mrs. George Hesch, and she has a pay ticket to cash." He slid the ticket to the paymaster, who inspected it, glanced at Mama, and opened a hefty, leather-bound ledger. He turned a few pages, then moved his finger down a column searching for something.

"Here it is. Hesch, George." The man twirled the book to face EB. "Can she sign?"

"Mama, you need to sign the book." I squeezed her hand to revive her.

EB supported her around the waist as he half carried, half dragged her to the counter.

The paymaster pointed to a block in his ledger book. "Sign here, Ma'am."

EB dipped the pen in the inkwell and handed it to Mama. It took two tries before she could grip it and scribble her name.

"There you go," EB said, guiding Mama back to the bench. He glared at a man occupying Mama's previous seat. "Move, dammit."

I stepped into EB's spot at the counter.

"Who are you?" the man asked.

"I'm Martha Hesch," I said, nodding towards Mama and indicated Papa's name in the ledger. "Her daughter and his."

"Is her address correct?" the paymaster asked me.

I peered at the information next to Papa's name and confirmed our address at the southwest corner of Linn and Oliver. "Yes, it's correct."

The man nodded and counted out thirty-five dollars in coin and paper currency. I put it in my pocket.

We left the office, and Jane raced ahead to hail a cab. I settled Mama into the corner of the cab, propping her up so she could rest. EB insisted on accompanying us home and told the driver our cross streets.

In the cab, EB leaned forward, his elbows resting on his knees. "Martha, may I advise you on the safety of your money?"

"Did he want me to invest it? Put it in a bank? "I suppose."

"There in your pocket. Anything could happen to it. I suggest you get a handbag to secure it."

Jane jumped in, elated to help. "I have one I don't use. It's all yours."

Knowing Jane wouldn't take no for an answer, I agreed with a quiet "Fine," though I felt uneasy about continuing to accept gifts from the Mitchells. I appreciated their kindness, but I could not continue accepting their gifts. A purse, cab fare, helping Mama. Charity from church was one thing, but continued favors from this family might lead to unintended consequences.

As the cab rattled towards home, I contemplated how to get Mama upstairs without allowing either one of the Mitchells access to our rooms.

The hack driver reined in the horse at Locke's shop. Mama stirred, standing just long enough for EB to help her from the cab to the street.

"Where's your place?" EB asked.

"Above the shop. If you would get her to the bottom of the steps, I can take it from there."

"I'll carry her. It will be easier on her."

Lizzie bounded up to us with a cheerful "Hello!"

"Lizzie, meet Jane and EB Mitchell." No time for small talk with a half-dead woman in the middle of the sidewalk, I barked orders at my sister. "Lizzie, support Mama's left side. I'll take the right."

EB refused to let go. "I said I'd do it."

"And I said I've got her," I snapped, my composure on the brink of collapse.

EB's eyebrows shot up. He let go of Mama's waist and raised his hands as if a robber held a gun on him. "Fine, do it your way."

"Goodbye, and thank you," I said over my shoulder. I regretted mistreating him, but I had no time for good manners.

The carriage door slammed shut, followed by the driver's command "Giddy up."

"What was that about?" Lizzie asked.

"I couldn't let them come upstairs."

"Why not? He could have carried Mama."

How could I explain the shame of our sordid rooms? The smell, water spots on the ceiling, bare floors, secondhand furniture, and the crowded space. You could fit ten of our rooms into the first floor of the Mitchell house.

We made it up four steps when Mama's skirt caught under her foot. She tripped, pitching forward onto her knees. She slid down on her belly, landed in a heap and rolled over onto Lizzie. I lost my balance, momentum pulling me backward. With no handhold, I tipped back and landed on my side.

"Ow," Lizzie cried. "My leg."

"Mama!" I scrambled to my feet, my arm burning. Ignoring the pain, I put an arm under her shoulders, cradling her. Lizzie slid out from under, massaging her ankle.

"See if you can put some weight on it." She got on her hands and knees, placed one foot on the ground, then the other.

"It doesn't hurt."

"Thank heaven."

"How's Mama?" On her knees, she checked her head, hands, arms, and legs. "She seems fine."

Relief flooded me that Mama hadn't been injured. I frantically considered our options to get her upstairs.

"You're bleeding," Lizzie said, pointing to my left arm.

I glanced at my injury. The burning sensation was from a scrape along the bone in my forearm. "What do you think?" I asked, holding it up for her to check.

"You lost a few layers of skin, but you'll heal. I'll get some bandages." She started up the steps.

"No! We have to get Mama inside. I can wait."

"How will we do that?"

I tried to rouse Mama. She floated in and out of consciousness, her eyes fluttering open and closed, her head lolling from side to side."

"You should have let that EB guy take her up."

She was right, I should have, but he would see how we lived and how poor we were and the smell. Oh, the smell was the worst!

"Yes, well, that's water under the bridge, isn't it?"

"It's not my fault Mama's on the ground." Lizzie shot back.

"I know, I know. Let me think."

I passed Mama's head and shoulders to Lizzie and hauled myself from the ground, dusting off my skirts. Perhaps a passerby could help. I went to the end of our walkway to the street. For this time of day, there should have been scores of people traveling up and down Linn, but just my luck, there were none.

The door to Locke's shoe shop stood open. I'd sworn never to go near that man again, but Mama lay sprawled in the dirt, barely conscious.

"I'll be right back."

"Hurry!" Lizzie urged.

I entered the shop. Repaired shoes lined the counter, each with a paper tag attached for identification. A sign on the counter read, "Ring Bell." I picked up the bell by its wooden handle and shook it a few times. A trivial peal.

Locke appeared at the end of the hallway. He came straight away and wiped his hands on his apron.

"Ah, the little miss!" He recognized me. "You got rent money?"

"Yes, I do."

He leaned on the counter, waiting.

"Mama's fallen. I'll give you the rent as soon as you help me get her upstairs."

Unfazed, he raised an eyebrow. "You bribing me?"

I shrugged.

"I don't see her."

"She's at the bottom of our stairs." I wouldn't beg. "Can you come now?"

He rubbed the hair on his chin, considering.

"Mr. Locke, she's lying in the dirt and could be hurt, but I can't examine her until I have her upstairs."

"Fine." He came from behind the counter. I darted out the door, hesitant for him to get too close.

Lizzie and Mama hadn't moved, but Mama's eyes were open. At the top of the stairs, Henry wailed as Mary held his hand, her eyes round as saucers.

Lizzie glanced at me, puzzled, as if to say, "What in the world?"

Locke lowered to his haunches. "Hey, Retta. It's Joe. I'm going to pick you up and carry you up the stairs. Put your arms around my neck."

I tried to link her arms around his neck, but they slipped away, limp and uncooperative. As he gathered her up, I heard her say Joe, or perhaps it was Oh. Or a moan. I wasn't sure. His muscles swelled under his shirtsleeves as he tramped up the stairs, scattering Henry and Mary back inside. I came from behind and pointed to the bed. He gently lowered her onto the mattress.

"I didn't know," he said. "She's real sick."

"Yes, but the doctor says she'll get better." I'd learned to keep Mama's condition hidden to avoid difficult conversations, and Locke could throw us out if he feared the disease as most people did.

"Rent?" Locke stood before me, eager for his money, dismissing the sick woman.

I counted out fourteen dollars. "That pays us through June."

His eyes lingered on the greenbacks I hastily stuffed back into my pocket.

"Right."

"Thank you for helping with Mama," I said, though it stuck in my throat like glue on a shoe sole.

I opened the door and waited for his exit. Behind him, I slammed the door, bolted it, and slid into a chair.

Lizzie had the brown bottle of laudanum in her hand. "Gave Mama some to help her sleep."

Unable to speak, I nodded, a wave of gratitude washing over me. What would I do without Lizzie?

"Let me see your arm." She folded my sleeve back and blotted it with a cool, wet cloth. The burning eased. "Hold it there. Later, I'll bandage it."

"Where did you learn all this stuff, Lizzie?" I marveled at my almost nine-year-old sister.

"From you, silly!"

Chapter Seventeen

The morning of Independence Day brought cloudless skies and endless sunshine. Mama asked to sit in the yard, but after the incident on ticket cashing day, I declined. Instead, we shoved her bed next to the windows so the sun could warm her.

The holiday didn't hinder mending duties, and Mary hummed a tune as we sewed.

"Won't you sing it to us, Mary? Isn't that Blue Eyed Gal?" I asked.

She cleared her throat, and sang, tapping her foot to keep time.

Fly around my blue-eyed gal,
Fly around my Daisy,
Fly around my blue-eyed gal,
You almost run me crazy.

Mama tapped a finger to the beat. Henry danced a little jig, his feet clomping on the wooden floor.

"Remember the picnic in the park?" Mama said, a hint of a smile on her lips. "Papa couldn't stop singing that song to all his blue-eyed girls."

"He's got four of them," Lizzie said.

Singing, laughter, smiles - snatches of joy welcoming a brief escape from Mama's inevitable fate. I couldn't deny it any longer, but I could set it aside for one day.

"I have an idea." I picked out a few coins from the money tin, went out the door and clopped down the steps to Linn Street.

At Schneiders, I snaked my way through the boisterous crowd, the air thick with the sour aroma of stale beer and ordered a bucket of lager. Bucket in hand, I hurried home, doing my best to avoid spilling the beer. At the open door, I held it aloft, and asked, "Beer, Mama?"

I will never forget the light in her eyes as she licked her lips in anticipation. I brought a cup from the kitchen and dipped it into the bucket.

Her head shook. "All!" She motioned around the room.

Lizzie gasped, "Beer for everyone?" She raced into the kitchen for more cups.

With our cups full, Mama raised hers and declared, "Prost!"

"Prost!" Our hale and hearty voices filled the room, echoing her salute.

Mama took a sip, a foamy mustache stretching across her upper lip. Mary drank. Her eyes widened at the unfamiliar taste, but she swallowed. Henry, not to be outdone, touched his lips to the brew. He promptly spat it back in, his face scrunching in distaste.

"Someday you will like beer, little brother," I said.

Lizzie and I, as if in solidarity, tapped our cups. Putting my lips to the rim, I looked at her and arched an eyebrow. She nodded. In an unspoken challenge, we drained our cups, slamming them onto the table like Papa did when he finished.

"More, Mama?" I refilled her cup.

"You too," Mama said. "You're German. You must learn to like beer."

I did like beer, though my experience was limited to stolen sips, while Papa looked the other way. I felt light and carefree, a warmth spreading through my body - a sensation I hadn't experienced in ages. Perhaps another cup would prolong my euphoria.

"Mama, I wanna know something." My voice sounded peculiar, distant and hollow.

Roused from her usual lethargy, Mama raised her eyebrows.

"Papa explained why he left Deutschland," I waved my cup. "Why did you?" It seemed important. No, critical to know her side of the story.

"It's a long tale, Martha," she said, resting her head on Lizzie's chest who sat behind her with Mama between her splayed legs.

"I've got time," I said.

Mama's eyelids shut and I thought she'd fallen asleep. "I came because of you," she said without opening them.

I grappled with her unexpected statement. "What? Why me?"

"I met Papa in our village, and we fell in love. The plan was to marry at the summer solstice, but before it arrived, I found out you were in my belly," Mama spoke to the wall, out the window, up to the sky, never once meeting my eyes.

I knew this meant she was pregnant before they married, instructing me on how babies were made when I got my first monthly.

She coughed and wiped her mouth with the handkerchief Lizzie handed to her. "In my village, getting a baby in your belly before marriage is a sin. We could have married, but your Papa wanted more."

"More? More what?" I asked.

"He wanted a better life. You see, we had no prospects in our village. Papa's father farmed a small plot to feed his family. But the rains didn't come, and the harvests failed. Year after year. Neither of our families owned land or our homes. We kept a roof over our head by working the fields and tending the animals. With nothing growing, the animals starved, and soon we starved, too."

Mama had not strung this many words together in weeks. Her breath came quick and shallow as she paused to rest her overworked lungs.

Mary perched on the bed, entranced by Mama's story, if not by her words, but with her calm voice, her face, though pale and waxen, come to life.

"My parents could not bear the shame. They ordered me to leave. I packed my few belongings and said goodbye without a loving word or embrace between us."

"Oh." I put my beer aside and joined my sisters on the bed.

"We always said that Martha came when we needed her most. If you hadn't, we'd still be in Bavaria."

"Did you marry in America?"

"We sailed on the Peter Hattrick for four months, from Bremen to New Orleans with a hundred other souls. To get to Cincinnati, we steamed up the Mississippi and Ohio Rivers on riverboats. Papa heard of good jobs, and, in time, thought he could open his own shoemaking shop. We stepped off the boat at the foot of Vine Street and married shortly thereafter at St. Mattheus. A month later, you arrived."

"That's a long journey, Mama!" Lizzie said, enthralled with her parents' adventures.

"Papa and I have many stories about coming to America, and we are fortunate to be here."

"But Mama, we have nothing. We're poor and live on the charity of others," I said, glancing around our barren rooms.

"Martha, we may be poor, but we are richer for the opportunities. Papa joined the army by his own choice, not because he was required to though I am heartbroken by his absence. You run a mending business that is not possible in Germany. The market we go to is full of riches beyond my wildest dreams. In Bavaria, the stalls were skeletons. We ate what we could find, surviving on foraged nuts and berries."

I remembered the ache of my empty belly when we ate only twice a day. "So, we have it good here?"

"We have a community of folks like us who celebrate traditions from the Old Country yet are proud Americans. We have access to medicine. We can disagree with the government without fear of punishment. A man can take any job and make a fair wage."

A coughing spasm seized her, doubling her over at the waist.

"Rest," she croaked as she lay back, every inhale a battle, every exhale shallow, rattling its way from her watery lungs up through her exhausted windpipe.

Lizzie eased out from under her and lowered her head and shoulders onto a folded quilt. Henry crawled in next to Mama and a moment later, his soft snore buzzed in her ear.

Tears stung my eyes as I stared wistfully at my mother, once strong and fearless, traveling to a strange place for a new life filled with hope and endless possibilities.

And now, look at her. Skin and bones, pale as a sheet, stricken by a disease without a cure. I'd not done enough. I'd let other people tell me what was best. I could have spent the money on a different doctor or medicine or taken her somewhere she could sit in the sun to her heart's delight, its heat drying up the fluid slowly drowning her.

Mary squeezed my hand. "Motty."

"Mmm," I said absently.

Mary kissed her forefinger and touched it to my cheek. She held up her finger to show me. It was wet and shiny. "No cry," Mary said, and I saw she cried too.

"What will we do, Motty?" Lizzie asked. "Will we be happy like Mama and Papa wanted?"

I looked at Mama sleeping peacefully, then at my sisters. "I suppose we keep going. We work hard, make the best of what we have, and stay together. That's my dream of independence." An independence I prayed would cascade from my parents' dreams into a family dedicated to each other in good times and in bad.

"And take care of each other, like we take care of Mama," Lizzie said.

We held hands, a solidarity I'd never take for granted. A sudden burst of gunshots punctuated the air, reminding us of celebrations taking place across the city. Ours was simple, yet memorable. Mama's story coupled with resentful acknowledgment she wouldn't be here for the next Independence Day.

Chapter Eighteen

New respect for Mama blossomed in me like a flower opening in spring. She'd endured deprivation, banishment, and pregnancy during months of travel - all for the dream of America. I marveled at her optimism after years of living hand to mouth in a tiny set of rooms and now, with death on her doorstep.

But Mama was still the woman who barked at me for silly transgressions and fretted when Mary sang ballads instead of ones meant for dancing. Lizzie's jokes, usually able to lift her spirits, fell on deaf ears. Henry tried to snuggle with her, but she pushed him from the bed. To ease all our misery, I fed her a spoonful of medicine.

We took turns standing over the sick bed, fanning the flies away. At night, Mama whimpered, a coughing fit waking her from drug-induced sleep. When I checked on her, she bombarded me with complaints: heat, damp nightgown, thirst, loneliness, Papa, blood-soaked handkerchiefs, and her unrelenting cough.

One night, the children asleep in the bedroom, she tossed and turned, coughing regardless of position, I laid a cold rag on her head and stirred the air with a makeshift fan.

"Medicine, please."

I tipped the brown bottle over the spoon, but only a few drops spilled out. "It's gone."

"Give it to me." She snatched the bottle and sucked the dregs of tonic. "Get more." The bottle clunked as it landed on the floor.

"I'll talk with Mrs. Eiflert tomorrow."

"See that you do."

A moment later, she asked, "Where is my husband?"

Papa's letters arrived weeks late, the dates he'd scribbled at the top long past. I wrote weekly, begging him to return.

"In Alabama."

"Idiot. Why isn't he here?"

My mind worked in literal patterns, translating word for word, missing the subtle meaning of her question. Yes, why wasn't Papa here?

An uneasy silence fell between us.

"Martha, you must take them." The words slipped from her lips in a soft, sluggish stream, as if she talked in her sleep.

I recognized this tone - it often came after she took the drug, when the lines between reality and fantasy blurred. I considered ignoring her, but something in her tone made me uneasy.

After a long pause, she asked, "Did you hear me?"

"I must take who?" I played along.

"All of them."

"Them?"

"To the asylum."

"The children?" The fan in my hand ceased moving of its own accord.

"Damn it!" Mama's head jerked toward me, eyes bulging from sunken sockets in her head. "Take the CHILDREN to the ASYLUM."

Her words struck like a punch in the stomach. Time rewound to Mrs. Eiflert's visit a year ago when I'd eavesdropped on their conversation. No, no, no! I clapped my hands over my ears as if I could block out the memory and her callous desire to be rid of her children.

Her hand clawed weakly at my arm, trying to pull my hands from my ears, but it fell limply to the bed. Her head lolled to one side, away from me. "You must," she whispered. "They'll be better off."

Better off. I let my hands slip from my ears. Night sounds resumed. A cricket in a corner, a child's soft snore from the bedroom, the clip-clop of a horse passing on the street.

"You hear me?"

I shook my head, clamping my lips shut to stop them from…what? From screaming, from howling, from yelling at my dying mother?

"Mama," I croaked. "I can't."

"You must. Nothing here without your father. Without me."

"But I'm here." My voice quavered.

"You aren't their mother."

"No, but I mother them."

"Not the same." Her voice, raspy from the effort of speaking, held a hint of kindness, absent until now.

"Why?"

I waited an eternity for her answer.

"I don't want them to see me die."

Her confession rendered me speechless. Was this true maternal concern showing through at last?

"I don't want you to die."

"But I am. Soon." Not a threat. A fact. Reality. The truth.

Unsteady, I eased onto the bed beside her. Clasping her hand, I said desperately, "You can't. We need you. I need you."

A coughing fit overwhelmed her, and we exchanged clean rags for bloody three times.

Finally able to pull a shallow breath into her lungs, she spoke. "Come closer."

I leaned in.

"Promise?" Her eyes, sunken but intense, burned into mine, waiting.

Promising her would break the promise I made to Papa. But Mama seemed to need it, and I understood it would be difficult for the children to witness her last moments. Should I betray Papa or obey Mama? I couldn't tear my family apart. What would they do? What would I do? Could I send them away and get them back? Was that possible?

"Motty, please." Her raw throat scratched out the words.

"Don't make me, Mama." Tears coursed down my cheeks as I slipped to my knees.

She waited. I debated. How could I lose everyone I loved? How could God be so cruel? How could I refuse what might be my mother's last request?

I clutched her hands in mine, fists linked in prayer. "Dear God, help me do what I must."

Her hand released mine and it fell atop the quilt. A faint smile crossed her lips, her eyes closing in apparent satisfaction. I knew then that my carefully chosen words had sealed my fate. To her, I had made the promise she sought, even if I hadn't quite said the words.

I leaned over her still form, brushed a strand of hair from her cheek and pecked a kiss on her forehead. "I love you, Mama."

"Wuv you." And she slept.

Chapter Nineteen

A rumbling woke me. Having slept sitting on the floor next to Mama's bed, I arched my back, stretched my arms, and bent my legs, unlocking my knees. Rolling on my hip toward Mama, I saw her sitting up, staring out the window.

"Good morning, Mama," I pressed her arm. "Storm's coming."

She didn't reply. I squeezed her arm and under the sleeve of her nightdress, it felt cold and rigid. I shook her shoulder and put my eyes level with hers, but they were unblinking, sightless. Mama died sometime between when I kissed her goodnight and a minute ago. I gathered all my strength and closed one eye, then the other. The finality of the act shattered my world, revealing a harsh new reality.

I found her hand and laid her palm on my cheek, caressing the lifeless limb. "I didn't get to say goodbye." Her sudden absence left me unprepared for life without her. How would the children react? What should I do to help them?

"Motty," Lizzie said from behind me. "Is Mama better? She's not coughing."

Before she could reach the bed, I grasped her shoulders and stooped to her level. "I need to tell you something," I sniffed.

"Why are you crying?"

"I'm crying because Mama went to sleep last night and did not wake up this morning."

She glanced at the bed. "Did you try shaking her?"

I nodded. She slipped around me and darted to the bed. Shaking Mama's shoulder, she coaxed her awake. "Mama. It's me, Lizzie." Mama's head wobbled, then fell toward Lizzie. Inch by inch, Lizzie backed away, eyes wide with confusion, her gaze fixed on her silent, still mother.

"She won't cough anymore or be in pain," I said.

"I don't understand." Lizzie tipped her face up to mine, tracking my features for glimpses of an awful joke or the unvarnished truth.

How did you tell a child about death? One day your mother is talking and breathing and the next, a body without life. Lizzie needed it straight, without sugar coating. I gulped and said what I knew.

"The cough. It stuck in her lungs and took her breath away. Without air, your heart stops. And then…you die." Death in a nutshell.

Tears slipped down her cheeks. "But she looks fine. Like she's sleeping."

"Which means she died without a struggle and is at peace. She always wanted peace and quiet."

"How many times did we hear that?" Lizzie's eyes rolled. "I didn't mean that, Mama." She directed her comment toward the bed.

"I was with her last night," I said.

"Did she say anything about dying?"

"She knew her time was coming."

"Oh."

"But we talked about you and Mary and Henry."

Lizzie's head shot up. "You did?"

"She said she loved you. And she made me promise," my voice fell off as I hadn't meant to reveal Mama's request.

"Promise what?"

Since the children had not seen Mama die, I reasoned the promise made last night no longer had grounds. I chose to share the promise made to Papa. "To take care of everyone and keep us together."

"Is she in heaven?"

"I think so. You know about heaven?"

Pointing to the ceiling, she said, "Up there with God."

Mary and Henry padded into the front room. Though weaned a few months ago, Henry still sought out Mama in the mornings to snuggle. He climbed onto the bed, but held back from lying next to her, sensing something different, her body still and quiet.

Lizzie, always the one who looked out for her little brother, took charge and placed an arm around his boyish shoulders. "Mama's gone to heaven, Henry."

"Heaven? She's not sick anymore?"

"Not anymore."

My heart broke as his tiny hands gripped Mama's cheeks, turning her head side to side. Getting no reaction, he simply laid down next to her and patted her arm, fingers rhythmically tapping, comforting her as she did him.

I should have expected Mary's reaction. She knew what it meant for someone to be gone, like Papa was gone. But when I said Mama had gone to heaven, she chuckled and pointed to the bed. "Mama here."

Thinking how to show her instead of telling her, I led her to the bed and placed her hand atop Mama's. Mary lifted it and moved her fingers like the counting game she and Mama used to play. When Mama didn't respond, Mary slapped her hand. "Play!" she demanded and stomped her foot.

"Mary, she can't play anymore," I cajoled. "She's asleep for a very long time."

Mary understood sleeping, but not the permanent kind. "No sleep, Mama. No sleep." She shook her arm, then pushed on her shoulder.

Lizzie started yelling. "Mary, she's dead! She's not waking up. Ever! You're so dumb!" And she fled from the room. I let her go. Nothing I could say would ease her pain.

Mary looked from me to Mama. "Gone?" Mary asked.

"Yes. She's in heaven," I said soothingly. "Maybe Mama would like one of your kisses to take with her on her trip."

Mary kissed the tip of her index finger and pressed it to Mama's cheek. Mary found Mama's hand again and sank to the floor, her eyes vacant and glassy.

Henry left Mama and climbed into my lap. "Motty?"

"Yes, my darling boy." I smoothed his hair and breathed in his scent, soap and apples, with a trace of urine.

"Mama's pretty." He appraised her face.

"Yes, she is, isn't she?" Peaceful in repose, we examined a stranger. In life, her expression had rarely been without a pursed mouth or wrinkled forehead. We stared at the woman who, in death, regained some of her youth.

"Get dressed and I'll make breakfast." I chased them out so they wouldn't see what I had to do next. Taking the quilt from under her arms, I shook out the folds and laid it across Mama's body. I brushed her hair, untangling the matted places and braided it as best as I could. Mama would not want to be seen with her hair undone.

"Mama you are finally free of pain and in God's bosom. Watch over Papa, for I know how much you love each other. Help me with the children. Give me strength in body and spirit to do what's right for them until Papa comes home. Good night, my sweet, sweet, Mama." I kissed her brow. After a last long look through blurry eyes, I raised the quilt and covered her face. The finality of the act nearly brought me to my knees.

I found the lap desk, opened it, and arranged paper, pen, and ink.

Dear Papa,

Mama has died. We are alone. Come home.

Martha

The rain came as the thunder predicted. I sat next to the window, rivulets of water streaming down the pane, blurring my vision. Or was it my tears?

I needed to think. Mama had been dying for such a long time, I should have been prepared for the eventuality. But I hadn't. Even Mrs. Eiflert had not advised me what to do.

Lizzie would have to fetch Mrs. Eiflert and give her the new, but I hated sending her out in this storm. "Lizzie, I think we need Mrs. Eiflert. When the rain lets up, will you go to her house, and tell her," I inhaled, "tell her about Mama?"

"I don't want to."

"I know, but if you don't, I have to. You want to stay here with Mama and the children?"

Stomping her foot, Lizzie shouted, "Why do I always have to do the hard stuff?"

"You do the hard stuff? What about caring for Mama, holding her head, while she spit bloody slime into a bucket? Sewing till my fingers bleed? Making all the meals and —"

A tap on the door interrupted our quarrel.

Lizzie opened the door and nearly fell into Therese Eiflert's arms before she could close her umbrella.

Therese. Here, so I could make deliveries. I'd forgotten.

"What's this?" She asked. The grin on her lips faded at quilt covering the entire bed. "Oh!"

"She died during the night," I said.

"I was just getting ready to come find your mama," Lizzie said to Therese. "But you've saved me the trouble."

"I won't be making deliveries today," I said.

Looking like a drowned rat, Therese saved me the discomfort of asking her to go back out in the rain. "I'll bring Mother."

The girl returned an hour later, her mother in tow. Dressed in black, head to toe, Mrs. Eiflert rushed into the room. She headed straight for Mama, knelt beside her, hands folded in prayer. After a minute, she stood. "Tell me what happened."

I relayed the events of last evening and this morning.

"Let's get her into the bedroom." Mrs. Eiflert stood at the foot of the bed and threw back the quilt, revealing Mama's feet, mottled blue and gray. "Therese take her shoulders." They lifted her. Lizzie and I followed them into the bedroom.

"What are you doing?"

"Your Mama needs to be laid out, and this is the only suitable place." Mrs. Eiflert said. "Have you never been to a funeral?"

"No."

"Well, then, here's the plan." Mrs. Eiflert stood at the foot of the bed. From behind her, I took in Mama's bare feet angled outward and a hand dangling lifelessly from under the quilt.

Her tone matter of fact as if she recited how to bake a cake, she said, "We'll put her in her best dress. Black is best. Tomorrow her friends will come and pay their respects."

"Friends?" I asked. Mama didn't have many.

"I'll stop at the church and speak with Reverend Knochelmann on the rest of the arrangements."

"Rest?"

"Her burial, Martha." Mrs. Eiflert stopped rattling off her list. "I'm sorry, dear girl. All this must be difficult. Certain customs must be observed with a death in the family. You and Mary should wear black. If you don't have any black clothing, I'll see what I can rummage from the church donation bins. And Therese may have something she's grown out of that will serve."

"Not me?" Lizzie asked.

"No, you're too young. But boys wear a black armband. We'll fix one up for Henry."

"What about this, Mama?" Therese popped her head out of the wardrobe with Mama's only black dress. Mrs. Eiflert examined it, eyeballing the measurements of the waist with Mama's prone form on the bed.

"That will do. Now leave us, so we can prepare your mama."

Backing out of the room to escape the sordid scene, I gasped for air, clutching my throat as the room seemed to tilt around me. The stench of death and the suffocating room caused my stomach to lurch, like a trapped animal desperately seeking escape.

"Motty, you're white as a ghost," Lizzie gasped.

"Take her outside, quick!" Mrs. Eiflert directed.

My legs shaking, Lizzie propelled me forward. The bile rose in my throat, and I fisted my hand over my mouth. I reached the stoop before the contents of my stomach emptied over the rail into the yard below.

Lizzie sat me on the steps and ran to get me a drink of water. My breathing slowed. The choking sensation eased. I sipped and spat it into the yard, clearing the foul taste from my mouth. The rain had stopped. The fresh air revived me.

Mary and Henry, clearly unsettled by the day's events, joined us on the wet steps. Henry nestled between my legs while Mary sat on the step above, her arms around my shoulders.

"Where will we sleep tonight?" Lizzie asked.

"I don't know," I said, my head clearing but still weak from vomiting. "We should ask Mrs. Eiflert."

"She's taken over everything. I want to sleep here."

"Even with Mama? With her in the other room?"

"I'm not afraid. She shouldn't be alone."

I laid my arm around my brave and stubborn sister's shoulders. "Tomorrow will be a hard day. We have to say goodbye. Forever."

"Mary," I got her attention by squeezing her arm. "How are you?" I tilted my head back, and she stretched her neck forward, our eyes meeting upside down.

"Mama," her simple word brought it home to me. Her eyes seemed to look right through me. While she and Mama had been mortal enemies at times, Mary loved her and cared for her in her last days, the way this unique child could with songs to stir memories and distract Mama from her pain.

"I miss Mama," Henry said, picking a piece of lint from my skirt.

My heart broke as I knew it would a thousand times until each one of us came to grips with Mama's passing, which I expected to be a lifetime.

"I'll speak with Mrs. Eiflert." I rose, gripping the stair rail and went inside.

"Mrs. Eiflert." She pulled the sheets from Mama's bed. "We want to sleep here tonight."

"No, you must come home with me," she said, distracted by her task. "You can sleep in Frank's room."

Lizzie yanked on my sleeve, her eyes pleading.

"We'll stay here if it's all the same," I said, unapologetic and firm. "We don't want to leave Mama alone."

"Not a good idea. I heartily disapprove." Her gruff tone attempted to put me off.

"She's our Mama. We'll stay if we want." Lizzie snapped.

Mary added, "My Mama."

"Very well. Therese! Time to go." Gathering her belongings, Mrs. Eiflert added, "You'd better see to Lizzie. She's getting a mouth on her."

"Her mother just died. I will forgive her behavior and hope you will, too."

Mrs. Eiflert sighed. "Yes, yes, of course."

As she prepared to leave, panic rose in my chest. Had I made a mistake in insisting we stay? We needed her guidance, her experience in navigating this unfamiliar territory of loss. How could I, at fifteen, take care of three children? What if I failed? What would it take to succeed, to survive until Papa came home? Mrs. Eiflert's support would be invaluable. I could learn from her and seek her advice from time to time.

"Tomorrow?" I asked to be sure I understood what was expected.

"I'll come early. The children should be bathed and dressed. I'll bring some clothing, and we'll work out how to fit them."

"Thank you, Mrs. Eiflert. We appreciate your help."

"I know." Her eyes watered, her demeanor softening. "I'll miss your mama. She was a good woman."

We gathered at the windows and watched them walk south.

"Papa. Home." Mary said.

"Papa will come soon," I reassured her.

"Hungry," Henry said.

A pot of soup stood on the stove, ready to heat. I shot a look upward and mouthed a thank you to Mama, or God, for sending this woman to our doorstep.

Chapter Twenty

Clad in somber black, courtesy of Mrs. Eiflert, I stood vigilant at the threshold of our rooms. I greeted the few that came and directed them to the bedroom, where Mama lay. Everyone brought something: a basket of apples, bread, cheese, nuts. One man handed me a bucket of beer, introducing himself as the barkeep at The Republic, and said he'd known my parents for many years. The guests sipped beer and shared memories of Mama and Papa's early years in town.

The soft chatter in the front room was interrupted by Reverend Knochelmann. Tall and gray-haired, he bent to enter, offered his hand, and said, "I'm sorry for your loss. She was a fine woman."

"Thank you, Reverend."

"How are you and the children?" The Reverend's deep voice matched the solemnity of the occasion.

"Doing the best we can."

"Where is Mrs. Hesch?"

I pointed to the bedroom.

"Would you and the children join me in a prayer?" He pulled a small book from the inside pocket of his suit.

The children sat on the floor by the windows, leaving chairs for guests. Overhearing the Reverend's request, Lizzie shook her head, braids swinging.

"Not now, Reverend." I wanted everyone to leave, to let us grieve our mother in peace.

An hour passed and the guests departed one at a time until the chairs held Mrs. Eiflert, Therese and the Reverend.

He checked his pocket watch and said, "The sexton will arrive soon."

"Before he comes, can we have a moment with Mama?" I asked.

"Of course. Would you like me to say a prayer with you?"

I shook my head. We needed to say goodbye alone.

We stood around the bed. Mama's appearance had changed overnight. Her lips twisted, and transparent skin stretched over her skull, sagging beneath her chin and ears.

"Scary Mama," Henry said, and tucked his head into my skirt.

This horrible vision would forever be etched in my memory, fighting with those that conjured up her smile, rosy cheeks, and youthful vigor.

Closing my eyes, I said, "Mama, I pray heaven knows the prize they got. We'll be lonely here on earth without you. Watch over us."

"Mary, time to say goodbye." She hid her face, peeking through her fingers. My arm around her waist, for comfort and direction, Mary kissed her finger and tapped Mama's cheek. "Wuv you." She turned her back to Mama and leaned against my shoulder.

Lizzie, dry-eyed and calm, asked Mama a series of questions. "What's it like in heaven? Do you have delicious food to eat, a warm bed to sleep in, music playing? If not, then you are not in the heaven I've heard of."

I stifled a chuckle, caught between solemnity and amusement at Lizzie's never-ending curiosity.

When no answers came, I said, "Heaven is perfect. She has all that and more."

Lizzie nodded skeptically.

As we emerged from Mama's room, a stranger stood at the door.

"This is Mr. Kepple, the sexton," Reverend Knochelmann said.

"Sorry for your loss, Miss," he said, holding his sopping wet hat. Rainwater dripped onto the floor. I resisted an urge to grab it, keep the water from puddling on the wooden floor, but one glance at his muddy boots assured me it didn't matter. The man entered Mama's room as I ushered the children to the farthest corner of the front room, shielding them from the sight of Mama being taken away.

Mrs. Eiflert ordered everyone to get ready. Peering down onto the street below, I saw the sexton place Mama's blanketed body in an open pine box in a wagon. He fitted the lid and hammered a few nails into place.

The six of us piled into a black, enclosed carriage that followed the wagon. We climbed a long hill until we drove through a set of matching pillars inscribed *German Evangelical Protestant Cemetery* and stopped on a lane overlooking a vast lawn speckled with gravestones.

We exploded from the carriage, eager to be free of the cramped space, careless of the rain. A few feet away, near a stand of maple trees, the sexton placed the box with Mama next to a pile of dirt.

The Reverend instructed us to gather around the box. I followed him, gripping Mary and Henry's hands, steadying them on the slippery surface.

"Is Mama in there?" Lizzie asked.

I nodded and gulped.

Pointing to the fresh hole beside it, she asked, "She's going down there?"

The finality of Mama's passing and subsequent rituals puzzled Lizzie. I had no talent for telling her the whys and wherefores like Papa did. Mute, I nodded again.

The Reverend coughed to get our attention. "Let us pray."

He led us in the Lord's prayer and said words about heaven and God taking Mama into his arms. He finished the brief, rainy service with, "May she rest in peace."

Henry pulled on my skirt. "I'm cold. Can we go home, Motty?"

Lizzie turned on him like a cat hissing at a dog. "So what? Mama's dead. She doesn't care if it's raining. You shouldn't either."

"Lizzie, he's three. He doesn't understand," I said.

Henry's plea grew louder. "I wanna go home."

"Home." Mary joined the fray, damp tendrils of hair sticking to her cheeks, unable to stay close enough for the umbrella I held to cover her.

The Reverend checked his pocket watch and muttered about another engagement. The children and I needed time; time to come to grips with Mama being gone, in the box, in the hole.

With the service over, Reverend and Mrs. Eiflert retreated to the carriage. The sexton approached, shovel in hand.

"What are you doing?" Lizzie turned on the man. "You're not putting her in there."

"Yes, I am, Miss."

"It's cold in the ground. She hates the cold." Her tears blended with rainwater on her cheeks.

"Mama, cold." Mary echoed.

Henry said. "I'm cold."

"We're all cold!" Lizzie wheeled around and shouted. "Mama will be cold forever. Forever!"

Lizzie stomped to Mama's coffin and threw herself on top. The sexton took a step closer, catching my eye. I shook my head, and he paused. I moved to the grave, pulling Mary and Henry with me.

"Bow your heads." I led us in the Lord's Prayer, giving Lizzie time to come to her senses. Mary recited the few words she knew. Henry fidgeted with his hat. Lizzie lay prone on Mama, her lips moving as she prayed along.

"Amen," I said, laying my hand on Lizzie's back. I rubbed long, calming strokes. "We have to go now."

"No!" she yelled, her head rising from the box. Her red-rimmed eyes glared at me. "I can't."

"But you must. You cannot stay here."

"No, you cannot stay," the sexton said from behind me. "Your mama is tired and needs her rest."

The sexton moved to Lizzie, and I watched in horror as he put his hands around her waist. But she held fast until he grabbed an arm. With nothing to hold on to, she let go.

Lizzie reached for the box, kicking and screaming, "Mama! Mama!" The sexton placed her in my outstretched arms, but before I could embrace her, she scrambled away and ran down the hill.

"Lizzie!" I shouted. "Stop!" Over my shoulder, I commanded, "Mary, hold Henry's hand. Don't move."

I picked up my skirts. At the carriage, Mrs. Eiflert stepped into the lane. "I'll get Mary and Henry."

"Thank you. I'll meet you at home."

Over her shoulder, I saw the sexton tilt the box into the hole and maneuver it until it disappeared. He pitched a shovelful of mud in. I heard a muffled thud as it landed on the box.

"Goodbye, Mama." Pivoting, I spotted Lizzie at the bottom of the hill, running aimlessly. Taking care around the muddy spots, I picked my way down until I spied her behind a tall stone monument with *Gauspohl* etched on its side, where she sobbed uncontrollably. I wrapped my arms around her.

In between hiccups, she said. "That man, he's covering, her, with, dirt."

"Yes, he is. But under the dirt is only her body. Her spirit is here and here," I pointed to her heart, then her head. Saying it and believing it were two different things. An eight-year-old didn't deserve to go through life without a mother.

Sitting in the mud, a dull drizzle soaking us to the bone, I held Lizzie in my arms. I could not send my siblings to the asylum. I would be their mother. Give them food, shelter, and foster their spirit and confidence.

The challenge of learning to live without Mama was temporary. Once Papa came home, he would relieve me of the obligations I'd accepted when Mama was supposed to survive.

Chapter Twenty-One

Occupying Mama's bed alone, as the others refused to join me, I slept deep and dreamless. Dawn crept over the windowsill, and an unfamiliar silence seeped into my consciousness as I awoke on the second day of a world without my mother.

Mama and Mrs. Eiflert never discussed what to do after her death, ignoring Dr. Jenkins' dire prediction. The only planning done in the event of her death was Mama telling me to take the children to the asylum. With that promise set aside, I put pen to paper, making a list of what needed to be done, a method to help me gain control of my circumstances.

Papa: Write until he answers.

Money: Two month's rent in the tin.

Two customers: Get more.

Then, I added the what ifs. What if a pay ticket came made out to Mama? What if no pay came at all? What if Papa didn't get home?

Lizzie wandered into the kitchen, interrupting my list-making. "Morning."

"Mrs. Eiflert is coming today while I make deliveries."

"Can I go with you?"

I considered her request. What harm would it do? After yesterday, it would take her mind off Mama. And mine as well.

"I don't see why not."

"I'll get dressed." She scurried from the kitchen, her bare feet padding across the wooden floor.

Mrs. Eiflert arrived at noon and handed me a covered pot. "Beef soup."

Putting the soup in the kitchen, I lifted the lid, releasing the aroma of three or more meals for my family. I returned to the front room, where Mrs. Eiflert pushed her thumb onto the toes of Lizzie's shoes.

"Martha," she said. "She's outgrown these. Henry, let's see yours." She motioned for Henry to stand before her. "Same here. You must come to Turner Hall on Tuesday."

132

"What's at Turner Hall?" I knew it as a meeting place, gymnasium, and concert hall.

"The Relief Committee takes in donations and hands them out to soldier's families. You'll find clothing, shoes, and other necessaries. Tuesday is my day to volunteer."

"That's wonderful, Mrs. Eiflert. We're grateful for any help."

"Are you still mending for neighborhood ladies?" she asked.

"I have two customers. Another one or two would help." I bit back the words that without Mama to care for, I could handle more work.

"I'll ask the ladies on the committee for referrals."

Mentally, I put a check mark next to get more customers on my list.

Walking downtown, unfamiliar territory for Lizzie, I held her hand at crossings. In between, we chatted about the prospect of new shoes, and how lucky we were to have Mrs. Eiflert watching out for us.

"Mama is in the ground now, isn't she?" A statement more than a question.

"Her body is. Yes," I replied with caution. Yesterday's trauma at the cemetery, too raw and recent, kept me from saying more.

"How come she didn't get better? How come she had to die?" She spat out the last word, her voice sharp with anger and confusion.

"I can't answer either question, Lizzie." I stepped over a garbage filled gutter.

"Who has the answers?"

"I think God knows."

"But he never talks to us. I talk to him but get nothing but silence."

An innocent and accurate statement. "I talk to him too. And sometimes I get answers."

Halting abruptly, she yanked on my hand, stopping my forward progress. "You do?"

Turning to face her, I said, "God doesn't talk to me, but sometimes I figure things out just by talking out loud. To Him."

My arm around her shoulders, I nudged her to continue walking. "I, rather we, will never know why Mama got sick and left us. It's something we must accept."

In the remaining minutes until we reached our first destination, I schooled my sister on proper etiquette. At the Mitchell house, Lizzie gawked at the red brick exterior, wide porch, and long windows on the front of the house. "It's beautiful."

Entering the house through the rear door, we were greeted by an outburst from Rose. "We've been worried. How is your Mama?"

"She died on Thursday," I stated it flatly, as if reporting on the weather. If I went into detail, the threads that bound the seams of my grief would unravel.

"Oh, my poor, dear girl."

I gestured to my sister. "This is Lizzie."

Lizzie curtsied as instructed. "Pleased to meet you."

"And I, you." Rose's eyebrows arched upwards. In a conspiratorial whisper, she told Lizzie, "No need to curtsy to me. I'm just the help."

In the office, I prepared the finished goods for Jane's review. Lizzie ran her fingers over the elegant walnut desk, but the sight of shelves overflowing with books drew her in like a bee to a flower.

Jane appeared, the hoops of her rose-colored dress swaying as she swept into the room. She held my face between her hands. "Martha. I'm so sorry."

"Thank you." I peered into her kind eyes, sincere in her condolences and wished she'd been there to console me at Mama's funeral.

I sniffed. "Jane, meet Lizzie."

"Hello, Lizzie." Jane's full attention swiveled to the girl, giving me a chance to swipe at my eyes. Lizzie repeated the introduction she used with Rose.

"How is Mary?" Jane turned to me.

"She's fine, but I'm not sure she understands."

"Did you write to your father?"

"Yes. But as you know, it may be some time before we hear from him."

"Yes, the mail delays are preposterous. Would you like coffee?"

"Thank you, but we can't stay. We have another errand and Mrs. Eiflert awaits our return."

Lizzie's bottom lip jutted out at my refusal of coffee, a rarity in our household since the war began.

Jane picked up the inventory list, made a cursory inspection of the clothing, and retrieved her money purse from the desk drawer.

"Have you thought about where you'll go?"

"Go?" Lizzie and I asked at the same time.

"Well, yes, now that you have no adult in your home."

"I—er, we," I stuttered. Nowhere. I had rent money.

Jane peered at me, expecting an answer.

I blurted out what came to mind. "Mrs. Eiflert and I will discuss that today." My confident tone did not betray the lie that stuck in my throat.

"I'm glad you have a plan," Jane reached for my hand. "But Martha, you and the children must live with an adult. You know that don't you?"

I didn't. "Ready, Lizzie?" I asked, withdrawing my hand from Jane's. I needed to escape the confines of the office and my employer's intrusive questions.

Startled, Jane stepped aside. I brushed past and fled through the back door, plunging into the space between the houses.

"Slow down, Motty!" Lizzie gasped, plucking at my sleeve until I stopped at the sidewalk.

"What did she mean by where will we go?"

Facing her, heedless of pedestrians passing by, I said, "Something I didn't think about. I didn't realize…" Picturing my list, this problem topped them all, for if we had nowhere to live, nothing else mattered.

"Motty let's stay where we are. It's our home."

Putting my arm around her shoulder, I pulled her close. "Yes, it's our home," I said, refusing to share the obstacles to keep it ours.

Two blocks later, Mrs. Simmons opened the door to my knock.

"Hello Martha."

Without preamble, I said, "Mama passed on Thursday."

"Oh, I'm so sorry." She motioned us into the house. "Will you and the children be all right? Is your Papa coming home?" Mrs. Simmons pressed for details as I filled the canvas bag with her mending.

"I've written."

"You have relatives nearby, right?"

Not wanting to give more information than necessary, I said, "I've written them, too."

Lizzie came straight to the point as we exited the Simmons' house. "We have relatives?"

"Not that I know of."

"You lied?"

"It's none of her business."

She sensed my discomfort. "You don't like her?"

"She's our first customer and we need the money." Mrs. Simmons asked no more than Jane did about our future, but her manner didn't sit well with me. She judged, whereas Jane commiserated. I should have quit the Simmons business long ago because of her daughter's disrespectful treatment of Mary. Thinking of my list, I resolved to only keep the Simmons' business until it could be replaced.

At home, I shooed the children into the yard and took a chair next to Mrs. Eiflert.

"I lied today," I confessed.

Her eyebrows rose.

"I said we had relatives."

"And you don't." Her eyebrows fell.

I shook my head. "Miss Mitchell said we can't live without an adult. And now, Mrs. Simmons thinks I've written to some relatives."

"I see."

"We can't leave. We need to be here when Papa comes home. Besides, where would we go?"

Mrs. Eiflert studied me for a moment. "I'm sorry you are in this predicament. But you should think about the children."

I snapped my head up, eyes locking with hers." "I am thinking about the children. This is our home."

"You could find a job. And the children can go to the orphan asylum. Your mother spoke of it."

Indeed, she had. To her, and then to me the night before she died. "I can't. I won't."

"The German Protestant Orphan Asylum has an excellent reputation and many children whose fathers are in the Army are there."

Why did everyone want to take my siblings away? "I am perfectly capable of caring for them. I have income, we have the church's generosity, and Papa will be home soon."

"As you wish, Martha, but I'm not sure how long you can remain as you are." She gathered her basket and hat.

Contrite, I said, "Mrs. Eiflert, please don't misunderstand. I promised I'd take care of this family. If they are not with me, I cannot."

"Your mother had it hard with four children, and she had a partner. You do not. That's one reason I think the orphanage is a good idea. You deserve to live a full life, one that doesn't include raising three siblings on meager means of support and working your fingers to the bone. It's more than anyone should ask of a girl of...how old are you?"

"Fifteen."

"Fifteen! You should be going to picnics and dances, have girlfriends, a beau."

Mrs. Eiflert painted a picture of a girl nothing like me. I never dreamed of going to a dance or talking with a boy. But for just a moment, I imagined that girl. Laughing with friends at a picnic, twirling in the blue dress Jane gave me, a boy bringing me a cup of punch. The dream sequence faded into reality with the image of my siblings. Mary's mouth pouting when she didn't get her way. Henry's scramble for comfort in Mama's lap. Lizzie's cornflower blue eyes mirroring Mama's in color and curiosity. They needed me and were all I had left of Mama. The thought of sending them away made my chest tighten with fears and worries greater than missed dances or boys.

"Those are not for me right now. Maybe when Papa comes home."

"Yes, indeed." The older woman placed her fingers under my chin, tilting it left, then right. "You have pleasant features, Martha. Any boy will find you pleasing to the eye. And you're smart and hardworking."

Heat rushed from my hairline to my collar as I gently withdrew from her touch. "Thank you," I mumbled, averting my eyes.

"I don't know what it's like to be in your shoes, so I won't judge. I'll see you Tuesday at the Hall." She clutched the banister as she descended the steep stairs.

Despite Mrs. Eiflert's well-meaning advice, I would not separate our family. Not while any other option remained. For now, we had money to pay the rent, charity of the church to supplement our food supplies, and most important of all, Papa had to be on his way. He had to be.

Chapter Twenty-Two

An overnight storm cleared the smoke-filled skies and the unpleasant odors of the slaughterhouse, ushering in a beautiful Tuesday morning.

I steeled myself to pay the rent, determined to keep Mama's death a secret. Greenbacks in hand, I entered the shoe shop. Locke accepted the payment eagerly, his oily manner sending shivers down my spine as I escaped into the sunshine where the children waited, excited for our outing to Turner Hall.

That unpleasant task behind me, we made our way across town. The grand brick building towered before us as we fell in line with other women and children, entering a vast room where sunlight poured through floor-to-ceiling windows, casting beams that made dust motes dance in the air. The smell of fresh-cut pine filled the space, prickling my nose. Cheerful murmurs and friendly greetings echoed off the ceiling and walls, creating a pleasant hum of busyness.

I led everyone down the center aisle. Tables constructed of sawhorses supporting wooden planks were laden with clothing. I spied Mrs. Eiflert at the front and my siblings followed like ducklings.

As usual, Mrs. Eiflert took charge. She pointed to two bundles. "I put some things aside for you. Underclothing, blouses, skirts, and pants for Henry. Shoes are in the barrels along the wall. Wear what fits and leave your old ones on the floor."

Lizzie, excited about new shoes, dropped Henry's hand and shot over to the barrels. She tried to stick her head in but couldn't see over the rim.

Mrs. Eiflert chuckled. "Tip the barrel and dump the shoes onto the floor. Just clean up when you're done."

Lizzie and I pulled the barrel onto its side. Henry, small enough to fit inside, dove into the barrel and threw out shoes, laces knotted to make pairs.

"Mary and I will be at those tables over there." I nodded toward the other side of the room, where a large sign declared dresses and skirts.

Walking away, I whispered. "Mary, it's Lizzie's birthday soon. Can you help me find her a pretty dress?"

"Birthday!" Mary clapped. No one could match her enthusiasm for birthdays, especially hers. She delighted in the attention rewarded her one day a year. "Birthday, Mary." My sister pointed to herself.

I laughed. "Lizzie's birthday. Yours is coming soon." It wouldn't come until March, but she had little notion of time.

The clothing on the table lay in disarray, unfolded by searching hands. I sought red or pink to complement Lizzie's fair complexion and light brown curls. Shifting pieces from one pile to another, I found nothing. However, in a neat stack on the end of the table, I spied red. I pulled it from the stack and held it before me. A dress, flared below a gathered waist, with a bodice shaped to fit snugly across the chest. The width and length looked right, and the poplin fabric was clean and in good condition. Decorative stitching adorned the collar and the wrist of each long sleeve. I wondered who the previous owner had been.

"I have it! Look!" I turned my back on Lizzie and Henry, who continued to look for shoes, and raised the dress for Mary to admire.

"Pretty," she said, admiring the fabric with her fingertips. "Birthday. Me."

"Lizzie's birthday, remember? Your birthday next." It could be frustrating that Mary always wanted a birthday, but arguing with her made no difference. She only knew birthdays meant gifts and cake.

Mary pointed to a green dress on the table. "Me. Birthday."

Black was the only color she and I could wear for a year, the proper time for women to be in mourning. I pointed to her skirt. "Find this color," I said. "Black."

"Black," she repeated, but stared at the green.

Lizzie and Henry ran up to us, out of breath, each clutching a pair of shoes. Their arrival interrupted my color lesson with Mary. I hastily rolled the red dress into a ball and hid it behind my back. "Try them on."

With new shoes on, they stood, ready for inspection. Placing my thumb above their toes, as Mrs. Eiflert did, I assessed if the shoes had room for their feet to grow.

"Good," I said, approving their choices. "Did you clean up?"

Lizzie and Henry raced each other to the barrel, refilled it, and throwing their old shoes inside, turned the barrel upright.

Mrs. Eilflert bustled up to our little group. "Have you found what you need?"

Lizzie and Henry proudly displayed their footwear.

"Mrs. Eiflert, you thought a few ladies might have mending work," I said.

"Yes, my dear. Follow me." She walked away.

I instructed the children to sit on the steps at the foot of the stage. "Stay put. I'll be right back."

I joined Mrs. Eiflert and two other women who inspected and sorted clothing into piles.

"This is Martha Hesch," Mrs. Eiflert introduced me. "Mrs. Biedermann. Mrs. Ziegler."

Mrs. Biedermann, a stout woman with gray hair, a bulbous nose, and small, deep-set eyes, said, "Pleased to meet you, Martha. I'm sorry about your mother."

I murmured my thanks.

"Please call me Agatha," Mrs. Ziegler said. Younger than the other two women, I guessed her around Mama's age. Her bright smile reached her green eyes. I liked her immediately.

Dipping in a small curtsy, I said. "Pleased to meet you."

Mrs. Eiflert got down to business. "Now, Martha, these ladies have some mending. They know your work is high quality."

Mrs. Biedermann handed me a bundle wrapped in brown paper tied with string. She explained about a torn sleeve and missing buttons.

Mrs. Ziegler, in charge of mending clothing donations, held up a bag of socks that needed darning. "These will be sent to our soldiers in the field. It doesn't matter if they match into pairs."

"My sister Lizzie is an expert at darning. And Mary excels at buttons." I hugged the packages to my chest, awaiting further instructions.

"What do you say, Martha?" Mrs. Eiflert urged. "Can you return these items, say, next Tuesday?"

I mentally juggled this additional work with Jane and Mrs. Simmons' orders. With Lizzie home from school for another month, we could easily meet the deadline.

"Next Tuesday is good," I said. Thrilled at the promise of additional income, I mentally calculated another dollar in the tin.

"Thank you, Mrs. Biederman. Mrs. Ziegler."

"Agatha, please!" Mrs. Ziegler exclaimed.

"Agatha." I thanked Mrs. Eiflert for the introduction and donations. "We are in your debt."

"Never you mind," Mrs. Eiflert said. "We are here to serve our community and I'm happy to help." With a nod, she turned and rejoined the other ladies in sorting.

"Everyone ready to go?" Tucking the packages into the mending bag, I walked to the foot of the stage. On the steps, Henry, still learning to tie his shoes, twisted a lace into a loop that didn't hold. Lizzie, elbows on the step behind, admired her new shoes.

Mary was nowhere in sight. I scanned the stage, my heart leaping into my throat. "Where's Mary?"

Lizzie sprang into action, darting down the steps and into the aisle. "Mary!" Her voice cut through the chatter.

"Stay," I ordered Henry, his eyes wide with alarm.

I raced after Lizzie, my gaze ricocheting from face to face. The cheerful bustle of women and children browsing grated against my rising panic. Washington Park flashed through my mind: Mary lost, Papa leaving. Not again.

I met Lizzie in the middle.

Switching tactics, Lizzie adopted a sing-song voice, as if she were hunting her sister in a game of hide-and-seek. "Maaa-ry! Come out, come out, wherever you are!"

What if she'd gone outside? What if someone took her? The horrifying possibilities pressed on me like a vise, squeezing the air from my lungs. My eyes scanned the crowd, but black-clad women with buns at their necklines blurred together.

"You take that side. I'll take this."

We sang Mary's name, walking up and down the aisles. Women frowned or scowled, though some offered help. "Have you seen a girl with dark hair about this tall wearing a black dress?" Shaking their heads, I questioned another and another. Our search alerted the crowd to a missing child, and the vast hall quieted, our voices singsong, echoing Mary, Mary.

My next step would be to go outside and look for her. The thought of her leaving the Hall terrified me.

"There she is!" Henry, squatting on his haunches near the stage, pointed to a table at the side of the room.

Lizzie and I rushed over, the way clearing for us like the Red Sea parting for Moses. My eyes darted here and there, my body spinning in a circle, even so, I didn't see her.

"There, under the table," Henry shouted. I bent at the waist and searched. Mary sat amid a pile of clothing along the wall.

"Mary! Oh, thank God!" I sighed, picked up my skirts, and rushed to the table.

On hands and knees, Lizzie crawled under until she sat cross-legged next to her sister as if they were about to play jacks.

"Hello," Lizzie said.

Tears of relief blurred my vision as I joined my sisters on the floor, nestled under the table, oblivious of the display we were making.

Mary exclaimed, "Me. Birthday."

"You," I stuttered, worried she gave away Lizzie's surprise. "You found a birthday dress."

Mary held a garment of forest green printed with tiny white flowers, the one she admired earlier. "Birthday!"

She wanted a birthday dress too. Black be damned. Making Mary happy after losing her was more important. I hoped it would fit and if it didn't, I'd figure out how to make it work.

"You scared us," Lizzie said softly, stroking Mary's arm.

Henry crawled next to me. Huddled together on the floor, I realized how strange we must look. I chuckled. Then Lizzie laughed, followed by Mary, and then Henry, his giggles blending with our girlish hysteria.

Someone cleared their throat from above. "I see you've found her." Mrs. Eiflert poked her head in, her mouth and eyes arranged in a smile instead of a scowl. I crawled out and brushed sawdust and dirt from my skirt.

"We did." I looked around the room. The crowd's bustle and murmurs had resumed as if nothing unusual had occurred.

"It doesn't take long to lose a child. Does Mary have any sense of danger? Anything she fears?" she asked, her head tilted to one side.

She feared loud noises, spiders, and sudden surprises. I shielded her from dangers in the street, kitchen, and with strangers. But Mary's innocence and trusting nature could have led to disaster. What if someone meant her harm?

"You have two choices, Martha," Mrs. Eiflert said, heedless of her audience. "Teach her to be afraid. Or protect her."

I looked up sharply, meeting her intense gaze.

"For the rest of her life," she added.

I had no reply. I didn't want Mary or any of my siblings to be afraid - it didn't seem natural. Mrs. Eiflert had a point though, one I needed to consider.

We left the Hall in a line. I led the way through tables and barrels, while Lizzie brought up the rear, keeping the younger ones in between. On the street, I put a protective arm around Mary as she clutched the green dress tightly to her chest.

The green dress fit Mary perfectly. The red was a size too big for Lizzie but could be altered. Mary only wore hers at home and fought me at bedtime to take it off. Lizzie hung hers in the wardrobe, putting it aside for her first day at school.

On the fifth of August, we celebrated Lizzie's birthday. Henry wore his best shirt and pants, the girls their new dresses, and I the blue one from Jane last Christmas. It felt sinful to have a party so soon after Mama's death. But Lizzie deserved it, and Mary would be the happiest soul on the block.

I retrieved the Geburtstagskranz, the wooden wreath we used to celebrate birthdays. Made of pine, no wider than the length of my hand, small holes were hollowed around the ring, each with a number scratched beside it, one through fourteen. I put a candle in the hole by nine, another at ten, and lit them. As we did for all birthdays, we sang the birthday song in German. At the end, we yelled, "Alles Gute zum Geburtstag, Lizzie!"

Waiting for her to blow out the candles, I reminded everyone about the tradition that came from our parents' homeland. "One candle is to celebrate this birthday. The other is to make a wish for next year."

Henry nudged Lizzie. "Blow!"

"I will. You only get one wish, and I want it to be a good one."
Her eyes darted back and forth as she pondered this critical decision.

"I'm ready." She took a deep breath and blew. The flame
sputtered out, wax spraying on the wreath and the table.

"Mary. Birthday." She pointed to her chest.

The candles relit, we sang the song, and Mary blew out the
flames.

Chapter Twenty-Three

Trusting Lizzie alone with Henry, I took Mary along on delivery
day. Mrs. Eiflert's advice to teach and protect Mary stayed with me.
I would expose Mary to new situations, gauge her reactions, and
help if needed.

Mrs. Simmons opened the door to our knock. Her lip curled
seeing Mary at my side.

Mary felt none of the woman's disdain. "Hello!" she screeched.

Instinctively, I reached for Mary's arm, to ask her to lower her
voice, but I stilled my hand. Thanks to mending income from the
ladies at Turner Hall, I no longer needed this woman's business. I'd
let Mary be Mary, consequences be damned.

I gave her the package of finished work. "Fifty cents," I said.

"Wait here." Voices floated though the open doorway, one
whining, the other scolding.

A minute later, Mrs. Simmons' daughter Sylvia appeared in the
doorway, arms crossed over her chest.

"You brought her." With emphasis on her, she nodded at Mary.

Ignorant of slights against her, Mary curtsied. "Hello!"

Sylvia ignored her. "She's odd, you know."

What could I say to this spoiled brat that wouldn't get me into too much trouble? "She is odd," I agreed, then added, "But so are you." My lips yearned to curl into a smirk, but I maintained my dignity and a measure of seriousness.

Sylvia blinked, startled. "I'm not odd."

Mary's head swiveled between the girl and me.

"I have another sister younger than you. I find it odd that you are not kind or polite like she is."

Her mouth flew open like a baby bird, waiting to be fed, before she wailed and fled from the doorway. "Mama! Mama! She said I'm odd."

"Oh Sylvia, you must be mistaken." Mrs. Simmons cajoled.

Curious about the commotion, I peeked into the hall. Sylvia's voice rang out clearly, "I thought she wasn't coming here anymore. I don't like her. Send her away."

Footsteps clicked on the marble floor and Mrs. Simmons stepped onto the porch, her daughter trailing behind, eyes narrowed, and lips pursed. I imagined smoke puffing from her nostrils, the dregs of a dragon's fiery breath.

"What is all the fuss?" Mrs. Simmons asked as she handed me fifty cents and a small, wrapped bundle.

"I'm not sure." I put the money in my pocket. "Mary, are you ready?"

"Now, just a minute!" Mrs. Simmons put a hand on my arm, halting our departure. "Let's get to the bottom of this."

I yanked my arm from her grasp. "Ask her," I tipped my head toward Sylvia.

"What happened?" Mrs. Simmons bent over and gripped her daughter's shoulders.

"She said I was odd," Sylvia pouted. Her eyes gave away the half-lie.

"I did and I'll tell you why." My hand on Mary's back, I nudged her forward, bringing her into the conversation. "Mary is different. She is slow to speak words and sentences. She can be loud. In your daughter's eyes, that makes her odd. I would rather Mary be odd than have your daughter's poor manners."

Mrs. Simmons' eyes widened in disbelief at my calling out her daughter. "My word!"

"Let's go, Mary. We've outstayed our welcome." I returned the package to Mrs. Simmons and ushered my sister to the steps. I didn't care what the girl or her mother said or did as I showed her my back.

Undaunted by the girl's cruelty and lack of manners, Mary kept hers. A huge smile on her face, she waved and shouted, "Bye!"

At the Mitchell house, Mary's reception was the exact opposite. Cook handed her a cookie to keep her occupied while Jane and I conducted our business.

"Did you hear about Colonel McCook?" Jane asked, as I settled myself in the chair next to the desk.

"Robert McCook?" The leader and sole non-German in the Ninth Regiment.

"Yes. A band of guerrillas attacked the wagon he rode in. Despite his defenseless state, they mercilessly shot him, and he succumbed to his wounds."

"How awful! Papa held him in high regard."

"You can bet the Ninth will revenge his death."

The mention of the regiment reminded me of my own concerns. "Speaking of soldiers," I said, my voice tinged with worry, "any letter from Papa? I've written scores to him about Mama. Surely, one must reach him."

"Even if one gets through, it may be some time before he can get leave to come home."

"Get leave?" I didn't understand this word as it applied to the Army.

"Temporary permission to leave his company."

"Oh. Not permanent?"

"The way EB explained it, he'll have to submit a request for leave. If granted, he'll get a pass to travel to Cincinnati. How long depends on your Papa and the Army."

"Assuming he returns, I hope he'll stay for a while." Under my breath, I muttered, "Forever."

Jane nodded sympathetically, then asked, "Did you bring another letter to post?"

I pulled an envelope from my pocket and handed it to her.

In the kitchen, I put the canvas bag over my shoulder while Mary finished her cookie.

"Take some for Henry and Lizzie." Jane selected a few warm cookies from the baking sheet. She placed them in a clean handkerchief, tied it at the top, and handed the little bundle to Mary, who beamed, proud to carry cookies home to her siblings.

At home, I added my earnings to the eight dollars set aside for September rent. If a pay ticket came and Papa hadn't assigned it to Mr. Eiflert, it would be worthless.

Chapter Twenty-Four

At last! A letter from Papa arrived at the Mitchell boarding house dated August 20, 1862. Mama had been dead six weeks.

> Mama's passing has hit me hard. I have permission to come home. We are chasing a brigade of Rebels through Tennessee and when we reach Nashville, I am free to come home.

Papa, home. The next weeks buzzed with anticipation; his return meant everything. Each footstep on the stairs sent me rushing to the door. The wait for him felt like getting molasses from a jar in January.

However, the enemy's invasion of Kentucky in early September overshadowed my excitement about his homecoming. Marching unopposed to Lexington, the Rebels captured the town, a mere eighty miles from Cincinnati. Word spread quickly that our city was a target for a force of fifty thousand Confederate soldiers. Major General Lew Wallace declared martial law, forcing business owners to close their shops to protect its citizens. Backed by Ohio Governor Tod, Wallace ordered all willing and able men to join the army in building defenses and digging trenches on the Kentucky side of the river, while the soldiers arrived from all fronts, and prepared for battle.

Schools closed. The markets shut down, leaving us no access to fresh food. Therese Eiflert delivered a basket of provisions and a message from her mother to stay inside. Jane offered us a room at the Mitchell house, but I declined in case Papa came home.

After seven days of martial law, and with no assault on any Kentucky towns adjacent to Cincinnati along the Ohio River, the town relaxed. Just after dawn, on the eighth day, I sat at an open window cooling our rooms with morning breezes. The street lay eerily silent save for a single horse pulling an empty wagon, hooves clip-clopping as it left town. Most days, a steady stream of wagons rolled past with fruits and vegetables from the farms and meat from the slaughterhouses headed to the markets.

The faint yell of a newsboy fluttered up the street into the window. "Martial law suspended!"

Grabbing my reticule, I slipped out the door, careful not to wake anyone. At the corner, I fingered three pennies for the newsboy and read the headline. "All businesses, except those selling alcohol, may open until four o'clock, including markets."

Hurrying home, I pushed the unlocked door open. Lizzie sat at the table, slicing a sausage into bite-size pieces.

"I think it's over." I laid the paper in front of her, pointing to the headlines.

The knife halted as Lizzie brought a chunk of sausage to her mouth. Looking over my shoulder, she tipped her head forward.

"What?" I said and whirled around. A man stood in the doorway, morning light shining behind him, obscuring his features.

Oh, dear Lord. Locke had followed me.

"Get out!" I shouted, waving a hand, shooing him like a pesky fly.

"Motty," Lizzie whispered.

"Didn't you hear me, Mr. Locke? Get out!"

But the man, defying my command, stepped through the doorway, his nearness chilling my heart. Instinctively, I drew back and thought of my safety, then Lizzie's.

"Motty." Locke didn't know my nickname, and his voice was devoid of mocking laughter.

"Papa!" The knife clattered on the table as Lizzie launched herself at the man's neck. He stumbled backward as he caught her in his arms.

"Papa?" Here he stood. In our rooms. Holding Lizzie.

"Hello!" He pecked a kiss on her cheek. She scrambled down and ran from the room.

I'd last seen Papa proud and strong in his blue uniform. Now, a long, scraggly beard framed his dirt-smeared, sunburned face. Time and travel had ravaged him. This man standing in my kitchen was almost unrecognizable.

I stood frozen between the kitchen and the door, tears rolling down my cheeks. "I'm sorry, Papa. I'm sorry Mama died." I wanted to tell him about Mama and that day, and every day since. But Henry and Mary interrupted my intentions, surrounding him with hugs and shouts of joy and finger kisses. His eyes, soft and understanding, locked on mine and instead of blame, I found shared sorrow.

Expecting Papa to be hungry, I put out the remaining sausage, cheese, and bread. Over the scant meal, Papa shared stories about his travels and his new assignment. "When we reached Nashville, some of us from my company volunteered to defend Cincinnati from the rebel threat. We're here on detached duty."

Detached duty? Did this mean he would not be staying? Not understanding how the Army worked when someone needed to go home, I waited for Papa to explain.

But Lizzie needed him. "Papa, we did everything we could for Mama. But she was too sick. Can you go with me to see her?"

Lizzie's plain-spoken words hit me, hard. The wound of Mama's passing was still raw, triggering a lump in my throat.

Papa pulled Lizzie onto his lap. Staring off at nothing, he cradled her in his arms, her head on his chest. I watched my father struggle with his loss, much different from ours. He sniffed, wiped his eyes, and exhaled. "I miss your Mama very much. It's hard to believe she's not here."

"No cry, Papa," Mary said.

"No, no cry, Mary." He breathed deep and blew it out slowly. "You're right."

He pulled Lizzie's chin up and looked into her eyes. "We'll go see Mama soon."

"Thank you, Papa." She crawled out of his lap and left the kitchen.

"She's had it hard," I said. I sent Mary and Henry to play in the front room so Papa and I could talk in private.

On her way out, Mary gave Papa a finger kiss and smacked her lips.

"Nothing's changed with her," he said.

"She's grown. You'll need to spend time with her to see how much."

"I hope to do that when I'm not on duty."

"What's detached duty? Will you come home at night? Should I plan for you to eat with us?"

"So many questions! You sound like Lizzie." He pushed his empty plate away. "I'm not sure. I report to General Wallace's headquarters tomorrow for my assignment."

"Tomorrow? Already?" My complaint flew from my mouth without thought of how whiny and bitter I sounded.

"You should be glad experienced men like me have arrived to defend the city." Papa wiped his mouth on the back of his shirtsleeve.

"But we need you here, Papa!" I shot back, crossing my arms over my chest with a huff.

"I don't get a choice, Martha!" His voice boomed in the tiny kitchen.

Taken aback, I stared at the table, thoughts racing but words stuck. My emotions felt raw, on edge.

"Daughter," Papa said, his tone softer. Stretching across the table, he put his hand out, palm up.

If I put my hand in his, I would give up what little control I had, what I needed to survive. Ignoring his hand, I focused on a cobweb dangling from the ceiling. "You're not home for good, are you?" Waiting for his response, I forced myself to look at him, the gauntlet thrown down.

He withdrew his hand. His shoulders slumped and his body sagged as if his bones had turned to jelly.

"You sound like your mother," he sulked.

"Compliment or insult?" I asked, taking a bit of pleasure in my response.

He inhaled deeply, then exhaled with a long sigh. A minute or two passed, the silence between us, a chasm too painful for either of us to bridge.

"I'm going out." He rose from the chair. "Don't wait up."

I'd heard him say these exact words to my mother, particularly after she'd been nagging him. I sat motionless in the kitchen chair, remorseful but too proud to ask him to stay. I listened as he bid his children goodbye, and the door slammed, shaking the thin walls of our rooms.

"Damn," I whispered in the empty kitchen. I did sound like Mama. But he was selfish. Selfish for leaving after being home mere hours. Selfish for only thinking of himself. And when challenged, he ran away instead of being honest.

His answer, though unspoken, was clear. He'd not be staying any longer than his assigned duty would permit.

Chapter Twenty-Five

Assigned to guard a distant town in northern Kentucky, Papa left amid tears of grief at his departure, the day after his homecoming. A week later, the papers reported that the Confederates had withdrawn to Tennessee, taking the threat of invasion with them. Days later, reports trickled in about a major battle near Antietam Creek, in Sharpsburg, Maryland, where thousands on both sides were killed or wounded. Several members of the Fifth Ohio, organized in Cincinnati, were part of St. Mattheus' congregation, and Father Knochelmann led us in prayer for the families impacted by the devastating battle.

Papa returned in early October, looking fit and in good spirits. Removing his hat and coat, he ate a meal and read the newspaper as if he'd just come home from work.

"How long are you here?" I asked, avoiding my real question, if he was home for good.

"I've been assigned to a recruiting detail." The newsprint snapped as he folded it in half.

"How many do you need?" I asked, hoping the number was large and unattainable.

"Seventy. Will be difficult with new regiments forming. As you know, the Ninth is all German, so our focus is on the German community."

"Are you joining us for supper?"

"Actually, I have a friend, Joe Decker, on the recruiting detail with me. I'd like you to meet him."

"Oh?" I knew a handful of Papa's friends, but Joe Decker was not among them.

"He's got a wife and boy living up on Dayton Street." He paused, then added, "I've asked them to supper tonight."

Dropping my work into my lap, I closed my eyes, letting his news sink in before I said something I'd regret. How could he just waltz in, add three people to our meal, and think nothing of it? Did he have any idea what it took to feed that many people? The preparation, the cost, the space?

Knowing my complaints might anger him, I tried a different approach. "Very well. With what we have in the kitchen to eat, your children will go hungry," I said, as if I didn't care. "The market is closed. What do you suggest?"

He rubbed his chin. "I, uh, I," he floundered, "I think you should divide what you have among everyone. They won't mind."

They being his children, or the guests? Willing to concede, I nodded, but the meal would be scanty at best. "Where will we eat?" I pictured our tiny kitchen.

"We'll bring the table and chairs in here!" Papa's arm swept the room, proud of his innovation. "Make it a special occasion."

"Um, Papa, we have only four chairs."

"Ah, yes, right."

I had him there.

"We'll eat in shifts!" Papa stood, a satisfied smile on his face.

"Fine," I muttered, defeated, and resumed sewing. With Papa around, flexibility would need to be my master.

I scraped together enough for a meager meal and fed the children. After clearing the table and rearranging it for guests, a smart knock on the door announced their arrival. We scrambled to our feet, lining up by age.

"Come in! Come in!" Papa's booming welcome echoed in the room.

The man, leaner and younger than Papa, removed his uniform cap, exposing close-cropped blond hair. A young woman followed, carrying a child.

"George, thank you for the invitation." The men shook hands.

"Children, this is my friend, Joseph Decker."

"Joe, please." The man advanced, clicked his heels, and swept his hat in a low bow. Straightening, eyes twinkling, he said, "I've heard much about this family. It's a pleasure to meet you at last." Turning to the woman, he stepped aside and ushered her further into the room. "This is my wife, Dina. And this little man is Gus."

The woman dipped and nodded. She was young, perhaps twenty, while I guessed the man was around thirty-five. About my height, her slender figure was softened by recent motherhood, with a head full of carrot-colored tresses that fell loosely to her shoulders beneath a fashionable poke bonnet tied under her chin. Her loose hair puzzled me; it seemed an improper style for a married woman.

Lizzie headed straight for the baby. "I'm Lizzie, and I'm nine. How old is he?"

"One year." The woman's heavy accent revealed her recent arrival from Germany.

"May I hold him?" Dina passed the baby into Lizzie's extended hands and sat him beside Henry's basket of toys.

"You have a fine son, too, George!" Joseph stretched his open hand toward my brother. Henry, peeking from behind my skirt, shook the stranger's hand, then retracted it as if hot to the touch.

Joe nodded toward Mary. Unaccustomed to strangers, she gaped at him, eyes round as saucers. "This your crazy girl?"

Crazy girl? What had Papa told this man? I rankled at his remark and fixed my father with a piercing look.

"Mary." Papa brushed past Joe's comment. "And this is Martha, my oldest."

I acknowledged the man with a nod and asked, "Papa, shall we go to the table?"

"Yes. Let's eat." Papa motioned his guests to be seated.

Joe helped his wife into a chair and took the one next to Papa.

I brought out a plate of sausage, bread, and cheese. Alongside, I put a sharp knife to cut off whatever they wanted. Papa looked at me over his guests' heads, confused by the meal.

"I'm sorry, there isn't more. With short notice, I had no time to market."

Papa's brow furrowed, his face darkening. I ignored his warning and studied Joe's reaction.

"This is fine, Martha," he said to me, then addressed Papa. "We could have done this another time, George."

160

I thanked him silently for getting me off the hook. I brought out a kettle of tea and poured it into our chipped and mismatched cups.

While we ate, Lizzie and Mary played with the boys, reciting a favorite poem. "Pat-a-cake, pat-a-cake, baker's man." When Lizzie said, "Mark it with a G," she poked Gus in the belly. His giggles rang out like musical notes.

As the last bites disappeared from plates, I angled my chair to listen to the adults with an eye on the children. I picked up a dress from the mending basket.

"You sew?" Dina asked, peering over my shoulder.

"Yes. Do you?" I asked to be polite.

"This dress I make. You like?" She planted her hands on her hips and twirled around so I could admire her handiwork.

"It's nice." It was nothing special.

"Me help?"

"Help?"

She pointed to the basket.

"Oh, no, thank you. You are our guest." Mama would flail me for letting a guest do my work. Something about this woman rubbed me the wrong way.

She dragged her chair next to mine, leaned over the basket, and riffled through the stack. "I help."

I stopped sewing and watched her rifle through the neatly folded clothes. "What are you doing?"

"This one!" She held a man's shirt aloft, the collar dangling from the yoke.

"I think not." I snatched the shirt from her hands and tucked it in my lap. My stern cold stare warned her to keep her hands to herself.

Surrendering, she slumped in the chair. Ignoring her, I refolded everything.

"What's this?" Joe asked. "Dina, are you crying? What's happened?"

I stopped folding and peered at the woman. Aghast, I saw a single tear slip down her cheek. She was crying. Over what? My insistence she behave as a guest should. Out of the corner of my eye, I spied Papa observing the scene.

"I help!" Dina pointed to the basket, then jabbed her finger into her chest. "I sew! I fix!"

Using his thumb, Joe brushed the tear from his wife's cheek. "Miss Martha," he said, "my wife does not speak English very well. I believe she wants to help you sew."

"Thank you but it's not proper for a guest." I applied what I learned from watching Jane about polite behavior. Turning to Dina, I laid my hand on her forearm and used simple English words to convey my meaning. "You are kind. But I do not need help."

Papa rose from his chair, hovering on the fringe of the conversation. "Everything all right?"

"We are." Mr. Decker smiled at me, smug and dismissive as if mildly amused by the scene, forgiving me for berating his wife.

I bit my tongue and held back the words I wanted to say but knew I shouldn't. How dare he?

"George, thank you for the invitation and the fine meal. Time to go, Dina."

The men descended the stairs to the yard below. With Gus in Dina's arms, Mary plucked at her sleeve. "Kiss!"

Dina whirled around, yanking her arm from Mary's grasp. "Kiss? What?"

Mary put her finger to her puckered lips and reached toward Dina's cheek. She recoiled, arms tightening around Gus.

Her finger in the air as if suspended by a string. I redirected it to my cheek. "Kiss!" I smacked my lips.

Mary pointed to Dina. "Kiss."

"No touch, du Heide!" She spat, using the German word for heathen.

Hiding Mary's hand in my skirt, I squeezed it. My words dripped with honey, "You are kind to offer a kiss to our guest, sister. She doesn't understand you are being friendly."

My eyes locked with Dina's in open challenge. I forced a mask of friendliness, while Dina's glare bore into me, her eyes narrowed to pinpricks beneath a furrowed brow, her lips moving in silent fury.

Mary squeezed my hand. Her beautiful face, serene yet eager, waited for me to tell her what to do or, what not to do. "It's all right, my dear. You meant no harm."

A grin tugged at my lips even as my free hand curled into a fist, nails biting into my palm, barely restraining me from slapping this woman. Maybe Dina meant no harm, but her rejection of my sister's farewell gesture, on top of butting into my business, put me in a foul mood.

Dina threw a haughty look over her shoulder as she flounced out the door and down the steps.

After cleaning up the remains of supper, I set Mary up with some button work and resumed sewing the dress. Dina was rude, taking liberties she had no right to, and I disliked her treatment of Mary. I hoped I'd never see her again.

Chapter Twenty-Six

After persistent pestering from Lizzie, Papa agreed to visit Mama and borrowed a weathered horse and farm wagon for the ride up the steep hill. After church on the last Sunday in October, Henry in his lap, Papa slapped the nag's back to start our journey. My sisters and I clung to the wagon sides in the back, every rut jarring our teeth, threatening to bounce us into the road.

We paused at the crest, the flattened hill revealing unrestricted land and forest, thick with oaks and maples displaying their autumn dresses. Having been encased in the carriage the day of Mama's burial, my first view of the city from this elevation stole my breath.

At the furthest point on the banks of the Ohio River, Kentucky's riverside hills sprawled as far as the eye could see. God's paintbrush had splotched them, dabbing gold, orange, and red haphazardly across the landscape. Cincinnati lay below, eighty years of progress crowding its seven hills with businesses, churches, and houses.

A little further on, Lizzie pointed to the entrance. "See those pillars on the left? That's the way in."

Papa steered the wagon through, and I directed him up the lane to the top of the hill. "Over there," I said, nodding toward a rise of dirt at the end of a line of markers.

Before Papa could halt the horse, Lizzie jumped down and dashed to Mama's grave. Mary on my one hand, Henry on the other, we joined her beside the hard-packed dirt while Papa remained in the wagon. A cool breeze carried the earthy scent of fallen leaves and newly turned dirt.

"Hello, Mama," I said.

Lizzie knelt and put her hand on the dirt as if she lay it on Mama's head. "I miss you."

Papa approached the grave. His steps were reluctant, but resolute.

Mary put her hand in his. "Mama sleeping."

Papa pinched his nostrils shut, his breath hitching as he struggled to maintain his composure. "Yes, Mama's sleeping."

Seeing my father hold back his tears triggered mine as I replayed her funeral in my mind, remembering that rainy morning. How Lizzie threw herself on the pine box, afraid to leave Mama in the cold, dark hole. How lost and alone I felt, responsible for the lives of three children. Wondering where Papa was, when he would come home, and how we'd survive until then. I silently thanked Mama for sending him home and prayed to God he would stay.

At the end of a row of plots, I leaned against the rough bark of a tree, musing on the months since Mama left us.

Papa's cry interrupted my thoughts. "Oh, Retta. My poor, poor, Retta." One hand covered his face, his shoulders shook, but he continued to hold Mary's hand. Or perhaps, she was she holding his.

Having never witnessed Papa cry and astonished at his display of emotion, Lizzie wrapped her arms around his waist, and Henry's tiny hand patted his stomach. They sought to console him, and by doing so, found solace for their own grief.

Papa found his handkerchief, wiped his eyes, and blew his nose. He noticed me under the tree and motioned for me to join them. I shook my head.

"Let's find something to put on Mama's grave," Lizzie said. Beneath the broad branches of a maple tree, the vibrant colors of fall leaves lay scattered on the ground. Mary and Henry presented Lizzie with choice specimens. She twirled them by their stems, inspected their worth, and discarded any that failed to meet her standards.

Papa came to stand beside me, and we watched his children work together.

"I don't know what it was like for you," he nodded towards his children, "or them."

"Her death was a blessing." I hated saying it, but she'd been in so much pain. "She could hardly breathe at the end."

"I've seen men die, some in my arms. It's tragic, horrific. But I didn't know them, not like you and your Mama." He paused. "You are brave, Motty."

"It wasn't bravery. It was necessary," I said, dismissing his compliment. "The nights were long, her cough agonizing and uncontrollable. She grew thinner until her clothes hung on her like a scarecrow's rags. And hardest of all, I lied to them." I tipped my head toward the maple tree. "Telling them Mama would be well— but knowing," I blinked hard, holding back tears, "knowing she was dying."

Papa pulled me close, and I lay my head on his shoulder, his uniform rough against my cheek. Like a creek breaking free of its logjam, my resistance loosened. Tears flowed unheeded. Pent-up grief soaked into his blue jacket.

"Motty, it's all right." His firm hands stroked my back.

"It's not. It will never be all right." My sorrow spent, I refused to be comforted, to be coddled. Then, as if possessed, my hands fisted, and I struck his chest. "Why didn't you come?"

I pounded again. Then he snatched my fists in midair.

"I thought I had more time."

166

I yanked my hands free. "You ignored what the Doctor said? A few months? Did you think he lied?" I paced, my fury needing an outlet.

"I tried," Papa said. "I didn't know she'd died until the end of July. I asked for leave several times, but we were deep in southern Tennessee, the enemy surrounding us. McCook himself denied my request."

"Harrumph! I don't believe you." I strode away from him, arms crossed over my chest, tired of his lame excuses.

"Motty."

I rolled my eyes at his use of my nickname and whirled around. A weary sigh punctuated, "What?"

"I lost her, too." His gaze wandered to the children laying colored leaves on Mama's grave, a fall quilt covering the dirt.

His helplessness nearly undid me, but my ire, built to a roaring fire, refused to be vanquished. "I know. But we watched Mama die. Little by little. One cough at a time until she spewed her lungs into a bucket." My chest heaved, breathless and angry, distraught at the memory of the day I awoke, and she did not. Suddenly, I felt the anger drain away, leaving only hollow grief and weariness.

Unable to look at him and done with his lies, I turned my attention to the children. "Finish up. It's time to go. Henry, did you pick up the leaves or roll around in them?" I smiled to take the sting out of my reprimand and brushed him off.

"That's a fine blanket you made for Mama," Papa said. Lizzie beamed from ear to ear.

Around Mama's grave, we clasped hands and said the Lord's Prayer. Without prompting, Mary started the sleeping prayer, the one we said on our knees before bed. A perfect prayer, because in her mind, that's what Mama was doing. Sleeping.

"Now I lay me down to sleep. I pray the Lord my soul to keep. If I should die before I wake, I pray the Lord my soul to take."

I found and placed a gold leaf near the head of Mama's resting place. One by one, my sisters and brother did the same, each choosing a different color.

"Bye, Mama," Henry muttered as he grasped my hand and waved with the other. I wondered how long he would remember Mama despite the stories I told to keep her memory alive.

Dry and brittle, the leaves crunched under our shoes as we walked to the wagon. We waited while Papa stood at the foot of Mama's grave. His lips moved, hands gesturing as if he were talking to her.

On the way down the hill, Lizzie leaned over the wagon seat. "Papa, most of the other graves have a marker with a name on it. Can we get one for Mama?"

"As soon as I have the money."

Delighted, Lizzie placed a sloppy kiss on his cheek.

Descending the hill, Papa ignored the view, his chattering children, and Henry's endless requests to drive the wagon. He drew into himself, shoulders slumped, shutting us out.

Before the war, I thought him an open book. We spent hours discussing the political events reported in the newspapers. When he enlisted, he gladly shared his reasons, giving me a sense of how his mind worked. I felt sure I knew him. Over the weeks since he'd been home, I asked him straight out to stay home, leave the army so we could be a family. He responded with vague assurances that all would be well. Ambiguity and I were not friends.

At the cross street near the Deckers, Papa dropped us off. "I'll return the wagon and be home later."

As I watched him drive away, I wondered if I had ever truly known him at all. We were at cross purposes. I wanted him home. He needed to escape.

Chapter Twenty-Seven

The recruiters met the quota in early November. Papa could be called back to the regiment any day. His pay had yet to arrive, and fortunately, we could live on mending money.

With Lizzie in school, Mary and I bore the brunt of the work, struggling to meet deadlines for several weeks in a row. I had two choices: cut back on the work or bring in someone else. As I sorted through a pile of torn shirts, an unexpected solution came to mind.

We had shared another meal with the Deckers, and that time Dina behaved, keeping herself busy with Gus and doting on Henry. Although she hadn't made a good first impression, Dina might relieve the stress of meeting our commitments. Like Papa, Joe hadn't received his pay, and they could use the money. Plus, it would please Papa.

"She says she can sew," I told Jane.

"Make her prove it. Give her a low-value piece and ask her to fix it. Don't tell her too much. See what she can do on her own."

"What should I pay her?"

"Give her seventy-five cents on the dollar. Keep the quarter for doing pickup and delivery."

"She'll be no good with customers except those who speak German. I think she's only been in America a few years."

"Where did she come from?"

"Somewhere around Munich. Joe brought her home with him when he returned from a trip."

"What do you think of the husband?"

"He's attentive to his wife. Adores his boy. Papa likes him. He's charming. Almost too charming. Something doesn't sit right about him. Her either, to be truthful."

"In my experience, Martha, when something feels off, don't ignore it. Trust your instincts."

"I'll take it slow." I had to or risk delivering sloppy goods.

"That's my girl!" Jane rose and put her arms around me. I stiffened in surprise. Quick and tidy, her affectionate gesture unsettled me, the physical contact strange but not unpleasant. Our relationship had changed over the months since Mama's passing, gradually shifting from business formal to friendly. Could I do business with a friend? Could I confide my fears in Jane without jeopardizing our working relationship?

Stammering my goodbye, I opened the back door and stepped into the yard, the crisp autumn air clearing my jumbled thoughts.

"Martha!" EB shouted.

He walked toward me with casual charm, his self-assured posture holding my attention. "Hello. How are you?" It had been some time since I'd seen him. He looked sharp in his dark suit and crisp white shirt, green eyes dancing under his dark lashes, cheeks pink with exertion.

"I'm well, and you?"

"The same."

"I'm heading north on an errand. Can I give you a ride?"

His offer caught me off guard. My heart quickened. "Well, if it's not out of your way."

"It's settled then. Come with me." I followed him through the back gate.

EB intrigued me. Spending time with him would be pleasant, but eight years my senior, he offered a kind gesture, nothing more. Despite our differences in age and social standing, I couldn't help but imagine a world where we were equals, where his kind gestures might mean something more. The fantasy was sweet, even if unrealistic.

Lifting me into the carriage, he flicked his whip over the horse's back, jolting us forward. Saturday traffic clogged Fourth Street, but EB, an experienced driver, expertly tugged the reins, weaving us past slow wagons and pedestrians who strolled heedlessly across the street, ignoring his shouts.

"How's your father?" EB asked.

"He's well. They met their quota."

"He'll be leaving soon, then?"

"I believe so, though he's not said for certain."

We rode in silence, the carriage wheels bumping over ruts in the road.

Picking at a spot on my thumb where I'd gotten a splinter, I stole a quick peek in his direction. "Can I ask you a question?" Perhaps he had answers to the questions I posed to Papa but had failed to pry out of him.

"Of course."

"Can a soldier leave the Army for good?"

"It depends." He pulled the reins to the right, steering the horse away from an oncoming wagon.

"On what?"

"On the circumstances. I don't know for sure, but as I understand it, he can ask for an exemption."

"What's an exemption?"

"It's a reason you can't serve your term of enlistment. Usually, it's because of an injury or illness. A doctor needs to approve those. Another kind is hardship, which would be the most relevant in your case."

"Hardship," I repeated.

"As your mother has died, your father is the sole provider for the family. He could ask for an exemption and be relieved of duty because there is no adult other than him to care for his children."

My pulse quickened. That's it! Papa needed to apply for an exemption.

"But Martha, I warn you," his voice lowered a notch, turning serious. "Your father's recruiting doesn't bode well for him getting out. The army needs every man they can find."

"How does one go about filing for an exemption?" I pushed to know more about keeping Papa home. "Can I do it?"

EB chuckled. "No, I'm afraid it's up to the soldier himself to present his case."

The carriage approached the intersection near home. "Let me out here. I'll walk the rest of the way."

He reined in the horse and guided it to the side of the street.

Alighting from the carriage, I placed my canvas bag over my shoulder. "Thank you for the ride and the information."

He smiled broadly, touching his fingertips to the brim of his hat. As he clicked his tongue for the horse to move, I felt a mix of gratitude for his help and a twinge of regret at parting.

After church, I walked to the Decker home. Dina answered my knock, Gus perched on one hip.

"Hello," I said.

Dina invited me in. I glanced around and Joe was nowhere in sight. The living quarters were cramped, a single room with a bed in one corner opposite the stove in another. The smell of fermenting cabbage permeated the space.

"I need your help," I said, coming straight to the point. I opened my bag and removed the garments I'd selected. "I have more work than time. Can you do some mending?"

She nodded eagerly, like a dog anticipating a treat. Putting Gus on the floor, she watched me lay out what I brought.

I showed her the pieces. Two split seams, the hem on a pair of pants that needed lowering, and two pairs of socks with holes in the toes. This mix would allow me to assess her skills.

"Can you finish these by Tuesday when I go to the Hall?"

"You bet. I meet you there."

"Ten o'clock." I held up two hands with all fingers splayed.

"How much money?"

"Fifty cents."

Her nostrils flared. "One dollar."

"Dina, this is a test. You said you could sew. Now, you must prove it. If you do quality work and deliver on time, you will have earned fifty cents and the right to do more. Is that fair?"

"I see. You try me."

"Yes. Are you willing?"

"Yes. If good work, I do more?"

"I'll decide on Tuesday." I opened the door.

"Thank you," Dina said as I descended the stairs to the street.

At home, Mary and I prepared supper. She loved helping in the kitchen and I kept her tasks simple and safe, gradually increasing complexity as she learned to handle a knife and other kitchen tools.

I warmed the meat in the skillet for drippings and Mary took over. Adding flour, she stirred in water, a spoonful at a time, smashing the floating flour with a fork.

"No lumps!" She smiled at me over her shoulder. It had taken a year and scores of trial and error, but Mary had perfected a smooth, thick gravy, saving me time and getting meals on the table sooner.

As we filled our plates, Papa came in. "What smells so heavenly?"

"Beef and vegetables," I said, lifting Henry into my lap freeing up a chair for Papa.

"Did you see Mrs. Decker?" Papa knew of my plan to try her out.

"Yes."

"Good of you. They need the money."

"I hope it works out."

Lizzie, with a mouth full of bread, mumbled. "Papa."

"It's not polite to talk with your mouth full," I said.

Chewing, then swallowing, Lizzie started again. "I want to know if you're home for good or if you have to go back to the Army." She shoved another piece of gravy-sopped bread into her mouth.

Looking at me, he said, "Lieutenant Kress received a request for us to return with the new recruits."

"When's that?" I dreaded his answer. Leaving. Not staying as I'd asked.

"The end of this week."

The room deflated, our cheery mood escaping like a burst balloon.

"Papa, have you heard of an exemption?" I asked, my tone inquisitive, as if I wanted to know how birds could fly.

"Exemption from what?"

I knew he knew, but he played ignorant. I tilted my head to the side, staring at him in disbelief. "Exemption from the Army. Get out for good."

"I've thought about it."

He had? My heart pumped faster, hope surging through my veins. Would I have to pull it out of him like a rotten tooth? "And?"

"If I say I'll look into it, will you stop nagging?"

His backhanded reprimand stung, and I felt its warmth travel from my cheeks to my neck. "Yes, it will stop me from nagging."

Chapter Twenty-Eight

Dina met me at the Hall as planned and her work was more than satisfactory. Neat stitches, flawless darning, and an ironed crease in the hem.

"This is excellent work, Dina!" I paid her as promised. "The ladies at the hall have promised more work. Let's see what they have."

I split the work fairly, but still, finishing this work and the rest would be difficult.

"I do more," Dina pleaded. "We need money."

Pitying her circumstances, and knowing I could use the help, I hesitated. "On Saturday, if I need help, I'll let you know."

"I do much sewing." Her hands joined like she was begging or praying. "I have idea, Motty."

I glared at her, my lips tightening. "Only my family uses my nickname." She hadn't earned the right, nor did I care for her accent emphasizing the second syllable.

"Oh, sure. Sorry." Abashed, she lowered her head.

"What idea?" I snapped, ready to go home and get to work.

I watched her swallow, gather her nerve. "I come to you. Sew faster. Gus have Henry."

It was a good idea. I could watch her work and give her extra as the need arose.

"Friday morning." She looked as happy as if I'd handed her ten dollars.

Friday arrived, as did Dina, who brought a good-sized chunk of sausage as a contribution for dinner.

"Go," Mary announced and went outside, leaving the door ajar to use the privy.

In the front room, Dina sat by the window, readying her sewing kit, unaware she'd taken Mary's chair. Maple with sturdy, thick legs and a high back, it fit Mary just right. No one sat in that chair except Mary. Ever.

This was an opportunity to see how Mary handled the situation and gauge Dina's reaction. I watched the scene unfold from the kitchen doorway. Mary, seeing Dina in her chair, vaulted into the room and halted before Dina, hands fisted on her hips.

"Mine!" Mary shouted.

Shifting back in the chair, Dina looked quizzically at Mary, then at me.

"Chair. Me." Mary grabbed one of Dina's arms and pulled on it.

"Stop!" Dina resisted and yanked her arm from Mary's grasp.

I could step in before anyone was harmed, but if Dina planned to spend time around our family, she would need to know the rules. No better teacher than Mary.

Stepping behind the chair, Mary gripped the spindles and, using all her strength, tried to tip Dina out. But the chair legs never left the ground until Dina stood and rounded on Mary. The chair regained its balance on the floor with a thump.

Mary plopped into the chair as if nothing untoward had happened.

"Ah. Mary chair." Dina smiled.

"Sew." Mary pointed to another chair tucked under the table.

Pleased with how the altercation turned out, I came into the room. "Thank you for understanding. When Mary gets stuck on something, you cannot move her."

"Or she move you," Dina joked. "Stubborn girl."

"She's a creature of habit. If her routine changes, she gets out of sorts. We have a certain way of doing things with her. Less trouble. More joy."

After Dina left, Papa swept into our rooms like the wind ahead of a tornado.

"Mary, give your Papa a hug." He folded her into his arms, a great bear clutching its young. A large smacking sound followed Papa's lips on Mary's cheek. She howled with laughter and wiped her face.

"Motty, I got leave!" He tossed my sewing to the floor, grabbed my hands, and pulled me into a lively polka, dipping and spinning us around the room.

"What in the world?" Lizzie asked from the doorway, her schoolbooks slung over her shoulder. Papa paused and bent down to Lizzie's height. "Remember that question you asked the other day? About staying home?"

She nodded.

"I've got leave. For three months."

"That's till," Lizzie counted the months on her fingers, "December. January. February. You'll be home for Christmas?"

And he'd be here for New Year's and my sixteenth birthday, too. Spending holidays with Papa was the best gift I could ask for.

"And I don't have to report for duty. I'll be around to help, and if I don't get caught, I might earn a little extra money working on the riverfront."

"Caught?" I smoothed my hair back into the bun loosened by dancing.

"I'm on the sick leave roster. Not supposed to work. Need to rest and get well."

"Are you ill?" Perhaps I hadn't noticed.

Papa coughed, hunched his shoulders, and started shivering as if cold. "I know how much you want me home, so I pretended to be sick. For two dollars, the doctor was happy to confirm my illness."

Two dollars for three months with his family. A bargain, to say the least.

"Guess what else?" Papa opened his wallet and removed a handful of greenbacks, spreading them on the table. "After I saw the doctor, I stopped at the paymaster. My pay arrived! Fifty-two dollars."

He counted out some cash and handed me a small stack. "Save that. I'll take care of the rent."

"What is Mr. Decker going to do?" Dina would be crushed if Papa stayed and Joe left.

"That's the beauty of it!" Papa grinned satisfactorily. "Joe got leave, too."

Lizzie yanked on Papa's sleeve to get his attention. "Remember you said when you had some money, we could get a marker for Mama?"

"I did. And we will get one." He tweaked Lizzie's nose as she wrapped her arms around his hips.

Fall colors, wood smoke, and the bite of winter's chill crept into our rooms. Mama liked spring best when everything came to life after the long winter sleep. But autumn was my favorite. Holidays, frosty mornings snuggling under quilts, evenings by the fire, pumpkins, apples, nuts, and hot spiced drinks. And snow!

As I prepared a celebratory dinner, I mused about life with Papa home for an extended time and the opportunities to do things we used to do. Sledding, holiday parties, church events. Mary could join the choir! She knew most of the Christmas carols sung at church and was ready. I made a mental note to talk to Therese on Sunday.

Papa surprised us with a bottle of elderberry wine. "Some for everyone, Motty."

He raised his cup. "Prost!"

I recalled Mama's toast on Independence Day with beer instead of wine. Sipping the wine, sweet, yet tart, I raised my cup. "To three more months of Papa."

"How is it you are staying home, Papa?" Lizzie asked.

"A fellow soldier told me to drink castor oil in tea. If I drank it all day, the doctor would think I had a stomach ailment."

"And it worked?"

"It did."

"You're pretty smart, Papa." Lizzie's top lip had a purple wine mustache.

Lizzie decided a sing along would add to our celebration. She and Mary led a rousing rendition of *Yankee Doodle*. Henry marched with the beat, his hand in salute position for the duration. They followed with other favorites, *Camptown Races* and, *Oh! Susanna*.

Papa cleared his throat and began one of Mama's favorites.

"Spinn, Spinn, Meine Liebe Tochter, Ich kauf dir Paar Schuh."

Papa stared into the dark beyond the windows. My eyes smarted with bittersweet memories as I sang along. Mary and Lizzie chimed in, singing the tale of a mother who bribes her daughter to spin cloth. Mama sang it to us as babes, a tune passed from her mother and her mother's mother.

We ended the evening in the yard, sitting by a fire Papa built. He regaled us with tales of his Army adventures: long marches, new places, and jokes suitable for young ears. He spoke fondly of the men, mentioning several whom he counted as friends. His faraway look told me he missed that life, the camaraderie of men like him, German by birth but very much American.

But we had him for now. For three months, he was all ours.

Chapter Twenty-Nine

With Christmas approaching, Therese spoke to the choirmaster about Mary joining the choir. Though she was warmly welcomed into the group, Therese, who had a fondness for my sister, took her under her wing.

True to his word, Papa investigated a headstone and reported his findings to Lizzie. "A granite stone is four dollars. The etching is two. I'm afraid it's more than we should spend right now."

They sat face to face, like partners discussing a business deal.

"Any other ideas?" Lizzie asked.

"I have one. Wait here." Papa went into the bedroom and emerged with a smooth oak plank squared at the corners.

"The stone cutter sold me this for fifty cents. He said with folks short on money, they make their own."

"I love the wood," Lizzie said, brushing her hand across the smooth surface.

Papa produced his carving tools. "I'll engrave her name and dates, and you add something pretty. What do you say?"

Lizzie turned the board over, inspecting it. "Temporary. Until we have the money. Agreed?"

"Agreed." They shook hands, sealing the deal.

Papa scratched the letters and numbers into the wood with a fine-pointed chisel, while Lizzie sketched Mama's favorite flower, a wild orchid, above her name. He showed her how to deepen the petal curves and finish it by using the burnt end of a stick to blacken the etchings.

"It's beautiful," I declared, proud of Lizzie's artwork and Papa making good on his promise.

"Can we take it on Christmas?" Lizzie asked.

"Weather permitting, we'll go after church," Papa said, then turned to me. "Just you and me. Agreed, Motty?"

I nodded. "It's fitting you two go."

At St. Mattheus on Christmas morning, I handed Mary over to Therese, and they took their places with the choir. The service opened with "Stille Nacht." Mary's soprano soared above the harmony and flute-like notes of the organ.

Afterward, on the church steps, accolades for her performance came from all directions. Most congratulated her openly, while others commented in hushed undertones behind gloved hands.

"Sings like an angel."

"Didn't even need a songbook."

"How could someone like her have such talent?"

Someone like her? The phrase made my blood boil. It took all my self-control to hold my tongue, infuriated by their narrow interpretation of Mary's talents.

But Mary only heard the compliments, and she basked in the attention, offering finger kisses to everyone. Most thought her gesture endearing, responding with their own finger kiss. Others stepped away awkwardly, avoiding her touch.

Papa approached me after congratulating Mary for a fine performance. "Lizzie and I will go now." His knapsack held an Army-issued shovel and Mama's marker.

Lizzie skipped up to me. "Merry Christmas, Motty. Thank you for letting me and Papa go."

On tiptoe, she planted a messy kiss on my cheek then ran to catch up with Papa. As they walked away, my fingers lingered where her kiss had landed. Despite this being our first Christmas without Mama, I thanked God for his blessings. Papa at home, Mary's gentle nature, Lizzie's compassion, and Henry, healthy and happy. In this moment, I had all I could want and would treasure it as long as possible.

To celebrate New Year's Day, 1863, I prepared a hearty dinner. As we sat around the table, Papa asked us to tell our Neujahrsvorsatz.

"What's that?" Lizzie asked.

Papa glanced at the ceiling, searching for a simple explanation. "It's a promise you make. Do something you've never done before, or do something better. If you want to be an artist, your resolution might be to draw every day."

"Oh, I see!" Lizzie said, her face screwed up in intense contemplation. "I have to think of one. Come back to me."

"Henry, do you have something you want to do better this year?" Papa asked.

With his chest puffed with pride, he declared, "Get taller!"

The room exploded with laughter.

"A good goal. You must stretch your muscles regularly." Papa put his arms over his head and reached for the ceiling. Henry mimicked him.

"You're taller already." Papa slapped him on the back.

"I have one for Mary." Turning to my sister, I asked her. "Would you like to do more singing this year?"

Her eyes lit up like a struck match. "Sing!"

Lizzie piped in, "I'll teach you all the songs I learn in school."

"And I'll ask Jane to teach you the ones she plays on the piano," I added.

"Sing!" Mary agreed, clapping her hands in delight.

"What's yours, Papa?" I asked, hoping his would be to leave the army and stay home.

"I have this fine new journal." He reached into his pocket for my Christmas present for him. "I'll write something every day."

I hoped my vague smile concealed my disappointment.

"I'm ready!" All heads pivoted to Lizzie. "I'm going to be a nosy Nelly."

"A what?" Papa asked, his forehead crinkling.

"It's what Mrs. Eiflert said. That I was a nosy Nelly."

Trying not to laugh, I asked, "Do you know what a nosy Nelly is?"

"Yup. Someone who asks a lot of questions. I want to know lots of stuff."

"You don't need a resolution for that. It comes to you naturally," I said.

Shrugging, she said, "Yeah, but this year, I'm going to read more books, ask lots of questions, and talk to people."

"No strangers," I warned.

"Of course not."

Papa turned to me. "And you, Motty?"

A few ideas occurred to me. Get to know the Mitchells better. Learn to make a dress from scratch. Take on a new customer. Get Papa to stay home. But the one I chose, my voice quiet, yet earnest, was, "I renew the promise I made when you left, Papa. I promise to take care of our family."

"That's what you do anyway!" Lizzie said. "You need something better."

"I think it's excellent." Papa's hand extended across the table, palm up. I laid my hand in his. "Thank you, daughter."

"Can you watch the children while I visit Jane? I want to attend their New Year's celebration."

"I made plans with Joe." He'd said nothing till now about going out.

"I know it's short notice, but I want to go. Can you meet him later?" Rarely had I asked for his help, but today I wanted to shed the shackles of responsibility and do something for myself.

"A few men from the Ninth are celebrating the Emancipation Proclamation going into effect today."

I flopped back into my chair.

"Next time," he said.

"There won't be a New Year's party next time!"

Possessed by anger, I tidied the kitchen, letting cookware bang and dishes rattle while cursing him under my breath. I'd sacrificed everything for this family. Went without food, nice things, a life. Just once I wanted to do something for myself. But no. Papa came first.

"Motty!" His bellow boomed in the small room, startling me as I set a teacup to the top shelf. My fingers jerked, releasing the cup. The impact sent shards skittering across the wooden floor. Two halves of a purple violet, Mama's favorite flower, lay at my feet. I stared at the remains. Broken, irreparable, trash.

I sensed Papa behind me and heard him exclaim, "Oh, no."

Laying his hand on my arm, I shrugged it off. "Leave me alone. Haven't you done enough for one day?" Turning on my heel, I left the kitchen. Papa studied me as I removed my apron and grabbed my coat and hat, desperate to escape the tiny, claustrophobic rooms. On the street, my tears blinded me. In my day dress and too upset to even consider attending the Mitchell party, I wandered north. I felt I could walk forever, and it still wouldn't be far enough to escape the frustration tightening my chest like a vise.

Mama. I wanted Mama. On Vine Street, I climbed the long hill to the cemetery, chastising myself. You're foolish. You're walking all this way to talk to a bit of dirt.

Lizzie's wooden marker stood straight and true at the head of her grave.

Margaretta Hesch

1823 - 1862

Her etching of a violet matched the one on the broken teacup and its loss pierced my heart. Careless of my skirt, I sank to the ground and wept, pressing my forehead to my knees. Tears flowed for my loss, for my mother, for my youth, ruined like the teacup, broken and in shambles.

I put little stock in dreams of marrying and having my own children, for I was too practical. I craved controllable realities which left no time for those ambitions. I devoted every ounce of energy to caring for my siblings. Who else would ensure Mary got the care she couldn't give herself, that Lizzie finished her schooling, and Henry learned to avoid risky situations? Surely not Papa, who thought only of himself.

"Mama," I said aloud. "I know I'm demanding."

I sniffed my tears back into my head. A puzzling thought struck me, and with no one to overhear, I kept talking to my mother as if she sat beside me listening intently. "I take care of everyone else.

Who takes care of me?" My forefinger jabbed my chest. "What about me?" The words were selfish and needy. At odds with my nature.

But I needed no one to care for me. I'd taken care of myself for years. My family meant the world to me, meeting their needs ingrained in my body and soul from an early age. Caring for them fulfilled me. And realizing this simple truth, a peacefulness descended upon me as if Mama's arms embraced me.

I remembered what she said in the days before she died, telling us the story of her journey to America: "Martha came when we needed her most."

The children needed me now. More than Papa. He could watch the children, carry heavy things, and stand between us and evil, but he couldn't cook or sew or teach Mary about a woman's body or Lizzie about proper etiquette. He could show Henry how to shoot, catch a fish, and cut wood. But Henry needed petting, cuddling, and kisses on scraped knees.

I'm here. Not off having a beer with friends or fighting a war.

A chill settled over me as the sun's warmth faded into the horizon. "Thank you for listening, Mama. I love you." I kissed my fingers and laid them on the violet, holding them there, making sure she felt my love, my gratitude for listening to my incoherent thoughts.

In the time it took to walk down the hill, I resolved to do one thing above all others. I would keep my New Year's resolution. I couldn't control Papa and knew I should stop trying. What I could do, however, was control myself and the care of the children. When they needed me the most.

Chapter Thirty

Although he failed to mention it, by my calculations, Papa's leave expired ten days ago. What were his plans? Would he be leaving soon? Could he get an exemption to quit the Army altogether or additional leave? Stop this. You said you'd let things go. Let Papa do what he needed to do.

But I couldn't let go. I had to know. Since Papa and Joe did everything the same, perhaps Dina would have answers.

Arriving at Turner Hall on our usual day to turn in our mending, I spotted her rooting through a table of clothing.

"Hello," I said.

"I have news." Without warning, she grabbed my hand and pulled it toward her stomach. I yanked it from her grasp, unsure of her intentions. This woman didn't stand on ceremony, nor did she have any concept of decorum.

"What are you doing?" I asked.

"Give me hand." She extended hers.

Tentatively offering mine, she clutched it, then placed it on her belly. "Baby." Her eyes sparkled.

I couldn't imagine anything worse than a baby coming at a time like this, but I pretended enthusiasm. "That's wonderful." I withdrew my hand.

"July, it come," she said.

I did the math. Five months away.

"Will Joe be here when the baby comes?" The answer to this would help me understand Papa's intentions.

She shrugged. "Not sure."

The only knowledge I'd gained from my visit to the hall was that another Decker child was on the way; I remained in the dark about Papa's plans.

At the Mitchells, I raised the subject with Jane.

"His ninety days are up. I have no idea what happens next."

"I bet EB would know. I'll get him." Jane left the office while I sorted the week's work.

"Martha!" EB said. "Jane said you had a question."

EB's eyes met mine, his expression serious in the sunlight streaming through the window. "I wonder if you might know about the consequences of not returning from leave on time."

"If you don't return, he's absent without leave."

"Oh." Having never heard the term before, I stared at him, waiting for him to continue.

EB motioned for me to sit in the desk chair.

I shook my head. "Thank you, I'll stand."

"As you wish." Moving some papers, he settled his backside on the edge of the desk, arms folded across his chest. "If a soldier doesn't return when his leave expires, it's considered a crime, and he can be court-martialed."

A crime? Court-martial?

Seeing my confusion, he explained, "If a soldier is accused of a military crime such as insubordination or absent without leave, an Army court determines his guilt or innocence. The penalty for being absent without leave is minimal, perhaps additional duty, or loss of pay. But I've heard some men were executed for not returning. Sends a message to the rest of the regiment."

"Executed?" My hand flew to my throat.

"I'm afraid so." EB stood up, pushing his hands into his trouser pockets. "Your father? His leave expired?"

"I believe so."

"Then I suggest he return or apply for additional leave."

I latched onto the latter. "More leave? He can do that?"

"He can try. He can even leave the Army. Lots of men quit, but it's a matter of discharge. Honorable or dishonorable."

My head swam with more terms I didn't understand. Overwhelmed, I dropped into the desk chair and stared out the window.

"My apologies. Honorable discharge is leaving the military with a favorable record, but the soldier can't carry out his duties. Getting wounded is an example. Follow?"

I nodded and shifted my gaze, focusing on EB's words and the manner with which he relayed the information.

"Dishonorable means dismissal for breaking the rules," he paused. "Desertion is considered a dishonorable discharge."

The military jargon in context with Papa's situation, I began to form a coherent picture in my mind. "Let me see if I have this right. If Papa doesn't return, he's deserted."

EB nodded, his neck stiff, reluctant to reveal the truth.

"And if the Army finds him guilty, he could be," I choked out the result. "Executed?"

"He's committing a military crime by not returning."

Papa could be shot or hung. The vision was too graphic, unfair, and illogical. With a full head of steam, I let the words fly. "How is it that a man who stays home to care for his family instead of going off to shoot strangers is a criminal? How? Tell me."

Calm in the face of my outrage, EB said nothing, letting me get it off my chest.

"It's obvious the army doesn't care about those left behind. The women and children who suffer as much, maybe more, than the soldiers." I fumbled for my handkerchief in my pocket and met his sympathetic gaze.

"EB, what am I to do? If Papa stays, he's a criminal. If he goes back, we're alone again." Tears sprung up unwillingly, I turned away, unable to bear him seeing me cry.

I lifted the canvas bag from the desk. EB took it from me and held it so I could duck under the strap. Adjusting the weight across my hips and shoulders, I prepared for the journey home.

"Can I take you home?"

"Thank you, but no. I am in your debt as it is. The walk will help me clear my head."

"No debt, Martha. After all, what are friends for?"

The following week, EB had an update. The Union Army was struggling with deserters. "Thousands of men have either disappeared from their units or, like your father, failed to return from leave. The military is threatening punishments like jail time."

I had news too. "Papa admitted his leave ended two weeks ago. He intends to stay home as long as possible but can't get his pay. He heard a soldier tried to collect his and got arrested right there on the spot.

"That's one way to catch the offenders."

"Papa will have to get a job eventually," I said.

"I may know someone willing to take on, a, um, someone like your father." EB fumbled.

"You were going to say deserter," I said, acknowledging the term laced with shame.

"Sorry, yes."

"No need." Leaving through the back door, I stopped and stuck my head back into the office. "Thank you!"

On the way home, I stopped at the market to shop for Mary's fourteenth birthday dinner after church. The Deckers were invited.

Therese relayed Mary's obsession with birthdays to the choir and after church, they handed her a package wrapped in newspaper, tied with red yarn.

"Me! Birthday!" Mary poked her chest and giggled. "Sing!"

The choir broke into the birthday song, harmonious and gay, right there on the church steps, heedless of March winds sweeping up our skirts and through our coats.

"Open it!" Therese urged.

Untying the yarn, Mary handed it to Lizzie for safekeeping. Disrespecting the paper, she tore it off, and it fluttered to the ground.

"Stitches!" Mary exclaimed. The gift was an embroidery hoop and several linen canvases with flowers sketched on them. A set of multi-colored threads completed her prize.

The gift could not have been more perfect. Mary loved embroidering, her fine needlework far exceeding mine. Everyone got a hug and a finger kiss, which were returned without reservation. The choir didn't tolerate Mary, they cherished her.

After supper, Papa and Joe stole outside for cigars, taking Henry and Gus along. I dismissed Lizzie to join the boys to play in the yard, the weather chilly, but dry.

Mary brought her new embroidery kit to me. "Stitch? Me?"

"It's your birthday! Do whatever you want." I popped a kiss on her brow.

Noticing Dina was quieter than usual, I said, "Dina, I'll clear.

You take it easy."

Going in and out of the kitchen, I noticed her and Mary head-to-head. Dina pointed to something on the linen and Mary peered closely. Content with their camaraderie, I returned to the kitchen.

"No! No! Stop!" Mary's screech pierced the air, sending a shiver down my spine.

Hurrying into the front room, I couldn't believe my eyes. Mary lay curled on the floor, hands covering her face, howling. Dina stood over her, shaking the embroidery ring, a piece of linen hanging from it. "Take!"

"What in the world?" I ran to Mary, my skirts puddling around me as I knelt next to her. "Now, now, it's all right, Mary. It's all right."

Over my shoulder, I shot Dina a glare that could throw daggers. My voice low and menacing, I asked, "What happened?"

"I show stitch." She shrugged, holding the ring where a needle dangled from a red thread.

"Mary never acts like this," I said, rubbing Mary's back as she sobbed.

"She mean," Dina said, her hands punched into her hips.

"Mean. To you." A statement, not a question, the words flat and emotionless, as if I didn't understand.

Mary sat up, saw the linen in Dina's hand, grabbed it, and tucked it under her body as she huddled on the floor. She'd acted this way with Mama; she was frightened.

"She's not mean. She's scared. What did you do?"

"I do nothing. I help. She stupid. No listen," said Dina, feigning innocent.

Closing my eyes, searching for patience, I said, "You have two choices. Go outside until Mary calms down. Or leave."

"I go."

Grateful she chose the one I preferred, I watched her gather her things and slam the door behind her.

"She's gone," I whispered, my voice raspy and hoarse as if I'd been the one screaming.

Safe from Dina, Mary flung herself into my arms, her heart-wrenching cries shattering my composure. How could Dina be so cruel? Couldn't she see how much Mary treasured her gift?

It took a while for Mary to settle. I dried her tears, helped her blow her nose, and drew her into my arms, rocking and humming her favorite lullaby.

Papa, Lizzie, and Henry came in just as I got Mary to the table.

"Joe and Dina had to go," Papa said. "I think she didn't feel well."

"That's too bad," I said, unable to keep a hint of sarcasm from my voice, but no one noticed.

"Mary?" I asked. "Are you ready for cake and candles?"

Her lower lip shook as she tried to smile because cake and candles were her favorite things on earth. And Dina had ruined it.

Papa lit a single candle in the Geburtstagskranz next to the number fourteen. When I handed him a second, he looked at me quizzically, as fourteen was the last hole.

"Mary gets to make a wish for next year. Put it in the number one, Papa."

"Ah, I see! Of course!" He lit both candles.

Mary's eyes shined in the candlelight, her joy trickling through recent tears. The four of us sang the birthday song, but she did not sing with us. Lizzie caught my eye, her brow furrowed with concern, nodding toward Mary. My glance said I'd tell her what happened later.

I whispered in Mary's ear. "You're fourteen. Here's this year's candle," I pointed, "Make a wish on the other and blow them out."

"Wish." Mary squeezed her eyes shut. The corners of her mouth turned down, her hands fidgeted with her skirts, tightening into fists, then loosening.

My jaw clenched as I fought back tears, thinking of how this woman, with no regard for others, had traumatized my innocent, loving sister on her special day. Dina was no longer be welcome in our home.

"Did you find a wish?" I asked.

Opening her eyes and mouth, she inhaled deeply and blew. The flames sputtered out. We applauded and cheered, "Alles Gute zum Geburstag!"

I served the cake, which everyone but Mary and I wolfed down. I pushed mine around my plate. Mary picked at the icing but left everything else.

"May I have your cake, Motty?" Henry asked.

I slid my plate to Henry, who devoured the cake in seconds, leaving only crumbs.

"No cake, Mary?" Papa asked.

"It's been a big day. She might eat it later," I said, and added her slice to the leftovers, covering them with a towel.

Mary cleared the table, shuttling dishes into the kitchen. Caught unaware, she enveloped me in a hug, her head on my shoulder, as tall as me, despite our two-year age difference.

"How are you?" I muttered into her hair.

I felt her head nod against my shoulder.

"Happy Birthday, Sister," I said.

"Motty. Wuv you." Her sad rendition of love you, bruised my heart.

We clung to each other, a lifeline in a sea of change, neither willing to sever our embrace.

Chapter Thirty-One

The weather, on the cusp of spring, was fickle and changeable. One day, winter had the upper hand, burying its rival in a snowbank. The next, spring revived and cracked old man winter over the head with a sunbeam.

Papa buttered a piece of bread and downed his tea. "I'm going down to the river to find work," he said, donning a heavy coat despite the sunny sky predicting a warm afternoon.

In less than an hour, the door opened. He stepped inside and rubbed back of his neck. "Martha, we must talk."

His tone urgent, his expression grave, he had my full attention. "What is it?"

"Outside." I followed him down the stairs. "It's a mess," he said.

"What's a mess?" I asked as he paced the short walkway in the yard.

"Lincoln. He's called for all men absent without leave to return to their regiments. I have to go back."

I froze, words flying from my mouth without consideration for his safety and welfare. "But you can't. We need you here."

"Martha, dammit! If I don't return, I face court martial."

I recalled the vile term EB described a few weeks ago. I stared at the street where the carriages, wagons, and foot traffic moved along. The rest of the world didn't stop because mine had come to a screeching halt.

"How long till you'll go?" I shivered in the cool March sunshine.

"There's a steamer going to Louisville tomorrow."

"Tomorrow." So soon. No time to plan, to come to grips with his leaving.

He placed his hands on my shoulders. "I have a plan. Dina and Gus will move in here. Joe is bringing them in the morning."

I shook my head in disbelief. "What?" Struggling to comprehend the incomprehensible, I shouted, "No!"

I thrust my arms between his, knocking his hands from my shoulders. "No way in hell!" The sensation of being held under water against my will left me gasping for air.

"It's a suitable solution, Motty," he said, expecting my nickname to soften my resolve.

"Why? Why is it a suitable solution?" Living with Dina wasn't suitable. It was revolting.

"Both households combined into one save on rent and fuel. Between my money and Joe's, it's enough for all of you to live on."

He's lost his mind, I thought. "There's no room, Papa."

"It won't be for long. People are saying with all the men returning, our forces will be strong enough to defeat the enemy in a few months."

How many times before had I heard this? Where was this miracle end to the war?

"I can't live with Dina. Not for a few months, not for one minute. Do you have any idea how evil she is?"

"Evil?" He scratched his head. "She's no such thing."

"You don't know, Papa! She undermines me, belittles Mary, and causes more trouble than she's worth."

His chuckle dismissed my concerns. "Martha, see it my way. She's twenty-one. She can make legal decisions and cash the pay tickets for Joe and me..."

I held up my hand, palm out. "Wait. Legal decisions? Cash pay tickets?" Rage boiled over. I'd had enough. Impulsively, I laid my hands on his chest and shoved him. He stumbled backward a few steps but caught his balance.

"You're giving that woman control over what happens to this family? After everything I've done to keep us going. How dare you!"

For good measure, I shoved him again.

"Enough!" His scream echoed off the walls of the buildings surrounding the yard. "I am the father. You are the daughter. I decide what's best for this family, and I've decided the families will live together." Nose to nose, he decreed my fate.

I pressed my lips together, preventing my tongue from voicing harsh thoughts and screams of rage. Papa had decided our fate—my fate—to live with this woman. Until what? She died in childbirth? I throttled her with my bare hands? I relished the vision.

"You'll make her welcome?" Papa asked a warning in the statement posed as a question.

"Over my dead body," I said, contempt breeding in my breast, as I mounted the steps to our rooms, soon to be a prison.

I lay awake that night and well into the morning. Thinking, worrying, plotting. I made a mental list of tasks to be handled before Dina arrived and rose as daylight bloomed behind the curtains.

Prioritizing our finances, I padded silently into Papa's room and slid the money tin from under the bed. Leaving the coins, I removed fourteen dollars, found a loose square in the quilt on the bed, folded the bills, and tucked them inside. Three quick stitches secured the money, leaving it accessible.

My next worry was Mary. I decided the best approach was to remove her from Dina's presence. This meant taking Mary on deliveries. With Lizzie at school, Dina would have to mind Henry, an easy chore with Gus as a playmate.

Of all my worries and fears, none was greater than Papa returning to his regiment, facing enemy fire, exposed to the elements and disease. All of which could mean his death. I hadn't bothered to ask him to stay, and he offered no alternative to leaving. In his six months at home, his presence patched the hole in our hearts left by Mama. I would miss feeling safe and secure with him nearby, as well as having him share the burden of raising three children.

The Deckers arrived after breakfast, toting all their worldly possessions in two carpet bags. Papa insisted Dina take the bedroom on the condition Henry slept there, sharing a pallet with Gus.

Initially, I balked at giving Dina the only private room. But our arrangement in the front room offered its own advantages: access to the kitchen, a window view, and freedom of movement.

Lizzie plied Papa with questions as he packed his knapsack.

"Why do you have to go?"

"The President wants everyone back by April 1. If I don't return by then, I'll get in big trouble."

"What kind of trouble?"

"Go to jail."

"Jail." She studied the word and what it meant for Papa. Moving on to her next question, I imagined her with a notebook and pencil, like a reporter drilling a witness for a news story. "Why are you going to Louisville? Is that where your people are?"

"My people are somewhere in Tennessee. And it's called a regiment. The Ninth Ohio Volunteers." Papa closed his knapsack, buckling the leather straps over the flap.

Her brow furrowed. "Papa, if you're a volunteer, can't you un-volunteer? Stay home? Quit?"

Her assessment made sense. Through the eyes of a nine-year-old, the solution was simple.

Papa sat and pulled her into his lap. "Volunteering for the army is a word that says you sign up of your own accord. I took an oath, and I get paid. Volunteers, for charities and such, don't get paid and aren't required to make a promise."

Lizzie tsked. "Then why call them volunteers? The army is strange."

He squeezed her, planted a kiss on her cheek, and lifted her from his lap.

Papa called for Henry, interrupting his work on his tower. "You are the man of the house. Like last time, I'll count on you to watch over your sisters and mind them. Will you do this for me?"

"Yes, Papa. I will." Henry nodded, his light brown curls dipping into his eyes, in desperate need of a haircut.

Papa stood straight and tall, clicked his heels together, and saluted. Henry imitated his father, but his heels made no sound despite three hearty attempts. Papa laughed, picked up his four-year-old son, and crushed him to his chest.

Putting Henry down, Papa offered his open arms to Mary and I. "Come here, you two." We buried our faces in his chest, our moist cheeks dampening his coat.

"Itchy!" Mary raised her head from Papa's wool uniform coat, rubbing her cheek.

"Here, let's try this instead," Papa said, scraping her cheek with his beard. "Better?"

"Soft." She tugged the short, curly hair on his jaw.

His eyes closed, arms encircling us. "You two have grown into fine young women. I will miss you."

"Me too, Papa. I'll take care of everyone, I promise." I let go of Mary and placed my arms around his waist.

"Thank you, Motty, for being the best daughter a man can have. I promise to get home as soon as possible."

"I love you, Papa. Stay safe and write." I tore myself away, wiping a tear from my cheek with the back of my hand.

"Joe!" Papa yelled toward the bedroom. Directing his attention to me, he said, "I've paid the rent for March and April and told Locke about Dina. I'll send my pay as soon as I receive it."

Joe emerged from the bedroom closing the door behind him. "My wife's upset. Best she's left alone for now." Gus hung onto one of his father's legs, making it difficult for Joe to move around. "Little man, I've got to go. You'll be good for Mama and Martha?"

Gus bobbed his head but clung to Joe's leg. Having his father for six months was all the memory the boy possessed. Henry had been the same age when Papa joined, and I knew the boy's pain would ease with the passage of time.

Joe ruffled his hair and reached for his knapsack. "Ready."

Mary, Lizzie, and I followed them down the stairs to the street. The men waved as they headed south to the riverfront, where a steamboat would take them to Louisville. They would arrive well before the President's deadline.

Their fate was just as uncertain as that of me and my siblings, left behind to wonder and worry.

Chapter Thirty-Two

Henry welcomed a permanent playmate. When not at school, Lizzie doted on Gus, while Dina wallowed in self-pity, crying in the bedroom and bemoaning her husband's absence. Meanwhile, I struggled with another woman's presence in our home and as the days passed, Mary withdrew into herself.

Our routine, disturbed by Dina and Gus, threw everything into chaos. The boys were rowdy and active, waking everyone early. Dina complained about everything. The mattress was too lumpy. Her room was too cold. The smell of my cooking made her nauseous.

One morning, a week after Papa left, I needed to escape. "Mary, Henry, let's walk Lizzie to school."

Mary shot out of her chair like a bullet from a gun, taking her coat and hat from the rack. Henry continued to play with Gus.

"Henry, let's go!" I nudged. Lizzie and Mary waited on the stoop.

"I don't want to go," he said, not lifting his head from his play. "Stay with Gus and Dina."

My eyebrows shot up. "You don't want to come?"

He nodded without looking at me.

Glancing into the kitchen, I asked Dina, "Can he stay with you?"

"Yes. He sweet boy."

After leaving Lizzie in the schoolyard, I vented my frustrations. Mary, ever the good listener, let me rant and rave.

"Dina's driving me nuts. Can't she shut up, and live with what we have?"

"Dina. No," Mary said.

"We're stuck with her." I gripped Mary's elbow as we approached an intersection.

Stepping into the street, she yanked her arm away, whirled on me, and halted, planting her feet wide. "No, Dina."

"Mary! What's wrong with you? You can't stop in the middle of the street." I guided her back to the sidewalk.

"Dina. Bad."

"I don't like her either."

Pointing to her chest, Mary said, "Me. Nice. Dina. Bad."

As we walked, I pondered ways to compromise. Perhaps getting to know Dina better would reveal some common ground.

Over dinner, I asked how she came to America. In halting English, she said she left because her village had no men to marry. A cousin with relatives in New York invited her to come. She met Joe on the ship coming over.

"We fall in love like that." She snapped her fingers. "Joe say no New York. Go Cincinnati."

I told her my parents arrived in New Orleans in 1846 and made Cincinnati their home.

"You born here?"

"Yes. Well, not in these rooms, but a few blocks away," I said.

"What happen her?" Dina tipped her head toward Mary, sewing next to the window.

"Nothing happened. She came two years after me."

"She not right."

Sighing, I thought about my response. Living together meant Dina had to understand Mary and be tolerant of her extravagances.

"Mary is just like you and me. She uses the privy, has her monthly, and is growing into a woman. She is physically the same." I let that sink in. "Over time, with lots of help, she can sew, cook, clean, and does them all well. Her embroidery work is extraordinary. She sings like a bird and remembers the words after hearing a song just once."

Dina's demeanor shifted as she leaned in, resting her chin on her hand.

"But she's slow to learn words and how to string them together into sentences." A thought about how to explain further struck me. "It's a little like you learning English."

Dina shook her head. "I no stupid."

Shaking my head, I said, "That's not what I meant."

I searched for another way to get my point across. "It's like Gus. He's two. As his mother, you teach him what's dangerous, what's safe. I do the same with Mary. I teach her. It just takes longer and sometimes many repetitions until she understands."

Dina mulled over what I'd said, a hand supporting her head. "We teach danger."

Did she misunderstand or did she toy with me? Nevertheless, this woman vexed me. "No. We protect her," I said, emphasizing protect. "She means no harm and is as gentle as a lamb. And like any child, she craves attention."

Getting up, she shrugged her shoulders. "Okay. I go." And she flounced out the door and down the stairs to the privy.

I stared after her, wondering if anything I said had an impact. Could she be kind and help Mary instead of calling her names? Offer support instead of ridicule? Only time would tell.

April came and went, marking two years since the war began. Papa wrote he was well and hoped we had settled into our living arrangement. No pay ticket accompanied his letter. I wrote that living with Dina required some adjustments, sparing him the details. A letter arrived from Joe and Dina read it aloud.

> The Ninth joined the Army of the Cumberland, a great mass of men who drill day and night preparing to fight as a unit. We have good food and lodgings and are grateful for warmer weather, though the rains mean drilling in mud.

"Drilling is good. No fight." Dina dropped the letter to her lap, heaving a sigh of relief.

"No pay ticket?" I asked.

"No."

The rent was due, but until Locke asked, the fourteen dollars would stay tucked away in the quilt and we'd live on mending earnings. Spring's warmer nights translated into fuel savings, and I reasoned we could make it another month without pay tickets. Issues between Mary and Dina arose from time to time, stemming from Mary's stubbornness and Dina's unwillingness to understand her. However, none were as serious as the embroidery incident.

As Dina's belly grew, she became increasingly uncomfortable. At seven months, she rarely left our rooms. I, on the other hand, took great pleasure in running errands with spring in full swing. Everywhere across the city, maple and oak tree branches budded, while at their roots, daffodil and tulip leaves poked through the thawing ground, heedless of frost.

On finishing a delivery with Mary, I spotted Mrs. Mitchell

tending a small plot of dirt in the corner of their yard.

"What have you planted, Mrs. Mitchell?" I asked, intrigued by the prospect of having a garden of our own. There was a perfect spot beside our building.

She pointed to one row, then another, naming the vegetables. "This is cabbage, lettuce, and peppers. On this side are cucumbers, spinach, radishes, and peas."

Mary crouched down, brushing a finger across the green leaves poking through the dark, moist earth. Mrs. Mitchell, unconcerned about Mary damaging the plants, asked, "Will you help me, Mary?" Kneeling next to her, she used a garden tool to release the dirt around a young plant. "Hold out your hands."

Palms up, side by side, Mary's eyes followed the actions of the older woman as she carefully lifted a plant, shook the dirt from its roots, and put it into her outstretched hands. "Martha, ask Rose or cook for some newspaper."

When I returned, Mary held two more plants.

"Put them on the paper, Mary."

"That one is lettuce. This is cucumber. And this is cabbage. Find a sunny spot, dig out the rocks, turn the soil, and layer dirt on top until you cover the roots. Water them when they are dry to the touch. Otherwise, let nature do the work."

She wrapped the tender plants, careful not to crush them. "Do you have a shovel or a trowel?"

I shook my head.

She handed me her trowel. "Bring it back when you're done. Let me know if you have questions."

Thrilled at fresh vegetables in our future, we thanked her and hurried home.

"Garden," I pointed to the spot in the yard with the best sun exposure. Planning to begin this afternoon, I laid the bundle of plants and the trowel on the ground. Mary and I climbed the stairs to change into work clothes.

Inside, I found a crying Henry cradled in Dina's arms.

"What? Are you all right?" I went to Henry to soothe him, but he buried his head in Dina's chest.

Annoyed at him dismissing me, but concerned about his welfare, I stooped to his level and rubbed his back. Almost knocking me over, Lizzie launched herself into my arms.

"He okay," Dina said. "Her. Not good."

"What in the world?" Two crying siblings. This never happened.

As I cradled Lizzie, I noticed Mary lowering and locking a window.

"Outside," I said to Lizzie, faking a sternness in my voice to fool Dina. I wanted Lizzie's side of the story without her two cents.

I steered Lizzie out the door, grabbing Mary's hand as we passed. Henry would have to wait.

"She put me in the corner. Made me stand looking at the wall." Her voice echoed off the walls of the buildings.

"Whatever for?"

"For shutting the windows," Lizzie screamed.

"Calm down," I said, sitting on the bottom step.

"The windows were wide open, and the boys, they," catching her breath, she paused, "climbed on the chairs and leaned out. Henry's belly was on the sill, his head and shoulders hanging over. And Gus, he did the same in the other window."

"How did they get that way? Where were you? Where was Dina?"

"I was reading my book. She was sewing. Sitting there, not doing anything. I pulled Henry back in and, of course, he bawled, but I didn't care. I closed the window. I grabbed Gus, had him under my arm, and then she hit me."

"Hit you?" I scrambled to understand.

"On the backside. Told me to put Gus down, which I did. Then I closed the other window."

My mind reran Lizzie's story and found nothing wrong with her actions. "She should not have hit you. What's this about standing in the corner?"

At this, my sister lowered her head, a sign of contrition. "I guess my mouth got the better of me, but I was so mad! I told her she had no right to hit me, she's not my mother. I thought she'd smack me, but she said I had to stand in the corner. But I didn't. I sat on the bed." A smile of triumph curled her lips.

"You disobeyed." I admired her gumption in the face of another reprimand.

"She has no right to punish me for taking care of the boys like I've been doing my whole life!" The tone of her voice rose an entire octave by the end of her tirade.

"But you ended up in the corner," I said.

"She pulled me off the bed and pushed me into the corner. I was afraid she might hit me again, so I stayed put. Then you walked in."

"Thank heaven." The image of Dina forcibly moving Lizzie filled me with a quiet fury.

"Motty, I did nothing wrong, did I?" She worried about my opinion.

"Not that I can tell if you are giving me the truth."

"I promise," she crossed her heart with a finger, then put her hand up as if swearing before a judge.

Nodding, I let her know I believed her.

"Motty!" Mary's delightful chirp startled me. She held up the trowel Mrs. Mitchell lent us. "Dig!"

"What's she doing?" Lizzie asked.

"Mrs. Mitchell gave us some vegetables to grow."

This time of day, the little patch glowed in the sunshine. Mary had scratched the surface free of debris and scooped the excess dirt into a pile.

"That's good, Mary!" I said as I plucked out a rock and told Lizzie about Mrs. Mitchell's garden.

"I can't go back in there," Lizzie said as she crouched beside Mary.

Dina had overstepped. Regardless of Lizzie's actions, I wouldn't tolerate Dina playing judge and jury with my siblings.

Leaving my sisters with their new project, I mounted the steps, steeling myself for the inevitable confrontation. Finding the kitchen and front room empty, I opened the upper windows to dispel the pungent aroma of cooked cabbage. The closed bedroom door didn't stop me from barging in, light from the hall piercing the gloom. The boys slept on their pallet. Dina lay motionless, eyes fixed on the ceiling, ignoring my abrupt entry.

"I need to talk to you," I said.

"Not now. Sleep."

"Now. Or I'll come in and wake the boys."

She rolled out of the bed, her belly preceding her. I waited by the windows.

From behind me, she said, "You mad. Sorry."

"You had no right to hit Lizzie."

Dina's hands fluttered around her head as if she brushed away a bothersome fly. "Sorry."

"You don't understand, Dina," I rose and stepped toward her. She stood her ground, staring at me with open dislike. "I'm responsible for my brother and sisters. If they need discipline, I'll dish it out. Not you."

"Fine." She turned to go, done with the conversation, done with me.

Anger and frustration seethed within me. How could I make her grasp the weight of responsibility for my siblings' welfare?

"Stop! Listen to me!" I stomped my foot, hands curled into fists.

She chuckled, clearly amused. "You funny."

"I'm funny?" Did she mean laughing kind of funny or odd kind of funny?

"You pout like baby when not get way."

"This is not about getting my way. This is about raising these children like my mother raised me. We do not hit or spank them. There are other ways to teach lessons and consequences."

"Okay. No more hit." She shrugged. "You done? I tired."

"No, I'm not done." I reached her in two strides, stood next to her, and pointed. "Those windows? You see them?"

She nodded.

"Only open them from the top. I don't care how hot, how smelly, how much the boys want to hang out of them. The only instance when the bottom is open is when the boys are not here, or we have a firm grip on their britches. Henry has come close to falling in the past."

A faint sign of realization sparked her eyes, and her lips parted. I continued my rant, interrupting her attempt to speak.

"That's why Lizzie did what she did. You don't punish someone for doing the right thing."

"No," Dina breathed the single word.

"In the future, let's talk about what happened, and I'll decide what punishment, if any, is necessary. I don't know if my way is the right way, but I've been minding these children all my life. I know them, I understand them, and they respect my decisions. Can we agree?"

"You good Mama."

Blown over like a feather on the wind, I laughed, releasing the tension in my body and the room. One minute, she declares me bad, the next, funny, then good.

"I don't know what I'm going to do with you, Dina," I said.

Chapter Thirty-Three

A month later, pushed to my limit, I realized something needed to be done. Dina's continuous offenses gradually eroded my patience, and the entire household grew weary of the constant tension.

When Henry sought comfort, he turned to Dina. A bump on the head sent him into her arms and only accepted Dina's kiss on his bruise. I insisted he eat what I set before him, but he looked to Dina for a reprieve, who granted it willingly. Mary's feelings were hurt when he refused to let her sing him to sleep. "Lullabies are for babies." I had no doubt where that came from.

We argued about money. Dina's contribution to rent and household expenses amounting to only a few coins per week. I fumed silently, wondering where the hell Joe's money had gone. Hadn't he provided for his family?

She sparred with Lizzie, inciting behaviors I'd never tolerated before. "You're not my mother" and "Thank God" were a constant refrain. Sometimes I interceded, sometimes I watched them fight like two cats in a bag.

One evening, as the dust settled from another skirmish, Lizzie confided in me. "I miss our old life, even before Papa was home. Things were simpler, and I didn't have to answer to her. Can we get rid of her?"

I thought of doing the same but hadn't figured out how.

"I'm going to speak with Jane this Saturday. Perhaps she has some ideas."

"Can I come with you? You always take Mary."

"How about the three of us go?"

At the Mitchell's, Mary rushed to the garden to check on the progress of the vegetables. Leaving her there, safe in the confines of the backyard, Lizzie and I went into the house.

Mrs. Mitchell and Jane stood at the kitchen table, hovering over a list of some sort.

"Hello," I said.

"Hello Martha," Mrs. Mitchell said. "Mary in the yard?"

"Yes."

"Jane, can you finish up?" Pulling an apron from the hooks near the door, Mrs. Mitchell opened the door and stepped outside.

Lizzie's eyes darted to the open door. "Can I go too?"

"Suit yourself," I said, and she bolted for the sunshine.

In the office, I watched Mary and Mrs. Mitchell in the garden on their knees, side by side, pulling weeds. Their heads together, Mary laughed, her rosy lips spread across straight, white teeth.

"Your Mama is a godsend for Mary," I said to Jane. "Giving us the plants and putting in a garden gave Mary a purpose, one I didn't realize she needed. Keeps her away from Dina, too."

"Mother loves your sister. She told me it's like having a child all over again without the unpleasantness of diapers and feedings."

Taking a step that could ruin my relationship with the Mitchells, I blurted out. "Jane, I need some advice."

"Yes, of course."

I sat on the old trunk, the list of Dina's faults and offenses tumbling out like water from a broken dam. To my own ears, the complaints sounded trivial, unworthy of exposure to my employer.

"Am I making a big deal out of nothing?" I fidgeted with the trunk latch.

"I think you have a right to be concerned. You're losing Henry. Lizzie's developing bad habits and Mary is suffering in silence. And you? What about you? After how far you've come, you can't let her ruin your life."

Happy she agreed with me, I blurted out, "How do I get rid of her?"

"EB has a pistol," Jane said. "That should do the trick."

Shock at Jane's suggestion must have registered on my face, because Jane added, "I'm teasing, silly goose."

I chuckled. "What else have you got?"

"Do you want to talk with Mother and EB? They may have some ideas."

I hated getting them involved, but it would take more heads than mine and Jane's to outwit Dina.

Jane ushered me from the cramped office into the parlor, where we waited.

EB strode into the room and took my hand, a welcoming gesture I'd come to expect. His shirtsleeves were rolled up, cravat untied, and breeches dirty at the knees. He waved at his attire. "Pardon my appearance. I've just left the stables where your sister brushed down Goldie. Good helper, that girl."

"I hope she wasn't in your way."

"No bother at all. She's fun to have around."

Mrs. Mitchell took the chair facing the window.

"Martha is concerned about Dina and what it's doing to her family," Jane said, addressing the room. "I'll let her explain the details."

They listened as I laid out my complaints.

"Martha," Mrs. Mitchell went first. "Has this woman harmed your children? Hit or beat them?"

"She smacked Lizzie on the backside once, but nothing else." I fiddled with the strap of the mending bag.

"Has she ever left Mary or Henry by themselves?" Mrs. Mitchell leaned forward in her chair.

"I don't believe so. Lizzie's always around when Mary's home. I don't imagine she's left Henry alone. He's stuck to her like a puppy waiting for a treat."

"I see." The woman leaned back in her chair, examining some far away item.

EB cleared his throat. "Martha, I'm sorry you are going through this. Does your father know how things are at home? Have you written to him?"

I shook my head. "I hinted at problems but nothing specific. I'm afraid he'll tell Joe and make things worse."

214

"Hold off on writing him till we have a plan," EB said.

A plan. These nice people, who owed me nothing, would help me untangle my mess.

Mrs. Mitchell snapped back to the conversation. "What if we turned the tables? Offer her a place rent-free."

EB and Jane's eyebrows shot up.

I blinked. The proposal caught me off guard.

"Free rent is tantalizing for a woman like her," EB said.

"Would she move?" Jane leaned forward, her eyes brightening as the idea took shape.

"I don't know. How would it be free?" I asked.

"You let me worry about that." Mrs. Mitchell added.

The room quieted as I examined this possibility. "It's worth a try, I suppose."

"EB can meet her and get her reaction." Mrs. Mitchell offered her son's help.

"No, let me do it. I'd rather her take her wrath out on me than have you in the middle," I said to EB.

"Give me the newspaper," Mrs. Mitchell pointed to the *Enquirer* on the table. EB handed it to her and, flipping a page, Mrs. Mitchell said, "Here's one. Rooms for rent at Walnut and Eleventh. Six dollars a month." She lowered the paper and looked at me. What if I pay three months in advance? Then it's up to her."

"We could move there!" I blurted out.

"You're not old enough to rent without an adult. She can." EB stated the simple truth of how my age affected our future.

Mrs. Mitchell rose from her chair and stood at the window, passersby moving along, taking a stroll on this fine summer afternoon. "Martha, I have another thought. I think I understand how you feel about your family, but I feel I must give you the option."

Her tone, low and grave, caught my attention. "What is it, Mrs. Mitchell?" I held my breath, expecting bad news.

"Rose told us yesterday that she's going to be married at the end of July. I'd like to hire you in her place."

"Oh," I pressed my hand to my chest, fingers splayed, struggling to find words.

"I'll hire Mary too, but at half your pay because I expect she'll do half the work."

I looked at Jane for her reaction. She nodded in encouragement.

"What about Lizzie and Henry? Can they come too?" The flaw in her offer would suspend further consideration.

Mrs. Mitchell closed her eyes and shook her head. "I'm sorry, but we can't handle children their age."

"But I can't leave them with Dina!" I leaped to my feet. "I just can't."

EB and Jane said in unison. "No, of course not."

"Then what?" My eyes darted from EB to Jane and came to rest on Mrs. Mitchell, her mouth open, ready to say what I didn't want to hear.

"No orphanage. We must stay together. I promised."

"Martha." EB's voice was steady, trying to calm my fears. "Nothing's been decided. But you should consider it. For your future and that of the children. I don't want to see you continue to live with Dina."

"What a choice! Live with a wicked woman or rip us apart by sending my brother and sister to the asylum."

Jane moved close to me and put her hands on my shoulder. "Taking care of them doesn't mean you have to be with them all the time. Maybe their care requires a change, a difficult one, but a place where they will be safe and happy."

Tears stung my eyes.

Mrs. Mitchell pulled me into the circle of her arms. I stood in her embrace, stiff and silent. How wonderful it would be to lay my head on her shoulder and grieve my circumstances. It would be easy to wallow in self-pity, to acknowledge my inadequacies as a caregiver, to damn Dina for ruining what little happiness we had.

Sniffing, I eased away from Mrs. Mitchell and straightened my shirtwaist. At my feet, the mending bag lay in a puddle. Getting it over my shoulder, I faced the Mitchells.

"Thank you for your help. I'll see if I can get Dina to move."

"Let me take you all home," EB said.

"No, thank you. We'll walk." I needed to think.

The three of them followed me into the yard, where Lizzie and Mary sat by the garden. "Time to go," I said.

Hugging and shouting goodbyes, my sisters hadn't a clue how upsetting the day had been. I planned to keep it that way as long as possible.

The following Sunday, the congregation at St. Mattheus was abuzz with news of the brutal three-day battle at Gettysburg, Pennsylvania. Despite the heavy losses on both sides, the Union victory was celebrated by the citizens of Cincinnati, who viewed it as a crucial turning point in the war, rekindling hope throughout the North. Many families anxiously awaited word of their loved ones' safety or demise, their hearts burdened with uncertainty as news from the battlefield slowly trickled in.

With Papa safe in southern Tennessee, I thanked God for his

distance from the battle. I prayed for the countless souls lost on the battlefield, their grieving families, and the hope that this crucial turning point would bring the war closer to an end.

Mrs. Eiflert handed me a basket of food, having missed Saturday's community donations, owing to the extended visit with the Mitchells.

"How are things with you and the children, and Mrs. Decker?"

"We're struggling to get along," I said.

"Is there anything I can do?" She shaded her eyes from the sun as we stood on the church steps.

"I need another place for us to live."

Surprised, she put a hand on my forearm. "Is it that bad?"

I nodded, but held my tongue, unwilling to elaborate.

"All four of you?" she clarified.

"Yes, all of us."

"I only ask because you could send the younger ones to the orphan asylum. Your mother spoke of it after your father left. She would approve."

"No!" I backed away, putting distance between me and the idea of my siblings in the asylum.

"I understand. But Martha…"

I cut her off. "Please let me know if you hear of a suitable place. Or someone I could speak with. Have a good day."

Nearly tripping over my skirts, I darted into the churchyard. Taking quick, shallow breaths, I gathered the children and, eager to escape Mrs. Eiflert and her solution, commanded them to hurry.

That night, I dreamed of the children calling my name, crying and reaching for me as I ran from them, crying too. Startled awake, I blinked at the ceiling. The soft breaths of my sisters beside me drifted into my awareness. I hadn't left them, but my tears were real.

The next morning, I shooed the children outside to play. It was time to confront Dina.

"This baby come soon. Moving down." Dina motioned how the baby had shifted downward, the bulge slightly lower on her hips than a week ago.

I placed a cup of tea on the table beside her. Raising her eyebrows at the unexpected gesture, she sipped. "You say something?"

Holding my cup in two hands, I squared up to face her and gathered the courage to tell her how I felt and lay out Mrs. Mitchell's plan.

"Dina. I don't know about you, but I am very unhappy with our living arrangements. These rooms are too small for six, soon to be seven," I gestured toward her belly.

"You want me go?" She rubbed her belly. "Like this?"

I lowered my head in despair. "I'm sorry. But you must find another place to live."

"No money." She stared at me, waiting.

"I've found rooms for you. Near the Hall. Free. For three months." Nervous, I couldn't speak in complete sentences.

"Free? How this work?" She folded her arms atop her bump.

"My friend, Mrs. Mitchell, has offered to pay."

"Why me? Why you not go?" she asked, challenging the plan.

"Because you are of age and I'm not. A landlord won't rent to me."

"I see." She considered the offer, her lips pursed, a furrow appearing between her brows.

The children's voices drifted through the open door as I waited for her answer, fiddling with a loose cuticle.

"I take. But," she said, "I have baby here." She swept an arm around the room.

"After the baby comes. Then you'll go?" We could make do for a few more weeks.

"Yes."

Hearing of Dina's agreement, Mrs. Mitchell said she would find a place for her after the baby was born. There would be more rooms like those advertised.

"What if she's stringing you along?" Jane asked. "The baby arrives, then she says the child is too young, or sickly, or any number of excuses."

"But she said she would," I defended our pact.

"Just because you're honest doesn't mean everyone is. Especially that one."

"Only a few more weeks," I said, and prayed we could get along till then.

Chapter Thirty-Four

Locke knocked on our door on the first of July. He wanted eighteen dollars. I removed the last five dollars from the quilt. Dina contributed one.

"I need the rest by the end of July, or I'll rent to someone who pays." His gaze bore into me with a sly, unsettling hunger. "Or you can give me something else, Martha."

I slammed the door in his face, my heart pounding. His mocking laughter followed him down the stairs.

"He bad," Dina said.

"You have no idea," I said suppressing a shudder at memories of past interactions with Locke.

Lizzie reminded me of the anniversary of Mama's death and said we should visit the cemetery. Unenthusiastic about the long walk up the hill and back, I asked EB if he could take us. He agreed to come on Friday afternoon after he finished work.

On the morning of our planned visit, Dina moaned, "Baby coming!" Her hair was disheveled, face pale, and her belly drooped heavily with the baby's weight.

"I'll send for the midwife," I said, fearing she would have it before Lizzie could fetch her.

Mrs. Seibert examined Dina. "She's not ready yet. Will be a few hours at least, but I'll stay just in case."

In between moans, I told Dina we were leaving. "We'll be back before dinner. Do you want me to take Gus?" It wasn't the boy's fault his mother and I didn't get along.

"Yes. I no good." Her eyes squeezed shut in agony, and her face crumpled as a wave of pain pulled her knees toward her stomach. A vague memory flashed through my mind—Mama's glazed eyes looking through me, her face drenched with sweat just before Henry was born.

At first Henry declined to go, but Dina's moaning and whimpering scared him into getting ready. I distracted him with the news of a carriage ride with a fine horse to take us up the hill. This cheered him and he watched for EB with Lizzie.

"He's here!" Lizzie screeched.

"Lizzie, you go first and get everyone settled." They filed downstairs, one at a time, until only I remained.

I told Mrs. Seibert we'd return in a few hours. She nodded. "Nothing happening here. Might as well get out on this fine afternoon."

The rear seat of the carriage fit Lizzie with Gus on her lap while Mary held Henry. I sat in front beside EB. We chatted amiably as he directed our vehicle across town and turned north for the climb up Vine Street. In the cemetery, at the spot where Mama lay, we disembarked.

"Can I come?" EB asked, looping the reins around the carriage frame to keep the horse in place.

"Why, I suppose," I said, surprised by his interest.

Lizzie ran up to EB as we approached and guided him to the foot of the grave. "Papa and I made her headstone," she said, pointing. "I did the flower."

"It's splendid!" EB walked around the bare patch and crouched low to examine it. "It has fine detail."

I spoke softly, almost to myself. "A year already. It feels like yesterday, yet ages ago. I miss you, Mama."

Henry and Gus ran around the other graves, playing tag, then hide and seek. When Gus ran across Mama's grave, Lizzie yelled at him. "Don't do that again, Gus. You want me to run over your Mama?"

EB hid a smirk that threatened to turn into a full-out grin under his hand, but his shoulders shook, giving his laughter away. "She's a pistol."

Mary finger kissed the marker, then walked over and stood between EB and me. I took her hand and from the corner of my eye, I saw her touch her fingertips to EB's hand. He didn't flinch or look at her but linked his fingers with hers as if they did this all the time.

Keeping his eyes forward, his voice low and concerned, he asked, "You all right, Mary?"

"Good," she said with a vigorous nod.

After the boys exhausted their pent-up energy, they stood by the grave, the six of us surrounding Mama on three sides, the marker on the fourth. I led us in the Lord's prayer, then Mary started the sleeping prayer. Gus and EB didn't know how it went, but they kept their heads down and listened as we recited the well-worn verse.

We covered Mama's marker with finger kisses as we said our goodbyes. Lizzie lingered the longest. As she approached the carriage, she wiped her eyes with the back of her hand.

"How about you sit up front with EB?" I asked her, checking EB's reaction over her head.

"Really? Can I?" She bounced on her toes, waiting for permission. EB nodded his approval and assisted me into the rear and put Henry in my lap. A consequence of Lizzie in front meant I had Henry all to myself for the ride home.

Instead of taking the same street down as the one we ascended, EB turned west, then south.

"This way is different," Lizzie said.

"Vine is all right to go up, but down can be dangerous. I prefer this way, where the streets go back and forth, zigzagging down the hill."

Lizzie grinned at EB as if he'd invented the sun. "You are clever."

"That's the best compliment I ever had from a lady," he patted Lizzie's knee.

Though I couldn't see her face, I knew her cheeks would be pink, her blue eyes sparkling at his remark.

At home, Lizzie tied the horse to the street rail while EB hoisted the boys to the sidewalk and gave Mary and me his hand to climb out of the carriage.

From the windows above us, I heard screams. Screams of agony.

"Dina!" I gasped. "The baby is coming!" Turning to EB, I said, "Thank you. Lizzie, mind the children." I picked up my skirts and took the stairs two at a time.

Mrs. Seibert's knitting needles clacked.

"Is she all right? I heard screams."

"She's fine. This is the way it goes till it's born."

"What should I do with the children?" I hadn't thought how terrorizing Dina's screams would be for Gus and Henry, or the girls, for that matter.

"Don't know. Somewhere else is best."

I rushed to the window. EB's carriage still stood at the curb. Throwing up the lower window, I leaned out and yelled. "EB!"

He leaned out of the carriage. "Yes?"

"Wait, please!" Rushing down the stairs, I nearly ran headlong into Henry. "Stay put. Don't go in the house!"

EB climbed from the carriage and met me on the sidewalk. "What is it?"

"The baby is coming. The children. They can't stay here. Let me think." Where could they go? I paced to the right, then back, and stopped in front of EB. "Maybe Mrs. Eiflert could help."

"They can come home with me," he said, as if he were taking food home from the market.

"What? No. That's all right. Maybe…"

EB interrupted my rambling. "For one night, it will be fine. We'll have a party, and I know Jane will be thrilled."

"You'd do that? You and all those children?" I gaped at him. Images flashed through my mind: broken knick-knacks, spilled milk, Mrs. Mitchell's scowl.

"Lizzie will help, and Mary knows the house. If they misbehave, I'll make them sleep in the stable."

This family liked to tease. "Not much of a punishment for Lizzie or Henry. All kidding aside," I asked, "Are you serious? You would take them?"

He affirmed his commitment with a decisive tilt of his head.

"You're a blessing, EB. I'll come for them tomorrow morning. This damn baby should be here by then." As if on cue, Dina's howls and moans escaped from the windows above us.

"Don't worry, Martha. We'll be fine. Just get that baby here and your freedom is within reach."

Striding into the yard, EB called, "Back in the carriage. We're going on an adventure."

Dina thrashed about the bed until the early hours of Saturday morning when, amid Mrs. Seibert's commands to "push" and "now", the baby arrived. As agreed, I cleaned and swaddled the child while the midwife helped Dina move into the bed in the front room.

"She's beautiful," I said, handing her the child. "Do you have a name?"

Dina touched her baby's eyes, nose, and ears, then placed her palm on its full head of dark hair. "Amelia."

"I'm finished. Congratulations, Mrs. Decker." To me, she said, "Change the linens as soon as you can."

Trying not to disturb Dina or the baby, I parted the curtains, letting in the first streaks of dawn lighting the sky. I lifted the windows from the bottom, hoping a breeze would air out the warm, stuffy rooms. Settling into a chair by the window, I placed a sheet of paper on the lap desk, dipped my pen into the ink bottle, and started a letter.

11 July 1863

Dear Papa,

Let Joe know he has a girl. Amelia arrived this morning without difficulty. Dina and the baby are well. Mr. Locke has said he will throw us out if we cannot pay him by the end of the month. Please send any money you can. We visited Mama yesterday. It is hard to believe she has been gone a year. The children are well. We miss you and hope you are out of harm's way.

With love,

Martha

P.S. Do not tell Joe, but Dina is moving out soon. Living together is difficult, and we both agree it's best.

Down in the yard, I got a fire going under the wash tub and disassembled the bedding. On the floor, beneath the bed, something white and rectangular caught my eye. An envelope, but in the dim light of the room, I couldn't make out the address. I tucked it into my apron pocket and half dragged, half carried the mattress to the yard and scrubbed it with a hogs hair brush and lye soap.

While the soap did its work, I examined the envelope, my heart fluttering at Papa's handwriting. The address read "Mrs. Joseph Decker, Linn Street, Cincinnati." I plucked out a single sheet of paper.

> Dina,
>
> Here is my pay ticket. Please cash it and give the money to Martha. You have one from Joe coming too.
>
> Regards,
>
> George

The date? What was the date? Nothing on the letter, but the envelope had a stamp on it. Postmarked in Chattanooga, the date was undecipherable but what did it matter? Dina had a pay ticket from Papa and hadn't told me. I ached to charge into our rooms and attack her, my breath and heartbeat quickening. But I tamped down my tendency to act first, think later.

Why? Why would she withhold the money? Where was it? How long ago did the pay ticket come? Thinking the worst of the woman who always challenged my kinder instincts, I concluded she'd stolen our money.

I built up a full head of steam. Climbing the stairs, each footfall thudded sharply on the wooden steps, echoing around the yard.

"Dina, wake up!" I shouted upon entering our rooms.

She stirred, searched for the baby and, finding her near and safe, looked at me.

"Where's Papa's money?" My voice loud and shaky, I struggled to control myself.

"What money?" She pushed her long red hair out of her face.

"I found this." I waved the letter. "Where's my money?"

"I have baby. Not good time." Dina said, struggling to get out of bed. "I need bucket."

I blocked her path, "I. Don't. Give. A. Damn." Each word a sentence. On damn, I shook the letter in her face.

She fell back onto the bed, a yelp accompanying her landing.

"I want my money!" The bellow emitting from my mouth could have woken the dead, much less the baby. But it slept on, oblivious to the drama unfolding.

"Gone. I pay people." Her eyes flashed. Anger? Fear?

Gone? Not hidden or put aside? "What do you mean, pay people? Pay who?"

"Joe gamble. He lose and tell me pay." Dina twirled her wedding ring between her thumb and forefinger. "Or else."

"Or else what?" I asked. A bribe, a threat, blackmail?

"He hurt me."

"What?" I screeched. Her elaborate tale had no merit. "I'll kill you myself if you don't tell me the truth!"

"No lie." Lowering her head, her red and mussed hair shielded her face, hiding her lie or the shameful truth.

"When did you cash the ticket? How did you pay this man?" I wondered when she left the house, for she rarely went out.

"I cash and give man money when you at Mitchell house."

The weight of the news forced me to sit, my head in my hands, angry and despondent tears welling up, closing my throat, choking off my air supply. I threw my head back and screamed. Over and over, I wailed, a primal sound from a dark place inside I hadn't known existed. My throat raw, I needed another way to vent my anger. I picked up the mending basket and hurled it across the room, the feeble thump it made as it hit the wall unsatisfactory. Striding to the table, I hoisted the pot with remnants of this morning's oatmeal above my head and flung it, spattering oatmeal on the floor, the wall, and my skirt. Swiping my arm across the table, I cleared it. My breakfast dishes flew across the room.

"Stop!" she yelled, hands protecting her ears.

After a moment of contemplating other ways to express my anger, misery consumed me, deflating my fury. "Dina, you have ruined us."

The baby cried, and Dina picked her up. "I know. I leave, go to place you say."

"But don't you see? That doesn't matter anymore. Without Papa's money, we can't stay either. I can't pay the rent, and Locke will surely throw us out." Weary and helpless, my lowest day since Mama's last, I explained the cold, hard truth.

"I do what Joe say." She defended her actions.

"Did you pay the man Joe's money, too?"

She squeezed her eyes shut and nodded.

"How much do you have left?"

"None. Owe more."

"More! Good God, Dina. Joe is bad."

"You no say he bad."

"I don't give a damn," I spat the words in her face.

Checking the angle of the sun, I brushed the oatmeal from my skirt, and tidied my chignon, loosened in my tirade. "I'm going to get the children. When I return, this mess better be cleaned up."

I slammed the door and as I walked under the windows, Amelia began to wail.

Lost in the hell of Dina's making, I stepped into the street without looking as I walked to the Mitchell boarding house.

"Watch it, lady!" The carriage driver raised his fist.

I muttered an apology and retreated to the safety of the sidewalk. Leaning against a lamppost, my body shook as if caught in a snowstorm. Head bowed to avoid eye contact with passing strangers, my breath quickened, and a wave of dizziness swept over me. Clutching the lamppost, I sank to my knees as my stomach heaved. Oatmeal and tea joined the refuse in the filthy gutter.

Pressing my hand to my chest, I slowed my breathing, trying to regain control of my body. I squeezed my eyes shut to keep the world from spinning as I clutched the post and slowly rose to a standing position.

A couple passed, arm in arm, averting their eyes with lips curled in distaste as I spat into the gutter to clear my mouth. Gulping deep breaths, I steadied my trembling but fought dizziness as my stomach settled.

With no money and believing Locke would make good on his threats, we had no home, no relatives to take us in, and no money to go elsewhere. I helped deliver her damned baby. Fed and minded her boy. Held my tongue when she refused to give me money for food and looked the other way as she stole Henry from me. No! No more! Her poison, her selfishness, ruined me. Ruined my family.

As I entered through the Mitchell's side gate, the wind carried laughter, shouts, and squeals. Unable to face my siblings just yet, I leaned my forehead against the cool bricks. Gasping, trying to suppress my despair, I mourned the life I'd fought so hard to preserve, lost because Papa trusted an untrustworthy person, leaving us homeless.

Steeling myself to greet the children, I raised my chin, planted a smile on my face, and stepped into the yard.

"Hello!" I stretched the 'oh' at the end into a drawn-out

'helloooo,' as cheerful a greeting as I could muster.

"Motty!" Lizzie and Henry shouted, running into my outstretched arms. My hopes of retrieving Henry from Dina's claws soared as he hugged me.

Mary rose from her knees in the garden. Stepping gingerly over the rows of vegetables, her smile shone like the sun bursting from behind a cloud.

"What is it?" Lizzie tugged at my sleeve.

"What's what?" I thought she meant my tears.

"The baby, you goose!" Hands on her hips, she chastised me.

"It's a girl. Amelia."

Lizzie stuck her tongue out at Henry. "Told you it was a girl."

Gus ran up. "Mama?"

It was not his fault his parents were fools. "Your Mama is fine. And you have a pretty sister."

Their excitement at my arrival gone, the little ones resumed their play.

Mary hugged me, and I held on longer than usual. When she pulled away, her eyes searched my face. "Motty, sad," she said, her voice tinged with concern.

I forced a smile. "A little. But I'm happy to see you. Let's speak to Jane and go home."

Mary had a different idea. "No home. Stay." She must be truly happy at the Mitchell home, a stark contrast to our cramped rooms with Dina.

"Maybe," I conceded, as I headed for the kitchen, the screen door slapping shut behind me.

I waited in the office, observing the children at play. My heart broke for them. Their lives were about to change and not for the better.

"Martha!" Jane burst in and hugged me like a sister.

Longing to drown my sorrows in her shoulder, I stiffened, pulled away, and smiled. "How were the children? Did they behave? If not, they're in big trouble."

Jane rested a hand on my arm. "Relax. They were fine. After supper, they played in the yard, then we put them to bed in the room across the hall from Rose. With Lizzie's and Mary's help, the boys were no trouble. They've been up since the crack of dawn, but Rose brought them down and gave them breakfast. We're planning on dinner for them too."

"I can't thank you and your family enough." I looked around for Mrs. Mitchell. "Did your mother mind having them?"

"Not at all. She acted as home base for a game of kick the can last night." Jane's laughter eased my worries about her mother.

"Can you stay for dinner?" Jane asked. "EB will be home."

"Only if I can help. Making a meal for four children is quite the task."

"Deal." In the kitchen, she told Rose and Cook there would be five more for dinner.

"Can I peel some potatoes?" I asked Rose, a full bag in the sink.

"Knife's in that drawer. Peel away."

"I hear you're getting married, Rose. Congratulations."

"I am. End of the month." Rose's face lit up at the mention of her upcoming nuptials. "When I go, are you coming to work here?"

I shrugged. "I'm not sure. My priority is to keep my family together."

"I know, but this is a good place to work. And the Mrs. loves Mary."

"All good reasons," I said. After this morning's events, Mrs. Mitchell's offer held greater attraction.

EB arrived as we gathered in the dining room. He took an end chair and Mrs. Mitchell the other. Jane and I sat among the children keeping a close eye on the boys. Their chatter rose to a din no one minded, and I caught Mrs. Mitchell hiding a smile when Henry balanced a spoon on his nose for a full minute.

Mary and I cleared the table and assisted with kitchen clean up. It was the least we could do to repay the Mitchell's hospitality.

Jane poked her head into the kitchen. "Martha, can you come into the front room when you're done?"

Sending Mary out to play with the others, I removed the borrowed apron and stepped into the parlor. EB rose as I entered and motioned me into a chair.

"We thought it a good time for a progress report," EB said. "Now that the baby has arrived, Dina should be moving out soon."

Mrs. Mitchell's eyes searched for confirmation. Jane peered closely at my face, hers full of hope. EB, elbows on thighs, leaned forward, expecting good news.

Uncertain how to explain this morning's undoing of all my hopes and dreams, I fiddled with a button on my sleeve.

EB sensed my distress. "Something's wrong, isn't it?"

I nodded, but I couldn't speak. My throat choked with tears. Eyes closed, I gulped deep breaths, exhaling slowly.

"Water?" Jane asked.

Shaking my head, I took one more breath and, on the exhale, said, "Dina stole Papa's pay."

The only sounds in the room came from horses' hooves clopping on cobblestones.

I continued. "She said she had to pay her husband's gambling debts or the man he owed would hurt her."

"Gambling?" EB questioned, scratching his jaw.

"Both Papa and Joe's pay went to the man, and she says Joe owes more. I don't know if I believe her or not. But it doesn't matter. Papa's money is gone, and I have none to pay the rent."

"She'll not be getting that room." Mrs. Mitchell said. "You must come to work for us, Martha. You and Mary. There's nothing else to be done."

"Mother, let's take this one step at a time," EB said, helping me manage his mother's desire to help. She dropped into a chair, fingers tapping restlessly on the arm.

"Locke told us he wanted all the back rent by the end of the month."

"How much do you owe?" EB asked.

"Twelve dollars."

"I have it," EB said, his hand slipping into his jacket.

"No, no." I shook my head and EB withdrew his hand. "Who knows when Papa's next pay ticket will come? It could be months," I sighed. "And it doesn't rid me of Dina."

"I see." EB stood and paced, his hands in his pockets, pausing, opening his mouth to speak, closing it, and shaking his head as if his idea left him as soon as he tried to put it into words.

"Mrs. Mitchell," I straightened and faced the older woman. "I'd like to accept your offer, but is no way for all of us to live here? You've had them overnight and it went well. They love it here, and I promise they'll behave and not get into mischief." I had little hope my lies would convince her.

"Martha, as I've said already, it's not possible. They are too young and while I do like them, children require more care than one might think. You, of all people, know this." Her raised eyebrow challenged my promises.

"I need to think," I said. "A cannonball fell from the sky and destroyed my world today."

Sympathetic looks passed between them, but no new ideas emerged.

Rising, I stood erect, my head held high. "I'll not take your pity, nor your charity. Thank you for having the children. You saved them from a night full of screams that would give them night terrors for years to come."

"They are wonderful children," Mrs. Mitchell admitted.

"Yes, but they are mine. I hope you will keep the offer of employment open until I can figure things out."

"I will."

I turned to EB. "Getting four rowdy youngsters home will be a challenge. Is it charity or pity if you give us a ride home?"

His chuckle assured me it was neither. "Get them to the stable. I'll hitch Goldie."

"Jane, thank you for all you do for us. For me." My eyes watered, but I turned away from her, unable to look at her without tears.

"I'll see you soon, Motty," Jane said. Her use of my nickname touched me as nothing else could.

Resisting the urge to hurl myself into her arms, I paused, caught my breath, and gathered my courage to leave this house, this place I could call home. If I dared

Chapter Thirty-Five

The next day, I found Mrs. Eiflert at the hall.

"Do you have any news of a place for my family to live?"

She shook her head. "Nothing. I'm sorry."

"I have a job with the Mitchells if I want it."

"And Mary?"

"Will work there, too."

The older woman nodded. "I know that's important to you." Her lips thinned as her desire to understand the fate of the others flashed into her eyes. "Lizzie and Henry?"

"I have no choice. They will go to the asylum." Saying it aloud confirmed the painful reality.

"I'm sorry," Mrs. Eiflert said. "Have you been there? The asylum?"

"No, I…" I took a breath. "I don't know what to do."

"Matron Pfefflin is a friend. Let me take you to meet her. Best if you like her and the place before you commit."

I could have kissed her! "Can we? Can you?" I hadn't thought of checking out the asylum before deciding they would go.

"I can. Friday. Come to my house after breakfast and we'll go in our buggy. It's in Mount Auburn, so walking is out of the question for me."

Even in my darkest hour, people like Mrs. Eiflert offered help. Placing my brother and sister in a distant home hurt my soul like a thousand paper cuts. Still, I thanked God for the charity and grace of women like Mrs. Eiflert.

"I know this is difficult," she said, laying a hand on my arm.

"You've been through so much. I'm sure God has a plan."

She pulled me into her arms, and I let her embrace me. "What if I don't like God's plan?" I said, the words muffled in her shoulder.

Mrs. Eiflert's chest rumbled with a short laugh. She held my face between her hands, then kissed me on the forehead. "I'll see you Friday. Nine o'clock."

On the street outside the hall, a newspaper hawker yelled, "Circus parade tomorrow! Read all about Van Amburgh's Menagerie."

Without hesitation, I shelled out three cents and bought a paper, scanning it for news of the circus. The parade, touted as a mile long, planned its route across Liberty Street, a convenient spot for us to watch its journey to the exhibition spot and a diversion from our bleak future.

At home, Lizzie scratched a hopscotch court into the dirt. She didn't bother with numbering them today. When Henry and Mary played, we used them as a teaching tool.

"Play with me, Motty," she said, her usual partner, Mary, busy with her garden.

I almost declined, the early afternoon heat unbearable, but then reconsidered. "Find me a marker."

Lizzie yelped with joy because I rarely played, always something more important to do. She picked through the rocks at the base of the steps and found one for each of us.

"You go first," she allowed kindly.

We played the first few blocks, enjoying the simple competition. After her turn, she cleared her throat. "Tell me what's going on between you and Dina. You're both acting oddly." She hopped to retrieve her marker from the fifth block, then landed it squarely in the sixth.

I relayed the morning of Amelia's birth. "The money Papa sent is gone. We have no money to pay the rent."

Though it was her turn to throw, she stalled.

Reading her mind, I said, "I don't know what we'll do. I'm trying to find a place where we can be together. But, honestly, Lizzie, I've had no luck."

"But you must. Find us a place. Or get some money." She rounded on me, her eyes wide and vulnerable. "I'll work. Hawk papers or sit on the corner with a hat for handouts like other kids. I'll do anything!" All wound up, she reeled off the first things that came to mind, pacing back and forth, throwing out ideas willy-nilly.

"No. You will not," I said firmly, blocking her path. "You will go to school, you will have a girlhood, you will be happy."

"That woman stole my girlhood." She pointed to our rooms, her blue eyes, like Mama's, dark and threatening. "Damn her."

"You're not supposed to curse," I said, repeating her admonition to me.

"Neither are you."

"I know, but I confess it feels good."

"Damn! Damn! Damn!" She laughed. Toying with her hopscotch marker, she said, "I don't feel better."

"I know something that might." I held out the news sheet to her. "How would you like to go to the Circus parade tomorrow?"

Hundreds of people crowded the corner at Liberty and Elm. The atmosphere was charged with excitement and reminded me of Papa's regimental parade at the start of the war. Standing three or four deep along the walkways, men smoked cigars, women chatted with friends, and children ran to and fro.

I hadn't told Dina where we were going and didn't offer to take Gus. I wanted this for my family.

We found a spot on Elm behind a rope strung up to keep people from standing in the street during the menagerie's grand procession. After twenty minutes, a boy yelled to the crowd, "Here they come!"

A light but hot breeze carried a drumbeat from the east. Ba-dum, ba-dum, ba-dum. A shiver ran down my spine in anticipation. The drums silenced, and the crowd stilled, waiting, holding its breath. Then, with a burst of bugles, drums, and fifes, the menagerie band struck up *Yankee Doodle*. As the band came into view, its brass instruments glinting in the sun, the crowd sang along, boisterous and jolly.

Behind the band, a man in a red coat led the biggest animal I'd ever seen down the street with no rope or restraint. "Behold the greatest beast on earth. The African elephant!" Gray and wrinkled, with huge ears, the beast's enormous trunk swung up and the animal bellowed as if to announce his arrival. Henry backed into me as it passed, the elephant's girth filling the width of the street. Lizzie reached out to touch it, but I caught her by the collar to keep her from harm. Mary watched in awe, her mouth a silent O, eyes combing over the animal as if etching it into her memory.

"It's an elephant, Mary," I pointed.

"El-wa-fant," she said with care, repeating what I'd said as she added this new word to her vocabulary.

"It's magnificent!" Lizzie said. "A tiny tail on such a large animal."

Behind the elephant a cage on wheels rolled up. A lion paced back and forth, a crown of dark brown hair, matted with sticks and straw, circling its face. A man walking next to the cage poked it with a stick and the lion roared, not once but twice, fangs showing pointy and white in a mouthful of very sharp teeth. Henry pivoted into my skirts, burying his face.

A group of clowns, jugglers, and acrobats performed their tricks on the street before us, followed by a set of six trained horses with pretty girls in colorful outfits, balancing on their back.

At last, the giant golden chariot featured on the poster rounded the corner. A man wearing a suit of gold held the reins of eight jet-black horses, each with a tall white feather dancing on its head.

"Van Amburgh himself!" said a man next to me. "I hear he puts his head inside the lion's mouth."

Henry's eyes widened. "Whoa! I'd like to see that!"

And right there, the joy and wonder on the faces of those I loved the most deserved a treat. The cost of the circus was a pittance compared to the joy of sharing a memory to last a lifetime.

Dina overheard our chatter about the parade. With a huff, she confronted me. "You see parade and no Gus."

"I don't have to tell you what we do."

"But Gus, he like animals." Circling around me as I moved about the room, I stopped. She bumped into me, and seeing the black look in my eyes, stepped back. I didn't speak to her again until we were ready to leave.

"We're going to see the circus. Gus cannot go. He's too little," I said.

"Oh," she said and dropped into a chair, the fight gone out of her.

"If you hadn't stolen our money, maybe I'd take him."

Blue eyes flashing, Lizzie confronted Dina. "You're a liar and a thief."

"I do what Joe say." Dina muttered, hiding behind her stringy hair.

The parade was an appetizer for the main event, and our excitement could not be contained. Approaching the exhibition area at Seventh Street, a throng of people headed in the same direction. Men shouted, "Come see this" or "Come see that" grabbing our attention for displays of curiosity. We watched a man eat a stick of fire. Another, wearing only a turban and a cloth around his mid-section, lay down on a bed of nails. One threw knives at a pretty girl who didn't flinch when they struck beside her head. We shared a bag of popcorn and followed the crowd into the red and white striped tent. For ninety minutes, all kinds of acts entertained us under the big top, my mind full of wondrous sights, devoid of worries, happy to see smiles of joy on the faces I loved.

At home, we discussed our favorite acts, sealing them in our memory until, at last, Henry yawned and crawled in next to Mary, already snoring softly.

Lizzie and I changed into our night dresses. It would be all four of us in one bed, but I was grateful to have us together after our wonderful day. Especially Henry, who didn't whine for Dina.

"Motty, thank you for taking us to the Menagerie," she said through a yawn. "It was a grand time."

For a few hours, the circus suspended reality. Now, nestled next to my sleeping siblings, I lie awake, knowing tomorrow's plans would forever change their lives.

Chapter Thirty-Six

The next morning, I prepared to meet Mrs. Eiflert.

"Lizzie, I have an errand to run and need you to mind the children. I'll be back before noon."

"I watch. No worry. Please, I help," Dina said.

With her back to Dina, Lizzie said, "You can trust me to care for them properly." As Lizzie sauntered away, she childishly stuck her tongue out at Dina, just beyond her line of sight.

In front of the Eiflerts' small two-story house, the buggy stood ready. We climbed in and set out for the asylum, turning north on Sycamore. The street rose ominously before us, much like the way to the cemetery. This stretch of road was sparsely populated, with large houses scattered among stands of trees, set back from the road.

The steep slope twisted around one bend, then another, until the incline leveled off. Our grip on the buggy seats loosened as our fear of rolling backwards ebbed away. A few minutes later, an imposing building loomed into view, its stark silhouette etched against the sky.

"That's the Asylum," Mrs. Eiflert said, turning the horse onto a well-worn dirt path.

We dismounted in front of a red brick building adorned with white window frames and a wrap-around porch.

"This is the best part," Mrs. Eiflert said, standing on the porch, peering over the expanse of the hill we climbed.

"Oh! Oh my!" I uttered, speechless at the unobstructed view of the city. From the east, the Ohio River bent around Mount Adams, then straightened along the line of buildings on the waterfront. Waves of summer heat shimmered over the landscape, blurring our view.

A metal plaque set into the bricks beside the front door read: *German Protestant Orphan Asylum 1851*. Six rocking chairs lined the porch facing the view. I followed Mrs. Eiflert inside. The cool interior welcomed us after our hot, dusty ride. The floor was checkered with black and white tiles while the walls were papered with colorful birds native to the area. Robins, blue jays, cardinals, and finches adorned the walls, some in flight, others perched on branches with mates. I imagined Henry and Lizzie identifying the different species.

To the right, a wide staircase led to a landing. The steps were worn by countless feet and the railing was dulled by hundreds of hands sliding along its length.

"Matron's office is here." Mrs. Eiflert halted in front of a set of double doors and knocked.

The door opened, revealing a tall, robust woman dressed in black from head to toe. A silver chain was hooked to a button, leading to a pocket where I suspected a watch ticked against her chest.

"Hannah! How lovely to see you!" The women embraced.

Mrs. Eiflert drew away. "Matron Pfefflin, this is Martha Hesch."

I curtsied. "It's nice to meet you."

"What brings you all the way up the hill?" Matron asked, over the yells of two boys running through the hall and out the front door. "Please come in." She stepped back and motioned for us to enter.

Matron slipped behind her desk and motioned to two chairs facing her. The room, dark with walnut paneling and bookshelves, was formal but pleasant, with fresh flowers in a vase on a table. Children's artwork was clipped to a string with clothespins.

Mrs. Eiflert opened the conversation. "Martha has fallen on unfortunate circumstances which require her to look into a home for her siblings."

Matron nodded. "I see. Tell me about you, Martha."

"Me?" I asked, surprised at this odd start.

"Yes, I'd like to know about you and then hear about the children."

How to tell a long story to a stranger? Where to start?

"Papa's in the Army. The Ninth Ohio. Mama died last year. I've been taking care of the children, well, even before Mama died because she got sick."

A slight bob of Matron's head urged me to continue.

"Papa came home for a few months but had to go back in March and we were doing fine until," I paused, the weight of our situation pressing down on me. "Our money was stolen. I cannot pay the rent. The landlord wants us out."

"How old are you?"

"Sixteen and a half."

"You've been through a lot," Matron said.

"Yes, Ma'am, we have." I lowered my head and picked at a hangnail.

"How do you know them, Hannah?"

"George and Retta, her parents, have been members of St. Mattheus' congregation since they arrived in the late forties. The children were baptized there, and Retta was a good friend. Martha comes to the Hall every week, delivering goods she mends for the community."

"Very resourceful." Matron sat back in her chair, folding her hands over her extended abdomen. "Tell me about the children."

"I have three siblings. Henry is four, and nearly forgotten his Mama, and Papa leaving left a mark. Lizzie will be ten in a few weeks. She's stubborn but smart as a whip, loves the outdoors and reading. Her curiosity knows no bounds." I turned to Mrs. Eiflert. "Did you know her New Year's resolution was to be a nosy Nellie?"

Mrs. Eiflert shook her head in amazement. "Why on earth?"

"She said you called her that once and instead of taking it as a slight, she pursues it as a calling."

Mrs. Eiflert chuckled.

"Lizzie sounds like a handful." Matron observed.

"She can be, but she's also a great help. She rarely gives me trouble when I ask her to do something. I rely on her heavily."

"The third?" Matron asked.

I took a deep breath before answering. "Mary. You don't need to be concerned with her. She'll be staying with me."

"Tell me about her, anyway. She's important to her brother and sister."

I swallowed, for talking about Mary meant describing her in a positive light. "Mary is fourteen. She loves gardening and thanks to her, we have a good crop of vegetables. She has a fine hand at sewing and embroidery. She belongs to the church choir."

Mrs. Eiflert added, "She and Therese are friends."

"But," this would be the hard part, "She looks like any girl her age. Except her speech is different. Mostly one or two words. Sometimes more. We understand her, though, and she gets along fine."

"She sounds lovely." Matron said.

"Oh, she is!" I sat forward. "You could not find a sweeter, gentler girl. But she's not good when her routine changes. I don't leave her alone for fear she could get hurt. As she can't tell one direction from another or say where we live, she could get lost. She trusts everyone she meets."

"We can take in all three of your siblings. Mary might be challenging at first, since only Lizzie would understand her, but we'd manage."

"No thank you," I said. "I promised Papa to keep her with me until he comes home."

In unison, Mrs. Eiflert and Matron arched their brows.

"And if something should happen to him?" Matron asked.

"Then she'll be with me. Always."

"Always?" Mrs. Eiflert repeated, her eyes wide in disbelief.

"Always is a very long time," Matron said.

Mrs. Eiflert, stunned at my commitment to Mary, said, "You realize that keeping Mary with you limits your prospects for marriage. I know of no man who would marry one girl and take on a sister, too."

I'd thought of marriage from time to time, when a boy at church caught my eye and smiled, or I spoke to a young man at the market. Marriage for me would be a hill to climb later. When Papa came home.

I pushed those thoughts aside and explained. "I've found work as a domestic servant. They'll take Mary too. I've looked for a place for all of us, but there's nothing."

"That leaves Henry and Lizzie."

I pressed my lips over my teeth, a vain attempt at keeping my tears at bay. "Yes. They need a place to live."

A heavy silence filled the room. After a moment, Matron cleared her throat and picked up her pen.

"I'll need some information," she said.

I nodded, swallowing hard.

Matron recorded Henry and Lizzie's birth date, Mama's date of death, and that Papa had joined the Ninth in April 1861.

"I'd like to bring them the day after Lizzie's birthday. Let her celebrate at home."

"That will be fine. I'm making a note that you are their nearest relative, requesting their placement. Mrs. Eiflert is a witness." She raised her brows, waiting for our assent.

A thought occurred to me. "This is a temporary solution. How do I get them out? When Papa returns?"

"Let's talk about how things work here," she said, putting her pen down. "The children are assigned to a room with others of their gender in their age range. Three meals a day, a bath every other, and prayers before bedtime. Each child will have daily chores. For example, Lizzie might help in the kitchen and Henry could tote firewood or coal."

That sounded fair enough.

She continued, "They go to city schools to associate with children outside the asylum. In addition, we teach practical skills. Girls learn to cook and sew, and we teach boys wood working and animal husbandry."

"And when it's time for them to go home?" I asked.

"They will be released to an adult, you, for instance, or someone else, but only with your permission, in person, to verify their identity."

"Oh, good." That would keep Dina from taking Henry.

"When the child turns fifteen, we release them with twenty dollars to help them start out. We find them work as domestics or in factories. If they show skill in a trade, we arrange an apprenticeship."

"When can I visit? Bring Mary?"

"We prefer Sundays when there are no scheduled activities. Most visitors come after church, stay the afternoon, and enjoy the grounds, weather permitting. On holidays, we have special programs the children perform in, and at Christmas and Easter, we offer a meal in the dining hall where families eat together."

Children to play with, structure, and all manner of learning. I marveled at the life Lizzie and Henry would have. It would be far better than what I could provide. "I like what you've described, Matron."

"We take great pride in what we do here, helping children through a difficult time, ensuring their minds and bodies are cared for." Matron smiled, her hands clasped, resting on the desk.

"May I have a tour?"

Matron glanced at her timepiece. "I'm afraid I have another engagement. You can return another time or tour with the children when they arrive."

I felt comfortable with what I'd learned. "I'll tour with the children when they arrive."

"Very well." She stood, and we followed suit. The three of us stepped into the hall. "I'm sorry you're in this predicament, Martha. Rest assured, Henry and Lizzie will be safe and in good care."

Matron extended her hand, and I shook it. Turning to Mrs. Eiflert, she said, "Hannah, it was good to see you. How is Frank?"

Mrs. Eiflert's face changed as if a cloud passed over it. "He wrote a few weeks ago. The thrill of the Army has faded, the grind of marching endless miles and sleeping out in the open not to his liking. But he's doing his part."

Matron drew her friend into a hug. "I hope to see you again soon.

Give my regards to Mr. Eiflert."

"I will," Mrs. Eiflert said.

At the front door, Matron excused herself and went down a hallway toward the back of the house. As we settled in the carriage, Mrs. Eiflert asked me to keep a hand on the brake during our descent. "Just in case."

"The asylum appears to be well run. The Matron is kind, the house is clean, and the grounds are perfect for two children who love the outdoors."

"I'm glad you like it."

Calculating the number of days until Lizzie's birthday, I said aloud, "Nineteen."

"Nineteen?"

"Days left till I bring them."

The old woman nodded. "Not long."

"I've got to tell Lizzie." My stomach knotted at the thought.

"How do you think she'll take it?" Mrs. Eiflert glanced at me sidelong as she maneuvered the carriage through traffic.

"Not well. She knows we have no money. Offered to sell her soul to stay together," I chuckled at my sister's willingness to do whatever it took. "She must go to school. Have a childhood."

"Something I'm afraid you're missing out on, my dear."

"I'll have mine later when Papa gets home. When we're a family again."

Chapter Thirty-Seven

Mrs. Eiflert dropped me in front of Locke's shoe shop. I went inside and waited for him to finish with a customer. The landlord eyed me over the customer's head, his brows lifting, a sly grin tugging at his mouth.

"Miss Hesch," he said after the customer left the shop. "To what do I owe the pleasure?" The balding man leaned on the counter, his eyes raking over me.

It was all I could do to stand my ground. "Papa's pay has not come. Unless you can let us stay till his next one arrives, we'll be leaving."

He pondered the ceiling for two seconds, considering my plea. "No. Pay me by the end of July or you're out."

"Very well, we'll go. But I'd like to ask one favor. The very last I'll ever ask."

Curious, he came around the counter. "A favor. Maybe we can trade favors."

I understood his meaning and inched back. "If I give you a dollar, can we stay until August the sixth?"

He crossed his arms over his chest. "What's so magical about that day?"

"It's the day I take Henry and Lizzie to the orphan asylum."

"Orphan asylum?" His eyes squinted.

"Yes." I didn't owe him an explanation, but did enjoy his consternation.

"Uh, sure," he said, flustered at this turn of events. "Keep your money. Sorry to hear about the children." His arms dropped to his side, and he stuck his hands in his pants pockets.

"Yes, me too." I turned to leave.

"What about the other one?" His head jerked toward the rooms above his head. "Is she leaving too?"

"You'll have to ask her." I stepped out of the gloomy shop and went upstairs, where the door to our rooms stood open. Dina sat with the baby at her breast in the front room.

"We're moving," I said. "I've just told Locke."

She jerked her head up, displacing Amelia's mouth. "I not move?"

"No. Because of you, we have no rent money. We leave in two weeks."

Dina lowered her head over the baby. I hoped she was ashamed about what she and her husband had done to our family.

I extended a hand to my baby sister. "It's time, Lizzie." I glanced at Mary and Henry. "Be good while I talk to Lizzie."

Henry stayed put, but Mary left her sewing and followed us down to the yard, settling on her knees next to the garden. She would miss her garden dearly. But Mrs. Mitchell's, many times larger, would soon take its place.

I led Lizzie to the stone bench in the shade. "Locke won't let us stay. I've looked and looked for a place where we can all live together, but I've found none."

Lizzie scuffed the toe of her shoe in the dust. "What now?"

I took a deep breath. "Mrs. Mitchell has offered me and Mary jobs at the boarding house. We will work and live there."

Her eyes lit up. "I like the Mitchells," she said, her voice edged with excitement.

Here it is, I thought. The point of no return. I stepped off the ledge and took the plunge. "Though she dearly likes you and Henry, Mrs. Mitchell does not have a suitable home for young children. You can't come with us."

She said nothing, wrestling with the fact that she wasn't good enough for Mrs. Mitchell to give her a home. "You're going to live there without me and Henry?" Her voice dropped in pitch, dread diluted her excitement.

"Lizzie, I tried everything I could think of to keep us together." I turned to face her, my despair evident as I braced myself to break her heart. "I've arranged for you to go to the orphan asylum."

"I'm not an orphan!" she screamed, leaping up from the bench. "Papa's alive."

"Lizzie, I'm sorry. We, I, have no choice." Tears welled in my eyes, unbidden.

"I don't understand." Her voice was shrill and loud. "Why do we have to go to an orphan place?"

"It's an orphan asylum," I replied, taking the easy road to correct her inaccuracy instead of addressing her question.

"Whatever you call it, we won't be together."

"There's no other way." Silent tears streamed down my cheeks at losing my brother and sister. "I'm sorry."

Lizzie slumped back on the wall and crossed her arms over her chest.

The silence between us lasted a few minutes, each of us lost in thoughts of a future where we would not see each other every day.

"I'm so sorry, Lizzie." I reached for her hand and gratefully, she let me hold it. "We're lucky we've stayed together this long. We could have gone to the orphan place after Papa left or when Mama died."

She picked at her skirt.

"I promised Papa I'd take care of everyone." I choked on my tears. "You are young and strong and so is Henry." I squeezed her hand and peered down at the tears streaking her own cheeks. "I hate we are going to different places. But Mary. She needs our consideration the most. Going with me means she's cared for and understood. No one knows her better than you or me."

"I don't want her to go to one of those places," she affirmed, wiping her tears with the back of her hand.

"This is a sacrifice for her. And remember, when Papa comes home, we'll all be together again," I said, looking for something cheerful in our future.

Lizzie wasn't convinced. "Papa could get hurt or die."

"He won't..."

Henry interrupted, calling from the landing. "Mary needs help in the kitchen."

The spot where Mary knelt by the garden a few minutes ago was empty.

Lizzie got up. "Stay. I'll go rescue her before Dina does something stupid." She picked up her skirts and climbed the steps.

I still had to explain this to Henry, a four-year-old whose only worry in the world was finding his lost ball. Instead, I had to tell him he was leaving the only home he'd ever known. Mary would be content in the Mitchell house but confused about her missing siblings. I felt confident those two would adapt to their new environments. But Lizzie. Lizzie was my wild card, the one to keep an eye on over the next few weeks.

Chapter Thirty-Eight

Jane handed me a letter from Papa the day after my visit to the asylum.

4 July 1863

Tullahoma, Tennessee

Meine liebe Kinder,

Yesterday we chased rebel troops. Today we march on muddy roads in boots with holes. It has rained every day for two weeks and we worry about crossing the swollen Elk River. Pray for our safe deliverance to the other side.

Pay tickets are delayed again.

You are missed with all my heart,

Papa

Apparently, Papa was unaware of the Decker's deception.

I finished my business with Jane, then asked to speak with her mother. Mrs. Mitchell came into the office and closed the door.

"Lizzie and Henry will go to the orphan asylum," I spit it out like a foul taste in my mouth.

Mrs. Mitchell tilted her head to one side. "I know that's a difficult decision for you."

"It is. But after meeting the Matron, I think they will be in capable hands for the time being."

"I'm glad to hear it. Are you able to accept my offer?"

I grinned. "Yes, I'd like to. Very much."

"Good. Here are the terms."

Terms? I realized I'd agreed without knowing the details. I felt foolish for not asking first.

"Since you and Mary have no experience, I'll pay you two dollars a week and Mary one. You'll have food and will share a room. If after one year, I feel Mary has improved enough, I will pay you each two dollars a week. You'll work Monday through Saturday with Sunday and holidays to do as you please. Do those terms suit you?"

Room and food, and three dollars a week suited me fine.

"I understand how you feel about Mary. She'll need time to learn. I agree."

Mrs. Mitchell raised her chin, glad to have the matter resolved.

"On one condition," I said.

Intrigued, the woman sat back in her chair. "And what might that be?"

"That I continue my mending business. I promise it won't interfere with our work and if it does, I will cut back or quit altogether."

She thought for a long moment. "You'll have to do your deliveries on Sunday, your day off."

"I can arrange that. We'll continue going to church at St. Mattheus. Mary sings in the choir and the ladies we sew for are members."

"When can you start?"

"We'll start the afternoon of August sixth, the day we take the children to the asylum."

"That's agreeable."

Opening the door, Mrs. Mitchell ushered me to the back door. "I hope you'll be happy here, Martha."

As we stepped into the yard where Mary worked in the garden, I dismissed thoughts of my happiness and nodded toward my sister. "She'll be happy here."

On Tuesday, with an intricate and laborious mending job for Jane due on Saturday, I asked Lizzie to deliver the mending to the Hall in my place. "The walk will do you good. Take a penny and buy a sweet for yourself on the way home." With a job on the horizon and no rent to pay, I could afford a penny.

Lizzie smiled at the thought of a treat.

"You remember the way? At Mrs. Eiflert's, go down to Walnut and you'll see the building on the right."

"I remember." We packed the canvas bag, heavy with goods, but Lizzie said she could handle it.

"Go straight there and come straight home," I said. "Once in the Hall, find Mrs. Eiflert. If she's not there, ask for Mrs. Ziegler. The inventory list is in the bag. You should get a dollar thirty-five. See if there's any more work and bring it home. Do you understand?"

She said nothing. I put my hand under her chin and raised her face to look into her eyes. "Be careful and go straight across the canal. Don't loiter on the banks. I've heard of vagrants living there."

"Yes, Martha," she said. Using my formal name assured me she understood, or she was tired of being told what to do.

I expected Lizzie to return around noon, but when the bells chimed the hour, she hadn't appeared. I sat sewing by the window, keeping occupied, but any movement below distracted me until I leaned out to see if it was her or not.

Another hour dragged by. Antsy, I needed to go out and look for her. Without knocking, I opened the bedroom door. "Dina, I'm going to find Lizzie. Come out and watch the children."

I jabbed a pin through my hat, anchoring it to my chignon. The streets were busy. Carriages, drays, and men on horseback going east and west, with no order whatever. Pedestrians walked by on their way to and from the market or running errands. None were Lizzie.

Berating Lizzie in my head as I walked to the hall, my thoughts swung between thrashing her to within an inch of her life and fearing she might be lost or hurt. Oh, God, where is she?

At the Hall, Mrs. Ziegler confirmed Lizzie had been there. "I think around eleven thirty. She gave me the finished things and took another batch. Not very much this week, I'm sorry to say."

"Did she say anything about going anywhere else?" I asked, glancing around the room as if she'd pop out of a barrel or from under a table.

"No, not that I recall," Mrs. Ziegler said. "I'll keep an eye out for her."

"Thank you." I zigzagged through the tables to the door and stepped into the glaring afternoon sun. The clock on the church across the street read half-past one. Two and a half hours since Lizzie left. A simple mending delivery. Why did I send her? I should have taken Mary and done it myself. Why did I think she could be trusted?

I thought of where else she might go. The canal was off limits, but I checked the usual spots where we watched the boats. Nothing. I stopped at Mrs. Eiflert's, but she'd not seen her.

With nowhere else to look, I retraced my steps. My pace to the Hall had been fast, full of hope of finding her, but now I trudged homeward, defeated and scared.

At Linn Street, I quickened my step, eager to get home, to see if she returned. In front of Locke's shop, a man climbed down from his horse. He looked a lot like EB. Maybe the sun played tricks on me, but the stature and movements of the man were very much like EB, the way he swung the reins under the hitching post, wrapping themselves around twice.

A half block from the man and his horse, I squinted. In the

saddle, someone leaned down as the EB-like man grasped his passenger at the waist and set them down on the sidewalk.

"Lizzie?"

Shading my eyes, I hurried to the man and the small person. The one lifted from the saddle, faced me, eyes wide, biting her lip.

"Lizzie?" I said, her presence a miracle.

"Martha," a male voice interrupted my disbelief.

Swiveling, I saw it was indeed EB. "Dear Lord! Lizzie! EB!" I stood rooted, shocked and struggling to comprehend the scene before me. My sister had been on a horse with EB. What in the world?

Closing my eyes, I shook my head, as if to wake myself from a dream. When I opened them, the man and the girl were still there. Relief swept over me and at that moment, I didn't care why she'd been gone so long.

I scooped her up, crushing her to my chest, peppering her hair and cheeks with kisses, silently thanking every power that brought her home safe and sound.

"You're all right?" I pulled back and examined her, my eyes raking over her face, her body, ensuring no harm had come to her.

Lizzie slipped her arms around me, shaking her head.

Over my sister's head, I met EB's gaze and mouthed, "What?"

He shrugged. "I found her in our stable."

My mouth dropped open, then shut, then opened again as I sorted through a multitude of questions about his declaration.

"Motty, I'm tired," Lizzie said, dropping her arms from my shoulders to get her feet on the ground.

"Where were you? What happened? I was so scared."

"With EB. I'm fine. I had to do something." Her responses

258

yielded no useful information.

"Martha, if you'll permit me to intervene," EB said, putting a hand on Lizzie's shoulder. "I think going upstairs would be best for her. You and I can talk."

"No, I want to hear what happened from her." Putting my hand under her chin, I lifted it, so she had to look at me. "I was scared to death. You were gone too long. I had thoughts no one should ever think."

"I'm sorry," Lizzie sighed. "I didn't mean to worry you. It's just. Just that I had to…I had to see." Her words drifted off, her meaning incomplete.

"See what?" I asked, determined to know, needing to understand what was so important to go off like that.

"The orphan place. I had to see where I'm going to live."

"You went to the asylum?" I gasped at the outrageousness of the act.

"Let's talk in the yard." EB grabbed my elbow and directed us from the sidewalk, where passersby dodged past.

In the yard, Lizzie asked again. "Can I go upstairs? I want to see Henry and Mary."

Grabbing her and holding her tight for a few moments, I released her and watched her climb the steps.

I walked to the stone bench in the yard, shock and confusion covering me like a heavy cloak.

EB followed. "She's a resourceful young girl," he said.

"I forgot," I murmured. "I forgot how curious she is, how she searches for information until satisfied."

EB, next to me, removed his hat, and held it on his lap. "I think you figured out why she did what she did."

"Yes, but why didn't you let me know she was with you? I was worried sick!"

He raised his hands, palms out. "She said you sent her. That I was to take her and bring her home."

"And you believed her?" I scowled at his innocence.

He hung his head, twirling his hat between his fingers. "I realize now I made a mistake. But putting that aside, let me tell you what happened. Then you can be mad at me or Lizzie or the entire world. All right?"

"Fine. Leave nothing out."

"I came home for dinner as usual and when I entered the stable, she was there saying she needed to go to the orphan place. Said you thought it a good idea for her to see it firsthand and I was to take her.

"Thinking I should honor your request, I set Lizzie in front of me on Goldie, and we were off. I knew its location, having been to Mt. Auburn many times. Once there, I settled her in a rocking chair and got a girl to fetch the Matron. I admired the view from the porch while Lizzie watched the children on the front lawn. A group of boys played tag, and some girls had a hopscotch game going. I think that's what it's called. The girl who went to find Matron asked Lizzie to play and she was gone in an instant.

"Matron came out and I explained our visit. She knew Lizzie was coming in a few weeks and was happy to give us a tour. I must tell you Martha, after speaking with Matron and watching the comings and goings of the children, it's an excellent place. If I were your Papa, I'd be relieved to know they are in good hands."

"Yes, I think he would approve. What happened next?"

"Lizzie returned and met Matron, who asked a few questions. What she liked to eat, her favorite games, and school subjects.

"Matron showed us the grounds, the outbuildings, and the kitchen, where girls of all ages prepared food. We visited the dining hall then the library, where hundreds of books were shelved floor to ceiling. By far her favorite, she said she could spend hours and hours in the library and never tire of it.

"Matron told Lizzie she looked forward to her stay. I liked she said stay instead of live, acknowledging her time there was temporary. Our tour finished, we said goodbye, climbed on Goldie, and rode here.

"Now you can be mad at me. But don't be mad at Lizzie. If you were in her place, you'd want to know where you were going, who would be there, and if you were going to like it or not."

"I only wish she'd told me. I could have taken her myself."

"She knows that. But for a girl who has absolutely no control over what happens to her, she needed to be in charge of something." EB's head tipped toward me as if he had a secret to tell. "She doesn't want you to worry about her."

"Not worry about her? Of course, I worry. She ran off without a word."

"She wanted to like the orphan place so you could stop worrying. And lucky for her, and you, she does." He ended on a confident note.

"I couldn't have asked anyone better than you to take her," I said, then teased, "except maybe Jane."

"I'm starving," he said, rising from the bench.

I thought to offer him something, but not in our rooms. No. I couldn't let him up there.

He saved me the trouble. "I'll be off. See you on Saturday."

"Oh! EB," I said, staying his progress toward his horse. "Could I impose on you to help me get the children to the asylum on the sixth of August? That's when they are going."

"I'll let you know for sure on Saturday."

"Then you can bring Mary and me to your house. That's also the day we move in with you and your family."

"I look forward to seeing you both in our home."

I followed him to his horse. He swung into the saddle and tipped his hat. "Good day."

"Thank you," I said and watched him bounce in the saddle as Goldie trotted away.

Glancing up, I caught my siblings' faces pressed against the windowpanes and managed a weak wave. At the bottom of the stairs, I paused to sort out my feelings.

In two weeks, Lizzie and Henry would sleep where I didn't, where I couldn't hear their calls for comfort in the night. No more kisses on skinned knees. No hugs when a friend turned to foe or to celebrate an achievement.

Lizzie had every right to know where she was going. The signs were there, but I missed them. I hadn't considered how to help her with this monumental change, make her feel safe among strangers. Despite the way she went about accomplishing her goal, I was proud of her determination, curiosity, and courage. Qualities I envied. She would have a childhood. Maybe not in the same house as me, but she would get to live as a young girl should, with dreams of pretty dresses, boys, and fancy parties. Perhaps the orphan place would be a pleasant part of her journey to womanhood, and I could rest easy on that score.

Chapter Thirty-Nine

The days leading up to our move blurred in a flurry of sorting and packing. We donated clothes we'd outgrown and Mama's few dresses to the Hall. I placed her remaining keepsakes, a tarnished cross, letters from Bavaria, her mourning shawl, and a handful of mysterious buttons into her sewing basket. Henry left his toys with Gus, except his beloved blocks. Lizzie boxed up our modest book collection, planning to deposit them into the asylum library. Mary and I packed our sewing baskets, Mama's quilts, and the lap desk. Papa's handmade sled, a relic of our childhood winters, tugged at my heart as we left it behind, a casualty of the move.

Mrs. Mitchell's invitation to celebrate Lizzie's birthday and spend the night at their home was a welcome kindness, solving multiple dilemmas at once. It offered a chance to mark Lizzie's special day away from Dina's watchful eyes and provided Henry and Lizzie a glimpse of Mary's and my home.

The morning of our departure dawned with my whisper to Mary, "Today, we say goodbye to Dina."

Her gleeful chant of "No more Dina" echoed through the last of our packing, Lizzie and I struggling to maintain composure as Dina's face flushed crimson.

As EB's wagon appeared at the curb, Lizzie's eyes swept the front room one last time. "I'll miss this place," she murmured, her voice thick with emotion. "I had my Mama and my Papa here." The weight of her words hung in the air.

My siblings gathered their belongings and descended the stairs, leaving behind the only home they'd ever known.

I leaned out the window and yelled to EB at the curb, "Here they come!"

"Good luck," I said over my shoulder to Dina, plucking my hat from the rack, the last of my possessions.

Her voice wavered. "I see you sometime?"

"No. I don't think so." We had no reason to cross paths, our joint mending finished.

"I come Mitchell house." A furtive gaze crept into her eyes.

"No," I said sternly. "That is my place of employment and not for you to visit. If you want to see me, come to St. Mattheus on Sundays." I regretted the invitation as soon as it left my mouth.

"Yes, I come," Dina said, eager to express her desire to see me.

My fingers brushed the kitchen doorjamb where Papa had etched our growth, the final marks made on Mary's birthday before he enlisted. I was fourteen, Mary twelve, Lizzie seven, and Henry two. Rubbing my fingers over the pencil marks, I pictured us lined up, stiff and tall against the jamb. We grew up in these rooms, once brimming with love, joy and family. Now, all that remained were memories. Some, like Mama's death, were painful to recall, while others filled me with melancholy and longing for what should have been.

I shut the door on our old life, the click of the latch final and heavy. Our wagon joined the flow of carriages and drays, the children's excited chatter rising above the din of the city street. Their joy was a stark counterpoint to the ache in my chest. Every familiar storefront and street corner we passed felt like another goodbye. This neighborhood had been our battlefield - where we'd scraped and saved, where I'd fought to keep us together. Now we were leaving it all behind. The thought of starting anew, without Lizzie and Henry, pressed down on me like a physical weight.

The short journey to the Mitchells' passed in my haze of

bittersweet memories and anxious anticipation. Before I knew it, we were in the stable, unloading our meager possessions.

I gasped when EB lifted the sled from the wagon bed.

"Where did that come from?" I asked.

"Henry begged me to bring it. I figure we can go sledding on the hill at the asylum."

As EB joked with the children and directed the unloading, an unbidden thought startled me. I loved this man. Instantly, I recoiled, rationalizing it as the love between friends, akin to my feelings for Jane. Not boy and girl love. The kind you had for someone you trusted and cared for.

Thrusting that uncomfortable thought aside, I led the children up the back stairs to our room. Jane arrived with extra blankets and pillows. "When you're settled, come down to the kitchen. We'll tell you the plan for the day."

Two beds flanked opposite walls, a high round window barely illuminating the otherwise shadowy room. Lizzie sprawled spreadeagle on the down-filled mattress while Henry, delighted by the springy bed, bounced gleefully, sending feathers drifting like lazy snowflakes. We stored things and clopped down the steps to the kitchen.

Mrs. Mitchell laid out the plan. "First, we have a few things to do to get ready. Rose has already gone off to get married, so we must all pitch in. Mary, can you go out to the garden and get some carrots? Martha, you and Lizzie put a tablecloth on the table and help Jane set it. Henry, let me think." She tapped her finger against her cheek.

The swinging door whooshed open as EB strode in.

"EB!" she grabbed his arm. "Henry needs a job. How about something in the stables?"

"Sure," he said, rolling his eyes at his mother. "Let's go Henry, I'm sure there's a horse we can feed. Or something."

Mrs. Mitchell chuckled.

The next hour flew by in a flurry of dinner preparations. Mrs. Mitchell called everyone to the table, and we took the same seats as the day Amelia was born.

Cook served a sumptuous meal of pork chops, apple sauce, and carrots. After we finished, Mrs. Mitchell brought in a cherry pie and a bowl heaped high with heavy cream topping.

Henry's eyes nearly popped out of his head. "Oh my."

"Mrs. Mitchell, we have a birthday ritual. Do you mind if we do it before pie is served?" I asked.

"Not at all. I'm curious." She pulled the pie and topping to the side.

I laid the Geburtstagkranz in the center of the table, put a candle in ten and one in eleven.

"Do you have a match?" I looked at the adults.

Jane opened a drawer in the sideboard and handed me a box. I scratched a match, then put it to each of the candles. "Mary, will you lead the birthday song?"

Mary sang the first notes. Henry and I added our voices. Glancing around the table, I could see that neither EB, Jane, nor Mrs. Mitchell knew the German words, but they bobbed their heads in time with the beat.

Lizzie radiated joy, her gaze fixed on the flickering candles, oblivious to the world around her. I knew she was considering her wish, which she took seriously. Last year, Mama's death overshadowed her birthday, and this one had another black cloud. Lizzie's birthday, from here on, would evoke memories of loss and significant change.

We waited as the candle wax dripped down the sides.

"What are we waiting for?" Jane asked.

Lizzie pointed to each of the candles. "This one is to be thankful for last year. The one is to make a wish for the coming year. I have lots of wishes to choose from." Her brow furrowed, mouth twitching in indecision. Then she set her jaw and blew out the candles. I wondered what she wished for.

"Me. Birthday!" Mary poked her index finger into her chest. I relit the candles, pushed the wreath over to Mary, and she started the birthday song.

The Mitchells exchanged puzzled glances before turning to me. I raised a finger, silently urging them to wait as we finished the song. They sang along, the words repetitive and easy to remember. Mary blew out the candles, not bothering with wishes or nonsense like that. Everyone applauded.

"Why?" Mrs. Mitchell asked.

"Mary loves birthdays. We sing the song and light the candles for her on every birthday."

"So, let's see. She's about eighty in birthday years!" EB chuckled.

Everyone laughed as Jane served the pie.

Later, in our room, we decided Henry and Mary would sleep in one bed with Lizzie and me in the other. After arranging blankets and pillows, we huddled on the floor, recounting the day's events in hushed tones.

"Look!" Henry pointed to the wall, where a half-moon shone through the round window.

A memory of a school lesson surfaced. The waxing moon was

symbolic in some cultures, representing abundance or prosperity. In other traditions, it was linked to new beginnings. Was the moon signaling that change was required to be prosperous? The notion lingered until Henry yawned and we knelt for prayers.

Tucking Lizzie under my arm, I snuggled close, facing Mary and Henry on the other side of the aisle. I loved seeing them, us, together. Sorrow engulfed me as I pondered when we'd next share a room, a home.

"Motty?" Lizzie asked.

"Mmm?"

"Papa's definitely coming home, right?"

I wrestled with how to answer. "He'll do his best," I offered.

"But if he doesn't, because, um, something happens, we'll be all right, won't we?" She fiddled with the string on her nightdress, betraying her anxiety.

"I can promise you this. As I've done since Papa left, since Mama got sick, I will take care of you. There is nothing I won't do to keep you safe until Papa gets home."

She nodded. "You can let me take care of Henry. I'll keep him safe." "She rolled to face me, her features solemn in the shadowy moonlight.

"Are you old enough, strong enough, to handle his crying and grumbling when he doesn't get his way?"

Lizzie laughed, "Well, maybe the nurses can help."

"I think that's a fine compromise," I said. "Ready to close your eyes?"

"Good night."

We rose early as EB needed to get to his office. After a quick

268

breakfast, I made sure Henry and Lizzie had everything in the wagon. They said goodbye to Jane and Mrs. Mitchell, who gave them kisses and a bag of sweets.

Near the crest of Mount Auburn, Lizzie pointed to the asylum. "Henry, there it is! Our new home."

"It's gigantic!" his mouth formed an O as his eyes took it the building and the grounds.

EB halted the wagon at the porch steps and said, "You find Matron. I'll stay with them."

At the top of the steps, I glanced over my shoulder and saw EB pointing to something as the children took in the view. I heard the words snow and sled, and Henry looked up at him as if he were a god.

I found Matron in her office, and she came out to greet everyone. Henry, shy and awkward at meeting the woman, clung to my skirt.

"Let me show you to your rooms, get your things put away, and take a quick tour. Would that be all right, Henry?"

He nodded. We climbed to the third floor and entered a room with single beds lining three sides, a large open area in the middle.

"A bed to myself?" Henry asked in awe, when we stopped at the foot of a well-made bed.

"All yours. This is for your clothes," Matron said, pointing to a small trunk at the bottom of the bed. "I warn you, that all toys are shared. It's not fair for one child to have something the others do not."

Henry nodded. "That's all right. I know how to share."

We stowed Lizzie's stuff in her room on the second floor, the same layout as Henry's. Her bed was on the end, closest to the door.

We walked about the grounds, taking in the stable and other

outbuildings. The tour ended on the wraparound porch, and it was time to say goodbye.

I knelt before my brother, so small, too young. "Henry, my darling, I will visit you every other Sunday." If I cried, I'd be lost. "I know you will be a good boy. Lizzie is here, and you'll see her all the time."

He nodded. "I'll be good." Then a thought struck him. "Where will you sleep? Will you be here too, like Lizzie?"

"Remember last night, the room we slept in? That's where Mary and I will sleep." I bowed my head, gathering the strength to leave this boy with virtual strangers. "I'll be here," I said, pointing to his head. "And here," my finger touching the place over his heart. "Just as you will be in my head and heart."

Henry sniffed and tried not to let the tears come. But one or two escaped and rolled down his cheeks. I brushed them away and kissed his pretty mouth. He kissed me back, throwing his tiny arms around my neck. I clutched him briefly, for if I held on too long, I feared I would be unable to let go.

"Mary, say goodbye to Henry." I nudged him toward his sister.

"Bye Henry," she waved to him. She didn't understand the profoundness of this moment, but Lizzie did and guided her into Henry's arms.

Leaving Lizzie proved easier than I imagined. Or so she wanted me to believe. Perhaps a ruse, she seemed happy to be staying at the asylum. Perhaps she refused to show me how much her heart hurt. We parted with only a few tears, mostly mine. Mary waved, but Lizzie hugged her sister like she'd never see her again. Mary would have a hard time in the next few days without her sister and brother, so I left them, stepping from the porch to join EB at the wagon.

"I'll be back on Sunday for sure. Is that all right, EB?" I checked with him to ensure he could bring us.

"That's fine, but at some point, I think you'll have to learn how to drive a horse and buggy yourself. I'll speak with Mother."

I glanced back to the porch. Lizzie walked with Mary down the steps, then touched her finger to her lips and placed it on Mary's cheek. Mary returned the kiss, and they embraced once more.

Lizzie handed Mary over to me, then grabbed me in a fierce hug. "Goodbye Motty," she said, her voice muffled against my body.

"Let's not say goodbye. How about, see you soon?" I tipped her face up to mine, planted a kiss on her forehead, and swatted her bottom. "Off you go."

As EB flicked the reins, Mary and I waved to my beloved sister and brother, half-orphans, half of my family.

"See you soon!" I yelled as the wagon rolled around the circular drive toward the exit.

"Soon!" Mary waved until the children were specks on the horizon.

PART THREE

Chapter Forty

Nestled in our attic room, I tossed and turned, yearning for Henry and Lizzie's soft snores and sleepy babble. Instead, door hinges creaked, boots thudded on carpeted stairs, and muted voices drifted up from below. I wondered if my siblings had settled in, minded their manners, obeyed the staff.

Mary awoke disoriented and searched under the beds and in the wardrobe. "Henwy? Wizzie?"

"They're in their new home. We'll see them soon," I said.

Soon had no relevance for Mary. I devised a simple method of making a soap mark on the mirror, one for each day leading up to a visit, and erased one each morning. By the third morning, jumping out of bed, Mary did the erasing.

Under EB's guidance, I learned to handle the horse and buggy. On the second Sunday after leaving the children, we went to church. Mary sang with the choir, I exchanged mending with Mrs. Eiflert, and steered Goldie up the hill. As the asylum loomed into view, a broad smile stretched across Mary's face, her eyes glimmering with recognition.

The children were excited to see us, and I noted no trace of regret. Lizzie attended public school while Henry learned his letters and numbers in a room with children his age. In his assignment of kitchen helper, he took out the garbage, retrieved water from the well, and obeyed the commands of the kitchen staff. Lizzie asked Matron if she could straighten the library shelves and alphabetize the books by subject or author and Matron, pleased with the outcome, assigned Lizzie the permanent duty of librarian.

Matron reported good behavior except for minor infractions, such as talking after lights out or running in the halls. She noted they were a delightful addition to the home's ninety-two other children.

Life at Mitchell House was packed with duties echoing our Linn Street routines, but on a grander scale. We made and changed beds, set and cleared the table, managed the laundry, and helped Cook in the kitchen. Mending, once a paid activity, became another duty.

We learned the basics, and I supervised Mary with new tasks until she mastered them. Sometimes Cook gave Mary instructions, but when Mary's words weren't clear, I was asked to translate. She responded well to Mrs. Mitchell, who used simple words and demonstrated how to do something rather than just explaining it.

I protected Mary from sinister glances and snide comments by keeping her busy in the kitchen during meal service. She practiced serving and clearing at the noon meal when the diners were limited to the Mitchell family.

But we did had run-ins with guests. Once, as Mary scrubbed the entryway floor on her hands and knees, the heavy front door swung open, toppling the pail, causing water to spill across the floor. Hearing the metal bucket clink on the tiles, I rushed in from the kitchen and skidded to a stop at the edge of spreading water. A young man stood in the puddle, his face a mix of surprise and bewilderment.

"Don't move," I commanded.

Before I could reenter the kitchen to fetch a mop, the man said, "Why don't you get up? You're all wet."

Returning to the scene in less than ten seconds, I dropped the mop head on the spreading water.

"You're stupid!" The man said. He'd moved from the floor to the bottom step of the stairway.

"What's going on?" I asked as I hurriedly mopped the floor, squeezed the water into the bucket, and mopped again.

"She's just sitting there. Soaking wet. What's wrong with her?"

"I'm sorry, sir. We'll be out of your way in a moment."

"Doesn't she talk?"

"Yes, she does. What do you want her to say?" I focused on mopping, lest my face reveal my growing irritation.

At my question, I caught him off guard. "I don't know, something, anything, an apology, I suppose."

"Mary, tell the man you're sorry his shoes got wet." I frowned at the shallow patch of water under his shoes.

"Sorry. Shoes," Mary pointed to the man's shoes, spattered with mud.

"That's it?" A flip of his wrist asked for more.

Eager to avoid getting Mrs. Mitchell involved, I changed my tack. "Mr.?" I asked.

"Franklin. Ambrose Franklin," he replied, with a hint of arrogance, as if he shared the same bloodline as the famous Benjamin Franklin.

"Mr. Franklin, I'm Martha. Please accept our apologies for the mishap. If you like, I'll polish your shoes to make things right."

"Now that's the ticket!" he said. "I accept." He took off one shoe, then the other, and placed them on the step. "I expect them done by supper."

"Yes sir," I replied, as he tromped up the stairs. I offered a mock salute to his retreating form as he vanished around the bend.

We mopped the foyer with no lasting damage. I sent Mary to change out of her wet skirt and stockings, while I figured out how to shine the shoes. I recalled one of Mama's tricks: warm a small sliver of lard in your palm, work it in with a soft cloth, and buff.

As I used a damp cloth to clean the seams and uppers, Mrs. Mitchell came in, but I failed to hide the shoes in time before she peered over my shoulder. I explained what happened with Mr. Franklin and that shining his shoes would make amends.

"You're doing this because he tipped the bucket over?" Mrs. Mitchell asked.

"It wasn't his fault. And Mary didn't get up and out of the way like he thought she should," I said.

Mrs. Mitchell's eyebrows drew in over her eyes, creasing the skin between her eyebrows. "Still, that's no reason to clean a man's shoes. Give them to me."

"I'm nearly done," I said. "If his shoes are polished as promised, perhaps he'll be more understanding of Mary's behavior in the future."

Mrs. Mitchell laid a hand on my shoulder. "You are wise beyond your years, Martha. All right, I'll do as you say, but if any boarder ever confronts you or Mary in the future, you must tell me right away."

"I will."

I finished the shoes. The next day, as Mr. Franklin strode toward the dining room, he acknowledged me with a nod and a crisp, "Good morning, Martha."

Two letters arrived from Papa. In the first, he supported my decision to put the children in the asylum and praised my efforts to ensure their safety and care.

The second arrived a week later, recounting his regiment's preparations for what appeared to be a major engagement with the enemy. They camped in Tennessee near Chattanooga, a few miles from the Georgia border where a great number of supplies had arrived, the entire Army of the Cumberland drilling day and night. The same day the letter arrived, Cincinnati newspapers reported a battle in Chickamauga, Georgia, where heavy casualties were expected. Battle news trickled in, and anxiety for Papa's safety gnawed at me. EB delivered the paper daily, and I devoured every article, as Papa and I had scrutinized the Republikaner when the war began. A full week elapsed before the Army supplied the number of casualties to the papers. Six hundred killed and two thousand injured.

As the military updated their grim tally, Union losses mounted: seventeen hundred men killed and eight thousand wounded over two bloody days in the forests near Chickamauga Creek. In early October, the names of officers and staff killed and wounded filled two columns, representing regiments from nine states in the Union.

With Papa's fate uncertain, I was grateful for household routines, finding solace in familiar duties. On Sunday, we drove the buggy to church, a bag of mending on the seat between us. Our earnings were a dollar or two a week, which I added to the pay from Mrs. Mitchell. With few expenses, the money tin held thirty dollars. At this rate, I'd have a tidy sum saved for our own place when Papa mustered out and we rescued the children.

The congregation buzzed with news of the battle. Women who had donned cheerful blues and greens the previous week now wore somber black from head to toe. Mrs. Stickler, the woman who bartered pork for mending, cried in fits and starts throughout the service, mourning her son's death. Mrs. Eiflert had no news of Frank. Reverend Knochelmann consoled the mourners, gave hope to those who had no news, and led us in prayer for all the brave men from our community.

I exchanged mending for the Hall with Mrs. Eiflert, who promised to let me know if she heard anything from her son. I loosened Goldie's reins from the hitching post when someone shouted my name.

"Martha!" Dina's voice, familiar but different somehow, halted my preparations for our journey to the asylum.

She dragged Gus by the hand and cradled Amelia in one arm. "Wait, please."

"Hello," I said cautiously. Dina's appearance startled me. Wisps of unkempt hair escaped her bonnet. Baby milk darkened her bodice, and her skirt was dotted with stains. She'd been crying, her eyes red, nose pink, and cheeks pale and drawn.

"Are you all right?" I asked, not wanting to care but unable to help myself.

"Joe." She wailed, letting go of Gus's hand to adjust the baby. "He dead."

"Oh, no." Nausea surged through me, and I steadied myself against the buggy. "Papa?"

"I not know." She shrugged. "But my Joe. Killed at that Chicka place. Captain Gluchowski write me."

"I'm sorry, Dina." I wanted to console her, but she and Joe had done irreparable harm to my family.

She sniffed loudly. "He no meet Amelia." Dina tucked her forehead against the baby's. "Gus have no father. What I do?"

Wary of entanglement in her troubles, I shook my head. "I don't know."

"Henry and Lizzie?" switching from her troubles to inquiring about my siblings caught me off balance.

"They are well," I said. "We miss them, of course."

"That good. Your job?"

What was she fishing for? "It's good."

"Oh." Dina sniffed again, less dramatic than the last. "You come back. Live with me." Her tone commanding, not inquiring.

A startled laugh escaped me. "You must be out of your mind!"

"No money, how we live?"

"I don't know, but I'm not supporting you." I turned my back and climbed into the buggy beside Mary.

"Martha, I sorry. Please. Help." Her cries pricked at my heart, for there were two innocent children involved.

"Ask Mrs. Eiflert." It was all I could think to tell her.

I tapped the switch on the horse's flanks, and we pulled away. I didn't look back, but Mary did. "Dina. Sad."

My heart ached for Gus and Amelia at the loss of their father. Wondering if we'd lost ours too, I prayed that no news about Papa was good news.

Chapter Forty-One

In the days that followed, reports on the Battle of Chickamauga dwindled to a trickle. The papers reported that General Rosecrans, having blundered the pursuit of the Rebels, with loss of life second only to Gettysburg, was removed from command. General Henry Thomas, the commander of Papa's brigade, replaced him at Chattanooga, where the Army of the Cumberland took up residence in defense of the city and struggled to oust the enemy from southern Tennessee for good.

A few days after I'd seen Dina at church, a knock at the front door interrupted my preparations for marketing with Cook. I'd inherited Rose's duty of greeting visitors and learning their intentions. Removing my apron, I tidied my hair and opened the front door a foot or so, assessing the visitor as taught by Mrs. Mitchell.

A young soldier stood on the porch. My mind flashed to Dina receiving news of Joe, and I bit my lip, struggling to contain my rising panic.

"May I help you?" I asked, trembling.

The soldier removed his cap and offered me a white envelope. "I have a message for Miss Martha Hesch."

No, no, no. My head twitched, defying the news. I withdrew from the doorway, unable to face what the envelope might contain.

"Is Miss Hesch here?" he asked. "If not, I can leave it with you."

"Please, no, please," I stuttered. I wanted to hide, to cover my head with a pillow, and make believe I was dreaming.

The soldier shifted from foot to foot. "I'll just put it right here, on the floor."

I watched him place the envelope at my feet. He shoved his cap onto his head, then said before leaving the porch, "I'm sorry, Ma'am."

I closed the door, my eyes fixed on the stark white envelope lying undisturbed at my feet. Swallowing, I leaned over and saw my name scrawled across the middle over the Mitchell's address. I examined it further, and it looked different from any letter I'd received before. It had no stamp or postmark. At the top left corner, printed, not handwritten, the return address said Washington Park Hospital.

Washington Park Hospital? The one by the canal? My paralysis lifted. I scooped up the envelope and tore it open. Glancing at the salutation, I recognized Papa's handwriting and the loveliest words I'd ever seen. "Dearest daughter." Clutching the paper to my breast, I raised my eyes to the ceiling and thanked God. The letter was dated today. I wiped my tears with the back of my hand and read his beautiful words.

> At Chickamauga, I injured my leg and, unable to walk, the enemy captured me. Me and Lieutenant Kuester, an officer in my company, were taken to the Rebel camp along with hundreds of other Union men. After caring for my wound and finding it not serious, Kuester arranged a prisoner exchange which required me to swear I'd never fight against the Rebels again. The exchange took place in Chattanooga, and now I am here at Washington Park. Please come when you can. If you have not heard, Joe Decker was killed on the battlefield.

Putting all thought of going to the market aside, I gave the letter to Mrs. Mitchell and asked if I could visit him today.

"We have an important event this evening," she said, returning the letter. "If he's at the hospital, he'll not be going anywhere today."

Disappointed, I went about my duties. Thoughts of Papa coming home for good raced around my head. My day off tomorrow, I'd visit, and plan for our future.

Mary and I walked to the temporary hospital built at the start of the war for injured or sick soldiers returning home or destinations beyond. At the entrance to the one-story pine edifice on the south end of the park, I told the man behind the desk that we were there to see George Hesch, of the Ninth Ohio. He found Papa's name in a ledger and signaled to a woman wearing a dark green dress covered by a stained apron.

"Please take these young ladies to see Private Hesch. He's in Ward One," the soldier said.

"I know him." She introduced herself. "I'm Mrs. Wolfe."

The woman led us down a narrow corridor. The smell of fresh pine barely recognizable, other odors, putrid and foul, assailed our nostrils, reminding me of our rooms during the last days of Mama's life.

Mary covered her nose with her gloved hand. "Stinky!"

Barely tolerating the stench, I followed Mrs. Wolfe into a room where an acrid blend of urine and feces made my eyes water. I held a gloved hand over my nose, but it did little good.

"You get used to it," Mrs. Wolfe noted and led us down the aisle of a room lined with five beds on each side. Lit only by the light coming through a single window on the north, a square of park greenery beyond it offered a pleasant view.

I scanned the beds for Papa.

Just as Mrs. Wolfe pointed to the bed at the end nearest the window, I saw him. Propped up by a pillow, he wore a dingy gray undershirt. His beard, streaked with gray and thicker than ever, covered his face. Greasy, lank hair straggled past his chin, and his cheeks were red and raw from prolonged exposure to the sun.

Taking caution not to scare him, I approached the bed and whispered. "Papa?"

His head shot around, eyes squinting in confusion. Recognizing me, his white teeth emerged from the gap in his beard. His arms opened, and I threw myself into them.

"Motty! How good it is to see you," he mumbled into my hair, one hand caressing my head, the other rubbing my back. He reached for Mary.

"Papa!" she shouted and fell upon him, hugging him and me at the same time.

"Oh, my dear, dear girls," he breathed. "I've missed you."

Tears streaming down my cheeks, I disengaged myself from his arms and stood beside the bed, basking in the sight of him. I couldn't be sure if I cried with relief, happiness, or the dam of my emotions, held in check for months, had burst at his return. Papa was home and everything would be right again.

"Papa, are you hurt badly?" I asked through the blur of my watery lashes.

He pulled the sheet back, exposing a white bandage on his left thigh, just above the knee, a yellow spot staining the center.

"The doctor says it's nearly healed," he replied. "A cannonball blew the limbs off a tree, and the explosion drove a branch into my leg like an arrow shot from a bow."

"Papa, ow?" Mary asked, touching the edge of the cloth.

"It hurt at first, but now only when I walk. The bandage will come off soon." He covered his leg.

"I'm sorry about Joe." I laid a hand on his arm.

His face crumpled. "I still can't believe he's gone."

"What happened?" I asked.

"We held off the Rebs all morning. Then Kammerling ordered us to drop our knapsacks and ready ourselves for a charge into the woods. On the Captain's command, we entered the forest, bullets whizzing all around us. Joe and I advanced together. He went to one tree, and I took another further ahead." Papa paused, wet his lips, and started again. "I waited for him to pass, but seconds ticked by with no sign. I called out, my voice drowned by gunfire and screams, but Joe didn't reply. I returned to the tree I'd hidden behind previously and found him lying on the ground, staring blankly at the sky. Blood gushed from his chest. He'd been shot in the heart."

I wanted to think kindly of Joe, but the gambling debt he'd forced on Dina still stung like salt in a wound.

Papa struggled for composure. "We left him there. Couldn't get any of our dead out of the forest with the enemy breathing down our necks. I don't know if he's been buried or not."

"Dina is distraught," I said. "She asked if I would move back in with her."

Papa tilted his head, curious to hear my answer.

"Not in a hundred years," I scoffed at the idea. "After all she did? Joe too. No. It's unforgivable."

"Joe didn't know she used your money. He swore it." Papa defended his friend.

"Not according to Dina. But it doesn't matter now, does it? My family's been torn apart because of the actions of people we trusted."

"I'll speak with her about it. I need to tell her something for Joe."

Turning my thoughts to the future, I perched my backside on the bed. "What happens now? With you?"

"As for my injury, I'm here until the doctor releases me."

"Oh. Then you're done with the Army?" Was it possible he was home for good?

"No, not quite," he said. "I have the rest of my enlistment to serve. Six months."

"You'll have to go back to your regiment? And fight?" I slipped from pure happiness to genuine fear of him facing the enemy again.

"The oath I took prevents me from fighting. I don't know where I'll be stationed after I'm released from the hospital."

"Since you're not fighting anymore, why can't you quit? I see lots of soldiers in town." My ambition for him to come home and make us a family outweighed the fact that his enlistment would be over in mere months. "The Army be damned. We need you!"

"Motty, you'll not swear!" he admonished, eyes flickering with a spark of rage.

"My cursing is all you got out of what I just said?" I challenged.

"No, but cursing at me is disrespectful."

"So," I folded my arms over my chest. "When are we going to be a family again? Get Lizzie and Henry out of the asylum?"

"I don't know. I can't just walk away from the Army," he said. "Everyone is fine where they are. When my time is up, I'll figure it out.

"Since you can't fight, what will you do?" Would he just sit around when he could be home, earn a living, and take care of us?

"I've requested duty at Camp Dennison. I think I'll be here a few more weeks before I get transferred. We can spend some time together. Maybe the little ones can visit me."

"Don't distract me with visits. I kept my promise, Papa. I expect you to keep yours. Cost me my girlhood, but here we are." I wanted to hurt him, to pierce his indifference with my sewing needle.

"You're just sixteen! You have lots of girlhood left," Papa replied.

"How is that? I'm in charge of Mary. We work six days a week from five in the morning until eight at night. I take in mending to save a few extra pennies, and as you can see, I don't have time for girlhood!" I challenged him, my voice rising with repressed rage.

When he did not respond, the sounds of the hospital ward filtered into earshot, reminding me he shared the room with other wounded soldiers. Men coughed, moaned, and spoke to each other. They paid no attention to us despite my raised voice.

"Papa," I took charge of the conversation, as he had nothing to say for himself. "It's time for you to make good on your promise," I said, putting emphasis on your.

Papa's head shot up. His eyes bore into me.

I wasn't done. "When you muster out, you'll find a job, a place for us to live, and we'll be a family again." I rattled off my thoughts on what he needed to do to satisfy the promise.

"And what if I can't make that promise?" He glared, icy blue eyes squinting, his mouth pursed in defiance.

Shocked at his retort, I recoiled as if he'd slapped me. "Can't or won't? What in the world is wrong with you, Papa?"

"I don't have to make promises to you. You are my child, not my boss." Indignation spurted from his mouth.

Tired and fed up with my father's inability to understand our loss, our suffering and that this family was his responsibility, I turned to Mary, who, for the entire time, watched my father and me attack each other.

"It's time to go, Mary. Say goodbye to Papa."

"Papa, bye," she gave him one of her kisses. I grabbed her hand from his face and yanked her away.

"We'll visit next Sunday," I called over my shoulder. "Maybe by then, you'll come to your senses and take charge of your family."

As we walked away, I heard him say under his breath, "We'll see about that."

We visited Papa twice more at Washington Park Hospital and on both occasions, I held my tongue, keeping the hope of his homecoming tucked away like a skeleton in the closet. His wound healed as expected and on our second visit, his bandage was removed. We took a turn with him through the park, a chilly day foretelling fall's procession into winter. Our conversation didn't stray beyond talk of living and working at the boarding house, the children's activities at the asylum, and news of the war.

I invited him to attend church with us on Sunday, and then to the asylum as he'd yet to see the children.

He agreed. "It will be nice to see them and some of my old friends."

Mary and I arrived in the buggy, excited about our outing with Papa. At the front desk, a soldier said he wasn't there. He'd been transferred to Camp Dennison Hospital.

"What? When did he leave?"

The man checked his book. "Yesterday."

Mary asked, "Papa?"

"He's gone." Then I had a thought. "Can I see Mrs. Wolfe? Is she here today?"

The soldier left his post and returned with the woman following on his heels.

"Hello. What can I do for you?" Something in her eyes held a warning. Or was it regret?

"We made plans to go to church today with my father, but he's not here. Do you know what happened?"

Mrs. Wolfe motioned us to the door. "Let's step outside."

Mary and I followed her to an ancient oak tree, where a bench had been installed under it.

"Miss Hesch, your Papa is in pain," she said.

"Pain? His leg?" I asked, bewildered at this turn of events.

"Not physical pain. The kind you have in your heart or your head. He's been through a lot in the past few years. Many soldiers who engage in battle, hurting and killing other men, fearing for their own lives, are not the same men as when they enlisted. The glory of battle and their fantasy of invincibility are shattered. I understand one of his friends died at Chickamauga, along with many others in his regiment. Your father is suffering. On the inside."

"I, I had no idea." My breath caught in my chest as the depth of his suffering dawned on me.

"He left yesterday." She paused and looked up at the remaining leaves on the old oak.

She had more to say. "And?"

"He requested to be transferred. Said he was ready."

"Oh!" My knees buckled. Mrs. Wolfe caught me under the arm and led me to the bench.

"I'm very sorry," she apologized. "He said to tell you he would write and visit soon. After all, Camp Dennison is not very far from town."

"Yes, I know," I said, my mind numb with disbelief that he would ask to leave rather than stay in the city as long as possible, be near me, Mary, see his other children.

Mrs. Wolfe sat with me for a few minutes, holding my hand while Mary patted my shoulder.

"We'll be going now. Thank you for sharing your thoughts on Papa's, um, pain." I stood, thanked her, took Mary's hand, and walked to the buggy.

"Papa?" Mary pointed to the makeshift building.

"He's not there," I said. "We'll see him soon."

"Soon?"

"Yes. Soon," I sighed. How soon, I couldn't say.

Six more months until he would muster out. With no clear path or plan for our future, my hopes and dreams for a family reunion lay like loose rocks on a fractured ledge teetering toward oblivion.

Chapter Forty-Two

A letter from Papa told us he'd been assigned to Camp Dennison's hospital. Attending to soldiers who spoke German, he read them letters and books, and assisted the staff with patient care, often acting as translator. The wounded continued to stream in from battles around Chattanooga and the siege at Knoxville, Union forces unsuccessful in pushing the rebels from Tennessee.

The annual party for boarders, tradesmen, and staff of Mitchell House was to be held on Christmas Eve. Mary and I helped with preparations for twenty guests and after Mrs. Mitchell approved everything, we changed into dresses for the occasion.

The blue poplin Jane gifted to me two years ago flattered Mary's figure. I wore a green plaid shot through with yellow and red, a castoff of Jane's. In honor of the holiday, I dressed Mary's hair with a knot at the crown, long brown locks cascading down her back. A sprig of holly berries pinned to the knot added a festive look to her outfit.

"Mary, you're beautiful!" Her blue eyes sparkled with my compliment. Almost fifteen, I'd overlooked how she'd blossomed into a young woman.

I pinched her cheeks to bring up some color. "Do this." I bit my lips with my teeth, upper, then lower. The tiny wounds flared her lips, red and full.

Pointing to me, Mary said, "Pretty, Motty."

I curtsied. "Thank you, my dear! Shall we go down to the party?" We stepped gingerly down the main staircase instead of the kitchen steps. At the bottom, I paused briefly to assess the scene before us. The front room buzzed with chatter, guests in their finery conversing, nibbling, and sipping. I recognized a few faces, but most were strangers.

"Here we go." I tucked Mary's arm through mine and stepped into the parlor.

Seeing us, Jane rushed over. "You two are pretty as a picture. Come. Have some tea. I have many people for you to meet."

"Stay by me," I whispered and tightened my grip.

"Have a seat. Today is your day to be served instead of doing the serving." Jane twirled around and rushed off to greet a guest.

Our full skirts brushed against each other, the soft rustle of fabric mingling with the gentle creak of the window seat. Bursts of laughter, the crackling fire, and utensils clinking on plates emitted not only the joy of the season, but the comfort and feel of home.

"Merry Christmas." The man whose shoes I polished bent at the waist.

"Merry Christmas, Mr. Franklin," I said.

"Permit me to apologize," he said, holding a dainty teacup balanced on a matching saucer. "Apologize? For what, sir?" I asked.

"I'll direct my apology first to," he tipped his head toward Mary. "Mary, is it?"

My sister sat forward and pointed to his feet. "Shoes."

Mr. Franklin chuckled. "Yes, that's me. The man who made a fuss about his shoes getting wet. My rudeness is unforgivable. I'm sorry."

I offered a small smile. "Thank you. The matter is forgotten." It wasn't, but the experience taught me how not to make an enemy.

Mary stood. "Kiss."

"Uh, no. Mary," I leaped up and snatched her elbow.

"Sorry," Mary said and with her other hand free, she touched her index finger to her lips and reached toward Mr. Franklin's face. He tucked his chin into his neck and withdrew a step.

I swiped my arm down over her forearm, deflecting her attempt to finish the kiss. "Mary, we don't touch people we don't know." I turned to Mr. Franklin. "Now I owe you an apology."

"What was that about?"

"When she hears sorry, she thinks she's done something wrong. Her way of making up for it is to give the other person a finger kiss. Like this." I demonstrated on Mary's cheek.

"Oh." He squinted at Mary, judging her. "Is she insane?" A nervous chuckle accompanied his bizarre statement.

The word insane extinguished any chance of my ever warming to this man. "No. No, she's not. Pardon us."

As I stepped between him and Mary, I nudged the hand holding his cup. It jiggled, spilling tea on his shoes. His eyes flicked downward, startled.

Oh, the irony! Hiding a bemused grin behind my hand, I guided Mary toward the dining room. Mr. Franklin glared at me. His mouth opened, closed, then opened again, a fish gasping for air.

"Bye." Mary wiggled her fingers at the man.

The Cook prepared small bites that Mrs. Mitchell called "dainties." Guests served themselves from overflowing platters and bowls. I wished more meals were like this, making our job easier and less time-consuming.

EB arrived late to the party, dashing in a dark suit, a red and green striped cravat tied at his throat. He looked both handsome and distinguished. My heart fluttered as he approached, then quivered as he kissed Mary and me on the cheek.

"Merry Christmas! You two are a sight for sore eyes." He laughed. "I've been dealing with farmers, dray drivers, and boatmen all afternoon."

"Did you finish?" I asked.

"Yes, all done till Monday." Noticing our empty teacups, he asked, "May I get you more tea or would you prefer punch?"

His consideration warmed me. "Punch please." As I passed him my cup and saucer, his fingers brushed mine. He turned away, unaware of my trembling hand.

Mrs. Mitchell tapped a spoon against a glass, the soft tinkle cutting through conversations and calling her guests to attention. She raised a toast, wishing all a merry Christmas with good health and fortune in the new year. The guests responded, "Cheers!" I muttered Prost into my punch, nostalgic for my parents' German toasts.

Jane played the pianoforte, her voice rising clear and sweet as she sang Stephen Foster's *Come Where My Love Lies Dreaming*. She encouraged the guests to join the final number, *O Holy Night*, a perfect close to the festivities.

As the last guests donned their coats and offered final holiday wishes, Mary and I slipped around the room. We gathered up discarded dishes and abandoned napkins. The familiar routine of tidying up felt comforting after the excitement of the party.

"Oh no, you don't!" Jane said, coming up behind me. "Give me those. You're not working tonight." She held out her hands for our possessions.

"I can't leave it to you to clean all this," I said, the instinct to help hard to ignore.

"EB!" Jane shouted over her shoulder. "Come get these two and keep them from clearing. Tie them up if you must."

"Are you getting into trouble, Martha?" EB teased, a playful glint in his green eyes.

"According to Jane, yes," I chuckled as the mantel clock trilled nine tiny chimes. "It's getting late. We have a big day tomorrow," I said.

"Going to the asylum?

"Church first."

"Is your father coming?"

"Maybe. He's not sure he can get away."

"Would you mind if I escorted you? I'd love to see Lizzie and Henry."

"You would?" I gazed at him, astounded at the suggestion.

"Christmas Day is pretty quiet here."

"Would you like to go to church, too? The service is in German, but Mary is singing with the choir."

"That settles it!" He looked around the room. "Jane?"

"Yes, brother." She scurried across the room and laid a hand on his shoulder.

"I'm going to church, then the asylum with Martha and Mary tomorrow. Want to come?"

"I wish I could, but I already made plans to visit Charlene Jacobs tomorrow. Next time?"

"Charlene? She's such a ninny." EB scoffed.

"Watch it, EB. She's my friend, ninny or not." Jane slapped his shoulder playfully.

We agreed on a departure time and bade good night to EB, Jane, and the few guests that remained. I thanked Mrs. Mitchell for the invitation and time off tomorrow.

"Merry Christmas." She leaned forward and pecked a kiss on my cheek. She touched Mary's cheek with her finger. These two had formed a bond over a garden. A blessing and an irreplaceable gift for my sister. And for me.

Chapter Forty-Three

After breakfast, EB drove us to St. Mattheus. He lavished praise on Mary's short solo, proclaiming her singing good enough to rival Jane's.

I introduced EB to the Eiflerts, Mrs. Ziegler, and a few other friends from the Hall. Mr. Eiflert and EB debated the whereabouts of the Ninth, who revealed that his son, Frank, had emerged from Chickamauga unscathed.

"Martha." A hand grasped my shoulder, a firm tap jolting me.

Mary saw her first and shrank behind me. "Dina! No!"

"Merry Christmas," she said, her voice lacking the spirit of the occasion. Her appearance had improved since I last saw her, but the dark circles under her eyes above jutting cheekbones betrayed her suffering.

"Merry Christmas." I nodded and held Mary's hand. "How are the children?"

She shrugged. "We all right. I apply for widow money."

At that moment, EB stepped in beside me. "EB, this is Dina Decker."

A brief grimace appeared on EB's face. "Good day, Mrs. Decker." No bow, no tip of the head, a complete absence of his usual greeting behaviors.

"EB Mitchell?" she asked.

"Yes," EB said. "I'm sorry for the loss of your husband."

"You help me," she blurted out. "I apply widow pay from Army. How long it come? You know?"

"Madam, I have no idea. The government moves slowly, so you may be waiting for some time."

Dismissing the woman, EB asked, "Are you ready, Martha?"

"Martha, please, your Papa. He home?" she pleaded, intercepting me as I turned to leave.

"He's at the hospital in Camp Dennison." I didn't bother to clarify.

"Oh. Sorry," she said, deflated at the news.

"Goodbye Dina." I didn't wish her a merry Christmas.

But Mary, being Mary, and despite her wariness of the woman, waved and said, "Bye."

At the asylum, we ascended the stairs to the weathered porch. Lizzie and Henry, watching from the windows, flew out to greet us. EB ruffled Henry's hair and chucked Lizzie under her chin.

The dining hall burst at the seams with children and adults. Long tables were piled high with food of all sorts. Half were institutional serving dishes, while the rest were contributions from visitors. I laid the Mitchell gift basket on the table: sausages, cheese, bread, and gingerbread cookies.

We brought presents. For Lizzie, an embroidered handkerchief from me and a bracelet braided from embroidery thread from Mary. For Henry, we knitted a matching hat and muffler.

Matron clapped her hands sharply, cutting through the chaos. Conversations hushed, and laughter faded as all eyes snapped to her, curiosity replacing the previous clamor. A group of children, including Lizzie, stood side by side at the front of the room.

"Merry Christmas! Thank you for joining us. These children, our nine to twelve-year-olds, have prepared a treat for you. We hope you enjoy it." She moved to the side of the group, turned to the children. "One, two, three."

Voices, low and melodic, wove perfect harmony as the haunting notes of *Stille Nacht! Heil'ge Nacht!* filled the room. The first two verses were sung in German, switching to English for the final one, Matron gesturing for the audience to join. Mary and I added our voices, and as the final notes faded, applause erupted.

"Did you like it?" she asked, running up to us after Matron dismissed the group.

"Oh, very much! I'm so proud of you!" I said into her hair, adding a kiss to the top of her head.

Someone tapped me on my shoulder. Thinking it was EB adding his congratulations to Lizzie, I turned. And froze. "Papa?"

He directed his gaze at Lizzie. "That was the most beautiful version of *Stille Nacht* I've ever heard."

She flew at him, and he scooped her into his arms. Lizzie entwined her arms around his neck, locked her legs around his waist, and clung to him like a lifeline.

Mary gaped, eyes wide with wonder, unable to believe it. "Papa! Home!"

"Where's your brother?" Papa said as Lizzie leaned back in his arms and caressed his cheeks under his bushy beard.

"He's outside running around," I said. "I'll find him."

But EB, who was standing behind me, gently stopped me with a hand on my arm. "I'll get him. You visit."

Papa acknowledged EB with a slight nod, which EB returned.

Papa enfolded Mary and me in his embrace, holding tight until Henry's shouts of "Papa! Papa!" interrupted us. He charged into the room and jumped into his father's arms, similar to Lizzie's greeting.

Invited to eat with the orphans, we filled our plates with food and found a spot where the six of us could sit together.

"It's nice to meet you, sir," EB shook hands with Papa across the table.

"And you, Mr. Mitchell." Papa took a seat across from EB.

"Please call me EB."

"George," Papa said with a smile.

Turning his attention to his children, Papa exclaimed, "It's good to see you! You've all grown so much." He forked a piece of ham into his mouth.

"You've changed too, Papa," Lizzie said. "Your beard's bushier, and your hair has more gray in it. You look smaller than I remember, too."

Papa patted his belly. "In some places, we ate well. But in others, especially in winter, we went without food for days. I'm lucky at the hospital. There's always something to eat."

Henry pointed to Papa's mouth. "Where's your tooth?"

Papa's smile unveiled a small but conspicuous gap in his bottom front teeth. "Somewhere in Tennessee, I believe."

"Hardtack get it?"

"Yes, my boy. Broke it right off."

Papa's teasing sparked laughter, rekindling memories of life before his departure nine months earlier. For a moment, time rewound as we savored his presence.

"Lizzie, how is it here?" he asked.

"I miss my sisters, but I have chores, and we go to school. I watch out for Henry and Matron put me in charge of the library. When my work is done, I read until the dinner bell rings or lights out."

"I can't imagine a better person in charge of books," Papa said.

"Henry, what about you?"

"I have a friend named Bill. He's older than Gus, so I don't do baby things anymore."

At the mention of Gus, Papa frowned. "Do you miss Gus?"

"I don't know. Maybe." He shrugged his shoulders. "May I be excused?"

"Yes," I said. "But stay close. We'll be leaving soon. Henry hopped up and ran out of the hall.

"When will I get to come home?" Lizzie probed. "I don't dislike it here, but I want to be with my sisters and especially you, Papa!"

"That's a good question, Lizzie. In late April, I am done with the army."

"It's December now." She counted. "Four months till April."

"Right," Papa said. "After that, I'll come to town and the first thing I'll do is get a job. Then find a place for us to live."

Lizzie rose from the bench, danced around the end of the table, and squeezed Papa from behind. "Thank you, Papa! That's a grand plan."

Grinning at this joyous news, I glanced at EB, who raised an eyebrow while keeping his gaze fixed on Papa, as though trying to measure his intent.

Papa pulled the journal I gave him last Christmas from his pocket and inside I could see greenbacks. He counted ten dollars and handed it to me. "Is Lizzie allowed to have money?"

Lizzie shook her head. "No. Matron says it might get stolen."

"I'll give yours to Motty. She can use it for something you need or want. Would that be all right?" he asked.

"Oh yes, Papa," Lizzie exclaimed.

"Mary, here's a dollar for you," he said, winking at me.

Mary accepted the greenback and rolled it into a little tube, put it to her eye, peered through it, and found Papa. "I see you," she declared.

"Funny use of a dollar." Papa laughed. "It's almost time to go. Show me the library."

Lizzie grabbed Papa's hand and dragged him into the hall, and they disappeared up the stairs.

The rest of us remained at the table. "Thank you for coming," I said.

"My pleasure," EB said. "Your Papa's news is, um, interesting."

I sighed. "I want to believe him."

He laid a hand over mine. "Stay strong." But a moment later, he rose. "I'm going to find Henry. Maybe we can play a quick game of tag."

At the window, I observed EB and Henry's dance, a flurry of tags and escapes. Mary ran up to EB, shoved him, and sprinted away, skirts flying. EB chased Mary, then Henry. I shook my head, marveling at EB - the boy within the man emerging, seizing a rare moment of boyhood fun.

"Where is everyone?" Papa asked, reentering the hall.

A nod toward the open field beyond the drive provided the answer.

"They're having fun," Papa said. "EB seems like a good man."

"The Michell family has been kind." I watched the game of tag.

"Does he mean something to you?"

I tore my gaze from the window. "Yes," I said cautiously, "He's a good friend."

"Nothing more?" Papa said, his brows raised.

Guessing at the meaning behind his questions, I shook my head. "Servants don't get involved with employers, Papa, you know that. No matter how I feel about him, he could never feel the same for me."

Papa nodded.

"Do you need a ride to the train station?" I asked, moving toward the door and stepping onto the porch. Seeing the sun low on the winter horizon, I thought it best we go soon.

"No, I borrowed a nag from camp. She's old, but I avoid the train ride and the long walk."

"I'm glad you came today, Papa." I looked up into his ruddy face. His blue eyes crinkled at the corners, deepening his smile. "And I liked what you said about when you get out. It's a dream come true."

I stepped into his outstretched arms. "I'm proud of you, Motty. You made good on your promise. I'm lucky to be alive, to be here on Christmas with my family and that is all because of your efforts. I'll do my best to get us back together." He kissed my forehead and held me at arm's length. "I'll say goodbye to the others."

I rounded up everyone but Lizzie and sent Henry into the asylum to find her. EB and Papa clasped hands, exchanging Christmas wishes. EB retrieved the buggy from the hitching post on the side of the building.

Mary and Papa traded finger kisses so many times, I lost count. Lizzie and Henry burst out of the building, colliding with their father in a whirlwind of hugs that nearly toppled him.

"Goodbye Papa," I said. A hug and kiss later, Papa handed us up to EB. He strode alongside the buggy, his hand entwined with mine until the lane's end forced our parting.

Chapter Forty-Four

Expecting the Ninth to be mustered out at the end of April, their three years completed, I waited for word from Papa. The newspapers reported no news of their recall from the field, nor did EB discover anything on my request. But Mr. Eiflert said he heard from Frank. The regiment having enlisted at the end of May 1861 had another month until their release. The first thirty days didn't count.

In late April 1864, Ohio called for thirty-thousand men to serve one hundred days, a directive designed to replace regular soldiers who guarded cities and forts. The "hundred days men", as they came to be known, allowed regular soldiers to join advancing Union armies, an attempt to end the war in a mere fourteen weeks.

EB shocked everyone when he joined the 137th Ohio, his second enlistment. His departure date was set for the first of May mustering in at Camp Dennison as First Lieutenant, three ranks higher than his rank of corporal in the Second Ohio.

Trying to convince his mother and Jane that his duty was not perilous, EB said he'd be stationed behind the lines of combat and the only danger he would face was illness and boredom.

"Write every day," Mrs. Mitchell implored. "I need to know you are safe."

Jane handed him a bundle of paper along with pre-addressed envelopes. "No excuses."

I gave EB a letter to deliver to Papa. The last time he visited the asylum was Easter Sunday in late March. "I hope you get to see him and find out how he's doing."

"I'll do my best," EB said.

EB wrote shortly after he arrived at Camp Dennison, noting that he'd not seen Papa, as he was busy training and outfitting his men. He planned to visit the hospital before they left camp.

In a letter to his mother, he informed her that his regiment had orders to travel to Baltimore, where they would serve as a garrison at one of several forts guarding the city. Though he assured her once again not to worry about his safety, I did. We all did. I couldn't imagine life without this kind, sweet man. After bedtime prayers, I added him to the list of people I begged God to bless.

At the end of May, the Ninth Ohio arrived at the riverfront, greeted by cheering citizens and a grand parade led by the Turners. Together with family and friends, the soldiers marched through the city, paused at Turner Hall, then departed for Camp Dennison.

With Papa's imminent return and the busyness of finding a place to live, moving, and getting settled, I decided Dina should handle all the mending from the Hall.

I spotted Mrs. Eiflert, radiant now with her son's return, prancing along the sidewalk in front of St. Mattheus. She approved of my mending plan. Leaving Mary with Therese to prepare for their performance, I waited on the steps for Dina, who had recently joined the congregation.

As the bells rang, calling everyone inside, Dina hurried toward the church, Gus clutching her skirt, Amelia on her hip. I approached her and extended my hand to Gus.

"Good morning, Dina," I said.

She tilted her head, wary of my approach, as I usually ignored her.

"I've talked to Mrs. Eiflert, and she's agreed you can have all the mending from the Hall."

Dina stopped dead in her tracks. "What you mean?"

"I mean, it's time for me to let go of the mending. With Papa coming home, I'll be too busy."

"Ah, yes. George." She walked toward the church doors. I fell into step beside her.

"Do you want the mending?" I asked. "There's a bundle in the atrium."

"Yes, I take." We stepped into the cool dim interior of the church. "Thank you."

I gave up Gus's hand to her and took a seat next to Mrs. Eiflert.

After the service, waiting for Mary, I watched with pleasure as Dina spoke with Mrs. Eiflert. She excused herself from the older woman and came up to me.

"Why you do this?" she asked.

"I told you. Papa's coming home. We'll be getting a place for all of us to live and I'll not have time for the mending with my job at the boarding house."

"I see your Papa," she said. "He no like your demands."

"What?" Taken aback, I frowned. "My demands?"

"Live here, work there, bring children home." Her raised eyebrows scoffed at me.

Those were topics I spoke with Papa about, but they weren't demands. Were they?

"When did you see Papa?" I asked, diverting the conversation and curious about why he discussed our future with her.

"Many times. He come. We talk." Dina said.

"How many times?"

She shrugged. "Not sure. He come after asylum."

He came to her after meeting us. Did they have a relationship? Did I care? Yes, I cared, I cared very much. Feeling betrayed once again, I regretted giving her the mending business. But it was too late. Hostile at Dina's meeting with Papa, I said, "Stay away from me and my family. That includes Papa."

I spun on my heel and met Mary and Therese at the buggy.

Mary scowled and pointed. "Dina."

"We're done with her. Let's go see the children."

I brought a letter from EB. On the envelope, Lizzie read, "To Lizzie and Henry".

Lizzie ripped open the envelope, pulled out the paper, made sure Henry sat close enough to see, and read.

"My dear Lizzie and my friend Henry." Lizzie paused and looked up at me. "I'm his dear." Her eyes sparkled, the affectionate address holding more meaning that I was sure EB intended.

> I am in the wonderful city of Baltimore. Use one of Matron's maps to locate it. We are charged with keeping Fort McHenry safe. It is on a peninsula overlooking the vast Patapsco River, four times wider than the mighty Ohio.

Lizzie looked up at me. "What's a peninsula?"

"It's a body of land that juts out into water all by itself."

Lizzie nodded, then read.

> Don't ask your sister what a peninsula is. Look it up.

Laughing, she slapped the paper with the back of her fingers. "He knows me too well."

"Go on, Lizzie!" Henry demanded.

> The area is famous for blue crabs, and we eat quite a lot of them. When they are alive, they are grayish blue, have a hard shell, with claws that pinch. Once cooked, they turn red. We crack the shell and dig out the meat from inside. You'll be happy to know they don't pinch while we eat them.

Henry stuck out his tongue. "Yuck! No crabs for me."

> I'll write again soon. Lizzie, I hope you are keeping the library in order and doing well in school. Henry, stay out of the hay loft and practice your alphabet. I expect it to be perfect when I return.
>
> Your dear friend,
> EB Mitchell

The man endeared himself to me once more. Of all the letters he had to write, he'd taken time to write one to the children. I missed him deeply.

As Papa's mustering out was only a matter of days away, I gave the children the good news. Expecting overwhelming joy at Papa's homecoming, Lizzie brought me up short with a question. "Do you think he'll survive being home?"

"What an odd question. Why wouldn't he?"

"Something he said when he was here last time."

"What did he say?"

"He said, I hope I can be a good father to you."

"Of course, he's a good father. Why do you think he said that?"

"We were talking about how I missed Mama, and he said he did, too. I told him it would be different when he got home."

I nodded, examining the undercurrent of Papa's words.

"He got sad. And when he hugged me, I could feel him shaking, like he was crying. I had to tell him to let me go. He was squishing me."

Papa's words puzzled me, but Lizzie's insistence on locating Baltimore on the library map diverted my thoughts.

On the ride home, I reflected on Dina's remarks and Lizzie's conversation with Papa. My demands. If Papa followed through, they weren't demands; they were promises he'd made—actions he'd assured us he would take. He said he'd make everything all right. Wasn't it his turn now? My turn was supposed to be over. But Papa's words to Lizzie lingered in my mind: "I hope I can be a good father." Why would he doubt himself?

Money wouldn't be a worry. With mending income covering our modest expenses, I'd saved over a hundred dollars. With his bounty and pay, we could afford a place of our own—maybe even one with two bedrooms. I could take in mending work during my free hours, and once Papa found a job, we'd be able to live comfortably.

I wished EB were here. He could help me unravel the meaning behind Papa's words. Why were my expectations considered demands? Why did he doubt his ability to be a good father? Jane might have a few thoughts, but I needed a man's perspective. I needed EB.

Chapter Forty-Five

I wrote two letters.

The first to Papa for news on when the regiment would muster out. "I'd like to arrange a meal with you and the Mitchells to celebrate."

The second to EB. I laid out a few sentences summarizing what Papa told Lizzie and Dina. "I don't understand Papa. What's wrong with him?"

The newspaper finally brought word of the Ninth, reporting they were at Camp Dennison, ready to muster out. At church, Mrs. Eiflert confirmed the report and said she heard the men would return to the city within a week.

I scanned the wanted postings for rooms and found one place of interest. Unable to decipher the 'men wanted' listings, I decided finding a job was best left to Papa. Unless, of course, I heard of someone hiring.

The week for Papa to come home came and went without a word of his whereabouts or when to expect him. Away from our old neighborhood, where familiar faces at the market or on the street kept us informed, I found myself cut off from news and gossip.

EB answered my inquiry about Papa's behavior but offered little consolation, as he had little time to write. "My guess is your father has been in the Army so long, he doesn't know how to be a civilian."

This made no sense. How could he not know how to be a civilian? Didn't Papa remember life before he joined? How he spent his time? When he had Mama. Yes, that part was different.

At church, Mrs. Eiflert confirmed the Ninth had returned to the city. She had no idea of Papa's whereabouts. After the service, I scanned the crowd for Frank Eiflert.

"Hello, Frank!" I surprised him by kissing him on the cheek. He blushed from his hairline to the tips of his ears.

"Martha, it's good to see you." He fiddled with his coat, buttoning and unbuttoning it.

"Have you seen Papa since you got back to town?"

"Saw him at the Republic Friday night, then at Turner's for the welcome banquet. It was a fine affair," he said and watched my face drain of color. "Are you ill? Here, sit down."

Frank eased me onto the top step of the church entry and called out urgently, "Mother, help!"

Mrs. Eiflert shuffled across the sidewalk. "Martha! You're pale as a ghost!"

"Papa." The word caught in my throat.

"What about him?" she asked.

Frank interjected. "I told her he was at the banquet last night."

"Oh, I think I understand. Frank, get your father and go on home. I'll be just a minute." Mrs. Eiflert shooed him off.

"Why?" I asked, tears streaming freely down my cheeks. "Why keep his return a secret from me?"

"I'm sure I don't know. It seems he would." Mrs. Eiflert patted my hand, oblivious to the curious stares around us.

A sudden thought struck me. On impulse, I blurted, "Can you mind Mary for me?"

"I suppose." Her affirmative nod was accompanied by a curious stare.

310

"If Papa's in town, which he is, according to Frank, he'll most likely come to the asylum today. Leaving Mary with you gives me a chance to speak with him alone. Papa's disregard for us has me fit to be tied. I mean to tell him how I feel."

"Well, I think Mary staying with me is a fine idea. I wouldn't want to be in the line of fire between you and your Papa."

"No, you don't. Thank you." I gathered my skirts and pushed up from the step. Holding out my hand, I assisted Mrs. Eiflert to her feet.

"I'll come for Mary this afternoon," I said. "And, by the way, your Frank has grown into a handsome young man."

"I agree, but as his mother, I realize I'm quite biased." She chuckled and left me to find Mary.

I reached the asylum early, finding Matron overseeing several boys prepare the hall for visitors.

"Martha, it's good to see you," Matron greeted me. "I'm not sure where Lizzie and Henry are, but I'll get someone to find them."

"Before you do, could I have a word?" I asked.

"Certainly." She led me out to the veranda, and we sat in rocking chairs facing the city below. "What's on your mind?"

"Papa's mustered out."

"That's great news!" Matron's voice reflected a joy I didn't share. "Do you have plans?"

"I do, yes. But I've yet to speak with Papa on the details," I said. "I think it could be a matter of weeks, and we'll take Lizzie and Henry home with us."

"That was your plan when you brought them," Matron smiled. "They are thriving here. I know you've seen it yourself, but Lizzie is a whiz at reading, and she started a story time for the little ones. They work on puzzles, draw pictures, and practice their alphabet and numbers. She's a born teacher or mother, or both."

"I believe it."

"And Henry. I confess, I worry about him. He's a physical boy. Quite fearless, too. He's climbed nearly every tree on the property, so we keep an eye on him. But he's happy with all this space. Even in winter, he goes outside except the worst of days. I fear you taking him to the city will limit his freedom."

I recalled several times he'd nearly fallen out the window. "Thank you for watching out for him."

"Martha, what I mean to say is that the children are doing well. I know you want them to be together but, consider this. You and Mary work and your father will, too. In the fall, the children will attend school. Who will get them ready, pack their supper, and be home when school is out? And what about holidays and snow days when school is closed? When school is out in summer?"

"Lizzie can handle all that. She's good with Henry."

Matron did not respond.

The stilted silence hung heavy between us. As her words slowly sank in, realization dawned. I whirled to face her, my eyes flashing and voice sharp with indignation. "Are you encouraging me to leave them here? They want to be a family again."

Matron looked out across the lawn, her foot tapping lightly as she pushed her rocking chair into motion. "Please don't take this the wrong way, but perhaps you're the one who wants to be together again."

Her words hit me like a sledgehammer in the sternum, knocking the wind out of me and reeling from her blatant intrusion on my affairs. "How dare you?" I rose from the rocker, looking to escape, but realized I had yet to see Lizzie and Henry.

Matron rose and brushed her apron down as if she could remove the wrinkles from sitting. "I'm sorry Martha. I just thought you might like another perspective—from someone who sees the children's potential and has experience in these situations."

Putting my back to her, I stared over the lush lawn of the asylum. "We have to be a family again. I promised."

"You promised who?"

"My father."

"What's your definition of family?" She asked, her voice quiet, leading my thoughts in a new direction.

I faced her again. "I guess, it's people who are related by blood that love each other." Wasn't it the same for everyone?

"Did you notice you didn't say live together? You said people love each other."

Having it put so simply, I grappled with the question: was living together and loving each other mutually exclusive?

"You don't have to live together to love someone. I have a mother in Columbus and a son in New York. We are a family, though we don't live together. And at our age, that's a blessing!" She chuckled at her own joke.

"But I promised," I pleaded, hoping she understood how important that was to me.

"It's between you and your father what the promise is expected to accomplish. You've been successful keeping your siblings healthy and safe. Mary, especially, has blossomed as much as Henry and Lizzie. And if you don't mind my saying, so have you."

My hands flew to my cheeks, a warmth rising under my skin. "I have?"

"No doubt about it," she said. "From the frightened girl I met last July to the strong, opinionated one standing here before me. I find you an inspiration. I think you should tell your story to our girls, what you've overcome, what you did to survive, knocking obstacles aside at every turn."

"I did what I had to do," I repeated what I'd told Mrs. Eiflert.

"Yes, you did. And look at you! You're still a nice person, you still care about others, your siblings, and your Papa, though I'm sure he's poked holes in the trust you have for him. Martha," Matron put her hands on my upper arms. "I'm not telling you what to do. But take some time and look at the other side of the coin. What's the worst that could happen if everything stayed the same?"

Tears threatened as her words challenged everything I'd battled for, clung to, and desperately needed to believe.

"I must get back inside, or the boys will wreck the hall. Have a seat and I'll get someone to find the children."

Numb, unable to focus, I fell back into the rocker. An inspiration. Family is about love. Mary blossomed. I tried to grasp the meaning behind her words, but they flitted away like butterflies struggling to alight on flowers in a strong wind.

From far away, I heard a squeal. "Motty! You're here!"

Matron's words echoed in Lizzie's cornflower-blue eyes—so like Mama's—and in Henry's impish grin, framed by Papa's lively auburn curls.

Chapter Forty-Six

Papa didn't come to the asylum. Lizzie wondered where Mary was and asked if Papa was out of the Army yet. I lied and said he had a few more days. Burdening a ten-year-old with the truth would only vent my frustration, a weight she didn't need to bear.

My conversation with Matron put crazy ideas in my head. One repeated itself over and over. What's the worst that could happen if everything stayed the same? I didn't like everything as it stood now. I wanted to see Lizzie and Henry every day, watch Mary work and play with her siblings, and feel Papa's tickles wake me in the morning. No, staying the same was not an option.

That evening, as Mary and I sat down to our evening meal, the door knocker struck the brass plate three times. Visitors at this hour were rare and the noise might disturb Mrs. Mitchell, who had already gone to bed. Rushing to the front door, I flung it open, expecting a boarder.

"Papa?"

Dressed in an ill-fitting brown suit coat over black trousers, he removed his hat. "I hope I'm not disturbing the house."

Stepping onto the porch and pulling the door nearly closed, I shook my head. "Most are abed. Mary and I are eating."

"I'm sorry I've not come sooner. Can we talk?"

Jane poked her head out. "You must be Mr. Hesch. I'm Jane Mitchell. It's nice to finally meet you!"

Papa bowed at the waist. "Thank you, Miss Mitchell. I'm pleased to meet you."

"Come in, come in!" Jane swung the door wide again. "Are you hungry? I'm sure we can rustle up something for you to eat."

"Papa? Would you like to join us?" I asked.

He hesitated, then nodded.

I followed Jane and Papa brought up the rear. As he entered the kitchen, Mary leaped from her chair and into his arms.

"I've missed you," Papa mumbled into her hair.

I added a plate to the table and scraped half my ham and beans onto it, pulled a chunk of bread from the loaf, and placed it in front of Papa, where Jane added a chair.

"Thank you," he told Jane, then me.

"I'll leave you to your supper." With a smile, Jane backed through the swinging door into the hallway.

Mary ate with one hand, the other touching Papa, making sure he was there and not a figment of her imagination.

A flurry of questions ricocheted through my head. Where have you been? How many times did you see Dina? When will we look for a place to live? Having been accused of nagging like Mama, I bit back my questions.

"You look fit," I said between bites. His beard, though long was neatly trimmed, was grayer than when I'd seen him last. I studied his face. Deep crow's feet crinkled at the corners of his eyes, uneven wrinkles etched across his forehead, and his cheeks were permanently flushed from years of sun exposure.

"Papa, how old are you?"

"What an odd question," he said, then his brow furrowed. "I think I'm forty-one. Or is it forty-two?"

In my mind, that was old. "When were you born?" I asked, prepared to do the math.

"July 1, 1822. When I got to America in 1846, I'd already had my twenty-fourth birthday."

"You're forty-one." But he'd be forty-two in a matter of days. "Glad your army days are behind you?"

Shifting in his seat, he inhaled. "Yes, but I miss my friends from the Ninth. And Joe."

I ate my beans and sopped up the juice with bread, waiting for him to speak.

"I didn't come sooner because I spent time with my friends. I've not seen some of them since Chickamauga, and when we got off the train from Dennison, free to do as we pleased, we ended up in a biergarten. The banquet was on Saturday night and, I," he paused, "I woke up too late for church."

"Many asked after you," I said.

"I planned to see you at the asylum, but I had no way of getting there but to walk."

"We waited for you."

"I'm sorry."

Beneath the table, my fist clenched, nails digging into my palm. It helped me keep a straight face, bite back a nasty retort, or worse, hurl my questions at him like bullets from a squad of rebels.

I compromised. "What's next?"

Papa wiped his mouth with the back of his sleeve. I handed him a napkin, but he shook his head and smiled. "Too many years without one of those to change course now."

Needing to do something while waiting for Papa's response, I stood and cleared the table.

Mary fingered Papa's jacket. "Blue? Pretty buttons?"

"I turned my uniform in. No more pretty buttons. No more blue." He pointed to Mary's eyes. "Except for your eyes."

Mary giggled, gathered the remaining utensils and dishes, and put them in the sink.

"Papa, let's go out back. There's a little daylight left, and we can sit on the stoop."

The screen door slapped against the frame as we stepped into the yard. Mary, yanking on Papa's arm, pulled him to the garden, where a mix of new and mature leaves sprouted in their respective rows. After a lengthy interest in the garden, he left her on her knees, moving dirt around, picking a weed here and there. Weeds had no chance, for she inspected and plucked them out several times a day.

"We usually go to bed right after supper," I said, looking for something to fill the silence. "We begin our day at five."

"I'm going to look for a job tomorrow," he blurted out. "But be warned—with the Ninth's return as well as other regiments, the city is flooded with men hunting for work."

I nodded, understanding that with six hundred men returning from his regiment alone, there would be more men than work. "What if you don't find one?"

"I'll find something. Might not pay well, but there must be something I can do." He stared at Mary puttering in the garden.

"I found a place for us in the newspaper. Can we go see it?" I said, trying to regain some momentum toward becoming a family again.

"No, let me find a job first. Else you'll get your hopes up." He patted my knee.

"I've already saved a hundred dollars. Did you get your bounty and pay?" I asked, suddenly aware he might think it was none of my business.

"Yes," he replied, offering no more than that.

"Where are you staying, Papa?"

"The Army is supplying rooms for mustered-out soldiers at fifty cents a night. It suits my needs for now."

"Mrs. Mitchell said you can rent one here for half the usual cost. A boarder's moving out in a couple of weeks." My voice rose with excitement at the prospect of Papa living with us.

"Martha. Stop." He held his hand up. "I'm barely back and you've already got plans. Too many for me right now."

"But Papa, I'm just trying to help," I huffed, my lower lip jutting out.

"I don't need your help. I'm a grown man and, as you've reminded me, forty-two years old. You are seventeen. Leave me be." His voice, though quiet, meant business.

I blew out a frustrated breath, exasperated by his lack of urgency. Standing, I faced him, glaring down as he stayed sitting. "You promised. You promised when you got home, we would all be together."

Papa stood, and the balance shifted, him looking down at me, his voice quiet yet commanding. "I said I would do the best I can. With how you're acting, I'm not likely to keep that so-called promise. Living with you would be more miserable than a winter in the trenches. I won't do it!"

A silence fell between us, broken only by the monotonous croak of a tree frog. I swallowed unbidden tears and swung my gaze upward. The dusky sky closed in on itself, grayish black, a single star twinkling over the northern hills. Fireflies fluttered in the yard, their yellow lights blinking.

"Motty." Papa kept his voice low, mindful of the late hour and people asleep in the house "I'll look for work starting tomorrow. Does that meet your demands?"

Demands. Dina used that exact word. "Papa, I don't mean to demand anything. I'm only asking you to do what you said. How is that a demand?"

"I don't know anymore. I'm tired. Tired of fighting with you, tired of worrying about money, a job, my children." Papa seemed to shrink before me, his shoulders drooping, head bowed.

"I'm glad you worry about us," I said, ignoring his fatigue. "That's been my life for three years. Even when you were home, it still felt like it was my job to make sure we had food, a bed, and money coming in."

His head seemed to droop a few more inches, my accusations adding weight.

Mary no longer looked for weeds, nightfall obscuring their presence. She listened to our angry exchange. "Papa?" she said, the darkness concealing her facial features.

He strode over to his middle daughter and helped her to her feet. "It's time to go in. Your skirts will get wet with dew."

"Sleep? Here?" Mary pointed to the Mitchell house and looked hopefully at Papa.

"Not tonight," he said.

Letting Mary down easy could be misconstrued as a promise for the future, and I couldn't allow it. "I'll tell her the truth." I grabbed Mary by the shoulders, forcing her to square up to me. "Papa's not staying here. Not tonight. Not ever."

Mary, frightened by my bitter, vengeful tone, one I'd never used with her before, began to cry.

320

"Martha, that's enough!" His hands fisted.

I shrunk back out of reach, frightened he would strike me.

"I'll not hit you, Martha, but you deserve a whipping. You need to remember who's in charge."

Unfazed at his threat, I clasped Mary's hand. "Let's go, Mary. Goodnight Papa. There's a gate on the side where you can let yourself out."

"Papa?" Mary cried, reaching out to him as I dragged her through the door.

I found the lamp and turned up the wick, lighting the kitchen. Mary hovered by the door, staring out at her father, his heartbroken face peering back at her. I drew her inside, slowly closing the door on Papa's illuminated figure, watching as the sliver of light narrowed until he stood alone, in the dark.

Chapter Forty-Seven

The next morning, the ramifications of how I'd treated Papa bore down on me like a leaden cloud, darkening my thoughts and dampening my spirits. I slept off and on, waffling between my indignation at Papa's inability to be true to his promise and my guilt at the pressure I put upon him. Who was right? Who was wrong?

The day began with sunshine trying to lift my spirits, but a late morning rain drenched any hope of a good mood.

"No wash today," Jane said. "Let's tackle the mending."

Jane made room in the office for Mary and me, setting up chairs in the cozy space. Jane wrote in her ledgers while we sewed.

"A letter came from EB yesterday," Jane said. "He's still in Baltimore but reassigned to guard the fort at Federal Hill. He's well but bored. I'm writing to him now. Anything I should tell him?"

I shook my head. "No, I wrote yesterday."

"How was your visit with your father?" Jane asked, folding her letter and slipping it into an envelope.

"It wasn't what I hoped. He's looking for a job. But the prospects are dim with all the other soldiers looking too. Once he has one, he said we can look for a place."

"That's a step in the right direction," Jane said.

Bending over a ripped shirt cuff, a tear slid down my cheek onto the white fabric.

"What's wrong?" Jane asked solicitously, standing her pen in the ink well and turning her attention to me.

Keeping my eyes on my needle, pulling it out, pushing it through, I sighed. "I'm afraid."

"Afraid?" Jane wondered. "Of what?"

"That Papa won't keep his promise."

"Oh," Jane said the single word without surprise or recognition. "Martha, put down the mending. Let's talk. Woman to woman."

I stuck the needle into the cuff and laid the work on my lap. Meeting her eyes, I felt another tear trickle down my cheek and brushed it away. Jane didn't pry into my affairs often, but today I welcomed her invitation to talk.

"Have you heard the story of Achilles? The Greek warrior?"

I shook my head. "No."

Mary paused her sewing to listen.

"Achilles was renowned for his strength, skills in combat, and winning battles, leading his troops to victory. His reputation as an

322

immortal warrior spread far and wide and before long, he too believed he was invincible. One fateful day while in his prime, Achilles was struck down by a single arrow. It pierced the one vulnerable spot on his body, his heel. He fell and the once unbeatable warrior met his end."

"What does Achilles have to do with me?" I asked.

"Like this. The story is a metaphor for having a weakness despite great strength. The story of Achille's heel reminds us that even the mightiest have a flaw that can lead to their downfall."

"And?" I opened my hands, palms up, pleading for the moral of the story. Flaw? Downfall?

"I think your father is your Achilles' heel. He's the weakness that will be your undoing."

"Undoing?"

Jane paused, then said, "You trust your father blindly. If he told you the sun sets in the east or flowers bloom in winter, you'd believe him. Now he says he'll get a job, and you want to believe it despite the odds. Your weakness is trusting him when he tells you what you want to hear. And when you don't like what he says, you prod him until he concedes or shuts down."

When she put it in so many words, I rejected her assessment. But recalling Dina's comment about Papa not liking my demands lent weight to Jane's words.

"He's a fish out of water, Martha. He's lost his wife, his prospects for work are limited to hard labor for pennies, and he faces raising children without his mate, who did everything for the children. He's back from the Army where he rents a bed for the night, seeks solace with fellow soldiers, and a daughter who won't let him adjust to this new and confusing world. You've been through your own hell, I know. But it's time you see his side. Imagine how you'd feel facing insurmountable obstacles with no skills."

At this, I leaned forward, thrusting my needle at Jane. "That's exactly what I've done. Faced impossible challenges with no experience."

Jane nodded, folded, then unfolded her hands, laying them flat on her knees. Her calm reassured and frightened me at the same time. "But he's not you. And to be frank, he's a man. Men are tricky creatures that don't think like us and if we try to get inside their heads, they deny our notions as silly and inaccurate."

"I don't want to get in Papa's head."

"But you must! If you row the boat against the current, you'll exhaust yourself before reaching your destination."

Another analogy I didn't understand. What did rowing a boat have to do with Papa coming home? Or Achilles?

Jane continued. "How about this? What if you stop rowing? Let the current take you where it goes. Pushing your father to do something he doesn't want to do will lead to unhappiness. Imagine you're all together in a place with Lizzie and Henry. And let's say your father hates his job but stays because he has no choice. He'll go out and drink up whatever money he's made, and then there's no money. And you know very well what happens without money."

I recalled Papa stumbling home drunk before the war. Was he unhappy about his job? Mama's nagging? Did he join the Army to escape?

"Let him find his own way. You've found yours." Jane leaned back in her chair, waiting for her advice to sink in.

With all the information Jane had given me in the last few minutes, my mind raced to make connections. But this last part confused me even more. I'd found my own way. Had I? What is my way? I wished EB were here to unravel his sister's puzzles.

"Motty." She used my nickname, something she did rarely, so I paid attention to this woman, this friend, who had never caused me harm and only had my best interests at heart. "Instead of constantly demanding he make good on the promise, try to let him go. Give him time to adjust to his new reality."

That night, I tossed in bed for an hour, mulling over Jane's advice on shifting my perspective and trying to let go.

Imagining myself in the rowboat of Jane's design, I controlled its path and destination, pulling the rough-hewn oars—this way when it drifted too close to shore, that way when it veered toward the opposite bank. Zigzagging from shore to shore, I made no progress. Blisters formed on my hands, forcing me to pull the oars in. Floating aimlessly, a breeze swirled around, shushing the trees along the banks. I closed my eyes, trying to relax, but fear of running aground made me peek. The little boat held steady in the center. Tilting my face to the sun, I let the gentle sway of the boat lull me into a peace I'd never known.

Was this Jane's point about letting go? Not just for Papa to figure things out, but for me too. Smothering, demanding, and cajoling Papa into doing what I wanted hadn't worked, and the effort wore me out and wore me down. For the few moments on the creek of my imagination, I let go of my worries, my fears, and settled into the present. Unfettered by my self-imposed needs, I inhaled deeply, releasing my breath slowly, then opened my eyes.

The round window cast moonlight into our tiny room, and Mary's soft snores pulled me back. Smiling at the memory of my vision—or dream—I rolled onto my side, promising to ease up on

Papa. A daunting task, but something had to change. Since I couldn't change him, I had to change me.

Chapter Forty-Eight

The promise to bring our family together again, I grudgingly admitted, was of my making. I'd taken his original promise to come home and altered it to suit what I wanted because I thought all of us together meant happiness. And Papa, badgered and bullied, strung me along, telling me what I wanted to hear, a father giving his daughter hope for the future she desired. How could I fault him for that?

Lizzie and Henry were safe and healthy, and I had to admit, happy at the asylum, not trapped in tiny rooms. Mary thrived under Mrs. Mitchell's tutelage, Jane's guidance, and always someone on hand to watch out for her.

My plan was simple. I'd tell Papa I'd leave things as they are until he was ready. But no. I couldn't say till he's ready or the pressure remained. He had to know I supported him and would wait until he'd figured things out.

With a few free minutes between supper and dinner service, I penned a letter to EB.

> I hope you are well and know how much you
> are missed. Your Mama worries constantly, as
> does Jane. And me. Please stay safe, for I could
> not imagine you not coming home.
>
> Papa has mustered out and is looking for a job.
> We argued and I regret how I treated him. I've
> promised to be kinder to him, put myself in his

place, and try to understand what it must be like to have his problems. Your sister told me about this man, Achilles, and his foot, and how Papa is my Achilles. I'm not altogether sure what it means, but I think it's that Papa can bring me to my knees.

Writing this seems absurd, don't you think? How could my father bring me down? But he vexes me and I do anger him with my pleas to get our family back together. I've vowed to stop badgering him and let him know I love him for who he is and not who I want him to be.

At least I'll try. I wish this war was over.

Yours, Motty

The door knocker clacked rapidly, halting my search for an envelope and stamp. Leaving the office, I checked my apron, my hair, and reached for the handle, just as another set of knocks tapped in rapid succession.

"May I help you?" I asked automatically as I opened the door. Startled at the visitor, I yelped in alarm. "Dina?"

"Martha, talk, please!" Her words choppy and quick flew from her mouth.

I nearly slammed the door, recalling my warning for her never to come here. But the sight of her flushed cheeks, hat askew, and her shuffling from foot to foot overrode my instinct.

"What is it?" A million calamities crashed into each other inside my head, like carts jostling for position on a crowded day at the market.

I stepped onto the porch and closed the door, keeping her and what she'd come for from the prying eyes and ears of the household.

"Your Papa."

I still had no information, but a shiver ran down the back of my neck. "Tell me now," I demanded.

"He say he join again." Tears welled in her eyes. "He tell me last night."

"What? Join the Army? He's just gotten out."

"He say he get good money. No find work."

"How much money?" I couldn't help being curious about what it would take for Papa to even consider enlisting again.

"Eight hundred dollars." Her chest puffed out like a rooster in the hen house.

I released Dina, gasping. Eight hundred dollars was a fortune. "Is he serious?"

"German brewer not go. Pay for substitute, he say."

"Substitute?" I'd read of men who could pay a fee to delay their service, but not for one man to pay another to go in his place.

"I tell him no. You not go, George." She shouted as if Papa were within hearing.

I paced the porch, turning over Dina's words in my mind, trying to make sense of it. Papa going back to war? He'd done his time. He was needed here. The whole idea of joining again was absurd.

Dina, head lowered, fiddled with loose threads on her shabby reticule. "He promise Joe. Help Gus and Amelia."

"What? Promise Joe?" My head swam with this new information. Papa said when he first got back, recovering at Washington Park Hospital, he needed to talk to Dina about Joe. Was this it?

"I say no join, I have widow pension coming."

"Dina, stop. Sit down and tell me everything."

I got the next bits from her as she rocked vigorously. Papa and Joe had promised that if anything happened to one of them, the other would make sure their family was cared for. Dina said that the man Joe owed for gambling had shown up, demanding the remaining fifty dollars. George found the man and paid off the debt.

Head lowered, staring at her reticule, she muttered, "He say he marry me."

"What?" The question sprang from my mouth involuntarily and a knot of apprehension tightened my stomach. Oh dear Lord! Please no! This woman would be my mother over my dead body.

"I say no. I marry, pension gone. But I tell him no go. Joe die. You no die! Stay home. With your family."

Why, she's on my side! Expecting her to want Papa for herself and shun his responsibilities, she, to my amazement, thought it best for him to be with us.

"Do I have time? Time to talk him out of it?" I asked, panic rising in my throat cutting off my air supply. Each second that ticked by was a lost chance to change Papa's mind.

She shrugged. "He no say. But his mind is made."

"Do you know where he's staying? I'd must find him."

She shook her head.

"Thank you, Dina," I croaked, thrusting out my hand in a poor imitation of Jane's businesslike manner. My fingers trembled in Dina's clammy palm. She left the porch, shuffling along the walk, shoulders slumped under the weight of my father's unthinkable proposition.

Reenlist? He had to be stopped. But how? I didn't know where to find him and rejected the fleeting thought of going saloon to saloon searching for him. My best bet was to start at church tomorrow, then the asylum, and pray he showed up at one or the other, before it was too late.

We needed him home. With us. Together. My plan to ease up on Papa, let him find his own way, flew out the window. Obviously, his rowboat floated in the wrong direction, where we might never be with him again. I'd not allow it. I would promise him anything to stay. Anything.

Chapter Forty-Nine

Papa did not attend the Sunday service. After shaking off Dina's request to go with us to the asylum, I said, "This is family time. If he shows up, I'll be trying to talk him out of this nonsense. He won't like us ganging up on him."

Dina nodded. "I hope he not go."

The children, including Mary, joined a game of hide and seek on the property while I paced back and forth on the porch, checking the eastern horizon for a rider on a lone horse. Thinking what to say, I tried to keep my anxiety in check but worries about his return to the battlefield consumed my thoughts. In danger once again. He'd made it out of the Ninth with a minor injury. Would he be lucky again?

On one of my orbits around the porch, my back to the lane, Henry yelled, "Papa's here!"

My siblings gathered around the horse, a dust cloud obscuring their excitement. Papa dismounted, tousled his son's hair, pecked Mary's cheek, and thrust a package into Lizzie's hands. She unwrapped it and handed something to her brother and sister, which they promptly popped into their mouths.

Coming down the steps, I smiled, determined to be nice, to let the rowboat go with the flow. "Any for me?" I asked.

Lizzie cracked off a corner of peanut brittle. I savored the crunch of peanuts in sweet hard candy. "Yum."

"How are you Motty?" Papa asked. He stood beside me while the children indulged in the rare sweet.

"I'm well. You?" I placed my hand gently on his forearm, conveying my intention to be a supportive, non-judgmental daughter.

"No job," he said, scuffing a boot, resembling a scolded boy.

"Something will come up." I forced a smile that hid my disappointment.

His head snapped toward me, eyes narrowed, perplexed at my lack of concern.

I walked to the spot where the flat yard began its descent. "It's a lovely day," I said, my earlier thoughts on what to say abandoning me.

Papa fell in beside me. "It is."

Despite my apprehension about his reaction, I plunged in. "Dina came to see me."

"That's nice. How is she?" Papa replied.

Oh, so he wanted to play games! I kept my eyes on the view. "She's, um, worried."

Papa said nothing.

Frustrated by his silence, I struggled to control my trembling voice, to pretend disinterest, while every fiber of my being ached to grab him by the shoulders and shake the truth out of him. "She said you are thinking of re-enlisting. Is it true?"

"Yes."

The word, the simple affirmation that he thought of going back to the Army, to war, undid me. "Seriously? You're considering enlisting again? Are you mad?" I was losing the fight, my voice escalating with each word.

"Maybe."

"Maybe? Is that all you have to say?"

"Maybe I am mad."

We gazed at the valley below, where the Ohio River meandered past the city. A distant steamer's trumpet blared, heralding its departure with a cargo of supplies or men. Soldiers who might never return to Cincinnati or wherever they called home.

"It's done, Motty." His words pierced the place in my heart where all truths come to die.

My head fell forward, neck muscles buckling along with the rest of my body. My bones unable to support me, I slumped to the ground. I waited for tears, for the inevitable choking sobs, and racking pain that accompanied them. But I had none.

Papa leaned over to help me up, lifting me under my arms, but I fell away from him, a rag doll, limp and unyielding. Giving up, he sat beside me. Henry tugged on his arm, trying to get him to play, but Papa said to give him a minute. Mary, catching her breath from playing tag, plopped down next to me.

"Motty?" she asked, one hand pushing my chin to turn my face to hers.

"I'm all right." I took her hand in mine. But I wasn't all right. I was as far from all right as the sun from the moon. Mary's presence, her fingers laced in mine, held me speechless, my throat constricted, tears smarting behind my eyelids, pulling my lower lip between my teeth to keep it all in check.

"I signed up yesterday," Papa said.

"Is it too late?" I forced my gaze to meet his, challenging the truth.

His imperceptible nod shattered my composure. I blew out my breath, tried frantically to check my tears, and squeezed Mary's hand. "I'm sorry, Papa. I've been a bad girl, treated you horribly. Please get out of it. Please don't go. I'll do anything. Anything." My eyes met his, sending an urgent message. Please stay. I love you. I'll be good. I promise.

Papa's hand cupped my cheek, his palm cradling my jawbone, fingertips grazing behind my ear.

"Please!" I wailed and, let go of Mary's hand, and launched myself into his arms. "Papa! I love you. I've always loved you. I just didn't know how much. That promise. That stupid promise. It's all my fault. I've sent you away. I've made it so bad, you want to go."

"No, no, Motty." His hands brushed my hair and patted my back in reassurance. "It's not your fault. Please don't cry."

Sobs wracked my body, tears soaking Papa's shirt. Alarmed, Mary comforted me with tender strokes on my arm.

"If it's anyone's fault, it's mine." I barely heard him, the fog of my wrenching sobs distorting his voice, muffling his words.

I pulled back. Confusion squinted my blurry eyes. "How is it your fault?"

"Come here, Mary," he said, pulling Mary in. "You're a smart girl. I'll tell you, too."

We huddled close, hands intertwined, and heads bowed, mirroring the solemn prayer circle from Mama's passing.

"I'm trying to figure out how to say this. And it's hard. But here goes." Papa took a deep breath, exhaled, and spoke.

"I'm enlisting again for several reasons. None of which," he paused and eyed both of us sternly, "have anything to do with anything you've done. They have to do with—Motty, you'll appreciate this—a promise I made."

I peered at him through tear-dampened lashes, stifling a sniffle as I awaited his next words.

"Joe Decker was my friend. A good friend. About a week before Chickamauga, we knew a major battle was coming and might mean injury, capture, or death. We made a pact to take care of the other's family should anything happen."

The promise Dina told me about and now, Papa confirmed his intention to make good on it.

"Joe died, God bless him. And because I'm a man of honor, I'm bound to help his family. Not by law, mind you, but by honor. The kind of honor between men who become brothers in the face of war's horrors, who take care of each other—no matter what."

"Honor?" Mary latched onto the word Papa emphasized.

"Yes, Mary. The kind of honor your sister shows for you. She'd never abandon you, never let any harm come to you, and would lay down her life for you. That's honor."

I had honor? Like Papa?

"When the man came around Camp Dennison asking for volunteers and the money offered was enough to take care of Joe's family and mine, I thought about it. Yes, it's about the money. But that's not all."

A random thought occurred to me. "What about the oath you took at Chattanooga? That you would not fight the rebels again?"

"Well, that is a bit tricky. Enlisting in a different unit lowers the chances of getting caught."

Papa's casual dismissal of his sworn oath stunned me. What if they caught him again? Would he be executed? Imprisoned and die of starvation or disease?

Lizzie plopped down next to us. "Why are you sitting on the grass?"

"Join us," Papa said. "Henry! Come here. Might as well tell you all at the same time."

"Tell us what?" Lizzie asked, as Henry squatted beside her.

"Get in a circle so we can talk. We used to do this in camp." Making sure he had Lizzie and Henry's attention, he said, "I've rejoined the Army."

Lizzie's face contorted in confusion. "Huh?"

"You're leaving again?" Henry, now five, had become accustomed to Papa coming and going. Their relationship was stitched together with hellos and goodbyes.

"Yes, I am. I'll tell you what I thought about before deciding. Most important is knowing each of you is happy and well cared for. Two. I'm not the father I need to be without your Mama. I miss her terribly and I know you do too, but being a father without a mama is a tough job. Right, Martha?"

Papa poked me in the ribs and I smiled weakly.

"Motty's a good Mama and a good Papa," Henry added, checking my reaction to be sure I took it with the humor intended.

"And lucky you are, Master Hesch!" I retorted, a scowl on my face to scare him, then relented with a smile.

"Three. Like me, many other soldiers returning from their service cannot find a job. The Army just raised a soldier's pay to sixteen dollars a month from thirteen. So, I'll earn a little more."

Three dollars more a month for sacrificing your life. Hardly a worthwhile raise.

"Four. The war should be over soon. President Lincoln has asked for more men and with those recruits, we'll whip the Rebels and be done with them in a matter of months."

I prayed daily for the war to be over, not just for Papa's sake but for EB's and all the other boys and men in our community.

"The last reason I just told Martha and Mary. You remember Joe Decker?" Four heads nodded. "Before Joe died, I made a promise to take care of his family. The pay I got for joining will help Dina, Gus, and Amelia. But it also helps us. I'll put most of it aside for when I get home. Then we'll get a place to live and be together."

I cringed inwardly. He'd done it again—kept his promise to Joe but delayed making good on the one for his own family, the one buried beneath layers of broken promises like fallen leaves piling up in autumn.

Lizzie burst the bubble. "What if something happens to you? We've lost Mama. We can't lose you too." She crawled into his lap, and he gathered her in his arms.

"I know, my sweet. I made it through three years. I can certainly do three more." His enthusiasm fell on reluctant ears.

"Let me show you." Papa pulled his journal from his pocket, a wad of paper money between its pages. "Martha, hold out your hand."

Counting aloud on the last bill, he said with a flourish, "Five hundred."

Never having held more than ten dollars before, the weight of it was the same as a paper pamphlet, representing a king's ransom. Dina said eight hundred for his substitution. I wondered what happened to the other three.

"That's a lot of money," Lizzie gaped. Then a bright smile lit her face. "Enough to get Mama a real headstone?"

"You bet. Martha's in charge of the money until I return." Papa handed me the bills. "You two can figure out the best headstone for Mama."

Lizzie hugged him tight. "You did what you said, Papa."

As I folded the greenbacks and deposited them in my reticule, the knife of Lizzie's words plunged into my heart. Tired of Papa making everyone feel good that he was leaving, I almost blurted out what came to mind. How is it you make good on promises to her, and Joe, and not me?

"When do you leave?" I asked.

"In a few days. I'm sorry. I must say goodbye today."

"But Papa, you just got here," Henry cried, clutching Papa's shirt, his fists white with effort to keep ahold of his father. Papa let him cling while Lizzie knelt beside him, arms surrounding his neck, planting kisses all over his face.

Finally, Papa gently freed himself from fists and arms, swiped dry grass from his pants, kissed his finger, and extended it to Mary. "A kiss for my big girl." Mary's bright smile rivaled the sun as she kissed her finger, and they touched each other's face to complete the gesture. "I'm proud of you. When I get back, I want to eat the vegetables you grow in your garden."

"Carrots? Beans?" Mary touted her favorites.

Papa's laugh started deep in his belly, then burst from his mouth. "Every single one."

My turn. My siblings milled around, waiting for this last goodbye. Dark thoughts flitted into my mind like bats disturbed by a chimney sweep. I hated him, cursed him to the devil. Go ahead, get yourself killed. See if I cared. How could he go? Honor be damned—how could he so blithely set us aside? Wasn't it honorable to care for his family?

I composed my face to mask my crumbling heart, the fear of him never coming home. "It's too sudden. We've had no time to get used to you leaving," I said, placing a hand on his rough cheek. "Please be careful, Papa. You're not invincible." Just as Achilles was not, I mused.

"Don't worry. The war will be over before you know it." I'd heard that so many times, like one of his promises, yet it went on and on and on. "You're a good girl, Motty. I'm proud of you."

And what did his pride get me? I'd done it all, kept the children safe if not together, so he could come home to his loving family only to leave again.

He kissed each of us once more, then mounted his horse. With a wave and a tip of his hat, he began his journey into the city. At the end of the lane, just before the turn onto the main road, he removed his hat and waved it over his head. I thought I had no tears left, but my eyes welled up as Papa disappeared down the hill.

I felt something missing in his farewell. What was it? I thought back over our parting words and it came to me. He hadn't asked me to take care of the children. Nor did I ask him to bring his family together when he returned.

He trusted me to take care of everyone, and I trusted him to come home. I conjured the image of myself in the rowboat, oars untouched, floating aimlessly, the current in control of my destiny.

Chapter Fifty

Everyone commiserated with me on Papa's reenlistment. The Eiflerts were stunned. Frank's eyes lit up at the amount of money being offered for veteran substitutes, but his parents squashed any thoughts of him joining again.

Jane and Mrs. Mitchell's annoyance with Papa helping Dina was nearly as great as their distress about his reenlistment.

"Honor be damned!" Mrs. Mitchell said with a sneer. "Why would he help that woman after all she did to you and the children?"

I shrugged. "Papa says honor is important."

"Humph," she snorted.

Jane asked how I handled the news. I told her I'd promised to do anything if he stayed, but it was too late. He'd signed the papers.

"And the children? How did it go with them?"

I thought back to the afternoon. "It went better than I expected. Perhaps they've gotten so used to saying goodbye, they don't realize it could be a long time till they see him again."

I pulled the wad of bills from my pocket. "I need to put this somewhere safe. What do you recommend?"

"I'll go to the bank tomorrow and inquire how you can open an account," Jane said. "Better yet, come with me and we'll do it together."

EB replied to my letter about Papa being my Achilles' heel.

It comes down to trust. You kept your word, but he's not keeping his. The more you push him to make good on his promise, the more he feels you control him. This cycle has repeated itself time after time in your relationship. It's time for you to do something different, and I think Jane's advice is sound.

Returning EB's letter, I wrote:

It is all too late. The arrow pierced my heel, and I am undone. Papa reenlisted.

Papa left Camp Dennison a week later, but I didn't know this until a letter arrived dated July 2. He wrote of his train ride to Columbus, Ohio, where he met other recruits joining the 110th Ohio. Some were draftees, some enlisted on their own, and a few, like him, were substitutes.

After a few days at Camp Chase, we boarded a train bound for Petersburg, Virginia. An officer from our regiment met us and escorted us to camp where Captain Dennehy welcomed me to E Company, a unit of seventy men.

There are only a few in my unit who speak German. All commands are in English and the officers use hand signals different from the Ninth. Some men were not pleased to see me. Behind their hands, I heard insults to me and Germany. It is a very different regiment from the Ninth where we were brothers in arms.

The area we are going to is a hotbed of Rebel activity. I've heard to expect skirmishes as we march, as we are in the heart of enemy territory.

I will be careful. You can trust me on this.

Papa

A hotbed of activity? Skirmishes? Where is Petersburg? I wished for the map in Lizzie's library to locate this place.

Every day after supper, I read the *Cincinnati Enquirer* front to back. There was no mention of the 110th or EB's unit the 137th. However, Confederate troop movements were advancing toward Baltimore and Washington City, leaving General Grant with a decision to continue his reach for Richmond, the rebel capital, or protect the Union capital. EB would be in harm's way should the Rebels attack these key cities.

On a sultry July morning, a letter arrived, addressed to me. I didn't recognize the handwriting but noted the postmark, Frederick, Maryland. Ripping it open, I noted the date, July 12, 1864. It was signed by Miss Katherine Hollen, Nurse, Frederick General Hospital.

With shaking hands, I held my breath and read.

Dear Miss Hesch,

I regret to inform you that your father was wounded at Monocacy three days ago. A gunshot to his lower right leg resulted in the doctor removing it above the knee. Private Hesch is resting after the surgery. His wound should heal

over the next few months, and he will stay here
until a more suitable place is found. Please send
any correspondence in my care and I will see he
gets it.

Papa shot. His leg gone. But alive. The prospects of Papa coming
home and getting a job evaporated at the loss.

Rereading the letter, I considered my initial reactions. How
could I be so selfish? Thinking only of what Papa's fate meant to
me, how it impacted my plans. What did it do to a man who could
not walk on his own two feet? The agony of the saw, the mental
anguish of finding one foot instead of two at the end of your legs.

Three weeks. Only twenty-one days from the day he enlisted to
the day he was wounded. After three years and surviving multiple
battles, including Mills Springs and Chickamauga, he fell in his first
battle with the 110th.

I lowered myself onto the steps in the foyer. Monocacy. The
Enquirer reported a battle by a river with this name, but details were
scant. The Union lost, but their efforts were said to have stalled a
massive Rebel Army long enough to shore up defenses around the
Capital.

I needed a map, for I didn't know where Frederick was. Perhaps
I could go there. Papa's money would buy a train ticket, and I'd help
him recover, be his right leg where he had none. Help him mend, sit
by his bedside and tend to his every need.

Mrs. Mitchell, hearing of my idea of going to Frederick, pulled
out a large bound book from a shelf in the parlor. She flipped it open
to a map of the United States.

"Here we are," she pointed to Cincinnati, then found Baltimore. "Here's EB."

"That's quite a distance," I said, tracing an imaginary line from town to town.

Mrs. Mitchell turned a few pages. "Here's Maryland and here's Frederick." She pointed to a spot on the map not too far from Baltimore and Washington City. She knew the area well, having referred to it when her son sent news of his unit's movements.

"Martha, be sensible. Besides the distance, there are inoperable rail lines, one army or the other destroying the tracks. Even if by some chance you get through, by the time you get there, Frederick could be in Rebel hands, and you'd be heading straight into enemy territory. The nurse said a few months for recovery. I say let's see how he does."

Jane interjected. "Your Papa is a proud man. It will take some time for him to come to grips with losing his leg. Might feel less of a man and won't want you to see it."

"Have you written the nurse yet?" Mrs. Mitchell asked.

"Not yet. I wanted to say I was coming, but you make sense. I'll wait until I hear about his progress." I concurred with her assessment, but waiting for Papa to mend would be excruciating.

"Wise move," Mrs. Mitchell commented.

"I'll write. Tell him how we're doing and the children's activities. Take his mind off his predicament." Looking pointedly at Jane, I said, "And I'll steer clear of scolding him."

"Another wise move," Jane echoed her mother.

Dashing off a letter to EB, his unit within miles of Frederick, I asked him to discover what he could about the battle and Papa.

Worry. That's all I could do was worry and write. Daily, I penned two letters to Miss Hollen. One in English, the other in German. Papa spoke decent English but wasn't very good at reading and writing. I urged the nurse to find someone who could read his letters aloud.

My first note read.

> Dear Papa,
>
> Is there anyone who speaks German at the hospital? It pains me to think you are not hearing our beautiful language as you recover. Please ask Miss Hollen for help.

I said I'd yet to tell the children about his injury, that time to heal was important before saddling them with a worry they could not impact. On a lighter note, I begged him to come home and taste Mary's homegrown vegetables. Keeping my fears and hopes to myself, I never once asked when we would be a family.

Two weeks passed with only one letter, short and in Miss Hollen's handwriting, dated August 1, 1864, three weeks since the amputation.

> Your Papa says to tell you he is feeling better. A young man, healing from a scrape with a minie ball, reads him your letters in German, which bring him comfort. He sends his love to you and the children and he's looking forward to coming home as soon as he can.

Cautiously thrilled at Papa's speed of recovery, my spirits lifted at the prospect of his homecoming. However, as I traveled about the city, my heart sank. For the first time, I truly noticed the number of men missing an eye, an arm, or a leg—and countless others bearing invisible scars. Papa now shared their fate.

EB wrote what he knew. The night before the battle, a small portion of his regiment moved to Fort Carroll to relieve soldiers called to defend Washington's north and west perimeters, less than forty miles from Monocacy. He had no news of the 110th, but heard there were many casualties. The Union's dead, wounded, or captured were over thirteen hundred, twice as many as the Confederates.

At church, Mrs. Eiflert shook her head as if she'd known something awful would happen to Papa. "I'll pray for his recovery."

Learning of Papa's survival despite being shot, Dina's face twisted in a mix of relief and exasperation as she muttered, "Verdammter Dummkopf!" However, she changed her tune when I told her he'd lost his leg. "Oh, mein Lieber Gott! I help. He stay with me."

"Whoa, wait a minute, Dina," I said. "I'll take care of him. He's my father."

"How you do that?" Hand on her hips, she challenged me. "Think, Martha. He need many help. Till he learn how."

"He's a grown man. I'm sure he can figure it out."

"Ok. Steps. How he do that?" She pointed to the five steps into the church.

Taking in the entrance, I saw no handrail and, therefore, nothing for Papa to hold on to. "Oh," I muttered, then I turned it on her. "There are steps up to your rooms."

Her mouth twitched uncertainly before she grudgingly admitted, "No good."

"But you're right, Dina. He'll need help when he gets home. I need to think about this."

"I help. Whatever you say. He save me." She touched my arm, and I placed my hand over hers.

"We'll figure it out." When did Dina and I become we? Without thinking, I'd included her in my plans for Papa's future.

At the asylum, I stayed silent about Papa's injury, choosing not to spoil Lizzie's eleventh birthday celebration. I lit the candles in the Geburtstagskranz while Mary poked herself in the chest. "Me. Birthday. Mary."

"Your turn after Lizzie." I smiled at Mary being Mary.

We sang the song while Lizzie contemplated her wish. "First, I want to thank whoever granted last year's wish. Papa is safe." She blew out the one on the eleven.

I grimaced at Lizzie's assumption that last year's wish had been granted. Papa was alive, but not out of danger. Injured, but not whole.

Lizzie stared at the candle on the twelve, inhaled and blew it out. Everyone clapped, and we repeated the process with Mary.

"Have you heard from Papa?" Lizzie asked as we prepared to go.

I removed the feedbag from the horse's nose and shook my head. "Just that one letter about going to Petersburg." The harmless white lie spared her any distress, allowing her peace of mind without the burden of worrying about Papa's recovery.

"I've written two letters. No reply." Her downcast mouth and scowling eyebrows betrayed her disappointment. "EB coming home soon?" A different topic altogether, but Lizzie adored the man.

"His service ends later this month. Won't be long till he's back."

346

"I miss them." Lizzie sighed, taking in the hilltop view of the city.

"Me too." I hugged her, mounted the buggy, took the reins, and turned it around in the drive.

"I'll see you in two weeks. Happy Birthday!"

"Birthday!" Mary shouted and waved to her sister as we drove down the lane.

Chapter Fifty-One

I went about my duties waiting for word on Papa's progress. My mind wrestled with the reality of losing a part of the body. A lost arm, though devastating, would be an inconvenience, but a missing leg altered the mechanics of movement altogether.

I did as Jane suggested and tried to put myself in Papa's place. What would it be like to have only one leg? With Mary's help, I bound an old sheet around my waist and secured it to my right ankle, my foot above the floor in a clumsy imitation.

Holding onto a table, I could only hop forward. Backwards was out of the question. I tried it standing and doing dishes, leaning on the sink for balance. But the muscles in my left leg, fatigued after a few minutes, cramped. The biggest hurdle of all was using the privy. I didn't dare descend the three steps into the yard, for I had nothing to hold on to but Mary. What would it be like to depend on someone to take care of your basic human needs?

"Jane, Papa is going to need a great deal of help when he gets home," I said when she saw me all tied up in the kitchen.

"Yes, he will, but there's one thing you haven't added to your experiment." She nodded at my replication of a missing leg. "A crutch and," she continued, "he can have a leg made that will strap onto the bottom of his stump."

The word 'stump' sent a shudder through me, its harshness all too real, the image of Papa without a leg painfully vivid.

"Martha, when your Papa gets home, he'll need constant care and a place to live with limited steps. How will you handle that?" Jane asked. "You'll continue to work here, I hope."

"Yes, I plan to stay," I said. "I'll have to find a place for Papa to live. Dina said she'd help."

"Dina?" Jane's brows knit over her nose.

"It may come to that. But I don't know. I think it best to wait for word on when Papa will get home, then I can plan. With his opinion, of course."

Jane's lips curved into a knowing smile as she acknowledged my decision to defer planning.

It seemed if it wasn't one thing to worry about, it was another. A never-ending stream of obstacles to overcome. With proper money management, we could survive on the money Papa left. But it meant that we could not have Henry and Lizzie with us until we worked out Papa's needs.

"Get in the rowboat, Motty," I told myself. "Float. For now, there is nothing to be done. Let the current take you. Your course will become clear."

The mail arrived and, in the pile, I recognized an envelope with Miss Hollen's handwriting. I tore it open, hope fluttering in my chest for good news.

> August 8, 1864
>
> Dear Miss Hesch,
>
> Your father took a turn for the worse last

week, and after a battle with an infected artery, he
died at ten o'clock this morning.

"Died?" I said aloud. But. He was recovering. I reread the
sentence. The words on the page wavered, blurred, hid their true
meaning.

> Delirium consumed him these last days. But in
> the days prior, he spoke of his children and his
> pride, especially for you. He muttered the name
> Retta many times before the end, and I assume
> this was his wife.
>
> I am told by others who fell at Monocacy that
> your father fought bravely. When the rebels burst
> from the cornfield, with no time to escape the
> oncoming forces, he took a bullet in the leg,
> disabling him from retreating with his comrades.
>
> A man in the hospital read your letters in
> German, which pleased your father immensely.
> He slept with them under his pillow.
>
> In closing, I am humbled to have attended
> your father. The doctor minimized his suffering
> with morphine. Knowing he was a religious man.
> I am sure he died with God in his heart.
>
> Please accept my heartfelt condolences,
> Miss Katherine Hollen

The next thing I knew, Jane hovered over me, grabbing the letter
with one hand and fanning me with the other.

"Your father?"

I nodded.

"Oh Martha, no." Jane slipped down onto the floor beside me. "May I?" she reached for the letter.

She read while tears slipped down my cheeks unchecked. I wished for morphine to dull my pain.

Jane held my hand. Mine lay in hers, limp and numb.

"He's with Mama now."

The thought that consumed me was Papa calling for Mama in his final hours. Mama died without Papa, but we, her children, were by her side until the night before she left us. Papa had no one except nurses and other soldiers, surrounded by moans, screams of pain, and soft prayers muttered with hope. Whereas Mama knew she was dying, did Papa? Did he see the doctor and nurse shake their heads after examining him? I prayed he slipped away without pain, but with her name, Retta, on his lips to let her know he was on the way.

Jane squeezed my hand. "I'm sorry."

"It's over."

"What's over?"

"Everything. We'll never be a family again."

Jane didn't refute the statement. Getting up, I dragged my fingers across my cheeks, clearing the wet streaks. I reached for Jane's hand to help her up. She returned the letter.

"Mary won't understand. When Mama died, she saw her body, said goodbye at the cemetery." I turned to Jane. "We don't have Papa."

The realization struck me - how could we honor Papa without his body, as we had done for Mama? "Where is he?" I begged Jane for an answer. "What will they do with Papa?"

The swinging door opened, and Mrs. Mitchell stepped into the front hall. "Jane? Martha?" She looked from her daughter to me, then, spying the paper in my hand, said, "No."

"He's gone. My father is dead, and he's never coming home." I slumped into the older woman's arms, jabbering the same words over and over. "Gone. Never coming home."

"Tend to Mary," Mrs. Mitchell said to Jane. "No need for her to see Martha like this."

Jane left to find Mary while her mother led me into the front parlor, sat me on the window seat, and perched next to me, laying an arm around my shoulders.

My sobs punctuated the rhythmic clip-clop of horses outside, the relentless ticking of the mantel clock, and Mrs. Mitchell's soothing murmurs. "Now, now. It will be all right."

Sitting up, my anger flared. Her arm dropped to her lap. "Nothing will ever be right again."

She brushed the tears from my cheeks with her handkerchief. "No, it won't be the way you wanted it. You are a strong woman. God only sends us what we can handle."

"Ha!" I scoffed. "I've heard that before. Haven't I handled enough already?" Mama's death, Papa's retreat from us and return only to put himself in harm's way once more. And then die.

"More than your share."

"It's all too much."

"Why don't you take the afternoon off? Do whatever you want. But maybe wait to talk with Mary until you are, um, calm."

I shook my head. "I need to keep my mind occupied. It will be hard enough when I go to bed tonight and the questions with no answers will roll around in my head."

"Very well, but if you need to go out, feel free to take the buggy."

I looked at Mrs. Mitchell, no longer just my employer, but a mother figure I'd come to cherish. "I, I'm lucky," I choked out. "You, Jane and EB are a comfort to me, to all of us. Thank you."

"It is I who am lucky." A beat of silence followed. The weight of my loss settled between us like a heavy cloak.

I peered at her in confusion.

"If not for you and Mary, my garden would be barren, and my mending done poorly."

I let the corners of my lips curve upward, grateful for recognizing our contribution to her household.

"But seriously, Martha, you are a lovely person and I'm grateful to know you for what, three years now?"

"Three years. Just after this damn war started." The war that stole Papa, leaving us destitute and alone to fend for ourselves.

"I'll say prayers for your father's soul, and I have a little more room to pray for EB's safe return. Let's not lose another loved one to this damn war."

After supper, a few hours of daylight left on this August evening, I took Mrs. Mitchell up on her offer of the buggy, deciding to give the news to Mrs. Eiflert instead of telling her at church the next day. I had no desire to break down in front of the entire congregation, particularly since many of Papa's old friends would ask after him.

Mrs. Eiflert answered the door, and disregarding formalities, I fell into her arms. She knew at once. "There, there, my child." In the bosom of Mama's dear friend and mine, her gentle murmurs of sympathy seeped through my muffled cries.

"Come in. Tell me all about it." A cup of tea in a shaky hand, I explained the letter, arriving only today, the news fresh but dated somehow as if it had happened weeks ago or to someone else and I'd just now understood.

"Remember, Mrs. Eiflert, how you helped with Mama's funeral and burial? Papa is likely buried in Frederick. We'll never get to visit him like we do Mama." This would be important to Lizzie.

Frank relayed what happened after the battles he fought. "Most soldiers are buried where they fall. In a cemetery close by, or like Mill Springs, a burial ground is laid out on a portion of the battlefield."

Mrs. Eiflert said, "I'll let Reverend Knockelmann know. He'll make special mention of him in the service."

That's it? Dying so far away stole the chance to honor a friend, a member of the congregation, a father of four, and a soldier who served his country not once, but twice. There should be a service or something, but I hadn't the strength to puzzle it out tonight.

I left the Eiflert's and decided to tell Dina. After telling me about Papa reenlisting, she deserved to know his fate. The windows were open from the top and I smiled, knowing that Gus and Amelia, now a toddling one-year-old, were safe from falling onto the street.

I clutched the rail, my eyes traveling from the steps to the landing, as memories flooded over me. The wooden stairs smoothed in the middle, concave from tiny shoes and big boots going up and down to church, the market, school, errands, and mending deliveries. Papa leaving, returning from West Virginia, then off to Kentucky, then Tennessee. Lizzie and I struggling to help Mama, her strength sapped by consumption. The last time my feet touched these stairs was the day before Lizzie and Henry went to the asylum.

I stared at the door handle. How many times had the turn of it granted me entry into these girlhood rooms? Hundreds? Thousands? Crossing the threshold to discover Mama's mood, Papa railing at the South for their foolish ways or praising Lincoln as the next leader of our country. Mary cowering from Mama or playing Cat's Cradle with her sister. Henry at Mama's breast or crying at her door, hungry and afraid. Lizzie clip-clopping down the stairs, trading the confines of the tiny room and Mama's sharp words for fresh air, sunshine, and sky.

Why had I come to tell Dina about Papa? Why did she deserve to know when she'd been the catalyst for separating our family?

Before I could knock, the door opened. "Martha?"

"I...I came." My brain and voice stumbled over how to say the unspeakable.

Dina's hand flew to her mouth. Turning away from the door, she left me standing on the stoop. I went in, closing the door behind me.

Gus and Amelia played on the floor. A wave of melancholy washed over me as ghostly images appeared: Henry stacking blocks by the window, Lizzie's chalk scratching on her slate, and Mary in her chair, needle in hand. The memories caught in my throat, a lump forcing me to swallow before I could speak.

"His leg got infected. He died last Monday," I said, tearing at a ragged fingernail.

"Joe. Now George." She reached for my hand across the table. "I sorry."

"I had big plans, Dina. I was going to find a place to live with no steps and take care of him. I put aside my dream of having the children with us because I knew Papa would need time. Time to heal, to get used to not having a leg, time to come to grips with his impairment."

Dina's eyes welled up. Lowering her head into her hands, elbows on the table, her shoulders shook. Of all the unimaginable things, I laid a hand on her shoulder, consoling the woman who betrayed me.

"Dina. Did I do this? Did I chase Papa away? Make it hard for him to come home, be happy with my plans? My demands?" Her interpretation of how Papa felt about my expectations still stung.

Dina looked skyward, sniffing, her mouth rounding as she exhaled. "Yes, he mad you want him home," she interjected, seeing the guilt on my face. "But he lost. Miss your Mama. He not know how to be father without her."

I'd heard this before. Jane? EB? No, it was Papa. "He said as much before he left."

"He love your Mama. Talk of her all the time." Dina snorted in derision. "Too much, I think."

Another layer of Papa revealed itself. As much as my parents fought, argued, disagreed, they loved each other. A misconception of love had taken hold of me, a belief that it meant doing good for the other, making sure they were happy, elevating each other to king or queen status. But my parents did nothing of the sort.

Their fights were terrifying, making up legendary. I cringed as their words cut like swords, reveled in a kiss on the forehead, rebelled at teeth bared in contempt, and sighed with relief at the door closing behind Papa.

How could their union be anything but destined to fail? A juxtaposition of needs and wants running in parallel lines, eternally misaligned.

By the time the war began, Mama and Papa had weathered fifteen years of marriage, four children, and countless struggles. But it was Papa's need to prove something that ultimately broke them. Was it loyalty to America? A commitment to abolish slavery? Or simply an escape from daily drudgery? I had only hints, never certainties. Perhaps even Papa didn't fully understand his own motivations—just a vague, restless urge for something different, something more.

I told Dina I'd let her know when I found out more. Gus hugged me while Amelia hovered behind her mother, clutching her skirts to steady her thirteen-month-old legs. I smiled at the girl I'd helped deliver and admired her shocking red hair, the same hue as her mother's.

Dina pulled Amelia from behind her. "This my friend, Martha. She special to me."

Tears threatened to spill over, and I hurried from the room, before my composure crumbled entirely, mumbling a promise to visit soon. The three Deckers stood in the window above me, now open wide from the bottom, Dina with a firm grasp around their waists, waving and yelling goodbye. I returned their wave, wiped my face with my sleeve, and flicked Goldie's back, steering the buggy down Linn Street. Toward home.

Chapter Fifty-Two

"EB! He's on his way home!" Jane held a telegram aloft as she rushed into the dining room, where Mary and I set the table for supper. "He'll be here tonight."

"EB!" My sister applauded, rising on her toes.

"In time for supper?" I asked, counting the table settings for the number of planned guests.

"Doesn't say," Jane said, reviewing the notice.

"I'll put an extra setting on the sideboard in case."

"Good idea. Mama will be ecstatic."

Mrs. Mitchell would indeed be thrilled. Her face drained of color at every knock, only to flush with relief when no ill news of her son arrived. EBs safety became more important to me after the news of Papa, for he was the only man in my life, the only male I wanted to trust. Should I? Did I need to?

Mary finished the silverware placement and tapped me on the shoulder, asking for my approval. I gave her a bleak smile and nodded. "Very good. Go help Cook."

Mindlessly roaming around the table, centering a plate, lining up a fork with its mates, I compared EB to my father. The younger coming home, surviving his hundred days while Papa's enlistment ended in half that number. Since Miss Hollen's letter arrived, I'd thrown myself into work and caring for Mary, allowing these tasks to consume my body while my mind wandered. Intrusive thoughts plagued me: his gunshot wound, losing his leg, his death in a distant hospital. A waste. All a damned waste.

Jane entered the dining room and found me sitting in the captain's chair at one end of the table, my cheeks wet. Seeing her, I wiped them away and stood.

"Martha, are you all right?"

"Yes. No." I would never be all right again.

"Sit, sit." Jane gestured for me to retake the chair. I lowered myself onto the fine tapestry seat. Jane waited.

"I'm glad EB is coming home." I picked at a scab on my knuckle where I'd lost a few layers of skin scrubbing a floor.

"Me too," Jane said.

The scab came off and a bit of blood oozed from the wound. I dabbed at it. "Papa didn't have to die. He didn't have to go again. He'd be here right now if he'd kept his promise!" My anger escalated at each statement. I slammed my fist on the table, dishes, silverware, and glasses clattered in discord.

Jane waited for my tirade to play itself out.

"Why, Jane? Why?" Anger and denial were constant companions after the initial shock of his death. "He said he'd come home. Even while in the hospital, he said he would come as soon as he could." My hands cradled my face, muffling sobs that threatened to seep through my trembling fingers. "I believed him."

"You wanted to believe him. You needed to," Jane soothed, "to survive."

I closed my eyes, focusing on Jane's statement. I survived. My body worked as expected. I ate, slept, worked, and had no aches or pains to speak of. From the outside, I seemed like any other girl of seventeen. Was this survival? It didn't feel like it.

Mary grew and flourished like the vegetables in the garden. Despite her impairments, they didn't stop her from learning. Jane taught her how to handle herself with strangers, and how to tone down her mannerisms so those same strangers didn't mock her. She had friends, people who loved her and protected her. Mary loved without judgment, the purest form of adoration ever bestowed on any human.

"Besides not telling Mary, I haven't told Lizzie and Henry. Better for them to think Papa is alive and well." I skipped my visit last

Sunday but had to go tomorrow or I'd miss my every-other-week trip up the hill. "Not only do I have to tell them Papa is gone, but that we won't be back together as a family for some time, maybe never. That dream perished with Papa."

Jane sighed. "Perhaps your dream can come true someday."

"What do you mean?" I couldn't fathom how with Papa dead.

"I see no reason why you can't all live together in the future. Both children are happy at the asylum and can leave when they are fifteen. That's only four years for Lizzie. By that time, you can take Henry out, too."

The front door opened with a click. Heavy footsteps reverberated in the entryway, interrupting my internal debate about whether my dream had a time limit.

"Where is everyone?" A man asked. I heard something heavy drop to the floor, footsteps coming toward us.

"EB!" Jane and I exclaimed at once and jumped out of our chairs.

Jane picked up her skirts and flung herself into his arms as he crossed the parlor. Watching their embrace, I wiped my face, tears of sorry mixed with tears of joy.

"Brother!" Jane had her arms around his waist, her head on his shoulder, and I pictured me there instead of her, feeling the steady rhythm of his heartbeat, his arms surrounding my body.

EB kissed the top of her head. Tilting her chin with his forefinger, he examined her face. "You look wonderful. A sight for sore eyes!"

"And you've lost weight. Didn't they feed you?"

"We hurried home through treacherous enemy territory with limited stops. We ate as we marched."

"Supper is soon, but I can get you something to tide you over."

"I'd like that. Anything will do."

Jane twirled and squeezed my arm as she swept past me.

"Hello EB," I whispered. His uniform trousers and coat were dusty and wrinkled, bearing the marks of long days in the field. Scruffy whiskers dotted his cheeks and chin, while a mustache drooped over his upper lip.

"My appearance is appalling, I know. I could have stopped to clean up, but I wanted to get home." He moved closer to me. "You look well. In spite, in spite of…"

"My outside is fine. It's my insides that are in shambles." Propriety rooted me to the floor, or I would have stepped forward to touch his arm, present myself for an embrace.

"To be expected," he said. "I'd like to have a word with you. Can we talk after supper?"

I knew he'd crossed paths with Papa at Dennison and since he'd not written of it, I assumed he'd tell me about that meeting. "Yes, of course."

"I'll go see Mother now." Turning his back to me, he followed Jane's path through the dining room, into the kitchen.

The swinging door's swish carried Mary's joyful squeal, her delight at EB's return momentarily brightening my somber mood. This man's homecoming meant so much to so many.

After supper, Mary and I lounged on the back steps, the summer air cooling as dusk spread shadows in the yard. Mary made tiny cross stitches on a piece of fabric stretched in the embroidery ring. Jane had sketched an outline of a wild violet, giving Mary a guide for her sewing. It resembled the flower Lizzie etched on Mama's headstone.

As I waited for EB, anxiety bubbled within me, my leg bouncing involuntarily beneath my skirt.

"Let's go in. It's getting dark." I wanted to know if EB still planned to talk this evening.

Mary shook her head. "Stay."

"Five minutes." Fireflies danced in the deepening twilight as I stilled my restless knee, savoring the silence of a day brimming with grief, excitement and anticipation.

The wooden screen door slapped shut behind us, jolting me from my reverie.

"Thought I'd find you here," EB stepped off the stoop and into the yard.

"Mama flower!" Mary announced, holding her work up for EB to examine.

"Pretty. Just like you!" EB chucked her under the chin.

"Me, pretty." Mary agreed, humility not a strong suit.

"Can I borrow your sister?" His habit of demurring to Mary pleased her to no end. Sometimes I wasn't as kind.

"Inside?" I asked.

"How about the front porch? We can sit in comfort."

"I'll join you as soon as I get Mary settled."

A few minutes later, I collapsed into the rocker beside EB. "I'm glad you're back."

"Miss me?" he teased.

I slapped his arm playfully. "I think being glad you're back means I missed you."

He nodded, rocking gently. Crickets chirped while fireflies twinkled here and there on the darkened porch.

"I went to find your Papa at the hospital."

Astonished, I sat forward and tried to make out his features. "In Frederick? When? How was he?"

"I'm afraid I was too late. He died before I arrived."

"Oh." Disappointment shrouded me like a veil, extinguishing my hope of hearing EB's account of meeting Papa.

"Let me tell you what I learned."

I stilled my rocking, intent on hearing every single syllable of his story.

"Near the end of July, I got your letter about your father wounded and at Frederick Hospital. We received orders to return to Dennison in the middle of August and when I learned our route would take us through Frederick, I went to the hospital the day we entered the city.

"At the hospital, I asked to see him and was told he'd died on the eighth. I missed him by a week. Knowing you would appreciate hearing about his final days, I asked to see his nurse or doctor and was directed to Building O, where I met Miss Hollen, the nurse in charge of his care."

"She's the one I corresponded with about Papa."

"She remembered George, mainly because of your letters in German. It was an unusual request."

"I wanted him to have a bit of home," I whispered in the dark.

"She thought it was sweet. She recounted the awful days after the battle at Monocacy. Your father came in with a gunshot wound on this right leg, below the knee. Many others needed immediate attention, so it wasn't until two days later, the bones damaged beyond repair, the doctor chose amputation to give him a greater chance of survival."

I cringed at the pain Papa must have experienced from the gunshot and the saw that took his leg.

"You all right?" EB asked solicitously.

"Go on," I replied, staring into the street beyond.

"Miss Hollen said George was healing well at first, but complications arose a few weeks after the surgery. His leg began to bleed, and despite the doctor's efforts, they couldn't stop it. At the end, your father drifted in and out of consciousness due to the infection and the morphine to dull the pain. Miss Hollen assured me he didn't suffer at the end."

In my mind's eye, Papa lay delirious on bloodstained sheets, in a haze of drugs, calling for Mama.

"I spoke with the doctor, too. The one who cut off, er, performed the amputation. He thought George had a fighting chance, but when infection set in, the only course of action was to wait it out or cut again. He opted to wait and sends his regrets that he could not do more."

"I'm sure he did his best."

We rocked in silence.

"What do you know about that battle at the Monocacy River? The *Enquirer* said it saved the Capital." I'd read columns of first-hand accounts of the battle but didn't understand its importance.

"Twelve regiments, under the command of General Wallace, made a stand at a critical railroad junction near the river. Though they lost the battle, their resistance delayed the enemy long enough for Grant to reinforce Washington and Baltimore. Your father's sacrifice, along with that of his comrades, likely saved our capital. According to the doctor, the 110th was one of the hardest hit. I spoke with an injured soldier from George's regiment who said the field was littered with wounded and dead. Overwhelmed by the Confederate Army, Wallace lost the battle but saved the Capital."

"So, Papa's death meant something," I murmured, a flicker of pride replacing the hollow ache of his wasted life. Papa being there counted.

EB reached over and placed his hand on my forearm. "His bravery and those of his comrades kept our country's leaders safe. Can you imagine if the Capital had fallen to the Confederates?"

"Papa wrote from Petersburg. He said the orders and signals differed from his experience in the Ninth. The men in the 110th barely concealed their animosity toward him because of being German. Is it possible those factors contributed to Papa getting shot?"

"I suppose," EB rubbed his chin. "It was a bloody battle. Just as many veterans died as green recruits. I'm sure the language difference made it difficult to understand orders and commands. It's hard to say."

"It doesn't change the outcome, but perhaps Papa didn't realize what he signed up for."

"From what I know, the Ninth was one of a kind. No other regiment was composed of all German-speaking men or the same level of training as the Ninth. Did you know that Colonel McCook was the only man who couldn't speak German? Must have been interesting leading them. All that aside, Martha, I agree. Your father must have felt like a fish out of water. I'm sorry he didn't make it. He should have."

"Papa didn't have to go," I whispered the fact. "He might have done something honorable, but still."

"I tried to talk him out of it," EB said.

"Out of what?" My head spun on my neck so fast, I had trouble focusing on him.

"Reenlisting. I wrote you."

Stuttering with disbelief, I said, "I didn't get that letter."

EB exhaled heavily, his hand rasping over his stubbly chin as he rose and paced the porch. "As you know, he was at Dennison with the Ninth when I went through on my way to Baltimore in early May. I gave him your letter. He told me an agent had approached him looking for men, especially veterans, as substitutes for draftees, men who didn't want to go for one reason or another. He thought he could get upwards of four or five hundred dollars."

"Eight hundred, including the Army bounty." I remembered the wad of bills he gave me the last day I saw him. "Five for us and the rest, I suppose, went to Dina. Possibly kept some for himself."

He whistled at the large amount. "At Dennison, agents stalk men mustering out, hoping for a verbal agreement to reenlist on behalf of a draftee when they return to Cincinnati."

"They approached him while he waited to muster out?"

Nodding, EB went on. "He thought it best under the circumstances."

"Circumstances? What circumstances?" I shouted, my voice echoing on the porch.

EB pinched his nose between his finger and thumb. "This might hurt, Martha."

"Tell me," I demanded, leaning forward in the chair. "And for God's sake, be still. Stop pacing."

A small smile flickered across his mouth as he leaned against the low brick wall, hands resting on the rail beside his hips. Shaking his head, he said, "I won't relay his words with justice. But in essence, he said he couldn't be a good father without your mama. He said it made little sense to pluck you out of your current living arrangements, where you were thriving. Besides back pay and the hundred-dollar bounty he received on mustering out, the substitute money would mean a new start. And if he didn't make it, then the money would be yours."

The scent of grass, the warmth of sunlight, Papa's earnest words, and Mary's hand in mine flooded back - a lifeline to that moment of truth on that last day at the Asylum. "He said much the same when he told us he'd joined again."

By this time, the fireflies had disappeared. Crickets chirped irregularly. EB returned to his chair, the rocker groaning softly as it tilted back, eased forward, then came to rest.

"How have the children taken the news?" His voice, a delicate balance of softness and anxiety, resonated with the care and affection he had for my siblings.

I blew out a breath. "I've not told them."

"Not even Mary?"

"I thought it best to tell them all together. It will be harder than Mama. They saw her. After."

"Yes, it's different." He understood.

My plan was to go to church tomorrow, then the Asylum. All of us would sit on the hill where Papa explained his reasons for enlisting. An idea occurred to me that would make it easier for me and for them. "Can you," I hesitated, "will you go with me to tell them tomorrow?"

I could feel rather than see his eyebrows arch in surprise, knowing him as I did.

Before he could respond, I pressed on, "The children would love to see you." I cleaned invisible dirt from under one fingernail with another.

"And I could use some help. I'm afraid I won't have all the answers to their questions, and you know how to talk to Lizzie, and Henry could use a man right about now." I stopped, running out of reasons.

I regarded him just as I had when we first met—in the cab he'd hailed during the rainstorm to take me home. Gracious, kind, and full of good humor.

"It would be my pleasure. I'm sorry you are dealing with all of this. Anything I can do to ease your burden is my priority."

"You do not know how much it means to me, EB." An overwhelming urge to reach out and touch him, to show him my gratitude, washed over me.

"I need to get back to the office, but work can wait one more day," he said, and just as I thought he might leave me on the porch alone, he offered his hand. "I'm exhausted. It's been a long day. I'm afraid I must call it a night."

He clutched my hand in his as we tiptoed into the foyer. My fingers burned, then iced over in the moment it took to reach the staircase.

With my free hand, I reached up and caressed his cheek, warm skin and soft stubble awakening an unfamiliar ache. An unnamed, desperate need gripped my heart.

His face tilted into my hand while he brought the other to his lips, brushing them across my knuckles. A powerful tremor rippled through me, head to toe, leaving me quaking. Fearing he'd noticed, I withdrew my hands and folded them together at my waist, grateful for the dim hallway hiding my flushed face.

He picked up the oil lamp and climbed the opulent stairway, pausing on the landing. The lamp's muted glow illuminated a subtle smile tugging at the corners of his mouth, a softness in his features, every curve reflecting tenderness. Was it a trick of the light or was it real? His voice, soft and full of affection, floated down the stairway to where I stood looking up at him, transfixed by his presence. "Goodnight, Motty."

I watched the lamp's glow recede from the landing and listened as his footsteps faded down the hallway to his bedroom. I kissed my knuckles where his lips had been and thought that yes, with time and abundant caution, I could trust this man.

I slipped through the swinging door, padded across the kitchen, and climbed the narrow back stairs to my room in the Mitchell house.

Epilogue

EB pulled back on Goldie's reins, bringing us to a gradual stop. The *German Evangelical Protestant Cemetery* sprawled before us, its lush summer lawn dotted with shady oaks and maples, sheltering a patchwork of grass-covered plots and freshly dug graves. Mary and Henry scooted out of the carriage and down the hill, to the spot where Mama lay in her eternal home. EB lifted Lizzie and I from the carriage.

"Ready?" I extended my hand, noting Lizzie's twelve-year-old frame was unexpectedly filling out in womanly ways. When had she grown to within inches of my height?

Eight at the start of the war, nine at Mama's death, ten when I left them at the asylum, and Papa dead at eleven. Gratefully, this year's birthday marked a happier occasion—the war was over. Though I saw no outward sign of tragedy after tragedy, Lizzie had a way of looking past it all, her curious nature set on the future, to something better.

The sun-bleached wooden marker, Lizzie and Papa's labor of love, slanted gently, weathered by the elements over the last three years. The inscription and engraving of a violet were difficult to make out, the edges smoothed by rain and wind and time.

Beside it, a broad granite base supported a matching stone purchased with Papa's money. I paid extra for the stonemason to come to the cemetery and sketch the flower, asking him to duplicate it as best he could. Though pleased with the stonemason's craftsmanship, I anxiously awaited Lizzie's verdict.

She read the inscription. "Wife. Mother. Margaretta Hesch 1823 - 1862." She stroked the etching, her fingers caressing the edges and crevices. "The violet is perfect, Motty."

I exhaled at her approval.

"My wish came true."

"Wish?" Lizzie put great stock in wishes, and a few had come true, including this one. But unlike her, I couldn't put faith in things beyond my control. Wishes only disappointed the wisher. Broken promises, however, hurt many.

"On my last birthday, I wished that by the time I turned twelve, there'd be a proper marker on Mama's grave." She lifted her eyes to the heavens, her blue more cornflower than sky. "Thank you, Papa, for keeping your promise."

The promise that I fulfilled. A spark of jealousy flickered behind my eyes at Lizzie's innocent words. Anyone could buy a headstone if they had the money and the will to make a loved one happy.

"And this year's wish?" Telling it could steal the magic, the promise of it being granted.

But Lizzie had no such superstitions. "I wished to see Papa. At that place you told me about. An-tee-dum."

After the war ended, EB returned to Frederick and found Papa's grave. In the hospital cemetery, two slabs of wood marked his head and feet—name, regiment, and unit in black paint, among hundreds of others. A cemetery for soldiers who died in Maryland at Antietam, South Mountain, Crampton's Gap, and Monocacy had been commissioned and the State of Ohio was raising funds to move its soldiers' remains. Anticipating Papa's would be moved there, the Mitchells contributed generously, and I set money aside for my family to visit Antietam when it was complete.

We gathered in a circle around Mama. I waved to EB who waited at the carriage, inviting him to join us. As we did every time we visited Mama, I started the Lord's prayer, then Mary led us in the sleeping prayer.

Now I lay me down to sleep.

I pray the Lord my soul to keep.

If I should die before I wake,

I pray the Lord my soul to take.

"Bless Mother Mitchell," Mary said, her voice carrying the reverence reserved for a beloved matriarch. At sixteen, lithe and freckled from working in the garden, she had adopted EB and Jane's formal address of "Mother", preserving "Mama" for her own. The contrast between the women was stark: while Mother Mitchell earned deep respect, Mary's relationship with Mama had been far more complicated. Though Mary's thirteen years with Mama could have been infinitely better, in the end, Mama cherished her

370

daughter's lively chatter, a voice made for praising God, and finger kisses.

These tender recollections clashed with the stark memory of Papa's impending departure in April 1861, when financial worries clouded our future. I heard Mama's naive yet enthusiastic words in my head as clearly as if she stood before me. 'We could put Mary in the lunatic asylum.' Papa's fury filled the tiny front room. He ordered me to never put Mary in an asylum, and I went a step further, eager to please and reassure him of his daughter's safety.

"Mary will be with me forever."

And then it struck me. All this promise stuff had its roots in that awful, terrible moment. Keep Mary from the asylum, ensure her safety, make Papa proud.

The result of my protection was Mary. A kind and loving person, despite people treating her rudely, who thrived instead of withering away in a lunatic home, and most of all, my best friend, whom I'd be with always. No regrets. No change of heart. And looking at the man beside me, I vowed that if EB wanted me, if he found me worthy, he'd have to take Mary, too.

Henry's voice jolted me back to the present as he asked God to bless his friend Stanley, who loved horses and playing tag as much as he did. The asylum provided him with much more than I could ever offer. Friends, a devoted sister nearby, and an open field with a stand of woods for endless adventures. I did my best to remind him of his father, but his memories were limited to hellos and goodbyes. Only three when Mama died, he had no shape, no form of her, except the tiny plot we visited.

Lizzie asked God to bless her family and her friends. "Oh, and my future husband." At this statement, she turned the full force of a hopeful smile on EB.

EB chuckled. "May I have a turn at this blessing thing?"

I raised my eyebrows. "You've never asked before."

"I know, but I have something to say. Maybe it's not a blessing exactly, but here goes." He cleared his throat and clasped his hands in front of him, solemn and respectful. "I'd like to thank God for Lizzie, for the day she ran away and came to me for help. Because if not for her needing my help, I'm not sure I'd be standing here. Each of you has changed my life and you have helped me understand how important family is. That family is much more than a place. It's the spirit of loving each other, of giving up, and giving in, to make the whole better."

He described my revised definition, based upon advice and reflection from some very wise women in my life.

"Well, that sure was some speech!" Lizzie exclaimed, breaking the solemn silence. "Motty, are you happy I ran away?" She didn't expect an answer. A giggle escaped from behind her hand.

"Would you all wait for me at the carriage? I'd like a moment with Mama."

Finger kisses rained down on Mama's markers.

"I love you, Mama." Mary said a full sentence. Love was love, not wuv. She'd come so far from when "Wuv you" was her best declaration of her emotions.

Standing at the foot of the grave, I spoke aloud to Mama. "Please ask Papa to forgive me. Or being you, just tell him to do it," I chuckled. "Ask him to forgive me for hurting him when all I meant to do was love him the best way I knew. I'm in the rowboat, floating where it will, and you know how hard it is for me to let go. Could you make sure the rowboat drifts in calm waters and peacefully toward a future filled with God's love and grace? For me, Mary, Lizzie, and Henry."

My gaze shifted between the weathered wooden cross and the pristine stone, and I realized how much had changed—not just the gravestones, but me. The beliefs I'd clung to as a child—Papa's infallibility, the power of promises, the simplicity of love and duty—had faded like the engravings on the wooden cross. In their place stood new truths, hewn from years of struggle and survival, polished by knowledge and experience. These realizations acknowledged human frailty, the complexity of love, the weight of duty. Unlike those childhood certainties, I knew these insights would endure. They were not etched in wood or stone, but in the very fabric of who I'd become.

A last finger kiss on the markers, I whispered the one truth that would never die. "I will take care of Mary and Lizzie and Henry."

The children waited in the buggy, eager to head to the Mitchell House to celebrate Lizzie's birthday—a rare occasion for all of us to be together.

"Are you all right, Motty?" EB asked.

Nodding, I let him grasp my waist and lift me onto the front seat. He climbed in beside me and guided the buggy with its precious cargo down the hill and into the city toward home.

THE END

Author's Note

Motty's Vow is deeply inspired by the lives of my ancestors, specifically my great-great-great-grandfather and his family. Much of what happens to Motty and her siblings is drawn from real events that affected my family during the Civil War, though parts have been fictionalized to fill in the gaps and explore the emotions they might have felt.

Writing this story has been my way of reconnecting with a part of my heritage I knew little about. Like many of the men and women of the time, George made difficult decisions, including enlisting in the Union Army, which left his children to navigate the world without him. Since much of the reasoning behind his choices remains unknown, I've taken some creative liberties to imagine what might have driven him—and what impact those choices had on those he left behind.

Through Motty's story, I wanted to capture the resilience and resourcefulness of young women and children in the 1860s, especially those from immigrant families, who often faced overwhelming odds. The historical backdrop of Cincinnati, the Civil War, and the German-American experience shaped every part of their lives, and I hope I've honored those struggles here.

While *Motty's Vow* is a work of fiction, it reflects the strength, love, and sacrifices that I believe many families, including my own, had to make. My hope is that this story sheds light on the resilience of ordinary people and offers readers a glimpse into profoundly moving moments in history.

Thank you for joining me on this journey.

—Diane Wahn Shotton

Real Faces Behind the Fiction: Motty and Mary

This photo was taken in 1934. The women seated here are the real-life inspirations for *Motty's Vow*—Martha "Motty" Hesch and her sister Mary. The vow Motty made in the novel—to never send Mary to an asylum—was real. They remained together for life. Neither Motty nor Mary ever married. They lived together until Motty's death in 1934. Mary passed away in 1942.

When I look at this picture, I don't just see family—I see survival. I see the promise that shaped a lifetime. And I see the heart of this story in two women who stayed side by side through decades of loss, change, and love. Motty's face may look stern (possibly annoyed at Mary's wish for another birthday), but I like to think it's the face of someone who kept her word—and didn't have time for nonsense. Mary, on the other hand, looks quietly content—her expression calm, perhaps even at peace. The contrast is striking. Martha carries the weight of responsibility; Mary, the softness of being cared for.

Lizzie, their sister, and Laura, Lizzie's daughter, are my direct ancestors. But it's Motty who is my north star—the woman whose fierce determination to protect her family and survive against all odds is the legacy I hope lives on in me. Her strength, her loyalty, and her unwavering promise continue to guide everything I write—and everything I hope to be.

With love to readers who carry stories—and promises—with them,

Diane Wahn Shotton

Mary and Martha "Motty" Hesch, 1934
Side by side,
decades after the promise was made—and kept.

Book Club Companion

Discussion Guide for Motty's Vow

Explore the promises, silences, and choices behind the story. Whether you're gathering with a book club or reflecting on your own, these questions invite deeper connection with Motty's journey—and your own.

Author's Note

When I began writing Motty's Vow, I was trying to understand a family mystery: why did my great-great-great-grandfather leave his wife and children to enlist in the Civil War? The real reason has been lost to time. Writing this novel became a way to imagine the lives shaped—and fractured—by that decision.

What I didn't realize was that Motty's story wasn't the end—it was the beginning. Readers kept asking, "What happened to the children?" and "What comes next?" I asked myself the same questions. That curiosity gave way to new stories, new promises, and the continuation of a legacy through Lizzie's Bond and Laura's Oath.

Each novel explores what it means to carry something forward: a vow, a burden, a family. I hope these questions deepen your discussion—and help you find the threads that connect your own story to theirs.

Discussion Questions: Motty's Vow

1. Motty makes a vow at age fourteen. How does this promise shape her identity? Was she ever truly free to choose another path?

2. What role does George (Papa) play in the novel, even in his absence? Do you see him as selfish, heroic, or something in between?

3. Much of Motty's strength comes from enduring loss while holding onto hope. What does the novel suggest about the emotional cost of resilience—especially for girls and women?

4. How do poverty and survival pressure Motty into adulthood? Were there moments you wished she had made a different choice?

5. Motherhood is a quiet presence in the story. What does Motty learn from her mother, and how does she carry that forward?

6. What does the orphan asylum represent—for Motty, for the children, and for society at large?

7. Discuss the role of silence in the novel—what goes unsaid between characters, and what truths remain buried?

8. If you could ask George one question, what would it be?

9. How does knowing that this novel was inspired by real family history affect your reading of the story?

10. Would you have made the same vow Motty did? Why or why not?

11. As the story unfolds, we learn more about George's choices and his reasons for enlisting again. How did this affect your understanding of him? Did your opinion of George shift by the end of the novel—and if so, when and why? (Consider saving this question until later in your meeting.)

12. Motty promises her father that Mary will never be sent to an asylum, despite the immense pressure and hardship that follows. What does her decision to keep that part of the vow reveal about her values and her understanding of love, duty, and protection?

Speculation Corner: The Rest of the Trilogy

13. Lizzie's story continues the legacy introduced in Motty's Vow. Based on this first novel, what threads do you hope to see carried through in her story?

14. Do you think Motty ever found peace with her father's decisions? How do you think her experience shaped the next generation?

15. What do you imagine happened to the children after the novel ends? Did any secondary characters leave you wanting more?

16. The author has confirmed a sequel and trilogy are in progress. What do you hope to see in the next chapters of these characters' lives?

Acknowledgements

As I bring Motty's Vow to a close, I can't help but reflect on the journey that led me here. What began as a curiosity about my family's past turned into a deeply personal exploration of resilience, love, and loss. This book is not only a story of one young woman navigating the hardships of the Civil War but also a tribute to the strength of the real people who lived through it.

Many of the characters in Motty's Vow are based on real members of my family. My great-great-great-grandfather served in the Union Army and left behind children whose lives were forever changed by his decisions. I'll never know the full truth behind his motivations for reenlisting, but through research and reflection, I've woven a story that attempts to answer those questions in the context of the political, economic, and cultural climate of the time.

Writing this novel has been both a challenge and a gift. The challenge came from balancing historical accuracy with the emotions and struggles I imagined my ancestors faced. The gift has been the opportunity to bring their stories to life, filling in the gaps with my own interpretations. Though much of the narrative is fictionalized, the heart of it remains true to the spirit of those who lived through such tumultuous times.

This story also allowed me to explore themes close to my heart: the weight of promises, the bonds between siblings, and the often-overlooked lives of women and children left behind by war. These themes shaped Motty's Vow, and in many ways, they mirror the experiences of people still facing hardship today.

Along this journey, I've had the support of many wonderful people. I'd like to extend my deepest gratitude to my husband for his unwavering support throughout this process. Without his encouragement and patience, this book would not have been possible.

I'm indebted to Peg for reading this manuscript in its early stages and providing valuable insights, and to Dave for his help with the cover. Thank you for joining me on the trip to Maryland, where I gained a deeper understanding of the horror of war and the tragedy of one soldier's injury and death.

Thank you to my wonderful beta readers—Dan, Safi, Tanya, and Mary Alice for your thoughtful critiques and suggestions. Your input made this book stronger in many ways.

I am deeply grateful to the Cincinnati Museum Center's staff for their assistance with the German Protestant Orphan Asylum records and for access to the treasure trove of documents about the Ninth Ohio Volunteer Infantry. To the Facebook group The Ninth Ohio: A Living History—thank you for providing invaluable information about the unit and the men who served in it.

Finally, my heartfelt thanks go to three incredible people who inspired a significant part of this book. I'm truly grateful to be on life's journey with you.

Thank you to the readers for sharing in this journey with me. Whether you're here for the history, the characters, or simply the story, I hope Motty's Vow has touched you in some way. This is just one chapter in the larger story of my family, and I hope to continue sharing their experiences in future works.

—Diane

About The Author

Diane tells stories about ordinary people navigating extraordinary choices—strong women, complicated families, and the quiet heroism that history too often overlooks. Her work explores the grit and love of everyday sacrifice, the weight of generational legacy, and the emotional cost of injustice.

She's drawn to the small, domestic histories that rarely make headlines but shape lives in lasting ways. If you've ever wondered how personal stories intersect with larger historical forces—or longed to find yourself in the quiet strength of those who endured—these stories are for you.

Her debut novel, *Motty's Vow*, follows a young girl's courageous stand to hold her family together during the Civil War. Her latest work, *The Dictograph Case*, is a historical thriller about buried truths, dangerous propaganda, and the price of silence in a small American town.

Born in Covington, Kentucky—just across the Ohio River from Cincinnati, she finds her stories rooted in the places and circumstances that shaped her family. Diane lives in Cave Creek, Arizona surrounded by her family.

Follow Diane:
Instagram: @dianewahnshotton
Facebook: facebook.com/dianewahnshotton
Substack: dianewahnshotton.substack.com
Website: dianewahnshotton.com